Volume Sixteen

of

THE
DECLINE AND FALL
OF THE
AMERICAN NATION

Also by Eric Larsen

The End of the 19th Century (a novel, 2011)

*The Skull of Yorick: The Emptiness of American
Thinking at a Time of Grave Peril—Studies in
the Cover-up of 9/11* (2011)

Homer for Real: A Reading of the Iliad (2009)

*A Nation Gone Blind: America in an Age of
Simplification and Deceit* (2006)

I Am Zoë Handke (a novel, 1992)

An American Memory (a novel, 1988)

Volume Sixteen

of

THE
DECLINE AND FALL
OF THE
AMERICAN NATION

BY

ERIC LARSEN

THE OLIVER ARTS & OPEN PRESS

Larsen, Eric, 1941-
The Decline and Fall of the American Nation

ISBN: 978-0-9883343-1-1
Library of Congress Control Number: 2013932416

The Oliver Arts & Open Press
2578 Broadway, Suite #102
New York, NY 10025
http://www.oliveropenpress.com

For my friend -- and
once my student -- Valter Alas "
who may recognize much of
what's in this book --
with affection and
best hopes and wishes for
the future me "

For What Was

[signature]
4/18/14

CONTENTS

Volume Sixteen

of

THE
DECLINE AND FALL
OF THE
AMERICAN NATION

A New & Revised Edition

(The Universities of Asia Press, Beijing, 2147
X. Jin Li, General Editor)

Entitled:

"The Role, Status, and Condition
of Intellectuals in Higher Education
During the Middle and Late Ante-Penultimate
Period of The Collapse"

Consisting of:

The Important Segments of the Larsen Papers:
Fragments I-VII and the Famous "Diary"
all in
The Bhāskara Presentation,
Newly Edited & Revised by
X. Jin Li,
General Editor
The Universities of Asia Press

A NOTE TO THE READER

Volume Sixteen of that indispensable and magisterial work of historical scholarship, *The Decline and Fall of the American Nation*, as every reader knows, consists entirely of the annotated and edited papers of Eric Larsen, M.A., Ph.D., member of the faculty of The Actaeon College of Institutional Analysis and Social Control, The University of New York (New York, New York, United States of America, The Americas), during what is now known to have been the Late Ante-Penultimate and the Early Penultimate Period of Collapse in that doomed nation. Evidence within these unique and famous papers themselves, along with a small number of very rare corroborative discoveries found through subsequent archaeological work in the layers of Actaeon's rubble, indicate that Larsen, during this specified period, was engaged in a highly ambitious project, to which he had given the general working title of "My Life in Education and the Arts Before and During the Gathering of the Great Calamity As I Have Experienced and Now Believe I Understand It." That project, as specialists in this area of The Collapse generally agree, consisted mainly of new work written for the occasion of the doomed project itself, but also of certain earlier pieces refurbished for inclusion in it. Whether or not the author seriously hoped for successful publication of so radical a work, and, if he did, exactly how he imagined that he could, at so late a time, safely bring it to the attention of such readers as still remained (those, that is, who, like Larsen himself, constituted the dwindling ranks of the unconverteds)—these are questions whose answers remain unknown.

It should be mentioned, in accordance with Volume Sixteen's title page, that the source used as the basis for this new edition is the famous "Ceylon Version" of 2110. We have made no changes in that edition's sequential ordering of the papers—have made no changes, that is, in the precedent set originally by the invaluable "Bhā-skara Presentation," which, as all know, was the first (after exhaustive studies using both chemical and textual evidence)[1] to break up the famous *"Diary"* itself into three sections, a change made in the belief—unchallenged to this day—that it allowed for a more holistic and less *linear* reading and thus for an experience much, much more in keeping with this strongly anti-Simplification author's own true aims.

Like all editors, scholars, and readers, we are thus indebted to the Bhāskara Presentation for having first organized the fragments in the sequence now universally believed to be that intended by their author rather than that reflecting only the order of their discovery (although, as tradition dictates, the sequence of their archaeological discovery does remain, expressed by the Roman numerals—I through VII—identifying each fragment). It must not be forgotten, either, that it was the Bhāskara Presentation's editors who, now so long ago, made an even more significant contribution by choosing to transfer the damaged Larsen documents to the printed page in such a way as to duplicate as exactly as possible the actual physical appearance of the originals at the time of their discovery, thus bringing about the now familiar and in fact even comfortable and often in various ways meaningful presence, throughout, of jagged beginnings or endings, sudden white spaces, various lacunae, and so forth.

We continue, that is—while deeply grateful for the many indisputable amenities and refinements contributed by the great Ceylon Version—to rely unquestionably upon the indisputable foundation underlying it, the invaluable Bhāskara Presentation of 2102.

X. Jin Li
The Asia Press
31076 M'tai Cordon
Beijing-AY38
10 October 2147 C.E.

---

[1] See Maximillian Shandra, *Dating the Larsen Papers: A Writer's Progress toward Calamity* (Bangkok, 2096).

EDITOR'S FOREWORD

In the "Late-Penultimate" and "Ultimate"[2] periods of the American Collapse—a fact familiar to even the most casual student of this massive subject—the greatest destruction of business, cultural, and scholarly archives (other than those maintained in secure areas by the military, the government, or great corporations) did not result from direct action by armed forces or through military armaments, whether domestic or foreign, as might logically have been expected. Instead, most archival (and other) destruction came about through the massive, ruinous, uncontrollable fire-storms that engulfed all of that nation's urbanized and most of its densely suburbanized areas, caused by the myriad blazes set by masses of raging and anti-educated members of the middle and lower-middle classes. (The only slightly less widespread acts of arson that were committed by the middle- and upper-middle-classes, predominantly by their males, differed significantly, the sole motive in these latter cases being malicious vandalism, not the blind and near-directionless rage of the lower classes. For a complete analysis of the mass psychology of the Middle and Late Ante-Penultimate and of the Penultimate and Ultimate themselves, see Volume Three of *The Decline and Fall of the American Nation* [pp. 493–572].)

Even by the time of the Late Preliminary, undeniably, all American universities modeled themselves to an irreversibly debilitating extent

---

[2] See Appendix, p. 303, for a chronology of the periods of the Collapse from the Early Preliminary (1950-1964) through the three stages of the Ultimate (2025-ca. 2085).

(as we see it from our own modern perspective) on the hierarchic model of the corporation or corporate state.[3] The universities, as a result, like the corporations, maintained fire- and even thermo-nuclear-resistant security and preservation systems for their own archives, vast numbers of which, as a result, have come down to us undamaged. Little of that archival material has proven to be of any true significance, however, in revealing the root causes of the Collapse. The reason for this failure is that, with extremely few exceptions, the purpose of corporate archives of the period was not to express or clarify, but rather to obscure and suppress any and all information that might be revelatory of the real workings, conduct, or aims of the corporation itself. The sheer meaninglessness, to the point often of what seems little more than intentional gibberish, of the vast majority of such archives remains an extraordinary aspect of pre-Collapse American communication and culture.[4]

In the corporate university structure, those in leadership and governing (that is, in "ownership") positions were housed at the top of an imaginary pyramid and designated not through accurate terms such as "owners," "governors," "regulators," "chiefs," or "bosses" but through the ingeniously neutralized term[5] of "administrators." These figures, in the university as in the corporation itself, were solely responsible for the ongoing creation of what was then known as "product," this being something that, among college or university administrators themselves, was referred to almost invariably (and, again, abusively) as "image." Any "product" of a traditional kind actually suitable to the university—"education," "learning," or "knowledge," for example—essentially disappeared from the university entirely as the administrators, in a complex and curious evolution, took over the roles both of owner-governors *and* producers. "Image," in short, became the sole "product" of the university, the administrators themselves having become at one and the same time the producers, controllers, and beneficiaries of it.

The word "faculty," meanwhile, did for a certain time remain in use, although it was a term that even by the Late Preliminary or Early Ante-Penultimate was separated entirely from its original "medieval"

---

[3] Some scholarship argues for later dates, as late as Early or Middle Ante-Penultimate, the second of these being the period of the earlier Larsen papers. The majority of views, however, hold generally for the Late Preliminary as marking the completed corporatizing of the universities.

[4] See Delia Nawrocki, *Language and the American Collapse* (Helsinki & Beijing, 2118).

[5] For analysis of this calculated abuse of language, see, besides Delia Nawrocki, George Orwell (*The Lost Orwell: Texts Restored and Rediscovered*, Pilgrim Press, Delhi, 2099, Iridhati Rushdie, General Editor), especially this inexplicably neglected English author's satiric novels *1984* (1948) and *Animal Farm* (1945).

connotation as designating both the university's governing *and* producing element (the body, that is to say, in charge of the gathering, maintaining, and handing on of "knowledge").[6]

In applying this corporate model to the university, the administrator-producer-owners found themselves with large numbers of useless "workers" or erstwhile "producers," these of course being the remains of their inherited faculties. Due to a byzantine complexity of legalities that were in place from approximately the Early Ante-Penultimate on, it was out of the question for administrators to dispense with these "faculty" in such simple ways as they may actually have wished, but they were forced to do so instead by relying upon far more indirect methods. Two of the most common of these were the encouraging of poor health and thus early death;[7] and the curiously-named concept of "attrition," which in fact simply meant making no replacements for those "faculty" who died. Other methods of eliminating these expensive and useless workers included the equivalent of surgical excisions of previously accepted or even once-prestigious areas of "knowledge" (history, literature, art, music, and philosophy most notably); the increase in numbers of "administrators" with a proportionate decrease in numbers of "faculty"; and, perhaps most common of all, the use of purely political means to *give the appearance* of there no longer being adequate "funding" for maintaining the university's previous numbers of "personnel" (as in the phrase "faculty personnel").

Important and effective as each of these methods was, still another aspect of "faculty-management" from the Early Ante-Penultimate onward is even more deserving of notice. This is the phenomenon of faculty members committing—and being encouraged to commit— intellectual suicide by themselves becoming administrators.[8] In some extreme cases, this was done by faculty members' voluntarily stepping

---

[6] The original model of the university was radically different from this later corporate and hierarchic "pyramid." The old European (and American) university could better be thought of not as a pyramid at all but as a group of gathered cottages or small houses, some perhaps finer than others but none significantly higher. It should be mentioned that by the beginning of the final quarter of the Twentieth Century, from the Late Preliminary on through the Middle Ante-Penultimate, very close to *all* memory of the original role and purpose of faculty had been lost, even by those faculty themselves who remained inside what was still popularly referred to as "academia."

[7] See pp. 32 ff. in "Fragment II," subtitled "Budgetary." [Editor]

[8] Influences that could be powerful enough to cause educated people to choose intellectual death by becoming administrators might seem unimaginable. As a guide to this aspect of Middle Ante-Penultimate intellectual enervation, perversion, and self-destruction, however, see especially Larsen's "Fragment IV" (pp. 127–192) , containing the ambitious and brilliant seventh chapter, "Despair Notes: How Deconstructionism Happened and What It Really Meant," of Alan R. Bloomgarden and Ira Margolies' *The Decline of Literature and Reason in an Age of Theory* (Yale University Press, 1992). See the Editor's Note to "Fragment IV" for a discussion of the authorship question.

forth and *requesting*[9] to be sent to special "schools" where they would be taught "how" to be administrators. Much more often, however, the suicide was accomplished not through full-fledged adminstratorhood but through faculty members becoming "fund-raisers" and "grant-seekers" of various kinds, thus being transformed, by definition, into demi-administrators and immediately losing their intellectual independence and integrity. Most frequently of all, however, intellectual death was accomplished by means of faculty members' taking up or embracing types of so-called "learning" or "knowledge" that in fact were nothing of the kind but that consisted actually (and only) of image rather than content, being thus by definition "product" rather than anything with genuine intellectual content, and thus being historically of no interest to a faculty member but only to an administrator.[10] Even through the use of such debilitating, corrupting, and deforming measures as these, however, faculty very seldom rose to the same entirety of privilege, power, "ownership," and reward that true administrators enjoyed. Nevertheless, the results were efficient in the elimination of "faculty" through neutralization, and therefore the methods continued to be held in great value by administrators. Notably, in none of the archival research projects undertaken since The Collapse itself has any archaeological evidence come to light identifying even one single "converted" faculty member who considered his or her intellectual suicide to have been a loss rather than a gain, or even to have recorded the thought, whether in public or private, that such a question could so much as even have arisen. Even so, there does remain the possibility that the converteds, if secretly in a state of humiliation and despair, could have been lying.

•

As mentioned previously, because of the university structure that prevailed from the Late Preliminary onward (or possibly from even earlier), such archival information as we do possess is almost entirely that generated either by administrators themselves or by "converted" faculty, these being the only two camps (other than certain numbers of researchers in the "hard sciences") that had automatic access to encrypted, vaulted, and supra-heat-resistant storage and retrieval systems capable of surviving the firestorms of the Collapse.

---

[9] Notice the case of "Dr. Socialism" (whose disappearance Larsen somewhat wistfully regrets) as alluded to in Larsen's famous *"Diary."* Dr. Socialism is known to have been one of those who "volunteered" for such a "special 'administrative school.'"

[10] Again, see "Fragment IV" for examples of "fields of knowledge" of these pseudo-academic types.

Truly "unconverted" faculty members, on the other hand, being perceived by administrators as insignificant at best (albeit burdensome) and as implicitly dangerous saboteurs at worst, were caused to remain invariably under-equipped and poorly treated, even their physical health, as mentioned already, being put deliberately (although of course never openly) in jeopardy in the anticipation of premature death and thus early departure. As for the matter of the information storage and retrieval systems that were made available to the unconverteds, these remained primitive even into the Middle Penultimate. Evidence has been found showing that a small nucleus of urban American unconverted faculty members labored on archaic pre-Stigler, base-non-unified, sensory-depletive systems *as late as into the Middle Ultimate itself!*

All of which leads us to the Larsen papers themselves. So well known are these famous documents that in truth they need no introduction even to the non-specialist reader. The incalculable good fortune of our even being in possession of them, however; the almost infinite odds against their having been discovered at all in the ruins and ashes of the great burned city where Larsen long ago lived and worked—surely these are matters that deserve to be acknowledged once again as causes of amazement and gratitude even if only in passing.

As must, too, the sheer uniqueness of the documents. In spite of the often badly damaged state of some of the papers—so that in many cases we possess only widely separated pieces—the fragments and parts of whole writings that we do possess give us a clear idea of the scope, ambition, and intensity of Larsen's aim, his undyingly passionate concern for the doomed and inimical age he lived in, and, more sadly, the toll that all of this took on a mind so fine as his, as we know from the intimations of panic and perhaps breakdown itself that are hinted at in certain of the later papers,[11] even though these nevertheless remain some of this extraordinary thinker's most brilliant works.

By the time Larsen set out upon his final project, life in the American university—and nation—had become intensely uncongenial to unconverteds, whose sheer numbers had diminished enormously and whose extant contributions are therefore now extraordinarily rare. The Larsen papers, thus, are a part of that merest handful of surviving written works that are incontrovertibly known not to have been composed by administrators or by converteds but by single individuals from among that small, dwindling, turn-of-the-century category

---

[11] Though admittedly not *only* in the later papers. See the Editor's Notes throughout Volume Sixteen.

of unconverteds who, like Larsen himself, continued until the end[12] to struggle against the steady and (as we can now so easily see) increasingly deadly erosions of learning, meaning, and conscience in the decades preceding the Collapse.

But let us allow Larsen's words to speak for themselves across the great silence that followed the Ultimate, bringing us their observations not only of the daily life of a true unconverted, with its pronounced rigors, losses, and hopes, but offering us also a candid record of the inside workings and structure of the American university as it existed in the Late Ante-Penultimate and Early Penultimate—knowing now, as the doomed Larsen never could—what incalculable, immeasurable, crushing sorrows and losses were so soon to follow.

X. Jin Li
The Asia Press
31076 M'tai Cordon
Beijing-AY38
10 October 2147 C.E.

---

[12] The time and cause of the writer's death are not known with any certainty.

A NOTE ON THE CONDITION OF THE PAPERS

The Actaeon College of Institutional Analysis and Social Control was spared destruction by fire no more than were those areas of the city around it, whether immediately nearby or quite far away. A number of factors, even so, contributed to the fortunate and relatively complete survival of the Larsen documents.

We know that the college itself was housed in two buildings, neither of them especially large, one four stories high and the other six, known, respectively, as Non-Presidential Hall and Presidential Hall. By the time of the Ultimate, however, these structures had been pressed in upon by a number of very high urban towers—ranging from fifty to as many as ninety stories. Even so, those massive piles rose up only on that side of Actaeon toward the center of the city rather than on the side away from the center. As a result, when the Collapse actually took place, the hurricanic winds of the great fire-storm, rushing into the vacuum that had been created at the city-center, caused the great towers to topple *away* from Actaeon rather than *toward it*, with the result that the college's site was far less deeply buried in rubble than were other parts of the city, even those immediately adjacent.

Further, there is the matter of the location of the papers inside Actaeon itself. Although most scholars believe that the author had retired from the institution a number of decades before the onset of the Early Ultimate in 2031 (it is unknown—though considered highly doubtful—whether Larsen was any longer alive by that point), his *office* remained apparently untouched between the time of his departure and the end. Whether this was due simply to neglect, or to the precipitate decrease by then in the number of unconverteds (resulting in a diminished need for the inferior office space given them), or whether it was a reflection of the institutional chaos and absence of leadership or control by that time—these questions can never be answered for certain. What can be known, however, is that Larsen used the office as a repository for copies of every piece—or so it is now thought—of the writing that makes up any part of what we refer to with familiarity as The Larsen Papers.

In addition, the *location* of Larsen's office proved of major importance in the preservation—albeit a preservation both partial and imperfect—of the materials. In an interior and windowless room (in this, the smaller of Actaeon's buildings, most rooms were windowless) on the ground floor, the office was situated *directly below* the paired men's and women's latrines stacked above it in identical locations on the second, third, and fourth floors of the building.

At Actaeon, as elsewhere in the city and nation, fierce and uncontrolled vandalism preceded and accompanied the widespread arson in the weeks and months leading up to the true firestorms and final Collapse. At both of Actaeon's buildings, very strong evidence shows that this vandalism began *in the latrines before spreading elsewhere,* with the wanton sledging of ceramic fixtures and tiles and the breaking open of pipes of the kind used both for fresh water and for waste. Archival, historical, or archaeological research has discovered no other site where *latrines* were the first target of destruction. Whatever its cause, this anomaly in Actaeon's case was of very great consequence in the preservation of the Larsen papers. During a period that must have extended over weeks and perhaps even longer—in the time, that is, leading up to the firestorms themselves—Larsen's office was saturated by a steady supply of water from above, both fresh and waste. This meant that when fire at last had its turn and swept through the college buildings, the papers, being sodden, stood a vastly improved chance of withstanding complete destruction.

Even so, given the extraordinary intensity of the fire-storms, some degree of burning inevitably occurred, depending mainly on the way the papers happened to have been stacked, clipped, bound together, tied, or piled up. Top and bottom sheets were the most susceptible to loss, with the result that the author's exact intent as to beginnings and endings is not always clear, with some beginnings and endings missing altogether. Larsen, further, must have sometimes stacked the papers in random piles (for whatever reason), with the result that pages are sometimes absent in the very midst of a narrative or argument, creating lacunae of sizes we can only estimate, can do nothing to remedy, and can only regret.

In regard to damaged primary documents, editorial policy throughout has followed long-standing tradition in transferring them to the printed page in such a way as to duplicate as nearly as possible the exact physical appearance of the original. This policy explains, throughout, the presence of jagged beginnings or endings of text, sudden white spaces, and the absence of entire sections altogether. Finally, during the estimated eight decades that the papers remained in the office before their discovery, additional forms of deterioration naturally took place, beyond those caused merely by fire and water.

—Ed.

THE DIARY

(Part One)

iii

My Life in Education:
What I Learned from Thirty-Five Years
in the
University of New York (UNY):

by

Eric Larsen, B.A., M.A., Ph.D.,
Professor of English
The Actaeon College of Institutional Analysis and Social Control,
The University of New York (UNY)
New York, New York
U.S.A.

Editor's Note:

Through pure chance, a greater proportion
of the final section of the Larsen papers (the
"Diary") remains intact than is the case with
most other sections—although the possibility
remains that we in fact have only a small part of
the *"Diary,"* in spite of its already standing as the
second-longest single section of the papers. But
the simple lower case Roman numeral "three"
preceding the title as it has come to us clearly suggests the very strong likelihood that what we have

---

[13] See Editor's note below.

is only one of what must have been at least three parts. Incontrovertibly, in any case, the extant segment possesses claim to the standing of endpiece if only by merit of its dramatic shape and the obviously concluding—and tragic—tone of its end.

A great amount of scholarship has been devoted to the ambiguities of the *"Diary"*— possibly more than to any of the other fragments comprising the Larsen papers. The reason for this intensity of interest lies, obviously enough, in the great explicitness the *"Diary"* provides in its descriptions of American academia in the Late Ante Penultimate, when the "Calamity," as Larsen most often called it, was well under way, and the Penultimate waited for only the next few desperate acts to occur before its own unfolding.

Aside from its revelatory detail and remarkable portraits of individual figures, however, the fragment poses another important and ongoing question that has consistently attracted chroniclers, scholars, and analysts—and this is, of course, the great question of the state of Larsen's own emotional/psychological balance at this point in his life and at the time of composition. That there is in certain and observable fact a degree of imbalance[14] is accepted universally, though strenuous argument still exists[15] as to its true severity or the extent to which it may have caused this fragment[16]—more than the others in the Larsen canon—to be less perfectly and entirely trustworthy than it might be, serving instead as a mirror of neurosis or even of deeper and more debilitating dissociative illness or even trauma.

---

[14] This is clear enough simply from internal evidence. Larsen, for example, begins as though actually delivering an address on the occasion of his retirement from Actaeon; and yet not only does the diary-format of the piece belie the probability of this being true, but Larsen himself quickly drops the pretense and from that point on seems, perhaps more than anything else, simply to be talking—however brilliantly—to himself.

[15] See Hong-Koestler, Irena, and Petra Gubar, *Apollo or Cassandra? Victim or Prophet? A Historically based Analysis of the Question of Paranoia Versus Prophecy in the Larsen Papers* (Beijing, History House, 2110).

[16] Although neither can readers ignore the strong contention surrounding the balance question in the vitally important "Fragment IV." [Editor]

Further, while the presence of *some* associative discord or pathology is agreed upon by all, the question of its cause or origin has by no means stopped producing new analysis or rigorous debate—debate that is not infrequently tantamount to outright quarreling, it must be said. The issue is a vitally important one, having to do, very simply, with cause and effect: did the *institution* of Actaeon, in other words, or of UNY itself, drive the author mad; or, on the other hand, did the author's madness, like that of many hundreds other of his colleagues and peers, serve instead to help bring about the eventual downfall of the college, of the university, and, by extension, the American nation itself?

While the issue, indeed, is both valid and deeply important, and while it poses a question not yet decisively answered, the present editor feels it a pardonable intrusion to remark that the *very great majority* of readers believe the madness to have originated within Actaeon and the world around it, and to have then been visited upon the suffering steward of those values that it itself had abandoned.

Finally, as mentioned previously, separation of the *"Diary"* into three sections appearing separately from one another follows the now-traditional Bhāskara Presentation of 2110 CE.

5/26/06 7:38 AM (Wed.):

My dear friends and esteemed colleagues: As you know, I have been asked to offer a few words—to reminisce for a moment with those of you assembled here—on the occasion of my retirement from the humanities faculty of Actaeon.

I'm pleased to do this, of course, perhaps even immoderately so, and I find myself also perhaps unduly flattered. Whether any of you will see merit in my words or find them beneficial is impossible for me to say. But I nevertheless eagerly grasp this opportunity to speak openly and in the strictest honesty of my thoughts, feelings, and memories at this personally complex and significant moment.

As all know who know me at all well, I have always and with extreme earnestness—as critic, thinker, writer, and teacher—made the utmost effort to be fair, analytic, and clear-minded. In that same spirit of rigor, candor, and honesty, I am now eager to look back over my many long years at Actaeon; to look back both at the institution and at myself; to consider such few contributions as I may have been able to make; and to consider also such ways as I myself may have grown and benefited in return.

My thirty-five years in the Department of English of the Actaeon College of Institutional Analysis and Social Control, UNY, may not seem very many (indeed, they now seem quickly gone), but they *have* been continuous. In fact, they would comprise an unbroken span if it weren't for one semester in 1991 when I carried no teaching load and was therefore not on campus. Nevertheless, with or without that break in service (if you will permit my using that curiously militaristic term), my tenure at the college by any objective measure may be considered a lengthy one.

And, like all of you, or for that matter like all of us worldwide, who have gone through equivalent experience, I can testify to the extremes of change that such a period of dedication and effort is capable of bringing about in a person.

When I joined the faculty of Actaeon back in the autumn of 1971, I was a young man soon to be thirty-one. Now, as I prepare for my departure from the college, I have grown old, even having traveled half a decade past Yeats's "sixty-year-old smiling public man,"[17] an extent of agedness that when I started at Actaeon I could not imagine. Now, however, I must of course accept it.

6/3/06 12:34 PM (Thu.):

To continue. My early career at Actaeon, if I may risk immodesty, was a model of what any young instructor of the time might have hoped for. I was lucky in that I took up my post with degree in hand, in that I was supported by unusually strong references (although in those days, of course, unlike now, we were absolutely forbidden ever to see or read our own letters of recommendation), in that I carried with me the advantage of five years' prior experience in the classroom, and in that I had already accumulated a small number of respectable if not in fact prestigious publications.

The university itself, as everyone here knows and many experienced, was in a state then of unprecedented and even historic expansion. Veritable crops of new faculty were being hired, and my own department at Actaeon, as a consequence, was generally young, my age of thirty being far from unusual among its members. This

---

[17] From William Butler Yeats, "Among School Children," one of the ten poems still extant and known to have been written by this otherwise almost entirely lost poet. [Editor]

convergence of ages allowed for a pleasant and useful commonality of thought, view, and approach to flourish.

But the department was homogeneous also in other and even more significant ways, a state of affairs that I well remember and still treasure, albeit only in increasingly distant memory. Those of us in the departmental ranks found ourselves happily unified in spirit and attitude and in our sense of what might be called a shared duty. The group was blessed, further, by a kind of natural affability, a general freedom from jealousy or spite, and by a readiness not only to recognize but to reward accomplishment and merit in colleagues. In my own case—again, to risk immodesty—I was elected quickly to major committees, drafted into curriculum planning, and asked to compose position papers for discussion by the department of issues that would afterward be sent up to college-level committees. At the end of my fifth year, I was made associate, at the end of my sixth granted tenure, and at the end of my twelfth made full professor. During that time, even as some few and faint signs of the Calamity[18] were becoming visible, I continued (conscientiously and industriously, I must say) to teach and write, to serve on committees, and to find considerable pleasure in my colleagues. My family life, also, was happy, and I found myself unable to imagine what could conceivably stand in the way of my finding a professional lifetime of fulfillment in an academic career at Actaeon.

6/4/06 1:05 AM (Fri.):

Other branches of the university, unquestionably, were far more attractive physically than Actaeon, some of them being blessed even with the luxuries of lawns, trees, and ivies of the kind familiar to me from my own wonderful student years at Carleton College and afterward at the universities of Wisconsin and Iowa.[19] Ever since that early time in my own intellectual and emotional life, I have associated the pleasures of such breadth, openness, and greenery as I knew then with the high and true values of composure, thoughtfulness, balance, patience, and quietness that are—or so I once was privileged to believe—essential and traditional parts of the academic life.

Actaeon, however, from the start, was extraordinarily unpleasant to all of the senses. Being a relatively new college (my own first year was the college's sixth), it of course could not have been expected to boast the lovely and appealing pleasures of mid-nineteenth-century

---

[18] Larsen's first use of this term, which, significantly, he apparently sees no need to define for his audience—if indeed he is addressing one. [Editor]

[19] None of them, of course, any longer in existence. [Editor]

academic architecture, rooms with high ceilings and cathedral windows, or the pleasantly softened tones of timeworn limestone, brick, or granite.

Actaeon, however, so aggressively bespoke the absence of features such as those that I was not alone in finding it sometimes difficult to quell a feeling of having been, as if through some insidious cosmic plan, singled out for abuse.

The college was housed in two separate buildings, and while one of them was unquestionably by far the more appealing, it was not the one that housed my own department, office, or classrooms.

"My" building[20] (known originally as "East Hall" though soon afterward, through a negative formation, invariably as "Non-Presidential Hall") was—is—low, rectangular, flat-roofed, and ugly. Filling the better part of a city block not far from the Hudson River, the west side highway, and the rail yards, it is fitted with long industrial-style windows inherited from the building's previous life as an assembly plant for electric motors, sealed bearings, and various lines of small home appliances such as kitchen blenders, water-pics, and vibrators—all of which may (I later came to think) have left their mark on the spirit of the place when, as home to Actaeon, it was dedicated to a kind of manufacture not greatly more elevated than its previous ones.

But I should not, I know, however faintly, allow scorn to find its way into my words on an occasion like this one, deserving as it is, in the tradition of such moments, of a dignified, balanced, and measured retrospection.

Actaeon, indeed—a fact of great importance—was only a single part of an enormous university that with the highest of aims, the year before my arrival, had thrown its doors open to any child of the city, whether excellently or poorly prepared, who wished to reach for the benefits, privileges, and opportunities that might be made attainable to the holder of a baccalaureate degree.

Without question, an expansive and ambitiously idealistic policy such as this, a policy of "open" admissions throughout the university, brought with it great numbers of complexities, rigors, and difficulties in the daily operation and organization of each college. Actaeon was no exception. And yet, difficulties notwithstanding, the new

---

[20] As the reader will notice, Larsen by this point has either given up or lost his opening premise that he was giving an "address." He might almost as well, from here on, be talking simply to himself. It is impossible to know whether he has "lost his place," as it were, or is deliberately putting into effect a subtle narrative plan that he has had in mind from the start—a question that is important to an understanding of the author's mental state, and to the extent of the moral, intellectual, and emotional strain he is experiencing by this point. [Editor]

admissions policy posed a challenge to which no educated person of progressive or tolerant mind could fail to respond—and I, by education, background, instinct, and temperament, was such a one.

6/5/06 4:34 AM (Sat.):

And so, no matter how nostalgic my memories of ivied walls, spreading lawns, and the weather-softened stones of academic buildings overlooking a meandering Iowa river, I had no delusion that such would make up a part of my new urban vocation. The great city itself was far different from the rural and semi-rural states where I had been educated and raised. And UNY itself, with Actaeon as a part of it, was reaching out into a new element of that burgeoning city's psyche and population, opening its arms now more widely and with a grander social purpose than ever before.

Or so I believed, so I believed, so I believed, as a result of my own native and learned idealism. My belief in turn served only to generate even more excitement, zeal, and sense of purpose. Here, I felt, residing in the heart of that moment, was a clear and welcome sense of social, political, and intellectual vocation. To use the word again, idealism was in the air, while at the same time everyone understood, realistically, that certain compromises would have to be made in order for genuine, real, practical academic success to be attained.

As a result, in those first years, it was easy for me to be tolerant of my building's deficiencies. Suffering them gladly in the name of the ideal, I suffered them also on the just and practical assumption that as time passed and the great experiment succeeded, they would be taken care of: in time, they would be transformed at least into the acceptable if not the outright appealing.

In this building, then, to be my academic home for longer than three decades, were outside walls not of 1860s limestone but of 1950s pale brick. Here were no leaded casements set into ivied stone, but factory windows with cyclone fencing across their faces. Here were no high ceilings but oppressively low ones of fiber-board instead; no open spaces, but constricted ones—rooms, cubicles, closets. Here were walls of plasterboard that fists and voices could pass through with almost equal ease. And here were rooms, in the huge majority of cases, without any windows at all.

Toward none of this, even so,

6/7/06 8:49 PM (Mon.)

was objection lodged or discontent expressed, if only because all of it was still new, the college young, the experiment just beginning. Certainly, as soon as possible, all the deficiencies—in order of importance, commonality, and severity—would be addressed, improved, or repaired.

But that was thirty-five years ago. Three and a half decades. *Twelve thousand seven hundred eighty-one days.*[21] And in all that time, there has been no change, not a jot or a tittle, none, not a particle.

6/8/06 3:56 AM (Tue.):

I return.[22]

In those early days, even the absence of simple, basic, essential things—the absence of breathing, for example, or of hearing; of speaking with ease, or of possessing reasonable freedom from airborne microbes; the luxury of urinating or defecating without substantially increased risk of illness or physical injury—the absence even of such things as these and of other fundamentals, in those early years, were met by all with forbearance, patience, and humor—with, that is, an *esprit de corps* now long since a thing of the past—in the certainty that they would be dealt with as the college found its momentum and got its footing.

In the meantime, however, so badly designed was the ventilating system that different parts of the building received its benefits either not at all or in such excess as to make, either way, entire areas all but unlivable.

For the greatest part of each year, classrooms were either far too hot or far too cold, so that students, sprawled or slumped in their seats, fanning themselves with papers, fell asleep one by one—or else they sat hunched forward like monks, conserving what body heat they could, never removing their coats, and taking notes (if they did so at all) with their gloves or mittens on.

Toward the end of the first decade or so, adjustments were often made, it is true, but always fruitlessly; and there was one unbroken period of nine or ten years when the ceiling vents blew air into the classrooms with such ferocity and in such quantities, whether hot or cold, that no one could bear to remain directly under them, while the deep, ship's-engine rumble of the stressed and vibrating air ducts, along with the roar and pouring-out of the air itself, set up so loud and steady a noise, like that in a wind tunnel, that no one could be heard except by shouting, or, on the worst days, and I add this without exaggeration, except by

---

[21] The figure has been adjusted by the addition of nine leap days. [Author's note]

[22] As usual, one cannot help but wonder at the curiously irregular hours kept by the author throughout the entire *"Diary."* For a consideration of this subject, see Chapter Two of the aforementioned Irena Hong-Koestler and Petra Gubar (*Apollo or Cassandra? Victim or Prophet? A Historically based Analysis of the Question of Paranoia Versus Prophecy in the Larsen Papers*, Beijing, History House, 2110).

6/9/06 9:37 AM (Wed.)
screaming.[23]

6/10/06 9:57 AM (Thu.):
I will never know with certainty, I suppose, which was the cause of which:[24] whether Actaeon's repugnant environment, through having the effect of lowering resilience and degrading morale, was what brought about the steady erosion in student self-assessment that I was to see over the years; or whether that same putrid environment was in fact a kind of policy statement—first issued from President Penguin-Duck's office—of what the students actually were like and were deserving of, the expression, that is, of a negative standard whose truth the students then in turn acknowledged by gradually, over the years, adjusting themselves downward to meet its prediction.

Either way, as change continued not to occur (as, to this very day, I quickly add, it has continued not to occur), certain unpleasant, ominous, and sometimes dreadful signs of the real nature of the situation began very gradually to become evident.

Those within Actaeon who were thoughtful and reasonable people, of course, were easily identifiable by the nature of their responses to those signs. Rational responses reflected rational minds, and without immodesty I believe that I was then and am still now able to place myself among the rational.[25] My own reactions to the emerging signs (and my own reactions to intellectual life at Actaeon generally) took form near the middle of the 1970s and have continued unchanged to this day. Specifically, I began, at that time, an assiduous effort to keep my bowels trained and my diet spartan and as near spiceless as possible, both measures undertaken in order that I could avoid ever needing to have a bowel movement during any given period of time that I was in the Actaeon building.

---

[23] See Hong-Koestler/Gubar, again (Chapter Eight, "Day by Day, Hour by Hour, Minute by Minute: Larsen's Narrative as Countdown to Calamity"), for a discussion of Larsen's irregularly "broken" narrative. [Editor]

[24] See Editor's Note at the beginning of this section. That Larsen found the question of cause and effect to be important in Actaeon's history and, by implication, his own collapse, has been taken by several analysts as evidence of his own probable freedom from instability or breakdown; others, however, have argued the opposite. See, for example, Frederik Nissen, "Negotiations with a Non-Future: Courageous Sanity in the *"Diary"* (*Annals of Lost Americana,* May 2130, pp. 34-51) and Lok-Ho Woo, "Madness Day by Day in the *"Diary"* of Eric Larsen: The Destruction of an Artist and Thinker in the Late Ante-Penultimate Period of the American Collapse" (*Studies in American Intellectual History,* August 2128, pp. 89–110).

[25] Readers, finally, must decide for themselves. The critical literature, however, is abundant and extremely rich. [Editor]

I began doing the same with my urine,[26] minimizing its production as far as possible by allowing myself no juice and only a single espresso on the mornings when I was to be in the building and, during the hours I spent there, by rinsing and spitting rather than actually swallowing water at the fountains (insofar as I was able to do this, since at certain times, after much screaming, the throat can scarcely survive without moistening, though even then I can occasionally satisfy it through gargling). As a result of these practices, I became dehydrated long before the end of a class day, and very often I became constipated as well, the cause being dearth of liquids. But the benefits of the regimen far outweighed its detrimental elements, since by keeping it I could avoid almost entirely—it occurring seldom more than once a month, usually not even once—the need to go into any of the Actaeon latrines.

And avoiding the latrines, in a word, was not merely desirable, but remained the only course dictated by intelligence and reason, due simply to the latrines' obvious unpleasantness and danger. During original construction—whether under specific orders from President Penguin-Duck's office, I am not certain—it was determined not that ventilation in the latrines, as in the classrooms, should be merely inadequate, but, more brilliantly, *that it should not exist in any way whatsoever.* This plan, adhered to unwaveringly in the thirty-five years that have passed, was doubtless made easier to implement than might otherwise have been the case by its having been clearly stipulated from the start that *all latrines throughout Actaeon* be placed in windowless rooms deep inside the interior confines of the building.

This policy's effects, as anyone can imagine and many of you here[27] know through experience, are numerous. One, in itself not harmful but merely unpleasant, is the ambient silence that persists in these rooms. Due to the intense quietness, you will hear in any of them, early or late, the sound of urine plashing into water. For the fact is, as everyone knows, that the all but universal laws governing the nature and demonstration of manliness dictate that duration and volume (both in sound and quantity) of urination are qualities directly proportionate to the degrees of manliness, extroversion, and confidence in the urinator.

And so it is that the widespread assertion of virility through demonstrative urinating is something that can't be escaped by anyone, no matter how retiring or mild mannered they themselves might be, who needs to enter any of the Actaeon latrines. Whether

---

[26] And still do. [Author's note]

[27] An interesting "slip" of understandable interest to analysts. Is the author hallucinating? Does he really "see" an audience? Nissen, Woo, and Hong-Koestler/Gubar all delve with fascinating results into these and associated questions. [Editor]

the feature of near-total silence in the latrines was part of the original college plan or a feature that arose *per accidens* as a result of airlessness is, is I have suggested, not known to me.

On the subject of urination, however, let me say just this much in passing:[28] that it is remarkably easy to evaluate not only character but the even more important "survivability-quotient" of individual staff members by the simple method of observing volume and pressure during typical urination. Obviously, a truly thorough and scientific study of urination would be of enormous practical value to those faced with making decisions about higher education policy. My own suggestion, however, is that it would prove even more germane to any serious evaluations of the well-being of the "college community" itself, including quality of personnel, level of morale, and, as mentioned, degree of survivability quotient.

Simply by watching[29] and listening as the urine is expunged, then recording the data carefully, one can arrive at remarkably accurate profiles not only of the temperament and personality of the urinator but also of the nature—or the total absence—of his interior life. The observations can be made with administrators and colleagues who differ as much, say, as Dr. Razor or Dr. Colon on the one hand and Dr. Gender, Dr. Blue-Collar, Dr. Muscle, or Dr. Ethnicity on the other; or Dr. Meek or Dr. Book on the one hand and any of the Deans Glad, Happyhand, Shark,[30] Dank, Rattle, or Slapster[31] on the other.

Obviously, in the case of President Penguin-Duck himself, information of this kind would be of extreme interest. But, while other faculty members may very well have seen and heard him urinate, it need hardly be said that I myself am not among their number.[32]

---

[28] An insufferable pun. If Larsen weren't an author who notices *everything,* a reader might guess that he failed to notice this one. [Editor]

[29] Stance, position, and body-attitude are obviously of great importance in revealing both character and survivability quotient, as are other observable traits of behavior—for example whether vocalization occurs during the act of urinating, or whether conversation is encouraged or discouraged. Are the eyes open or closed? If closed, what does this mean? If open, where are they directed? Downward, in an effort to achieve a semblance of privacy? Or upward, in entirely the opposite manner, as with those who arch themselves and throw back their heads during the act: are the eyes then kept open, cast as they are toward the ceiling itself? [Author's Note]

[30] Many years ago, I myself once observed Deans Glad, Happyhand, and Shark standing shoulder to shoulder at three adjacent urinals, all, as they urinated, with their backs identically arched and eyes flung to the ceiling. I have pondered the meaning of the sight ever since. [Author's Note]

[31] Who does in fact vocalize during urination. [Author's Note]

[32] And yet of course, while he may never have seen him urinate, Larsen was destined indeed to see President Penguin-Duck defecate—this during the President's betrayal of the author after Larsen's failed effort to expunge Sasha Brearly from his classroom. The entire famous and pivotal incident, as the masses of its readers know, takes place in the third and concluding part of the "Diary" (p. 235 ff.). [Editor]

6/12/06 2:06 AM (Sat.):

I must confess to having told an untruth earlier, at the beginning of this talk.[33] I'm shamed to admit it, though I can honestly say, at least, that it was only a lie of omission.

Remarking on my early career at Actaeon, nevertheless, I allowed the impression to remain that I had accepted my post of my own free will, as a matter of choice. In truth, this was in no way the case.

In 1971, the market for people with new degrees in the humanities was no less dwindling, barren, and meager than it was to become later on.[34] The three hundred fifty-nine applications I sent out during my last year of graduate study at Iowa City resulted in only four interviews and a single offer—that, of course, being Actaeon's, which itself wouldn't have existed either were it not for the university's enormous push into open admissions at the time.

I was in no manner lacking in merit, academic or scholarly. That was true. Nor, as I've said, was I unmoved by the challenge of my new position, or by the state of the university at the time, it being also true that my idealism was plucked and made reverberant by the university's great experiment.

But that I may have chosen Actaeon over other schools, few or many, is without the smallest grain of truth whatsoever. Like the jobs of most of my colleagues at Actaeon, mine was the result of free choice in no other way than that I was, indeed, entirely free to take it or leave it.

The careful listener, thus alerted, may begin to suspect other lies—of omission, only—in things I've said. Yes, the truth is that very quickly in those early years it became clear that my academic credentials held no currency elsewhere, making me essentially a prisoner at Actaeon, assuming I chose to remain in academics at all. Consequently, as the university's ideal of open admissions began to fail, its dream to dissipate and fade—and this happening far earlier, in truth, than I've allowed myself to suggest—the accompanying sense of despond was greater than it would have been had I—and my colleagues—been free simply to give it up and move on.

---

[33] See note 15, p. 12. Both Nissenson and Woo, though dramatically opposed in the substance of their arguments, remark on the feebleness of Larsen's maintaining the fiction of the *"Diary"* as a real retirement address ("this talk"). All agree that as he continues, the *absence* of audience and Larsen's resulting and extreme *aloneness* are in fact what become steadily more and more apparent. [Editor]

[34] Maximillian Shandra (*The Collapse of History: Statistical Analyses of American Fields of Study in the Early Penultimate* [Bangkok & Tokyo, 2099]) points out that by the year 2011 only *three* American universities still offered majors or degree programs in literary studies organized on historical principles. Everywhere else, such studies were organized by theme, race, gender, class, and ethnicity far and away the most common, for reasons utterly mysterious and impenetrable to us today. [Editor]

But we weren't. And despond on the desert island is quite different from despond in a land of plenty.

In this way possibly can be explained, at least in part, the malaise, disappointment, sorrow, exhaustion, and gloom that some of you may have detected as an undercurrent in my words from the start, try as I may have done to put a bright face on the occasion of my departure from the place that has been my professional home now for so long a time.

The fact is that the grim direction Actaeon was headed under the leadership of President Penguin-Duck became evident very early on indeed, however faint the first dreadful hints may have been.

The airlessness of the latrines, those godless rooms into which male colleagues, students, and staff made their way in order to reveal the quality of their characters through their manner of voiding urine—the absence of fresh or even moving air in the latrines resulted in greater degrees of unpleasantness than I have mentioned. While a person was in the latrines, it was natural to try not to breathe, although of course this was impossible for any great length of time, not long enough to urinate oneself, no matter how heroic an effort one made to hold off between gasping intakes (through the mouth, of course). The sounds alone that were to be heard in the latrines were a deterrent to the slightest lingering: not the urinary plashings so much as the more rigorously graphic sounds—farts, moans, expletives, splashes, plops, and, worst of all, the projectile diarrheic gushings—from behind the stall doors.

In the absence of fresh or even moving air, and in the confines of a room windowless and small, the scents, odors, and stenches created by moaning figures hunched in their solitary and straining misery behind rows of closed doors can easily be imagined—as can the laments of the others in the room who found it necessary—pitiably choosing life over death—to draw this fouled air into their lungs, across their taste buds, and as last resorts in through their nostrils.

In student life, neither healthful nor regular diet, of course, can ever be assumed. In the case of Actaeon students, however, it seemed to me, judging not just from the smells and sounds in the latrines but from other evidence also, that as their morale continued to drop, so did their attention to the maintaining of even residually wholesome diets. Not only did the stenches in the latrines become stronger and more omnipresent from a time early on, but other signs of discouragement among the students beyond eating poorly became evident as well. Not even I, as I mentioned, was always able to avoid the latrines, though I doubled my efforts at plainness and regularity of diet after discovering once, right at my elbow as I hunched in the gloom of one of the stalls, a rainbow-arc of human feces, thickly enough applied to the wall so as to be not yet fully hardened, the smallness and half-light of the booth necessitating that my eyes, in order to see, be only inches from it, the nose I smelled it with all too nearly touching the very substance. If ever member of mankind knew an incentive toward stricture of bowel and regulation of diet, it was for me that experience in that booth on that day—though an even more disconcerting portent of despair, murder, and malaise awaited me a time later, when I was forced into the latrine once again, this time by the workings of a cruel intestinal flu. Hunched again on the dank and foul stool in the vile little closet, I saw—inches from my eyes as in my straining misery I raised them to look forward—three bullet holes in the stall door. The holes formed a scalene triangle, its points two to three inches apart from one another. I positioned my eye cautiously behind one of them and saw a slightly larger but geometrically equivalent triangle on the wall between two urinals, where the unleashed bullets had blown away holes the size of half dollars in the ceramic tiles.

A major and vitally important element of Actaeon's academic "mission," as all know, is its dedication to the study of "social control" in its myriad manifestations and applications.[35, 36] Without question, it was entirely possible that whoever, sitting on this toilet in this stall in this latrine, discharged his gun three times to create these six holes, had done so as part of a research project or course assignment, although whether this may have been at the introductory or the advanced level, I have no clear idea.

I, of course, looked at the bullet holes from the point of view of a scholar trained not in the social sciences but in the humanities. And this could be why my own conjecture was that whoever put the holes in the door and wall did so most probably out of rage, madness, or despair, and that—I could not help but conclude—these passions had been brought about by a growing consciousness of the direction that Actaeon seemed to be moving under the guidance of President Penguin-Duck. Similar if less violent indications of abandonment and malaise were observable everywhere—in the sheer inability of the vast majority of Actaeon students, for example, to complete their class assignments on any regular basis, or on any basis at all; or in the case of the bright young man, a semester after graduating, who

---

[35] For a detailed discussion of the Actaeon "mission," see my unpublished paper, "Curriculum or Campaign? Politics and Intellectual Bankruptcy in College Curricula, with The Actaeon College of Institutional Analysis and Social Control as a Model." The paper is available in the Actaeon library on closed reserve. [Author's Note]

[36] One of the greatest sorrows of scholarship is that no remnants of this title have been discovered among the Larsen papers. Larsen's own, in fact, is believed to be the only known reference to it anywhere. [Editor]

returned for a visit and, having taken a chair in my office, sobbed help-lessly into his hands as he told me that Actaeon had prepared him for nothing whatsoever in the real academic or professional world; or, most alarming and foreboding of all, in the cases of the many young graduates who wrote to me saying that they missed me and that I had been *the best of all their instructors at Actaeon*—assertions that I took in every single case to be signs, if not of outright psychological imbal-ance resulting from the ravages of their time at Actaeon, then at best of clinical depression or of a deep, unreachable disorientation and detachment from reality.

The most shocking signs of despair and malaise, however, at least to me personally, were the death threats I received from students whose sense of self-worth had been so inadequately tended to or so severely damaged by their experience at Actaeon that murder actu-ally occurred to them as a potentially reasonable step in resolving the perversions and difficulties of college life. One such student was a pudgy but bright malcontent who had made no secret either in class-room or in conference of his strong animosity and indignant sense of injustice at being, as he saw it, patronized by my assumption that I knew more than he did about the material and my consequent insis-tence on leading class each day. Having come to see me in my office, he said, pausing at the door on his way out and looking back at me, "What you better do is just watch out you don't make me mad. Last time I got mad, the guy ended up with a hole for a face."

And out he went. After a cautious delay, I, on legs of jelly, tiptoed to the door; most, most quietly pushed it shut until I heard the latch click; then locked it firmly behind him.

That happened late enough in my tenure at Actaeon that I had already trained my bowels not to move during the day, although now, I must admit, in my terror at what had just taken place, I was hard pressed, even with sitting down again and clenching my buttocks powerfully, to keep them from their natural expression. I thought of the bullet holes in the latrine door, and I thought about my study of them. These thoughts now made all the more vivid the image I had been left with by my student—blood and fleshy bits sprayed across the wall behind my desk and I, other than being faceless, lying as if napping on the floor.

Of such frights, this was not the last in my time at Actaeon, nor was it the first—which, though far from the most dangerous of its kind, remains in my memory through its having been somehow one of the most frightening. Working at my desk quite early one morning, my office door left open in a professional gesture of my readiness to serve, I sensed that I was not alone. I had heard no sound of any kind, but, when I looked up, I saw, filling the entire doorway, an immense, broad, towering, muscular giant of a man whose coal-black eyes were fixed on me and yet seemed at the same time to be looking through me, fixed on nothing. He simply stared, and stared, and stared, as if he were sleeping while awake, or catatonic—or quite, quite mad.

It was like being gazed upon by death, or by the wish-for-death, or by the you-soon-will-be-dead. I spoke—the politeness in my voice seeming patently absurd—asking, "May I help you?" There was no response. When I spoke again—"Is there someone you're looking for?"—still none. By then extremely frightened, I found the self-possession to push my chair back slowly, as one might do upon finding a huge coiled snake at the door And as I pushed back, I also, more slowly still, rose to my feet.

And there we stood, he and I: he, through his piercing yet empty eyes, seeing in me I know not what; and I, I felt *certain,* seeing in him an abyss of nothingness, oblivion, and death. *Here* was a test for my bowels, the very bottom dropping out of them even as I stood petrified with fear. Had the ominous figure stepped toward me, pressing me into the corner of my shabby little office, I don't know what I would have done, unless perhaps kick my way through the plasterboard wall into the adjacent office, then through that one to the next, tunneling through the building like a blind rat chewing its way toward escape.

But, as silently as he had arrived, he simply withdrew, turned, and disappeared. As terror loosed its grip sufficiently to unparalyze me, I went and closed the door as quietly and gently as if I were putting a sleeping baby to bed, and then, scarcely able with my trembling hands, turned the lock.

This happened sometime in my fifth or sixth year at Actaeon. And never since, for three entire decades, have I left my door either open or unlocked during any time I am inside alone. And never have I opened it for any person until, no matter what time of day or night, they have told me, through the door, who they are and what they want.

FRAGMENT I -"BUDGETARY"

Editor's Note:

Known as one of the "collected and collated" pieces found among the Larsen papers, "Fragment I" is comprised entirely of memos, flyers, notices from internal Actaeon newsletters, and the like. We owe its earliest preservation, editing, and cataloguing primarily to the effort and scholarship of X. I. Wei, whose work in this area of the Larsen papers has been exhaustive. She has—here and elsewhere—kept all materials intact precisely as found or, in cases of unnumbered or otherwise damaged pages, has carefully recreated the sequence in which Larsen most apparently intended the items to be read. Many sheets, of course (in spite of their having been stapled or clipped together by the author), were separated when undergoing other heavy damage, and innumerable others can only be assumed to have been lost through complete destruction. Nevertheless, "collage" segments like "Fragment I" remain one of the most fascinating of the several varieties of projects found among the Larsen collection, for in them, as it were, the author speaks in silence.

He cruelly satirizes some of the most egregious, shocking, far-reaching, and destabilizing abuses within Middle and Late Ante-Penultimate academia, and yet he does so (very possibly as protection against recrimination from administrators or converteds) without uttering so much as a single word of his own. As the reader will discover, this "silent" or "hidden" method will be of even greater importance in "Fragment II," subtitled "Voicemail."

Damage to the sheets in both is regrettable, though fortunately it is less extensive than in other sections of the papers.

"Budgetary"

1

To: The Actaeon College Community
From: Dean and Vice-President Terrance Happyhand, Ph.D.
Subject: Flyers
Date: August 30, 1999

Sometimes department flyers are posted on walls, doors and in the elevators. Posting announcements in these locations in a sense does violence to the environment of the college community and sets a questionable example for student groups announcing their events.

As a community composed of faculty and staff, departments and student organizations the environment of The Actaeon College of Institutional Analysis and Social Control should be maintained at the highest level. There is a moral obligation that each part of the community follow the established rule it erodes the rule for the entire community.

Please accordingly inform those individuals who do your posting.

2

REPORT TO THE QUALITY OF LIFE COMMITTEE
(Attachment A)

(Committee Membership: Dean & Vice-President Roland Glad [chair]; Dean & Vice-President Terrance Happyhand; Dean & Vice-President

Don Hammerhead; Prof. Sally Mandrake; Prof. Warren Wetmore; Prof. Car Cleopatra)

The following concerns were presented as action items to the committee as a whole by Professors Mandrake & Cleopatra:

1. Fire safety: hallway on third floor of Non-Presidential Hall is used for storage, blocking exit.
2. Fire safety: stairwell C, leading to emergency exit, is filled with discarded lockers.
3. Fire safety: fire doors fail to close tightly, remaining ajar, and could not block smoke.
4. Quality of air in Non-Presidential Hall is deleterious, people often becoming ill after only a few hours.
5. NPH (Non-Presidential Hall) needs additional main entrance, crowds being an impediment to entering and exiting.
6. Newspapers and flyers are strewn daily across Non-Presidential Hall lobby floor.
7. Classrooms are filthy, littered with empty bottles, candy wrappers, food, spilled sodas, papers, etc.
8. Blackboards, tables, desks in classrooms need washing.
9. Many desks and tables in classrooms are broken.
10. Clocks in classrooms and hallways of NPH all differ, often by many hours.
11. Fifty percent of NPH classrooms are without clocks altogether.
12. Clocks need replacing on side walls, not front, so that both students and instructor can see them.
13. Classrooms in north end of NPH are without noise insulation: one class hears another.
14. NPH classrooms are intolerably hot, needing fans until permanent repair.
15. NPH classrooms are intolerably cold, needing supplementary heating until permanent repair.
16. Mouse droppings throughout NPH.
            cleaning desperately needed.
                in offices, after 24 years, in grave need of replacemen
                    ughout in need of painting.
                        broken for five years, since Spring 199
                        and men's rooms throughout in need of ventilati
                            ctioning faucets in Non-Presidential Hall men's and wom-
en's roo
                    and Women's rooms in NPH lack shelves for papers and books
in each stall.
            en's and women's rooms need shelves for books, etc., at sinks.

24. All men's rooms, in NPH and in Presidential Hall, need shelves for books, etc., at urinals.
25. Graffiti in NPH classrooms, halls, and rest rooms need
26. Toilet stall latches in women's rooms broken.
27. Toilet stall latches in men's rooms broke
28 Non-Presidential Hall 3rd floor men's room: stall for those with
29. Lighting in conference rooms dim.
30. Faculty Dining Room needs renov
31. Buildings during night classes lack secur
32. House phones to Security—as in Presidenti
33. Advertisements on wall
34. Telephone failu
35. Copy servi
36. Use o
37. Ap
3

3

To: Faculty of Actaeon College of Institutional Analysis
           and Social Control
From: Actaeon "Town" Meetings Planning Committee (Dean
           Smith Rattle, Chair)
Subject: "Town" Meetings
Date: August 31, 1999

Since 1990, "Town" meetings have become an intrinsic and invaluable component of the Actaeon community. It serves as a tool for healing and growth, giving students, faculty and staff an on-going forum for the exchange of ideas, concerns and ever changing information critical to the academic world of Actaeon, the university, and their world.

Please announce all meeting dates for the fall semester.

4

To: Dr. Morton R. Penguin-Duck, President, Actaeon
From: Dr. Orton Trulock, UNY Chancellor
Subject: Spending and the Actaeon Budget
Date: May 7, 2000

Dear Morton:

I have recently studied the projected annual income and outgo of moneys for our university colleges. After poring over this information for The Actaeon College of Institutional Analysis and Social Control and having found a record of gross over-expenditure, I have become greatly concerned about your institution's financial condition.

Attached is a copy of the data I have seen, consisting of reports received by me from the University-wide Budget and Fiscal Affairs Maintenance Office (UWBAFAMO), covering Actaeon's FY 1999 and FY 2000 budgets. At the present time, UWBAFAMO projects a year-end deficit of $3.4 million (or 9%) for Actaeon. This deficit is due to an under-collection of revenue in the amount of $0.05 million and a frankly hard to believe over-expenditure of $3.35 million. At present rates of collection and expenditure, UWBAFAMO projects for Actaeon's FY 2001 overspending of 2.8% in excess of that for FY 2000.

It is imperative that the college immediately develop a comprehensive financial plan to eliminate this deficit without failure or delay. Your plan cannot rely on additional resources from the university and must
within the scope
including fac
convert
who d
wis
h [37]

5

To: The Actaeon College Community
From: President Morton R. Penguin-Duck
Subject: Greetings for the 2000-2001 Year
Date: September 9, 2000

It has been a grand summer and a difficult summer. It has been a grand summer in that I was able to travel widely to a number of major cities in Europe, South America, and Asia, and, in response to the

---

[37] How Larsen might have come into possession of a letter such as this, from Chancellor to President, is unknown. Its tone, nevertheless, clearly suggests Trulock's distaste for and disapproval of President Penguin-Duck's over-expenditures. How these reached the extent of excess they did without being curtailed by higher authority is, also, unknown. Breakdown of exactly this kind, of course, became increasingly prevalent as the Late-Ante Penultimate gave way to the greater disasters of the Penultimate. [Editor]

many invitations we had received, to offer in those places, with the capable assistance of Vice Presidents & Deans Glad, Hammerhead, Happyhand, Shark, Dank, Rattle, and Slapster, our world-famous Actaeon Seminar on Being Human with Dignity, Maintaining the Right of Human Dignity, and Asserting the Rights of Being Nice (BHWID-MTROHD-AASTROBN).

It has been a difficult summer, however, as a consequence of controversial university-instituted tightening of budgets. This action on the part of the university, in regard to Actaeon, which I have resisted strongly, has resulted in our being required to trim $6.8 million from Actaeon's spending over the next two years. The Vice-Presidents & Deans and I, however, have already developed a budget-reduction plan and will be discussing it with the university—and with all members of the Actaeon College community—in the near future.

In the long run, I have every confidence in our plan and firmly believe that the Actaeon budget will remain, as ever, solid, strong, and purposeful, and that the work and business of the college, once again as ever, will go on with enthusiasm and strength. We have had a very good fall registration with a headcount increase of approximately 0.075-0.078% over last year's. Our objective in the future must be enrollment, enrollment, enrollment. In recent years, enrollment has gone down slightly and we have suffered badly. Therefore I will ask the entire Actaeon College community for assistance in raising our headcount, as I will also in our efforts to improve student retention. For now, as I have said, our objective must be enrollment, enrollment, enrollment.

While there are multiple strategies we must employ to achieve this objective, experience has taught me that a strong focus with the goal of exceeding expectations is an important characteristic of all world class institutions such as ours. Having a sense of urgency, creativity, the courage to make difficult decisions and bottom-line accountability are critical tools for success in situations of this kind as they always have been. Equally important, a willingness to change and to adopt new academic and administrative models is essential and I will be consulting with many of you on these questions throughout the coming months.

We are firmly marshaled to move forward as always. May we all have a grand year.

6

Message one, forwarded by extension 693462, was received at 10:10 am, Wednesday, September. 23rd:
It is with deep sorrow to announce the passing of Mr. Samuel G.

Coffey, who for many years served as Actaeon's Associate Registrar. Funeral services will be held as follows: Kinderhook Funeral Home, located at 4356 Horse Pond Road in Sunhill, New Jersey. Viewing will be Friday, September 26th, 2000, between the hours of 2 p.m. to 4 p.m., also 7 p.m. to 9 p. m. The funeral will also be held at Kinderhook Funeral Home, on Saturday, September 27th, at 11 a.m. Directions to Kinderhook Funeral Home is take the George Washington Bridge to Route 6-East, travel 10 miles to Hook River Road, exit at the bottom of the exit ramp, you bear left, travel one half mile, funeral home is located on the left side. If you have any further questions please feel free to give Irene Rojas a call at 7640 in President Penguin-Duck's office. Thank you. Goodbye.

7

Message three, forwarded by extension 693462, was received at 6:40 pm, Tuesday, October 14th:
This is a message to all members of the Actaeon College community. It is with great sorrow that we notify you of the passing of Dr. James Mooney, who for the past three decades has so capably served Actaeon as chairman of the Foreign Languages and Literatures Department. The wake[38] will be held on Thursday, October 16th, from 2 to 7 p.m. at the Thomas M. Carel Funeral Home at 89th St. between Amsterdam and Columbus. The funeral[39] will be held on Saturday October 18th at 10 a.m. at St. Joseph's in the nave at 490 3rd Avenue. For anyone who wants to send flowers notify them that for flower delivery the address at St. Joseph's is (212) 854-5122. Thank you very much.

8

Message four, forwarded by extension 693462, was received at 5:20 am, Friday, November 17th:
This is President Morton R. Penguin-Duck, I have the sad duty to tell you that Roberta Netley died on Sunday. Uh, Roberta Netley was in the sociology department since 1973. Um, she there will be a memorial service, uh, tomorrow morning, Wednesday, at the Esplanade Memorial Chapel at 55th Street and Lexington Avenue. That's Wednesday, uh, November 18th at 9 o'clock. She was a wonderful colleague and teacher. We will all miss her greatly. We send her family our deepest sympathy. Thank you.

---

[38] "The" wake? [Author's Note]

[39] "The" funeral? [Author's Note]

9

Message five, forwarded by extension 693462, was received at 9:45 am, Tuesday, December 21st:

This is President Morton R. Penguin-Duck. I am sad to tell you that Dietrich Lord of the History Department died on December 18th, Friday, at 4:30, of what is suspected, they think, a massive heart attack. The wake will be held at Claremont Funeral Home and the visiting hours will be today from 3 to 5 and 7 to 9 and tomorrow from 3 to 5 and from 7 to 7.30. There will be a funeral mass at the Church of the Annunciation at 8 o'clock Tuesday evening. Thank you.

10

Message one, forwarded by extension 693462, was received at 11:15 am, Monday, January 24th.

Message to the Actaeon College community. It is with sadness that we announce the passing of Leonora Susman. Dr. Susman joined Actaeon College in 1978 in the Department of Art and served there with
and personal attention to the needs of
students and remained
family has plan
the
n

Message two, forwarded by extension 693462, was received at 7:30 pm, Thursday, February 5th.

Message from the office of the President. It is with deep sorrow that we announce the passing of Dr. Rudolph Marley this morning community in 1966. Funeral services will
across from Marshall Plaza sho
ephone number at
prefe
t

12

To: The Actaeon College Faculty
From: Professor Archer Rash
Subject: Call for Papers
Date: March 19th, 2001

Considering developments within the college, the following call for papers may be of particular interest to members of the Actaeon faculty, who may find this new journal to be of professional interest either as contributors or simply as readers. Some may have seen the notice already. If so, I hope you will please forgive the duplication.

Call for Papers,
The Journal of Threat Assessment

Manuscripts are being solicited for the *Journal of Threat Assessment*, a new quarterly cross-disciplinary journal that will begin publication in late 2002, to be published in conjunction with The Hyslop Press. The journal will be devoted to the assessment and management of threats and violence in varying contexts. Relevant topics are to include homicide, stalking, obsessional harassment, assault, sexual offenses, group violence, hostage situations, kidnapping and abductions, suicide, serial and mass murder, implied or direct threats of violence, and protective measures for victims of all kinds. A wide range of contexts are addressed, including workplace violence, domestic violence, school, college, and university violence, threats against public figures and/or employees, domestic terrorism, and international terrorism.

The journal is to be a scholarly forum for those who are engaged in the practice of assessing and managing threats, including mental health professionals, law enforcement officials, government administrators, lawyers, school officials, corporate professionals, public and private security personnel, members of college faculties, and those responsible for developing and making policy.

Manuscripts that deal with
assessment, or management of threats are
Concise review articles and research studies
practice issues or have direct implic
practicing professional. Authors should
manuscript in a format that is ready f
the *Handbook des Artz und*
ualisches Verein (4th ed.). Pa
page, references, figures, and tables. Submis
the paper has not been previously publish
ncurrent consideration with another journal.

Submissions should be sent to:

Dr. Professor Franz Joseph Karl Reins, D.D., LLD., hil.

of Threat Assessment
31 Jose   trasse
  0 Wien
  TEREICH

13

Make Your Own Life Mask!

Join the Women's Center for a mask-making workshop on
November 16th. This program is open to students, staff, and faculty at Actaeon. Each participant will construct a mask molded
to her/his face, working in an environment especially designed
to encourage reflection, meditation, and security. Once your
mask dries, you can embellish it with paints, sequins, feathers,
shells, and your hopes.

Which aspects of your self do you project to the world? Who
are you on the inside? What would you like to increase or celebrate? How will you be remembered when you are gone? The
Life Mask also makes a lovely gift for a parent, child, or loved one.

Take some time to explore these themes! Sign-up for the
Mask-Making Workshop. You can stop by our literature tables
in the library lobby, The Women's Center office in Room 1043
Non-Presidential Hall, or call us at ext. 7319.

YOU are invited!!!

wednesday, February 29th
3:15-4:45 pm, fsdr*
QUALITY OF LIFE, FACILITY CHANGES, &
IMPROVEMENTS AT ACTAEON

tuesday, march 6th
3:15-4:45 pm, fdr*
CHANGES IN ACADEMIC STANDARDS:
HOW WILL THEY AFFECT YOU?
ARE YOU IN JEOPARDY?

monday, march 12th
4:30 pm-6 pm, fdr*
AN OPEN MEETING: SHARE YOUR IDEAS,
CONCERNS, QUESTIONS, & FEARS

*faculty & staff dining room, 2nd floor,
Non-Presidential Hall

from
The "Town" Meetings Planning Committee:

xavier quiñones (chair), james d'alone,
aida porch, anne lath, mary fox
morris arthur, car cleopatra,

actaeon college of institutional analysis & social control

FRAGMENT II — "VOICEMAIL"

Editor's Note:

Although many of its sheets were detached and widely separated from one another at the time "Fragment II" was discovered, X. I. Wei[40] argues persuasively that the segment is nevertheless without question one of the "collected and collated" examples of the Larsen papers. Through her well known methods of research, using both chemical and x-ray procedures,[41] Wei has made a perfectly convincing recreation of Larsen's intended ordering of the sheets. Without doubt, the result stands as one of the more revealing, impassioned—and ominous—of the author's "wordless" works. Its attack on the policies of President Penguin-Duck and his followers is equally notable for its subtlety and laudable for its diplomatic restraint, especially in light of the

---

[40] See especially *Silent Speeches: The "Collected and Collated" Portions of the Larsen Papers* (Guang Zhu University Press, 2113).

[41] See "An Example of Ordering through Scientific Method: The 'Miscellany' Section," pp. 48-62.

execrable circumstances that must, in reality, have pertained. The powerful ironies of Larsen's "found" method[42] are to be seen throughout: beginning even in the "Preface," with its obvious implication that the kinds of moral example expressed by one of the most beloved works in the nation's literature, *The Adventures of Huckleberry Finn,* have, in the academy of President Penguin-Duck and the America of the Ante-Penultimate, been, in a single melancholy word, abandoned.[43]

We are fortunate that damage to the sheets in this extraordinarily important section is relatively moderate.

Preface

1

You can't pray a lie—I found that out.
— Huck Finn

2

Above all, I congratulate you on the extremely positive rating of your stewardship of The Actaeon College of Institutional Analysis and Social Control that was reached by the group that recently undertook and completed the quinquennial presidential evaluation.

—University Chancellor Orton Trulock to President Morton R. Penguin-Duck, June 1999

3

Each one of us is absolutely confident that our quinquennial review of President Penguin-Duck's stewardship of The Actaeon College of Institutional Analysis and Social Control was conducted in a manner consistent with the University's policies and procedural guidelines,

---

[42] Except in titles, not a *single one* of Larsen's own words appears in all of "Fragment II." [Editor]

[43] See R. V. Tomsi, *A Morality that Could Look Only Backward: The Abandonment of Education, Taste, and Meaning in the Ante-Penultimate Period of the American Nation* (The Tibet Press, 2110).

that it was thorough and objective, and that it was inclusive and
highly participative.

— Head of the Evaluation Committee George S.
Newton, President, Topeka Junior College, to Ms. Natty
del Rosario, Assistant to Orton Trulock, Chancellor

4

Faculty uniformly shared a sense of pride in the college and repeatedly said "people are happy to be working here." They feel that
President Penguin-Duck provides real support for the faculty,
for their projects and for their research. They spoke of being fully
engaged despite the fact than many of their majors had been discon-
tinued years ago.

— From the Quinquennial Evaluation Report, entitled
"The Actaeon College of Institutional Analysis and
Social Control: A Special Place, with A Unified Campus
Culture, and an Extraordinary President"

5

The overwhelming response to the president was tested several
times by asking various groups, "Who are the president's detractors and what do they say?" Uniformly the individuals in the group
would get a very puzzled expression on their faces and invariably
someone would speak up and say, "There are no detractors."

— From the Quinquennial Evaluation Report of
President Morton R. Penguin-Duck

6

Our objective in the future must be enrollment, enrollment,
enrollment.

—President Morton R. Penguin-Duck, from his memo-
letter dated September 9, 2000, and entitled "Greetings
for the 2000-2001 Year"

7

Believe me, the budget will finally rectify itself. Only be patient. I
have ideas. [44]

— President Morton R. Penguin-Duck, in a meeting
with faculty early in 2000

---

[44] See "Editor's Foreword," pp. 1–6.

Dear Members of the Faculty, Staff, Alumni, and Friends:
You are invited to join us for a memorial ceremony and reception in tribute to the deceased members of our faculty and staff. At the ceremony we will unveil the plaques on which have been inscribed the names of those who have served The Actaeon College of Institutional Analysis and Social Control with distinction for an extended period of time.

— President Morton R. Penguin-Duck, from a letter dated May 3, 2003

Voice Mail

From the Office of President Penguin-Duck, July 28th, 2000:
Hi, This is President Penguin-Duck. This is going to be my midsummer letter to you, which I usually send, uh, in the mail but we didn't know that we had all your summer addresses so I thought you'd be calling in to get your messages. I just wanted to mention, um, a few things since commencement. Uh, the conference on human dignity in Santiago was extremely successful I think in every way and, uh, it was enjoyed by all and, and we were very fortunate to have the wonderful support of the Chilean government and one of the big themes of the conference, of course, was human dignity and organized crime, and only two weeks after we left there was that terrible bombing by organized crime in the midst of downtown Santiago which if it had happened during the conference or prior to the conference would have sabotaged it, so in a sense we were very lucky but it also underscored the problem of organized crime in world locations around the world. Speaking of international affairs also we have been asked since the conference by three additional foreign governments to again give the Conference on Being Human with Dignity and Asserting the Rights of Being Nice with Human Dignity...

From the Office of President Penguin-Duck, 8/6/00:
We regret to have to inform you of the death of Rexford Roberts, devoted husband of Leonora Roberts of the Bursar's Office staff. Mr. Roberts will be waked at the house of the Dale Funeral Home on Wednesday Aug 15th from 4 until 8 p.m. The funeral home is located at 2000 St. Christopher's Place at the corner of Satterfield

Avenue in Brooklyn. The funeral will be held at 10 am on Friday Aug 17th at Saint Mary's church which is located at 3410 Satterfield in Brooklyn. Thank you.

From the Office of President Penguin-Duck, 8/24/00:
It is with deep sorrow that we inform you of the death on Friday August 27th of Lawrence Wexler father of Peter Wexler Director of Building Services. A private service will be held at 10 a.m. on Sunday August 29th 2000 at Prior English and Merkin Funeral Home at 760 Third Street in Chappaqua New York. In lieu of flowers donations may be sent in Lawrence Wexler's name to the Chappaqua Reading Library 200 Gregg Avenue Chappaqua New York 10047. Thank you.

From the Office of President Penguin-Duck, 9/11/00:
The Actaeon DRC is pleased to announce a conference on "The Role of the University in Fostering Interethnic Coexistence on Campus, in the Community, and Beyond," on October 13, 2000 at The Actaeon College of Institutional Analysis and Social Control.

On October 13, 2000 the Actaeon Dispute Resolution Consortium (ACTAEONDRC) will co-sponsor a one-day conference with The Isaiah Fund entitled "The Role of the University in Fostering Interethnic Coexistence on Campus, the Community and Beyond." The conference will feature a keynote speaker, a plenary session with leading local, national, and international coexistence and dispute resolution practitioners and scholars, workshops highlighting diverse aspects of interethnic coexistence, and a town meeting focusing on "next steps" for those involved in coexistence work. The conference will also draw from a new book entitled the Compendium of Interethnic Coexistence edited by Dr. Eugenie Hamburg and published in April 2000 by Today Press.

From the Office of President Penguin-Duck, 9/15/00:
President Morton R. Penguin-Duck cordially invites all members of the Actaeon College Community to attend a reception in the honor of Robert A. Jandry former Vice President for World and Satellite Campus Affairs in a celebration of his dedicated service to the Actaeon College of Institutional Analysis and Social Control and especially the college's World and Satellite Campus Programs. The reception will be held on Wednesday September 19th at 5 p.m. on the 6th floor of Presidential Hall. Contributions of $25 towards his gifts are welcome, however I hope all members of the Actaeon College Community will join us on the 19th in bidding a fond farewell to our good friend Bob A. Jandry. Thank you.

From the Office of President Penguin-Duck, 10/28/00:
The department of Philosophy, Art, and Music (PAM) regrets to inform the Actaeon College Community of the death this past October 10th of Jeffrey Wheeler, father of Myra Wheeler Richards, administrative assistant for the department of Philosophy, Art, and Music (PAM) and of Professor Bimbi Wheeler, of the School of Hotel Management at the College of Floating Island. A private memorial has been held and the families wish that contributions be made in memory of Jeffrey Wheeler to the Breathing Free Fund 1090 Seventh Avenue, New York, New York, 10012. That's in memory of Jeffrey Wheeler, to the Breathing Free Fund 1090 Seventh Avenue, New York, New York, 10012, telephone 212-934-4475. Thank you.

From the Office of President Penguin-Duck, 11/10/00:
This is President Morton R. Penguin-Duck. I have been approached by a number of veterans to ask us to commemorate in a special way Veteran's Day since this Wednesday will be the eighty-second anniversary of Armistice Day the end of World War I. What they have suggested and I certainly support is that you might ask your students at around 11 o'clock or 11:05 when the class starts on the 11th hour of the 11th day of the 11th month, that you commemorate the men and women who died in the service of our country and particularly those who died in World War I that horrific war. So if you would do that I and the veterans would appreciate it very much. Thank you.

From the Office of President Penguin-Duck, 11/16/00:
The office of the Vice President for Non-World Campus Affairs is sad to inform you of the passing of Mr. Irving Silver on Sunday November 19th, 2000, father to Mrs. Betsy Bogin, special assistant to the Vice President for Non-World Campus Affairs. A memorial service will be held tomorrow, Monday, November 20th, at Parkview Chapel, 7492 Terminus Avenue near Fifth Avenue, Brooklyn, New York. The service will be held at 1 p.m. Shiva will be held at Mr. and Mrs. Bogin's home on Tuesday Wednesday and Thursday at 52 Oak Lane, Carfield, New York. For further information and directions please contact me Elaine Berinski, that's Elaine Berinski, at extension 7756, 7756. Thank you.

From the Office of President Penguin-Duck, 1/13/01:
The Department of Hygiene, Athletics, and Martial Arts (HAM) is very saddened to announce the death of Miss Zazua Ruiz's mother, Kassa Negawa—that's spelled K-A-S-S-A, N-E-G-A-W-A—in Swaziland on December 14th. Condolences may be sent to Miss Ruiz in care of the Department of Hygiene, Athletics, and Martial Arts

(HAM). Thank you very much.

From the Office of President Penguin-Duck, 2/8/01:
A reminder to the Actaeon College Community from the Registrar's Office and the Department of Buildings and Grounds. As per the spring 2001 academic calendar, on Tuesday, Feb 18th, Friday classes will meet; on Monday, February 24th, Tuesday classes will meet, and on Thursday, February 27th , the college will be closed due to the shutdown of electrical power required for upgrade of the college computer and voicemail systems. Please announce to your classes. Thank you.

From the Office of President Penguin-Duck, 3/30/01:
We regret to inform you of the passing of Charlotte Briarhill yesterday, March 27th, when she gave in at last to an illness that she had fought against bravely for years until she went into a coma and at long last now her family agreed to pull the plug.[45] The wake will be held on Wednesday, April 3rd from 2 to 5 and from 7 to 9 at Danziger and Conklin Funeral Home, 115 East 40th Street in Manhattan, telephone number 212-245-4358. The funeral service will also be held at Danziger and Conklin, on Friday April 5th at 11 am. Burial will be at Prospect Cemetery in Brooklyn, New York. After the burial on Friday at 12:30 refreshments will be served at The Colt on 63rd Street near Fifth Avenue. Thank you.

From the Office of President Penguin-Duck, 4/2/01:
Hello, this is Vice President Terrance Happyhand with an important message for the Actaeon College Community from the Department of Buildings and Grounds (D-BAG). On Friday, April 11th at 11 pm, a test of the emergency electrical generating equipment will be conducted. As a precaution, it is recommended that all personal computers be unplugged before the end of the working day on Friday. The electrical test will be completed by the beginning of the workday on Saturday, the following day. Thank you for your cooperation.

From the Office of President Penguin-Duck, 5/1/01:
It is with deep sadness that we announce the passing of, uh, Mr. Roberto Torres, father of Lourdes Torres-Carabajo of the student accounting and receipts, uh, division of the bursar's office. Funeral services will be held on May 3rd at Funereria Sangra, Aya Casa # 63, Myana, PR, 010412. For further information please contact Tony Perez at Actaeon College extension 3401. Thank you.

---

[45] See, again, "Editor's Foreword," pp. 1–6.

From the Office of President Penguin-Duck, 6/18/01:
The previously postponed meeting of the Consortium on Deadly Violence will be held on Wednesday June 23rd at 6:00 pm in room 3520 Presidential Hall. We are delighted to welcome Gillian Carmichael, author of *Deadly Violence: Observations on a Rising Crisis in the American Nation* and clinical director of the department of forensic psychology at Stanford Hospital of the California Medical School. Dr. Carmichael will present on "Sublimation of Impotence and Rage in Those Subject To the Manipulations of a Mass Consumer Society: The Unseen Links Between Intentionally Created Meaninglessness and the Individual Psychology of Resentment and Violence." Please join us for what promises to be a most interesting meeting. Refreshments will be served courtesy of President Morton R. Penguin-Duck and of the Office of the Vice-President for Public Relations. Thank you.

From the Office of President Penguin-Duck, July 7, 2001:
With great sadness we announce the death of Paul James Fitzmaurice, who served for many years as Actaeon College's Director of Security. The wake will be held on Friday, Jul 9th and Saturday July 11th from 2:00 to 4:30 and from 7:00 to 9:30 pm at Yeats Funeral Home 5th Ave. and 60th St. in Brooklyn, telephone number 718-634-8677. The funeral mass will be on Sunday July 12th at 10:00 am at St. Bardolph Church, 5th Ave. and 64th St. in Brooklyn. Thank you.

From the Office of President Penguin-Duck, August 15, 2001:
With great sadness we announce the passing of Miss Lilatta Jones Mulcahy, for a great many years head circulation clerk in the Actaeon College Library. Miss Mulcahy died on Monday August 13th after a long and brave struggle with illness that began in the spring. The viewing for Miss Mulcahy will be held on Wednesday August 15th between 4:00 and 9:00 pm at the Brent-Carlton Funeral Home on 5053 Borough Ave., between 182nd and 183rd Streets. The funeral will be held on Friday August 17th at 10:00 am, also at the Brent-Carlton Funeral Home. A College van will leave from the front of Presidential Hall at 9 am Friday morning. Please call Missie Kent at extension 5811 if you wish to request a seat. Thank you.

From the Office of President Penguin-Duck, October 10, 2001:
An announcement to all members of the Actaeon College Community: we are deeply saddened to announce the passing of Hazel Southworth, beloved mother of LaToya Wheeler. Memorial services for Mrs. Southworth will be held on Friday, October 12th

at 2:00 pm at Our Merciful Lord Church, located at 126th St. and 8th Avenue. In lieu of flowers please make donations to the Walter Dunphy Hospice Center, that's Walter D-U-N-P-H-Y Hospice Center at York Avenue and 62nd Street in New York, zip 10128, phone 212-420-2844, thank you very much.

From the Office of President Penguin-Duck, November 19, 2001: Good morning, this is President Morton R. Penguin-Duck. Is it my very sad duty to tell you that Reg Donaldson, the founding president of the Actaeon College of Institutional Analysis and Social Control, died yesterday. He, uh, had been in a coma for about ten, uh, weeks. Uh, he served as President of Actaeon College from its founding in 1965 until 1970. Uh, before that he was the Provost and Academic Dean here at the College and hired a large number of our original faculty, many of whom are now retiring or otherwise seeing their long and dedicated careers at Actaeon coming to an end. Uh, after its founding, he was able to bring the College to national prominence. A memorial service will be held in the Unitarian universalist church at Upper Winsock, New Jersey, on November 10th at 4:00 pm. Donations in memory of Dr. Donaldson may be sent either to the Actaeon College of Institutional Analysis and Social Control Reginald D Donaldson Scholarship Fund, which we have just set up, or to the University of Nebraska, Sioux City. It was his vision to join the liberal arts with the theory and practice of institutional analysis and social control that launched Actaeon College in its unique and uniquely profitable mission. After long service and patient mentorship to us all, may he at last rest in eternal peace. Thank you.

From the Office of President Penguin-Duck, December 19, 2001: This is President Morton R. Penguin-Duck. I'm very happy to be able to announce to you that the university board of governors has unanimously given final approval to Phase Two.[46] We will be now negotiating with the owner and moving forward. I am thrilled, as I'm sure we all are. I will keep you posted, as always, on every new development. Thank you.

From the Office of President Penguin-Duck, January 15, 2002:

---

[46] No documentation survives to let us know what was meant by "Phase Two" or for that matter by the "Phase One" that may be supposed to have preceded it. We can hypothesize only that it must have been a development plan of some kind. The Larsen Papers do, however, though at only a single point, make a passing reference (was it deliberately oblique?) to the ominous words "Phase Three." See *Financial Origins of Academic Collapse in the Early Penultimate* (Taipei, 2130), in particular Chapter Four, "Academics Betrayed: The Imperial Presidency."

To the Actaeon College Community: it is with deep sadness that we inform you of the death of Alexander Quincy Brandon, dedicated library staff member. Mr. Brandon died on this Sunday, January 13th. For wake and funeral information, please call Audrey Caull at extension 7423.

From the Office of President Penguin-Duck, February 21, 2002:
This is President Morton R. Penguin-Duck. As you may possibly already know, the Prime Minister of Great Britain announced this morning at 8:30 that the British government would accept and implement the Actaeon College of Institutional Analysis and Social Control plan for collaborative study of resources for the study of human dignity and the establishment of international seminars in institutional development in the arena of domestic and international social control with dignity, specifically utilizing an ongoing cycle of the Actaeon Seminar on Being Human with Dignity, Maintaining the Right of Human Dignity, and Asserting the Rights of Being Nice (BHWID-MTROHD-AASTROBN).

This is extraordinarily good news for us. There will be a few modifications in the Actaeon plan, but they will be very minor, and, uh, we've heard so far from the British government, the Scottish parliament, and the American government, and they are all very pleased, as I am, and I, um, want to thank each of you for your advice, counsel, support, and patience over these past two or three sometimes difficult years.

From the Office of President Penguin-Duck, February 28, 2002:
You are cordially invited to an important event tonight. Clara R. Cotter, author of
Violence and Inequality in the American Nation: Casualties of the Consumer State associate professor of sociology at Harv
on the extraordinary toll exacted
institutionalized or structural violence. Please join
most interesting
Presidential Ha
you.
m

From the Office of President Penguin-Duck, March 13, 2002:
We are saddened to announce the death yesterday of Mr. Nicholas Cullum, long-time member of our custodial staff. The wake for Mr. Cullum will be held Friday, March 14th from 2:00 to 4:00 and 6:00 to 8:00 pm at the Riverside Funeral Home, telephone 212-
on Saturday, March 15th at 11:00 o'clock at Our Holy Lord

From the Office of President Penguin-Duck, March 31, 2002:
The Center for Studies on Violence and the Diminishing Likelihood of Human Survival wishes to invite you to an event on Friday, April 5th at 6:00 pm in room 1743 of Presidential Hall. Professors Elizabeth Kremer and John Collier, both of Actaeon College's Institute of Social Philosophy, will present on "The Abolition of Prisons, Arguments, Counter-Argument, and Some Answers." With the nation's prison population exceeding 2 million, the subject could hardly be more p
Join us for what promises
timely, and interes
want to
wh

From the Office of President Penguin-Duck, April 17, 2002:
To the Actaeon College Community: There is a deep sadness that I inform you that Professor Norbert Small of the Department of Social Control and Legal Philosophy (SCALP) passed away[47] on Saturday, April 15th. Memorial Services will be held Thursday, April 20th, at 2:00 pm at the Bridgeview Funeral Chapel, 32-10 Fourth Avenue, Astoria, Queens, telephone 718-401-7205. Thank you.

From the Office of President Penguin-Duck, May 17, 2002:
The Center for Studies on Violence and the Diminishing Likelihood of Human Survival would like to announce an event on Friday, May 20th, at 6:00 pm in room 1743 Presidential Hall. We are delighted that Richard Lloyd-Lloyd, Professor of Human Development and Co-Director of the Family Life Development Center at the University of Southern California and author of numerous books on violence, communal violence, psychological violence, and institutional violence, will present on "Pathways from Childhood Aggression to Youth Violence in a Socially Toxic Environment." Please join us for what promises to be a most interesting and intellectually challenging evening. Thank you.

From the Office of President Penguin-Duck, May 21, 2002:
Hello, this is a message from the President to the entire Actaeon College community reminding you that the final Actaeon College Community "Town" Meeting of the spring semester is scheduled for May 24th at 4:00 pm in the third-floor student dining room, Non-Presidential Hall. This will be our last open meeting of the year, where all will have the opportunity to share questions, concerns, ideas, and

---

[47] Ibid.

of course compliments. Please bring a friend, colleague or classmate. We look forward to seeing you there. Thank you.

From the Office of President Penguin-Duck, June 24, 2002:
We are saddened to inform you of the death of Mr. Ray DeLorenzo, long-time laboratory assistant in the Department of Sciences. There will be a wake tomorrow night, Friday, from 5:30 to 7:30 and then a funeral at the Porter Funeral Home on Central Avenue in Queens. For more specific directions you can stop by the Department of Sciences, Sixth Floor, Non-Presidential Hall. Thank you.

From the Office of President Penguin-Duck, July 30, 2002:
This is President Morton R. Penguin-Duck. I regret to inform you of the sudden deaths yesterday, in North Carolina, of Professors Marvin and Jane Terrapin of the Department of Fine Arts. There will be no public funeral.

I hope that all of you are having a pleasant and productive summer.

DANGER!

DO NOT READ THE FOLLOWING PAGES: DOING SO MAY BE DETRIMENTAL TO MENTAL OR EMOTIONAL WELLBEING

The following pages are provided for the sole purpose of maintaining a historic and archival record of the events represented by them and for no other purpose. They will, consequently, fail to reward any effort whatsoever made to read them. Let it be noted that any degree of narrative or dramatic energy that *may* exist within these pages does so to an extent *slightly greater than the degree to which such energy was present* in the actual past years of which these sheets now comprise a fixed, unalterable, vacant, barren, and voiceless index.

Such energy, if any exists, results, of course, not from the pages' being organized chronologically (all nature being so) but from the small touch of structural artistry with which they are imbued through the device of their being arranged, in addition, alphabetically and also numerically. [48]

---

[48] The headnote is taken universally as being Larsen's own. In *Silent Speeches: The "Collected and Collated" Portions of the Larsen Papers* (2113), X. I. Wei devotes his entire fourth chapter to an analysis of the quartet of papers known collectively as "Fragment VI" (printed in four separate sections in all editions, of course, following the Bhāskara Presentation). Among the dozen or more scholars who so far have devoted themselves to the elusive mysteries of "Fragment VI," Wei remains unparalleled in his penetration, depth, and subtlety. His understanding, especially, of the powerful ironies expressed and contained by the fragment (and by its headnote) distinguishes his work from that of others, as does also the unvarying clarity of his expression. His explication of Larsen's keen and profound awareness of the paradoxes of narrative is especially insightful and informative, but his subsequent discussion of the role those paradoxes play in interpreting the *emotional content and meaning* of the Larsen Papers reveals him to be a critic unique in his abilities and in the simultaneous breadth and focus of his understanding. *Why did*

Larsen create "Fragment VI" only then to declare in no uncertain terms that it not be read? In Wei's view, the fragment is another in the category of Larsen's "found" pieces, this time in the form of a very nearly pure word-sculpture, intended not to be read but simply looked at just as any other sculpture might be. Paradoxically, though, the sculpture is made not of marble but of words. And therefore what Larsen has done, according to Wei, is *kill the words before transforming them into the unmoving form of the sculpture*. Thus it is, following a recognition such as this one (of the author's method), that the reader-viewer can at last "hear-see" or "see-hear" in these "unliving" words and in the static, ossified, "archival" form they have been given—the "reader" can at last sense clearly the long, forlorn, slow, melancholy cry of loss, regret, grief, pity, and sorrow felt by the author at the terrible loss of *life* represented by his wasted and unproductive decades amid the banalities of Actaeon under the leadership of President Penguin-Duck. But then, too, of course, there remains the larger, *universal,* interpretation of the work: The paradox of narrative (one of the paradoxes) is that narrative requires life for its existence but *it is not life.* It requires time, but *it is not time.* Narrative, then, in at least one very real sense, is *a record of absent life and can be nothing other.* How fitting it is then, on numerous levels, that "Fragment VI" cries out, as it does, in loss, in regret, in sorrow—and in silence. [Editor]

FRAGMENT VI:

MY ACADEMIC CAREER

Our objective must be
enrollment, enrollment, enrollment.
—President Morton Penguin-Duck

Quantity is quality.
—President Morton Penguin-Duck

I
Fall 1971

1
English 101, Composition I
section 01

Bernstein, Robert	Greene, Althea	Nwahiri, Matthias
Boyle, Suzanne	Gruspier, Charles	Perez, Franklin
Brown, Andrea	Hinde, John	Pomara, Francesco
Difrancisco, Karen	Lynch, John	Quinones,S Hector
Formanek, Patricia	Messana, Joseph	Russsell, Michel
Grandberry, Leslie	Montalva, Thomas	Sarach, Omar
Gundberg, Carl	Mueniere, Anne	Williams, Anthony

2
English 101, Composition I
section 02

`

3
English 101, Composition I
section 02

Asmus, James
Brown, Shanteil
Burgos, Gloria
Candelario, Elizabeth
Codd, Monica
Herbst, Michael
Jordan, Yvonne
Levine, Aaron
Lopez, Donna

Makebish, Marcella
Mcneal, Karla
Murphy, Merilee
Noble, James
Ponce, Denise
Rago, Jodi
Reid, Desiree
Rodriguez, Ana
Rodriguez, Maria

Rugbart, Stacie
Simorella, Paul
Soto, Maribel
Urzala, Giovanni
Weeks, Christopher
Wexler, Mia
Williams, Ina

4
English 101, Composition I
section 07

Anderson, Sharon
Arroyo, Margarita
Brns, Stephen
Donet, Jose
Espenkotter, John
Estella, Vincent
Finelli, Gennaro
Flores, Lorena
Gibbs, Christine

Gorman, Bartholomew
Kelly, Lawrence
Kerivan, John
Levine, Aliso
Long, David
Malave, Emily
Mckenna, James
Nawrocki, Marylynn
Reynolds, David

Rodriguez, Herbert
Spero, Anthony
Thomas, Peter
Times, Gilbert
Torrossian, Gilbert
Williams, Leroy
Yagual, Magali

5
English 101, Composition I
section 09

Amerson, Theresa
Bruckman, Wanda
Cordero, Samuel
Dallessandro, Kevin
De Latour, Patrice
De Los Angeles, Henry
Dillon, Lisa
Espinosa, Carola
Ferreira, Jeanette

Gonzalez, Danny
Goss, Ronald
Gutierrez, Sandra
Hoens, Eric
Johnson, Kimberley
Marrero, Mercinda
Mullen, Bruce
Nunez, Denia
Rumble, Tricia

Russell, Marsha
Sapig
Th
T

1
English 102, Com
section 10

Aponte, Ada
Beaton, Kathleen
Betancourt, Nantalie
Breton, Rochelle
Cesar, Shiela
Cochran, Althea
omo, Maria
Coombs, Sandy
Cortes, Andrey
Gardner, Kerr

Bejarano, Carolyn
Green, Don
Hernande
Hernan
Herre
Hum
Jo

Bacchi, Roy

Adams, Everett
Albino, William
Antoniuk, Agata
Arancherry, Jason
Camaj, Kole

Gor
Gu
H

—
A
Ar
Bow
Bradl
Braith
Brown,
Caramic
Cohen, D
Curry, Jose
Esposito, Car
Ferrigno, Vince
Fidanza, Antoni
Fraser, Kenneth A
Hahn, Robert R

Blackwell, John D
Collins, Kevin J
Conaboy, Thomas F
Conlon, Douglas B
Cotter, Joseph P
Eyman, Buster D
Fredericks, Walter T

G
Gle
Gord
Kowals
McRae, G
Rechenberg

Lit
Introduction to L
Section 03

Agront, Nelson L
Armao, Richard D
Baldofsky, Joseph Jr
Bess, Johanna
Cassidy, Timothy B
Colton, William J
Demarco, Michael
Dugas, Richard A
Faye, Christopher
Friel, Timothy J

Garcia, Zenaida
Geary, John
Gordon, Audrey, R
Lacovara, Joanne
Lane, Johnniemae
Leach, Richard B
Maher, John P

Mastro, John
Miller, Alton
Monfasani, Neil L

V
Fall 1973

1
English 101, Composition I
section 42

Antomez, Herbert Jr
Myers, William A

Osorio, Theodore P
Valentin, Elvin

Wermuth, Ezra C.

2
English 101, Composition I
section 48

Ackerman, Barbara
Brewer, Denise
Dinegar, Alan
Harper, Leonard

King, Hillary
Sanjurjo, Rennie
Santiago, Fred
Segalini, George

Simmons, William
Tisdol, Kevin
Van Nooten, Errol
Zagami, Bart

3
Literature 321
The English Novel

Banzer, Fred
Barbarisi, Lenore
Chapero, Alicia
Didonato, Nat
Fiskaa, Tom

Galagher, Judith
Glance, Simon
Hughes, Martin, J
Kowolski, Farland
Kozma, John F.

Levinsk
Rand
O'R
Sa

VI

Spring 1974

1
English 102, Compositio
Sections 23–24

Agulles, Christian
Ali, Judge
Ash, Susan
Augone, Charles
Bowman, Kenneth
Braxton, Vincent
Cahill, Patrick
Calahan, Robert
Carter, Louis
Colon, Antonio
Concepcion, Orlando
Connor, Gregory
Conway, Ladine
Cruz, David
Degarcia, Desdemona
Derosa, Vincenzo
Donnelly, Jeanne

Edkins, Gary
Farrell, James
Ferguson, James
Flickstein, Madelon
Ford, Le Bron
Ford, Rodrick
Garravito, G
Gay, Sam
Greenh
Hall, L
Harr
Lac
La
L

Alicea, William
Barrett, John
Brennan, Pa
Brown, Mel
Butler, Ty
Cambria,
Carrobb
Cassa
Cha
Chi
Co
C

—
B
Ban
Bara
Bergm
Beruldse
Bruggema
Casole, Mic
Ciaccio, Vince
Clarke, Michel
Colon, Nancy
Cordero, Lillian
Corvasce, Maur
Crooke, Eustace,
Delucia, Lawrenc
Demario, Frank M

Deme, Robert S
Dorritie, Raymond
Edelstein, Sheldon
Ferrara, Richard
Frazier, Mayetta

Aiello, Michael
Beech, Olive
Benedetto, Christophe
Brady, Billy B
Brancaccio, Donato
Brown, Gregory
Brownstein, Daniel   M
Burkard, Gary   Me
Camparella, Phyllis   Mon
Crenshaw, Frank   Mope
Delion, Ted   Napoli
Dennett, Phyllis   Neller, F
Edwards, Brian

Spring

1

Literature 103, The Enlightenment t
Section

Amato, Ronald   Felton, Ronald
Bartley, Glenn   Grafer, Bette
Basso, Richard   Hom, Diane
Bolliraz, Ramjit   Kolarik, Sean
Brennan, Robert   Kucinski, James
Breslin, Barbara   Lasala, Stephen
Britt, Deborah   Laskin, Edward
Brown, Joyce   Lewis, Derrick
Burns, Jerome   Lopez, Evelyn   R
Colgau, George   Lupu, Ben   Ru
Conze, Yves   Maltz, Barbara   Seub
Dagostino, Joseph   Mcleod, Gloria   Shiff
Dillon, Frank   Milliam, Lorenzo   Vera,
Dirocco, Dana   Mongelli, Donna   Willia

—

Ba
Bar
Car
Dunp
Falco,
 Falcon
Figueroa
Garvin, J

Aiello, Ra
Burke, Ca
Carter Jawa
Charon, Dar
Deazevedo, Is
Fallon, David
Felician, Tenor
Fleming, James
Folfinopoulis, Gus
Gonzalez, Doreen

3
English 216, Fiction Writing
Section 01

Actie, Winnifred	
Anderson, Linda	
Austin, James	
Bosetti, James	
Brown, Sharon	
Bruning, Howard	
Desanto, George	
Dorsey, Deborah	L
Dupree, Sharon	Lu
Farrell, John	Mar
Foley, Elizabeth	

English
Section 1

Avello, Barbara	Doller, Don	Phillips, John
Avello, Cathy	Feeley, Lind	Pittman, James
Baulkman, Joanna	Henry, Miche	
Brown, Tony	Jordan, James	
Cruz, Clara	Karl, Robert	
Cuccia, Frances	Miserendino, Jos	
D'allesandro, Paul	Ortiz, Edward L	
Dennaio, Judy		
Desalvo, Leonard		

English 101, Composition
Section 12

Balgovind, Satya	Mateo, Joe
Barrett, Junior	Mccray, Essick
Cassidy, Eugene	Mcparland, Gerrard
Cetta, Anthony	Mcqueen, Donalda
Conception, Narcisco	Ortiz, Edwin
Edmonds, Rick	Pallens, Gary
Graham, Lillie	Quinones, Sonya
Love, Christophine	Reid, Ethan

Literature 103, Medieval and Renaiss
Sections 03–04

Arnold, Jennie	Karma, Joyce	
Bole, Sheila	Kenniwbrew, Pamela	
Colavita Maria	Kipp, Edward	
Grant, Barbara	Longo, Tony	
Griffin, Thomas	Mandell, Jody	S
Hanania, June	Miller, Kenneth	Su
Hawkins, Carol	Montgomery, Valerie	Var
Johnson, Ralph	Murphy, Walter	Ward
Jones, Innie	Ng, Fay	Zadzie
Jones, Sheila	O'halloran, Sean	

XVI

Spring 1979
I

English 101, Composition I
Section 07

Anderson, Dennis	Coiro, Joseph	Robinson, Ernest
Babbini, Patricia	Flannery, Thomas	Rodriguiz, Marilyn
Bartalone, Maria	Holman, Diane	Sindab, Rosalind
Borvee, Ernest	Jones, Rodney	Washington, George
Boyce, Susan	Kroufle, Felix	Watkins, Kathy
Brady, Robert	Mirrione, Michael	Watson, Roosevelt
Briggs, Frank	Portuondo, Pablo	Woodley, Charles
Callahan, Shannon	Price, Gerald	

2
English 101, Composition I
Section 09

Abramowitz, Shelley	Hernandez, Jose	Molina, Desiree
Brinson, Allyson	Iadisernia, Philip	Rosa, Migdalia
Chavis, Rosezina	Irizzary, Danny	Thompson, Sa
Cunneen, Judy	Johnson, Keith	

3
English 216, Fiction Writing

Cassidy, Eugene
Chorens, Jos
Davidson,
Delgado

THE "DIARY"

(Part Two)

iii
My Life in Education:
What I Learned from Thirty-Five Years
in the
University of New York (UNY):
by
Eric Larsen, B.A., M.A., Ph.D.,
Professor of English
The Actaeon College of Institutional Analysis and Social Control,
The University of New York (UNY)
New York, New York
U.S.A.

6/16/06 3:00 AM (Wed.):
If the specter of death at my door was not really a full-fledged psychotic but only a tripping student, a young man driven to drugs by frustrations and sorrows, that at least was something understandable. But it was no less frightening, and obviously it was serious. I myself, in my decades at Actaeon, have more often than I probably ought to admit felt lured by the blessed release that drugs can bring, including alcohol, but time and again I have been kept safely away from that danger by my deep fear of the Actaeon latrines and my revulsion toward them.

A well-informed consciousness of the body and its needs is, after all, one of the major concerns of the Actaeon curriculum. Even I have become informed enough in matters physical to know that the prolonged and excessive use of drugs will bring about in time (something certainly true with alcohol) a weakening and unsteadiness of the bowels—which, were it to occur in my case, would force me again into the disease, stench, gunfire, and ostentation of the latrines, something that would doubtless even more steeply increase the odds of my premature death than would the use of the drugs themselves. And so I am fortunate, if only in this sense: that my desire for the latter is well controlled by my revulsion and fear as regards the former.

6/17/06 4:26 AM (Thu.):

The question of drugs, nevertheless, turns my mind naturally to the subject of my colleagues, since there can be no disputing this simple fact: that it is only natural and reasonable for any *thinking* person at Actaeon to crave the release provided by them.

Our departmental rate of mortality, it must be said, has been remarkably low. In thirty-five years, only eleven colleagues have died, with just *one* of their deaths *directly* attributable to alcoholism, and that relatively early in my time. The alcoholic who died, indeed, was a genuinely thinking person, in possession of a pliant, complex, and deep mind, a person mourned briefly and now forgotten absolutely, such being the nature of fate at Actaeon in cases of those who are thoughtful.

Deans who urinate with their backs arched are remembered longer.

Of my surviving colleagues, I can declare honestly that, with few and treasurable exceptions, they have avoided the ravages of alcohol less through the sheer exercise of will or fear of the latrines than through the more radical method of eliminating desire for drugs by first eliminating *thought* from their lives.

President Penguin-Duck himself, on the other hand, is

6/17/06 5:47 AM (Thu.):

another matter altogether and has been so from the beginning of his decades-long tenure. Leadership at the presidential level, after all, inescapably brings with it pressures and responsibilities that are far more taxing and weighty than those falling upon everyone else (though let it quickly be added that President Penguin-Duck has *never* been heard to complain or to express even so much as a single fleeting breath of self-pity).

It's a logical impossibility, consequently, for President Penguin-Duck to participate in my colleagues' type of drug-control program— that is, to eliminate the desire for drugs by eliminating *thought* from his life. For him, as commander, helmsman, and captain, this method is obviously and patently out of the question.

As President, after all, Dr. Penguin-Duck's task is vital and clear: he must never nod. He must *always* be alert; he must *always* be ahead of any kind of trickery or deceit, ready to perceive and out-maneuver it; he must *always,* without lapse, hesitation, exception, or failure, do everything in his power to fulfill the terms of his mandate—the inestimably important responsibility *of making things appear other than they are.*

A job like his, clearly, can be trusted not just to anyone, but it must fall only to a person of exceptional strength, someone who, like President Morton R. Penguin-Duck, by their very nature will remain unflaggingly thoughtful, alert, and awake.

By definition, in other words, *President Penguin-Duck is a thinking person,* a fact proven by the consistent, flawless, and ongoing exercise of his responsibilities over these many, many years. But the consequences of so continual an exercise of intellect must be faced unflinchingly: the fact cannot be avoided, that is, that President Penguin-Duck has no choice but to resist drugs only through exercise of will, since, as we've seen, to eliminate *thinking* from his professional life is out of the question. My colleagues may (and indeed they do) eliminate thinking from their lives whenever and as often as the impulse may seize them—even permanently. But a single fleeting moment of failed intellectual alertness in the president is another matter and of exponentially greater importance: the briefest lapse could, after all, deceive him into *blurting out the truth,* an error that could very possibly be catastrophic, wiping out with a simple and innocent phrase or two the entire carefully structured world of Actaeon altogether.

And certainly no voice of doubt has been raised[49] as to the stoicism, strength, and steadiness of President Penguin-Duck in the

6/17/06 6:47 AM (Thu.):

stalwart fulfillment of his job—a job especially demanding when one considers its intrinsic vulnerability to the solace—which is after all our subject here—of berry, grape, and grain.

For the entirety of my thirty-five years at Actaeon, President Penguin-Duck has been at the helm. And it is a credit indeed to his near superhuman strength that only in the past twenty-eight or twenty-nine of those years has his face taken on the rosy glow and sub-dermal puffiness that suggest the strength with which he has waged a battle against alcohol—a battle, surely, punishing and demanding enough to have felled a lesser man long, long before this.

One aspect of leadership undertaken always with utmost seriousness by President Penguin-Duck has been the task of keeping every

---

[49] Indeed, see p. 41, in "Fragment II": "The overwhelming response to the president was tested several times by asking various groups, 'Who are his detractors and what do they say?' Uniformly the individuals in the group would get a very puzzled expression on their faces and invariably someone would speak up and say, 'There are no detractors.'" (From the Quinquennial Evaluation Report of President Morton R. Penguin-Duck) [Author's Note]

member of "the Actaeon College Community" fully informed at all times of matters important to the college. In the early years, he communicated by means of mimeographed sheets sent out regularly to faculty and staff through inter-office mail. New generations of copy machines, easier to use and much less messy, replaced the mimeograph—and then, later still, came the advent of voicemail. With this breakthrough, President Penguin-Duck was able to speak to the entire college on a daily or even an hourly basis by the simple push of a button. His voice became a familiar and intimate part of our daily lives from then on, and, once again, it is nothing if not a powerful testimonial to the President's strength and dedication as chief guardian of the intellectual life of Actaeon that *only in the past ten or fifteen years* has that voice begun to reveal the slurs, elisions, and mispronunciations that show him *still not to have weakened* in his mission, *still not to have lost* the courageous struggle with alcohol, still not to have stopped focusing, in short, on his one single, indispensable, salient, and invaluable task: *that of making things appear other than they are.*

An even greater credit to President Penguin-Duck's unflagging strength both of character and intellect is the well-known fact that when his voice first began revealing its valiantly controlled garbles and slurs, it did so only late in the day. And even though it does so now even first thing in the morning, the President himself shows no signs of weakening, but continues instead with enormous strength to stand firm against the immense power of a drug that, as already suggested, would long before now have overcome armies of lesser men.

Simply consider the strength of will and depth of resolve necessary to continue serving Actaeon at whatever cost to body and spirit when even the first message of the day sounds less like the original

"Hello, this is President Morton R. Penguin-Duck"

than it does

"Hello, thiz Present Morn Are Peng'n-Duck"

or, later in the day,

"'Lo, thiz'z Prez Mor'n Pen-Duck,"

the words having taken on an international, perhaps French, Creole, even Vietnamese, tone, rhythm, and accent, although even then the man behind those words remains the same and unvanquished Morton R. Penguin-Duck, President.

6/18/06 7:46 AM (Fri.):
In my thirty-five years at Actaeon, I have never stopped finding it curious that the president's name should suit him so well as it does.

My many colleagues' names, over that same period of time, have been suited to them as well, but in their cases fate seems to have dictated matters differently than in the case of President Penguin-Duck. For among my colleagues, albeit with some significant exceptions,[50] names have reflected (and do reflect) not merely physical qualities (as in the case of President Penguin-Duck) but also, and most of the time *only,* intellectual or philosophic ones.

The times being such as they are, it became clear very early that *every*one on the faculty at Actaeon was at the beginning of a significant period of change: *all* of us, that is, had begun growing either thinner or broader, narrower or wider, and all of us were to *continue* doing so. A very small number, it's true, emerged as anomalies by merit of their going through repeated cycles in which they would first widen, then thin down again to a diminished point even narrower than at the beginning, only to widen yet again afterward.

Far and away most pronounced among the broadeners, and without question the earliest to have *begun* broadening, are Dr. Race, Dr. Class, Dr. Gender, and Dr. Ethnicity. Very, very close behind is Dr. Woman, estimable in the size of her growth but estimable too for being the most obvious anomaly of any on the faculty. Dr. Woman widens in *only half of her body at a time* while simultaneously narrowing in the other half. Her upper body, for example, will broaden at the same time as her lower body will begin to narrow and wane. Later, as this process reverses itself, her upper regions will wane and her lower wax (allowing Dr. Woman, for a brief time in passing, to possess a normally balanced shape) until the lower parts are once again Brobdingnagian and the upper parts Lilliputian.

Among others who have expanded enormously, and sometimes monstrously, in girth are Dr. Gay (though not Dr. Lesbian, who waxes and wanes like Dr. Woman), Dr. Black, Dr. Hispanic, Dr. Ghetto, Dr. Victim, Dr. Worker, Dr. Post-Colonial, Dr. Third World, and Dr. Asian, along with Dr. Gender 2, Dr. Ethnicity 2, Dr. Class 2, Dr. Blue Collar, Dr. Theory, and Dr. Muscle, though these last six, coming as they do from the ranks of junior faculty, are not yet anywhere nearly as wide as the others but are catching up rapidly. [51]

---

[50] Dr. Muscle, for example. [Author's note.]

[51] Strictly, I should not count Dr. Muscle indiscriminately among this group, since, though he is indeed one of the new generation, he widens at his own rate and in his own equally distinct ways. [Author's Note]

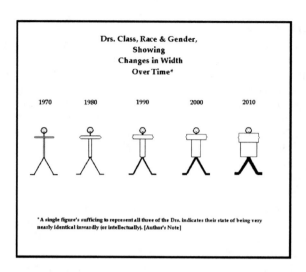

Drs. Class, Race & Gender,
Showing
Changes in Width
Over Time*

| 1970 | 1980 | 1990 | 2000 | 2010 |

*A single figure's sufficing to represent all three of the Drs. indicates their state of being very nearly identical inwardly (or intellectually). [Author's Note]

On the other hand, the dominant figure of the opposite kind, those who have grown only narrower, is Dr. Razor, my dear friend and also chair of my department for the past thirty-three of my own thirty-five years at Actaeon. Dr. Razor has become so narrow through over-work, professional despair, personal anxiety, domestic loss, literary sorrow, and the use of tobacco that, lately, when he greets me in the corridor I sometimes find myself at first unable to see him at all, being aware only of his familiar voice, until a glimpse from the side brings him into view once again (for, unlike the broadeners, he still has more depth than width).

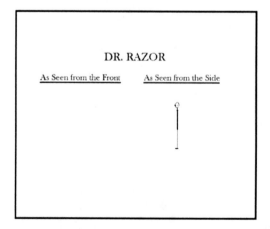

DR. RAZOR

As Seen from the Front   As Seen from the Side

Unique among the narrowing faculty is Dr. Socialism, who, to judge only by his appearance (reduced, as he is, almost to bones), might well have stopped being nourished decades ago. The singular thing about him, however, is that as he has grown physically narrower and narrower, his temperament has become proportionately only more mean, cantankerous, grasping, wily, spiteful, opportunistic, preening, narcissistic, and egocentric. As for his *thinking* or his *intellectual activity,* these have gradually become entirely undetectable, making all the more puzzling what reason there might be for the continued sharpening of his most unappealing personal traits.

Only he, in any case, has grown less pleasant in character while also wasting away. Those making up the rest of the narrowing group, unlike him, are mild in manner, kind and equable in character, balanced in view, gracious in argument and demeanor, while in temperament they are generous and unpresuming. Unostentatiously, they live balanced uneasily between a melancholy resignation to, on the one hand, the loss of meaning as they have known it and, on the other, a *very* faint hopefulness that the future may still in some way prove redemptive.[52] Some of them, at the same time, are poised upon the very lip of the precipice of despair, and one or two, thankfully no more, have already begun the dreadful fall into that unforgiving abyss.[53] This is the group that I myself am a part of, the group among which I count my own best friends. Of them, still living today, are Dr. Tic, Dr. Nerve, Dr. Rash, Dr. Colon, Dr. Meek, Dr. Good, Dr. Book, and Dr. Poem.

6/19/06 11:58 PM (Sat.):

As I said, President. Penguin-Duck's name, unlike the names of others, touched only on *physical* traits, offering no whisper of the man's philosophic or intellectual self.

Like Dr. Razor (though to a far less pronounced extent), he was narrower viewed from the front than from the side, although his shape itself was much less consistent than Dr. Razor's, and in this way he had more in common with Dr. Woman than with anyone else. President Penguin-Duck's width, I would estimate, ranged from near five inches to near twenty-five. A caliper, that is, might measure the distance from one of the President's temples to the other at approximately five inches, and the distance from one of his hips to the other at twenty-five.

---

[52] I myself pray that this is so; live on the assumption that it is; and yet fear that it is not. [Author's Note]

[53] I cannot easily bear to watch this happen, being as I am absolutely helpless to provide comfort and incapable of extending any kind of aid. [Author's Note]

President Penguin-Duck, indeed, was unusually shaped. His head was wider across the crown than it was from temple to temple; it widened again between temples and cheekbones, then still more across the lower face. His eyes were very small, further accentuating the narrowness of the face's middle point, while the handle-bar mustache he maintained had the effect only of accentuating the broadness farther down, leading many to express the sentiment (although never in his hearing) that the mustache was in fact not a flattering choice of fashion for him.

President Penguin-Duck was of only medium height but he had a surprisingly long neck. Below it, his chest widened in a barrel-like thrust and might have given an impression of strength except that his arms were extremely short and his shoulders sloping rather than square. His waistline was less notable than was the soft, widening, pronounced flare of his effeminate hips, below which his legs continued to the floor, conventional in every apparent way.

That Dr. Penguin-Duck was conventional either in appearance or demeanor could not in honesty be said. Observed from straight ahead—little eyes, ruddy cheeks, absurd mustache, head narrow at the middle, as if a constricting belt had been fixed around it in the womb as it grew—he looked preposterous. Looked at from the side, his appearance was even more curious, since this was the view that revealed most uncannily the remarkable accuracy of his name. He had a way of holding himself with his chin tucked in, shoulders thrown back, and chest puffed out that unquestionably suggested the carriage and posture of the Emperor Penguin. At the same time, quite possibly a result of the same inherited trait that gave him his soft flaring hips, the lower part of his spine possessed a saddle-like inward curve that served only the more to accentuate the rear-ward bulge of his very large buttocks and to give them the appearance of a counterbalance to his out-thrust chest, the entirety evoking no other shape in nature so much as the curved back, extended tail, and protuberant breast of the mallard, merganser,[54] or smew.[55]

So odd was President Penguin-Duck's general appearance, in fact, especially in the later years when his face had acquired its pronounced red color, that it invariably reminded one of the wondrous good luck of having been born into a modern, post-Enlightenment era like our own, with its philosophic foundations built on the solid footings of empiricism, relativism, and tolerance, freed of the benighted

---

[54] "A small Old World merganser (*Mergus albellus*), the male of which has white and black plumage and a white crest. ETYMOLOGY: Origin unknown." [Author's note]

[55] Any of various fish-eating diving ducks of the genus *Mergus* or related genera, having a slim hooked bill. Also called *sheldrake*. [Author's note]

tyrannies of spiritualism, witchcraft, and superstition. In previous ages—the late middle ages, for example, the age of Chaucer—an appearance like President Penguin-Duck's would have been taken literally as an outward reflection of what lay within. How lucky we are indeed to be blessed instead with a heritage that makes it a part almost of our very nature to judge not by externals but by internals

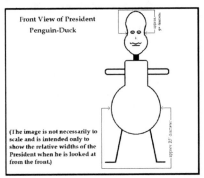

Front View of President
Penguin-Duck

(The image is not necessarily to scale and is intended only to show the relative widths of the President when he is looked at from the front.)

only; not by superstition, tribalism, or fear, but by the verifiable qualities of the true inner self; not by prejudice, dislike, or fear, but by the intrinsic and objectively judged merits of duty, dedication, and—above all—individual worth and achievement.

6/20/06 5:32 AM (Sun.):

I have always wished in a secret part of myself (although I would admit it to no living soul) that I too could be like my widening colleagues, so that, like them, I could also stop thinking altogether.

Imagine the ease, the simplicity, the effortlessness—the sheer dumb docility that itself can so wonderfully pass for thought—with which life could be lived if only a person were like them—like, say, Dr. Lesbian or Dr. Ghetto or Dr. Woman, Dr. Gay or Dr. Everybody's, Dr. Post-Colonial, Dr. Blue-Collar, Dr. Victim, or Dr. Follow.

For me, though, it remains only a dream: an impossibility, a thing that will never happen.

What stands in the way of it are my instinct, training, background, and education: all of these make it my destiny to be held forever among my narrowing colleagues, where I will now, given the world around me and those who govern it,[57] inevitably grow only thinner, like Dr. Razor, until at last I become nothing at all.

---

[57] A hint of subject matter that the author will take up in the hugely ambitious "Fragment IV" (see pp. 121 ff). Shandra finds evidence here suggesting a late date of composition for that major work (Maximillian Shandra, *Dating the Larsen Papers: A Writer's Progress toward Calamity* (Bangkok, 2096).

6/20/06 5:43 AM (Sun.):

Yes, the wideners will survive, the narrowers will not. Just as the cockroach will survive, the brook trout and ruby-throated warbler not.

6/20/06 5:44 AM (Sun.):

No, among the survivors will be none of my old lifelong friends, those who, tortured by the considerations of thinking and of thought, move wraith-like through the latrines and halls of Actaeon, less and less visible each day.

6/20/06 5:45 AM (Sun.):

And isn't it true, scientifically, that this is the way it must be? By natural selection? The surviving species, the adaptable species, remains the superior one, does it not? By definition?[58]

6/20/06 5:52 AM (Sun.):

The truth is this: from a time very early on, thinking became intolerable at Actaeon.

Thinking, after all, led to the truth. And the truth—a truth of cold, heat, screaming, airlessness, disease, stench, bullets, death threats, lassitude, despair—this truth, quickly enough indeed, revealed itself to be intolerable.

And, therefore, if *that* is the truth that one is led to by consciousness and cerebration, what could possibly be more reasonable than *simply to stop thinking?*

The truly most intelligent response, one that might have sprung fully armed from the foreheads of Deans Glad, Hammerhead, Happyhand, Dank, Shark, and Rattle themselves, was: *stop thinking.*

However breathtaking the brilliance of it may seem so far, there's even more to it. *For the real genius of the broadeners' response to truth has even deeper elements.*

Actaeon, after all, could survive (as President Penguin-Duck knew all too well) only if it continued to *seem* to be a college. And here can be seen what's truly the most genius-struck aspect of my widening colleagues' strategy. It was this: my widening colleagues, absorbing as if by osmosis President Penguin-Duck's brilliance at making

---

[58] In its tone, here is the most despondent moment to have been found in the "Diary" so far. And with it begins the long unfolding of the question of authorial balance. For opposing views, see Frederik Nissen, "Negotiations with a Non-Future: Courageous Sanity in the *"Diary"* (*Annals of Lost Americana*, May 2130, pp. 34–51) and Lok-Ho Woo, "Madness Day by Day in the "Diary" of Eric Larsen: The Destruction of an Artist and Thinker in the Late Ante Penultimate Period of the American Collapse" (*Studies in American Intellectual History*, August 2128, pp. 89–110). [Editor]

things seem *other than they are,* found a way no longer to think while at the same time still *seeming* to be thinking.[59]

In this way, through this one supreme, terminal example of the literary intelligence being used to cancel itself out[60] (and along with it any lingering perception of irony whatsoever)—through this ingenious process of self-lobotomy came the certain, irreversible, steady widening of Drs. Race, Class, Gender, Ethnicity, Woman, Gay, Lesbian, Black, Hispanic, Ghetto, Victim, Worker, Post-Colonial, Third World, Asian, Theory, et al—and simultaneously the steady, irreversible thinning of Dr. Tic, Dr. Nerve, Dr. Rash, Dr. Colon, Dr. Meek, Dr. Good, Dr. Book, Dr. Poem, and

6/20/06 6:11 AM (Sun.):
me,

6/20/06 6:53 AM (Sun.):
who in those years came to find life at Actaeon more and more excruciating, increasingly difficult, ever more closely approaching the impossible.

6/20/06 4:33 PM (Sun.):
I no longer used any alcohol whatsoever; I included large amounts of roughage in my diet; I supplemented this by fiber tablets twice daily; and I permitted myself only the tiniest amounts of liquids on any given day until the clock showed that less than an hour remained before my departure from Actaeon—the result of such measures being that I was able, by avoiding the Actaeon latrines, the better to protect the lingering vestiges of my mental and physical well-being. Further, I religiously continued the practice of keeping my door closed and locked whenever I was in my office alone, protecting myself if only through advance warning from the death threats that continued to arrive with roughly consistent frequency throughout my years at the college.

---

[59] Again, a harbinger of the theme of "non-thinking" as it is developed more fully in the impassioned and masterful "Fragment IV" ("A Letter to My Younger Colleagues"). There, Larsen shows how academic non-thinkers become *so expert* that they *no longer even know* that they are non-thinkers but continue to think they are thinkers.

[60] See pp. 170 to compare the widely-known passage on the extent of academic intellectuals' self-deception, where Larsen reflects on the omnipresent qualities of illogic and solipsism, "whose possessors no longer realize that *they have internalized a state of on-going infantilism,* the perfection of this retrograde achievement causing them to have lost the customary means of self-recognition—by the contrast of self *with things outside the self*—a loss causing them to be exactly as unaware of their own condition as a fish is unaware that it swims in water."

A very great obstacle remained, however, in that I was still unable to protect myself from exposure to the Actaeon classrooms themselves.

My livelihood, my professional commitment, and my dedication to the ideal of education all required that I continue regular attendance in the classrooms, and, furthermore that I undertake my work there with the same levels of energy and commitment that had marked my very earliest years of teaching.

And so I did exactly that, although therein lay the seed of my unwonted end, bringing ever and inevitably closer the day of my betrayal by President Penguin-Duck, the day of my brief moment of courageous clarity, the day of my attempt to expunge Sasha Brearly from the classroom, from my presence, from my life, and from "study" of *The Aeneid.*

How quickly—how very, very quickly—President Penguin-Duck made it clear to me that I had made a terrible and irretrievable mistake: That he, indeed, would side with Sasha Brearly and not with me, that *he would be a liar for her but not a truth-teller for me,* that my own fate was deserved and, however disastrous that might be or become, it meant nothing to him, while her fate—her fate being my sad, pathetic, ludicrous, principled, dedicated attempt to cause her to go away, to cause her to stop destroying class, to cause her *to stop wasting other people's time and throwing other people's lives away—* her fate was undeserved, *her* fate *would* be remedied, *would* be apologized for, *would* be set right, *would* bec [61]

6/21/06 2:22 AM (Mon.): [62]

Yes, if only I could have set my principles aside and become a widener—how easily I might have survived.

---

[61] Here is the only known example of the author's having broken off in mid-sentence—mid-word, in fact—and not having gone back later to complete what was begun, or not picking up with the same sentence in the next entry. Shandra, X. I. Wei, and others concur that the present truncation is *not* a result of damage done to the sheets during the Collapse, but that it can be attributed only to the intensity of the author's emotional state at this moment—Larsen is moving toward a description, after all, of the climactic event that, most scholars and commentators agree, in all likelihood brought an end to the writer's academic career and professional intellectual life, very possibly, as most again believe, breaking his spirit once and for all. That event itself, of course, and other events surrounding it, is described in Segment Three of the *"Diary"* (pp. 235 ff.). [Editor]

[62] What struggles and crises may have been taking place in the author's private emotional life during the composition of the *"Diary"* must remain a matter for conjecture, as so much else must remain also for readers of the Papers. Here, however, one can hardly avoid noting that a burst of writing occurred early on Sunday morning, June 29th, 2006, with Larsen making no fewer than seven entries between 5:32 a.m. and 6:53 a.m. Had he been awake all night? Did he sleep, then, during the midday hours? The next entry is made later the same day, 6/20/06, at 4:33 p.m. And then the final, extraordinarily emotional, entry is entered once again in the very small hours, now of Monday morning, June 21, 2006. Given hints such as these, we cannot avoid trying to imagine what agonies of intellect and emotion the author must have been experiencing. [Editor]

But as my life at Actaeon went on, I grew only thinner, albeit never as thin as Dr. Razor, who recently has become difficult to locate except by telephone.

In my own case, the truly vital and saliently important thing that I always half-consciously was aware of but never paid sufficient attention to—a failure so easy to see now, in retrospect—was this: *that my inner life was thinning at a rate commensurate to the thinning of my body.* Laboring in the false and thankless world of Actaeon and President Penguin-Duck was destroying me intellectually and spiritually, and this inward death, possibly at the very instant when I rose up against it in a moment of recognition—this inward death is what would cause the true difficulty for me, is what would ruin and destroy me.

6/21/06 2:46 AM (Mon.):
I remember exactly what it was that set me moving inexorably toward the end. And I remember, leading up to that awful end, how long a time it was, how terribly, dreadfully, unremittingly long a time it was at Actaeon, the chain of days, the months, the years, the years, the years, the years, the y [63]

---

[63] See note 61, p. 72. As before, Shandra and X. I. Wei agree here, too, that the truncation is not a result of damage to the page. The pathos is heightened exponentially by our knowing this to be the case. [Editor]

FRAGMENT III — "MY INTELLECTUAL LIFE"

Part One:
The Early Start Good Fortune Gave Me in
My Intellectual Life; Its Brief Duration;
and
Its Sudden End

Editor's Note:
Few segments of the Larsen Papers are more tantalizing than Fragment III, being, as it is, the most
intensely—and ambitiously—biographical section of anything else among the discoveries, with
the possible exception of the even more badly
damaged Fragment V. X. I. Wei has shown[64]
convincingly that the two fragments are part of
a deliberately planned single piece, one intended
in fact to have been a book-length epistemologi-
cal study of the relationship between the private
self and artistic perception, and, subsequently, of
the relationship between self and symbol, aesthetic microcosm and aesthetic macrocosm (that
is, artwork and world). Yanmei Ting has made
much the same argument, though declaring further—or differently—that the major "hidden
work" known to us only through these fragments
was in fact not an exercise in criticism at all, but

---

[64] "Parts of an Unseen Whole: the Aesthetic/Philosophic Biography Dormant in the Larsen
Fragments" (*Literary Studies in the American Ante-Penultimate,* Spring 2130, pp. 63–92).

an enormous, most likely multi-volume, novel. [65]

Some of the more exclusively biographical critics of the Papers have made hypotheses about the extreme extent of damage to the pages in these particular fragments, it being generally agreed that we probably have as little as a twentieth, or five percent, of the whole. The most persistent in this branch of scholarship has been Lok-Ho Woo. Persuasively, Woo has made the case that, remaining to the end an "unconverted" inside an increasingly uncomprehending academic world (and general population), Larsen grew inevitably despondent. In a number of extremely readable and moving passages, Woo makes the probability seem quite real that Larsen, in a desperate act of disillusionment and disgust, destroyed the novel himself, missing only the fragments left to us now.[66] Powerful controversy remains, of course, as to the premise that the author himself may have put his own work to the flame. If he did so, however, few other actions in that grim era preceding the Collapse could have deprived later generations of so much pleasure, of such value, so completely.

---

[65] See especially Chapter Seven, "Ghost of the Bildungsroman: the Haunting of the Larsen Papers," in Ting's *Darkness Visible: The Lost Novels of Eric Larsen* (Taipei, 2110). [Editor]

[66] Woo, "These Fragments I Have Shored Against My Ruins" (*Studies in American Intellectual History,* December 2134, pp. 59–174.

Part One:
The Early Start Good Fortune Gave Me in
My Intellectual Life; Its Brief Duration;
and
Its Sudden End

I

1

Then, all of a sudden, it simply happened: After good luck in birth,
family, and upbringing; after strong academic preparation; after signs
of genuine promise, my intellectual life (in the early 1980's, when I
was entering my forties) collapsed as if overnight into a pit of ashes.
And there, more or less—no: there, unremittingly, precisely, and
exactly, it has remained ever since.

Calamity. But I must point out that it was in no way an individual
matter. It was in no way something that happened only to me.

It was the whole world that began to change. The world I lived in,
the world I thought I knew so well—it suddenly changed completely.

Think of humans' lives being like the lives of fish in the sea, with
the difference that the human ocean is made of air, not water. When
the change came, it was as though the air had been depleted suddenly
of oxygen. Enormous kills took place. Dead "fish" by the millions
were washed up onto the shores.

By the millions. By the very millions.

Believe me.

•

A poisonous catastrophe, worldwide, perhaps even universal. I
still don't know the full scope of things, even now, at this late date.[67]

---

[67] Almost all dates of composition in the Larsen Papers are in dispute. Liechtenstein and
Claire, however (*Times of Doom: Chronologies of Culture from the Early Penultimate to the
Collapse* [Ho Chi Minh City, 2114]), make a convincing case that Fragments III, IV, and

Whatever did take place, I know this: I was in the midst of it, I observed it, I still do. And I have managed so far, in one way or another, to live through it. All this with the dubious result that here I am now, surviving however best I can in the barren, diminished, depleted world left to me.[68] I do this, mainly, by keeping out of sight as much as I possibly can and by doing my work quietly, insofar as that remains a possibility for me.[69]

And there's the rub, or one of them. Never have I been able to "teach" quietly. Nor have I been willing to, nor have I ever seen why I *should*. All around me, when I stroll through the halls, I look into rooms, on both sides of the corridors, filled with people asleep. This, apparently, is the way "teaching" is now done, or the way the experts do it. As if within the haven of sleep, no harm can be done. For me, the very idea is anathema. Never—not since my first semester, my first day, my first *class* at Actaeon—have I been able to abide it, the dozers in the back, the sleepers along the sides, their heads fallen against the walls, open mouthed, as if they had been made aghast and then knocked cold by the marvels of the things I'd shown them. So it has always been and so it is still, with me. I am driven into a rage against waste, sullenness, loss, emptiness and folly by the *sight even of a single person* asleep in one of my own rooms. Imagine fifty of them.

Classrooms. Somnolaria, they should call them.

And so it has come about, the use of noise. It isn't my credo, but it's the simple necessity of keeping it interesting, keeping them awake, keeping it productive, keeping madness and grief and humiliation and despair at bay throughout every hour no matter how much energy it may require or how great a toll it may take.

A note of explanation may be in order.

•

From the start, I knew I want [70]
graduated from high school, in 1959, I wa

V were all three most likely written between the end of the Late Ante-Penultimate and the opening of the Early Penultimate, or, that is, sometime between 2005 and 2012 (see Appendix One for a chronology of the Collapse). [Editor]

[68] So intense an impression of malaise and emptiness makes it almost impossible not to imagine Larsen in his Actaeon office as he writes. For the atmosphere of that office, see Part I of the *"Diary"* and also "A Note on the Condition of the Papers" in the Editor's Foreword. And of course see also p. 89 ff. of this present piece, "Fragment III" ("My Intellectual Life"), [Editor]

[69] That the fact of Larsen's making *noise* while doing his job became a central charge at the time of his betrayal by President-Penguin Duck (and by Drs. Correct, Long, Nose, Everybody's, Me, Cleopatra, Know, Race, Class, Gender, Muscle, and Victim) is, to us, of course, astonishing, inexplicable, pathetic, and entirely absurd. [Editor]

[70] The extremely poor condition of the sheets in this section of "Fragment III" deals a heavy blow to readers and scholars, especially those desiring information about the Larsen biography. For a convincing but by necessity hypothetical "reconstruction" of the life, see Maximillian Shandra, *Dating the Larsen Papers: A Writer's Progress toward Calamity* (Bangkok, 2096). [Editor]

from college, I was convinced my life would be ded
had been a sound one—in high school with teachers like St
with instructors like Scott Elledge, Reed Whittemore, Owen Jenkins
Harriet Sheridan, and others. As a result, I subscribed to the view tha
could, must, and do strengthen one another. So, I devoted the next
years, on and off, to graduate study instead of doing something el
say (though they never would have taken me any
a fly-fisherman or forest ranger.

    I got ready, in other w
begun publishing piec

ern Fiction Studies

The South Dak

        was honest but no money in it, a
      Needed support as I
        getting ready for all along.

    was how I came to New York City and Actaeon, age thirty
married, my dear wife pregnant for the first time, t
                1971, eage
    n the certainty (and belief) that here was a pl
        ould lead a literary life that was honest and
productive and   intellectual integrity and was *genuine.*
    Or so I thought. And so they let me g
for a certain brief time.
    And then, the calamity. And, with it
             ibble realization that what I had under-
taken for one entire side of my life's work was not teaching at all, but
it was "teaching." And that (two children by this time) there was no
going bac
emperor meanwhile more and more naked, t
Actaeon going more and more the
self-deluded in a nation itself
idly more and more insane
so that I, I, I unsuccessf
could have wished
again and again failing to learn
key thing how not to try, not make the effor
how not to increase my effort in inverse proportion to the
obvious and observable ignorance, lack of preparation *or of interest in a*

or result—in other words, could have become more adeptly self-deluding, learned how to shut my eyes, how to *widen.*

would anything, really, have turned out differently? Would I
feated, lost?
If I could only have found my way successfully int
—but then at least *what?*

ight have left me alone, the
r. Correct and Dr. Long, Dr. Nose
leopatra and the vile Dr. All, whom I
on to mention the administrative cohort, all
hand, Shark, Dank, and Rattle, and of
n-Duck himself.
have seemed a matter only of an alteration in behavior, a
emper, mood, pattern, practice. If it were other than
anage to come so naturally to all those who did
ollowness they were living in the very midst of?
g, neither at the beginning nor at the end, not in
ctice, or mood. Instead, it was a matter of
less than living a lie.[71] And this was do
he simplifying of what's there, until at
vens' "The Snow Man," one of the mo
and only at that time, as it is in the
istener, who, "nothing himself, b
hing that is not ther
the nothing that[72]
then it is po
only then
but not
who c
crim
les
ot
v

---

[71] See p. 40, "Fragment II," and the epigraph used there from *The Adventures of Huckleberry Finn.* The echo of it here is obvious. [Editor]

[72] The quotation, unfortunately truncated, remains unidentified, "The Snow Man" unknown. [Editor]

become, the one necessary thing above all
be revelatory without being perceived as
understood by the others as expressing truth, to
utter *only without sound*,[73] putting forth words that if heard at all
nly by their echoes," since in this way alone, through a
lost, can one hope to elude the simplifiers, with their childish
maniacally fierce puritanical wrath and narrowed minds, yet
at the same time seek out and find those other remaining few left
alive in a dying intellectual world who can still listen, still hear, still
respond, still feel, still *read.*

It *must be*[74]

7 [75]

Above all, I was trained to believe that in the artistic or intellectual life success invariably lay in solid and continued preparation, no
matter the degree of natural talent that may or may not precede it. As
a result, I set out to prove myself capable of great diligence by putting enormous effort into my own intellectual preparation and literary training. Or, to be exact, I did so once I was old enough to make
conscious decisions of this sort.

Before that, everything in my intellectual—and aesthetic—life
was of course the result of such nurturing as I received from my parents, family, background, and surroundings—in other words, the
blessings of fate.

•

The first time I *feared* failure, or remember fearing it, was in fourth
grade. I know the season was spring, and the year must have been
1950 and my age nine. My teacher then was Miss Stryk, pronounced
"Strike," a beautiful young woman with abundant, raven-black hair
who became our teacher again two years later.

I had been kept home for a fair length of time, in quarantine along
with my two sisters because we had all had whooping cough. The

---

[73] See part 4 of "Fragment VI" (pp. 217 ff.). Larsen's oxymoronic phrasing here anticipates
the subject of the so-called "aesthetics of silence" that is to become so very meaningful at
the end of the Papers. [Editor]

[74] So ends a justly famous fragment about *the meaning of literature* that is itself very beautiful in its "found" rhythms, however despairing in tone. The passage is taken as expressing
Larsen's idea that the essential and even radical irony of literature is that only in the deepest and often non-literal senses can or does it function with any lasting effectiveness as a
means of "communication"—an irony no longer perceivable to (and therefore rejected by)
the "simplifiers" and other converteds. [Editor]

[75] The last section number before this was "2." We have simply no way of knowing how
many pages have been lost between that section and this. [Editor]

time at home had felt less a deprivation than almost like a vacation, really, since the spring weather was lovely, none of us felt the least bit sick, and we were free to run about the farm however we pleased. For part of each day, our mother made an effort to keep us current with our lessons, sitting us down at the dining room table to do whatever work our teachers had given her for us up to that point. In my own case, however, something must have gotten lost or overlooked, because I suddenly found myself behind in arithmetic. The very day I went back, Ms. Stryk set us all to performing a set of problems in long division that I didn't have the faintest idea how to do.

This was the first time I remember feeling panic in school, and I'm not certain exactly why the sense should have come just then— unless this really was the first time I hadn't understood something expected of me by a teacher. The sheet in front of me seemed entirely meaningless, and as the others set about doing their problems, a powerful, unalloyed fear rose up in me, almost as if I were drowning. Our seating was alphabetical, so Richard Jensen was one seat away from me (normally, Patty Klingbile would have been sitting between us, but she was absent). I fought back tears and whispered in desperation, begging Richard to show me what to do.

I don't remember anything beyond that point (Richard always knew everything, so I imagine he showed me how to do the problems—or got Ms. Stryk to show me), nor do I remember wondering just why I had become so badly frightened. It may have been nothing but a child's terror of being left behind, separated from the herd. But it was, I realize now, the first time I had ever realized that school was not just automatic, that it wasn't something that happened to you and would take care of itself without any effort from you. But I saw now that some amount of care was involved and that you had to hold up your side of the project if there were to be any success. Twenty-two years after the fourth grade, when I began as an assistant professor at Actaeon, this understanding was so ingrained a part of what I assumed education was that the Actaeon students sitting there looking up at me with no anticipation or interest, no questioning air, but with listless boredom, slack-jawed sullenness, or often enough plain hostility—well, they seemed like creatures from another galaxy, people who had never been exposed to even a hint of such an idea about education as mine, let alone to any true experience of it, people for whom the entire proposition had been turned precisely and absolutely upside down, for whom there was no conceivabl

•

f course, at age nine or ten, I thought about it in a differe
ut the effect, still, was the sa

•

act is that for all my life I have been terrified of failing, or at least all my life after early

Which doesn't mean that I've always done the most reasonable thing to avoid it, or that by failure I have always meant the same thing as others may mean by it.[76]

Doubtless, i [77]

•

Four Things that Happened When I Was in the Sixth Grade

When I was in the sixth grade:

1) At the north door of the school, waiting in the group to go back in after lunch recess, I fell on the ice and was briefly knocked out.

Outside the door, a sheet of ice had spread out in an apron, and, through thawing and re-freezing, had taken on an undulant surface consisting, as it were, of hummocks, some the size of walnuts, others baseballs, still others as large as grapefruits. When I slipped (my feet simply went out from under me), I fell so that my right temple, with my body's weight behind it, hit a baseball-sized lump of ice. Instant blackness was everywhere around me. Then stars began floating across the velveteen blackness—five-pointed stars of different colors. When these disappeared and my vision began coming back, I saw that the last two or three sixth-graders—I'd been in the middle of the crowd of them before—were pushing their way in through the door and disappearing inside. It was as though for a few moments I hadn't existed. That bit of time—for me—had been snipped out of the universe.

2) Stephen Koch's father died. His father, a lawyer, had moved to Northfield from St. Paul in 1946 or 1947. He had an office on the west side of Division Street, on the street level. When he died, of heart disease, he was forty-four.

Later, in ninth grade, I became friends with Stephen and remained so for many years. Before that, however, I knew him only by sight.

---

[76] As an unconverted, Larsen of course saw Actaeon itself (and his being a part of it) as a failure, one reflecting a greater, macrocosmic failure, a failure of the cultural nation itself. To the converteds, however, this perception was completely different: they, too, saw failure, but for them, failure and its causes were *always in other people, never in themselves.* That perception—or blindness—helps explain the strange mixture in the converteds of a fiercely arrogant righteousness on the one hand and a blithe, shallow, almost solipsistic contentedness on the other. See Robert Pinckert's seminal work on the psychology of converteds from the Early Ante-Penultimate through the Late Penultimate (*From Empiricism to Narcissism: A Nation of Non-thinking Intellectuals,* Beijing 2113). [Editor]

[77] Again, an entirely unknown number of pages are missing. [Editor]

We had never spoken. He was in the "other" section of sixth grade. His classroom, although just across the hall, could just as well have been in the Antipodes.

But of course I knew about his father's death, and I have a memory of Stephen on what I believe was his first day back at school. The memory consists of nothing more than my seeing Stephen come out of the building at the end of the day. But I thought to myself, *"He is the one whose father died."*

He was at the top of the hill. I was at the bottom.

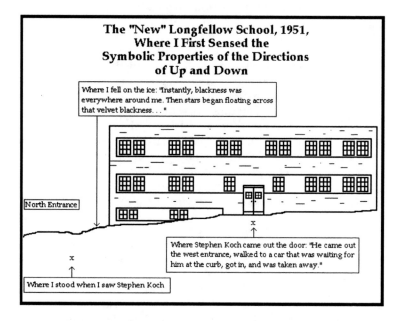

The "New" Longfellow School, 1951, Where I First Sensed the Symbolic Properties of the Directions of Up and Down

Where I fell on the ice: "Instantly, blackness was everywhere around me. Then stars began floating across that velvet blackness. . ."

North Entrance

x
↑
Where Stephen Koch came out the door: "He came out the west entrance, walked to a car that was waiting for him at the curb, got in, and was taken away."

x
↑
Where I stood when I saw Stephen Koch

The memory is vivid and permanent. Almost everyone at that time thought of Stephen as having a superior air, something that, to me, made him interesting and somewhat mysterious. It was true enough that he had an attitude and a posture. These came from the way he walked, moved, and held himself, and from the fact also that he wore glasses. He had a reputation, already, for being intellectual and bookish. Almost always, he held his chin slightly raised, adding to the impression that he was thinking of higher things, or that he felt burdened by the necessity of making his way through the crowds of lesser beings.

Three years later, our friendship began, and he became the second most influential person in my life intellectually.

I was nothing like him. I lived out of town, he lived in t

He came from a large city, I had never been close to one. He
with his life, while the very question hadn't even occurred
visited by disease and death, I had been touched by n
to have to live without a father.

•

built into a hill that sloped down from south to north,
so that this entrance was a full story lower than the east and we
him, at the close of the first school day after his fathe
the west entrance and walked to a car that was
myself was standing near the Secon
up along the gradient as I
car came down the h
I stood, turned an
past me.

•

ality of symbols, including the directions up and down. Heig
descent, a significance drawn from nature, unarguable, and
putably universal, archetypal, of a kind equally true an
inking, human existence, but not even these they
itrary in the simplifiers' rejection, seeing no need
in the case of the Green Knight, the example
only in attitude, not reason, the attitude that
were accepted, and therefore will be rej
simplifier asked what rationale
the very empirical basis of the
jected as erroneous, wron
ers like Stanley Fish
vile and hegemonic
in to a beast
nger.

•

ps an even more significant moment, symbolically: the time
Tom Rankin and I were stepped over by his father.

like me, born in 1941—and by then, his father,
in his second marriage, was far, far from being a young man, o
oments typical of her more apothegmatic side, was fo
that Tom's unusual intelligence was from his b
"child of aged loins."
What Mr. Rankin's age actually was, I don't know, b
past seventy, even older, by 1946. After other faculty posit

became professor of English at Carleton, and for some
chairman through the 1930s. After his retirement fr
still went to his college office each morning in o
then at midday walked back home ag
sidewalks shaded by the high elm
pleasant shade under branch
archways high overhe
autumn.

•

At one such moment, Tom and I were playing on the walk
in front of Tom's house. I remember that the sun was out, the day
was pleasant, dappled light and shadows were falling from the trees
above us—and we, in the manner of five-year-olds, were blocking
the sidewalk by lying on our sides, each leaning on an elbow in order
to gain some degree of elevation while also leaving a hand free for
whatever play we were involved in.

What that might have been, I don't remember—miniature cars
or trucks, or forcing ants to go on detours into their holes, or simply
pushing around blocks or sticks or some such thing.

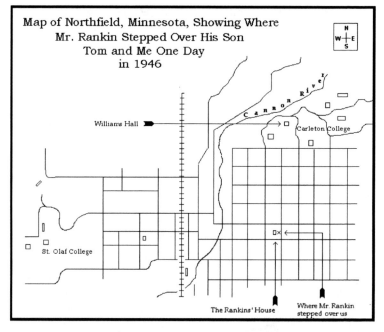

Map of Northfield, Minnesota, Showing Where Mr. Rankin Stepped Over His Son Tom and Me One Day in 1946

But I remember the rest of it perfectly: that Mr. Rankin appeared;
that, without altering his pace, without turning left or right, without

saying a word, without making so much as a gesture or nod, he lifted his feet and stepped over us. His pace unbroken, he then turned in at the front walkway, went up the two concrete steps, continued to the front door—and went in.

Again—just as in the case of Stephen Koch, the hill, and the automobile—the symbolism extends in all directions, in this case again the most pronounced of them being up and down. In the stream of generative power that rose upward from us (or from his son Tom, at least) where we lay on the sidewalk was the promise of futurity for Mr. Rankin: futurity for him, that is, in the form of the reward, pleasure, and promise provided by his own offspring. At the same time, downward to us *from* Mr. Rankin flowed all that he was and all that he represented: the authority, security, strength, and stability that had been gathered by him and stored within him through his intellectual harvesting of the preceding century's wealth, all of which now, by the very fact of its having existed, was being offered to us, *from* him, while we in return and at the same time offered ourselves to *him* as the potential means by which those things could be carried forward another step into time, into the future.

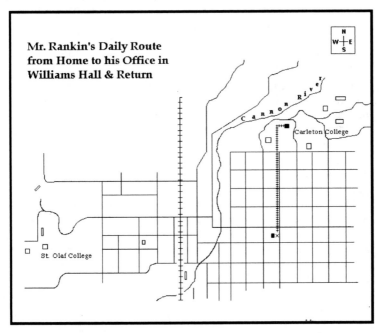

Mr. Rankin's Daily Route from Home to his Office in Williams Hall & Return

I came later to think of this as the moment when the 19th Century stepped over me. I have thought of it that way ever since.

Mr. Rankin—in his rumpled suit and tie, the old-fashioned air he had about him, his white hair sticking out and his scuffed leather briefcase—Mr. Rankin stepped over us as if doing so were the most natural thing in the world.

From below, he was enormous. He loomed above, dimmed the light of the day for an instant—and then was gone, had passed over us, was on his way to lunch, and everything fell back to being nothing either more or less than it had been before. Except that of course it wasn't the same and never would be, because Mr. Rankin had stepped over us and now he was gone, and I was never to forget that moment, ever.

•

And how ironic, therefore, the parallels between my own life and Mr. Rankin's. He there then, now gone. I here now, halfway through my fourth decade at Actaeon.

My life: three decades of it had existed before Actaeon, and now three and a half have existed in Actaeon.

The year Mr. Rankin stepped over me and Tom was 1946. The year now is 2004.[78] If Mr. Rankin was seventy-five years old in 1946, then I still have a decade to go before I reach the age he was when he came home for lunch and Tom and I were on the sidewalk, in his way, playing with trucks, or ants, or twigs.

•

Parallels. Mr. Rankin had *his* office, at Carleton, and I have *mine,* at Actaeon. Mr. Rankin's, doubtless, would have been in Williams Hall, that ancient, classic, modest, two-and-a-half story red brick hall that was constructed in the 19th Century, that for almost a hundred years looked toward the southwest from its rounded knoll, and that was torn down in 1960, nothing but bare ground left behind.

That was during my second year at the college, when they tore it down. How I grieved for that dignified, worn, dusty, comfortable, perfect old building.

Its own symbolism: reaching out in every direction simultaneously, simultaneously having things returned to it from every direction; looking out in every direction, simultaneously being seen from every direction. Then the enormous complexity added even to that, because there was the added symbolism extending also through time itself in every degree of past and future.

---

[78] See note 80. [Editor]

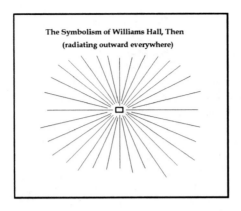

The Symbolism of Williams Hall, Then
(radiating outward everywhere)

But no one else understood, or saw, or cared, or seemed to think about it at all, so it was torn down and came to an end and ceased to be and was never to return or exist or be seen again, ever.

The Symbolism of Williams Hall Now

My own office at Actaeon, mine now for over three decades, and the place, as it happens, where I am writing these words[79, 80] —an unusual thing, since mostly I work at home, in my apartment, at my desk, in the pleasant quietness there, and only seldom here, although that's not so just now—so that, with a certain timely appropriateness, I remark on the symbolism of my office. Which means doing the opposite of what would have been done in the case of Mr. Rankin's.

---

[79] At 11:57 p.m., Saturday, November 20, 2006. [Author's Note]

[80] Is Larsen's note to be taken at face value? Is his identification, only one page earlier, of the year as 2004 an error? [Editor]

In mine, I must identify the symbolism of the place by identifying its absence of symbolism: the absence, that is, of any symbolism reaching outward, an absence well symbolized by the lack of windows in my office, as also by the lack of air—of any kind, that is, that's fresh, or from outdoors, or moving, as opposed to the kind my office is indeed supplied with, at temperatures conveniently either too hot or too cold: air already used up, stale, dead.

No, the symbolism of my room, unlike those rooms that lived on for a century in Williams Hall, finds its strength and greatest expression not horizontally or obliquely, but vertically. For in height and depth, in the directions of up and down, the symbolism of it is strong and deep. Consider: Below my office is the earth; above, three levels of latrines, stacked up like boxes of crackers.

Indeed, the extraordinary richness of symbolism of this kind is to be found everywhere, rooted as it is in the very life-forces of the vertical, the forces of downwardness and upwardness, of one, of the other, or of both simultaneously. The seed is pushed down, is it not, into the earth, and the sprout pushes up, does it not, into the light. Consider Mr. Rankin stepping over us on the sidewalk: his testicles hung down, yearning toward the earth, and we—the sprouts brought into being from plunged seed like his—we also then grew, aspired, rose upward.

Thus it has been also with my office at Actaeon, a coincidence of identically the same archetypes and symbols. In my office, there have been ambition and aspiration, growth of spirit and a surging toward light, all upward, in the form of my writing and thinking. Then, simultaneously, coterminously, indispensably, there has been the coming downward of the fertilizing element, giving strength and power to the seed and destined thus to aid the birth of further and additional new thought, inspiration, and composition.

Few other offices at Actaeon (if any) have enjoyed the fortune of such perfect placement as mine,[81] and the truth is that, as a result of that room's perfect location, my intellectual fertilization was so powerful over time that the effect grew evident not only in my own literary projects but in my pedagogic skills and ambitions as well. Not only was I able to manage increasingly complex materials, matters, and approaches in the classroom, but I was able also, albeit with ever-greater expenditures of energy and loss of fluids, to become louder and louder in my pedagogic methods and therefore more and more effective as an instructor. Success of this kind, however, as the reader knows, did not meet invariably with the approval of all of my

---

[81] I have now, I should mention, returned home, and I am writing these words in the comforting environs of my own apartment, my own room, my own desk. [Author's Note]

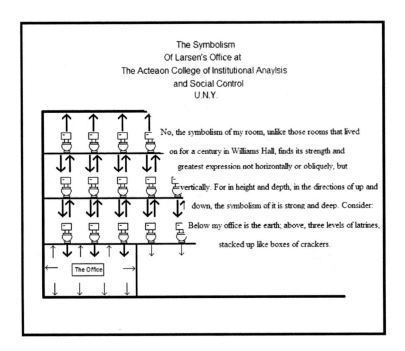

The Symbolism
Of Larsen's Office at
The Acteaon College of Institutional Anaylsis
and Social Control
U.N.Y.

No, the symbolism of my room, unlike those rooms that lived

on for a century in Williams Hall, finds its strength and

greatest expression not horizontally or obliquely, but

vertically. For in height and depth, in the directions of up and

down, the symbolism of it is strong and deep. Consider:

Below my office is the earth; above, three levels of latrines,

stacked up like boxes of crackers.

The Office

colleagues—for the real reason, I have always believed, that they were, in truth, *jealous* of it, although such a truth, of course, would never be spoken of. Either way, such questions remained moot for so long as I was able to keep my uses of quickness and loudness a secret known only to me—and, of course, to my students themselves.

But secrets are never easy to keep, and they're even harder, logically enough, when the issue has to do with *noise* or *loudness*—or when such loudness and noise happen to be located in the Acteaon College of Institutional Analysis and Social Control, UNY, where they might at any time be overheard by inquisitive and corridor-creeping colleagues the likes of Dr. Nose, Dr. Snoop, Dr. Correct, Dr. Cleopatra, and Dr. Muscle.

As clearly as if it were yesterday, I remember when this close-knit group of colleagues first overheard me—or the day they made it a point—if you understand—to overhear me. All five later claimed they were merely passing my room by chance on their return from lunch; though, in point of truth, I had previously, and more than once, had glimpses of them peering through the windows of my classroom doors, this at hours of the day nowhere even near lunchtime. Be that as it may, on the occasion in question, the Drs. Nose, Snoop, Correct, Cleopatra, and Muscle not only *heard* (and presumably saw) me being loud but reported *what* they had heard to Actaeon's director of security, Mr. Badge Worn, and afterward to President Penguin-Duck himself, with results that became very meaningful to me indeed. The loudness incident, after all, helped feed and develop President Penguin-Duck's subsequent impression of me as unreliable and a ne'er-do-well, making it all the more probable that he would choose rather to betray than protect me after my failed attempt to expunge Sasha Brearly from my class on the day of the *Aeneid.*[82]

Still, however calamitous the outcome may already have proven for me both personally and professionally,[83] it remains important, I feel, that the record show as clearly as possible that the loudness heard and reported by the Drs. Nose, Snoop, Correct, Cleopatra, and Muscle be *understood to have arisen for intellectual reasons and on an intellectual occasion that itself served perfectly legitimate pedagogical and educational ends.*

Therefore, let me put down here that the intellectual occasion consisted of a discussion of James Joyce[84]—specifically of his short story "Eveline," and, more specifically still, of these opening passages, which for accuracy and clarity, I quote:

> She sat at the window watching the evening invade the avenue. Her head was leaned against the window curtains, and in her nostrils was the odour of dusty cretonne. She was tired.
>
> Few people passed. The man out of the last house passed on his way home; she heard his footsteps clacking along the concrete pavement and afterwards crunching on the cinder path before the new red houses. One time there used to be a field there in which they used to play every evening with other people's children. Then a man from Belfast bought the field and built houses in it—not like their little brown houses, but bright brick houses with shining roofs. The children of the avenue used to play together in that field—the Devines, the Waters, the Dunns, little Keogh the

---

[82] For the extraordinary significance of Larsen's remark, see see "'The Diary,' Part 3," p. 235 ff. [Editor]

[83] The details of exactly what had become of Larsen by the time of this writing, or had happened to him, are unknown. Both Nissen and Lok-Ho Woo make clear the *extreme* unlikelihood that he was, by the time of composition of this section of the "Diary," still a member of the Actaeon faculty. (Frederik Nissen, "Negotiations with a Non-Future: Courageous Sanity in the *"Diary"* [*Annals of Lost Americana,* May 2130, pp. 34–51] and Lok-Ho Woo, "Madness Day by Day in the *"Diary"* of Eric Larsen: The Destruction of an Artist and Thinker in the Late Ante Penultimate Period of the American Collapse" [*Studies in American Intellectual History,* August 2128, pp. 89–110]). [Editor]

[84] Understood by most scholars to have been an Irish writer highly influential through the Late Penultimate, after which most traces are lost. The only known extract of actual work by him consists of the passage quoted here by Larsen. [Editor]

cripple, she and her brothers and sisters. Ernest, however, never played: he was too grown up. Her father used often to hunt them in out of the field with his blackthorn stick; but usually little Keogh used to keep nix and call out when he saw her father coming. Still they seemed to have been rather happy then. Her father was not so bad then; and besides, her mother was alive. That was a long time ago; she and her brothers and sisters were all grown up; her mother was dead. Tizzie Dunn was dead, too, and the Waters had gone back to England. Everything changes. Now she was going to go away like the others, to leave her home.

Home! She looked round the room, reviewing all its familiar objects which she had dusted once a week for so many years, wondering where on earth all the dust came from. Perhaps she would never see again those familiar objects from which she had never dreamed of being divided. And yet during all those years she had never found out the name of the priest whose yellowing photograph hung on the wall above the broken harmonium beside the coloured print of the promises made to Blessed Margaret Mary Alacoque. He had been a school friend of her father. Whenever he showed the photograph to a visitor her father used to pass it with a casual word:

'He is in Melbourne now.'

It is a sad, even a pathetic story—as all know who have read it—of inability to grasp life, failure to achieve emotional birth. It is a story of loss, fear, and a desperate sinking backward into lifelessness. It is a story, in short, very much like the story of Actaeon itself, of death overcoming life.

Throughout the tale—not unexpectedly, considering Joyce's monumental literary and intellectual gifts and achievements—ingenious uses are made of verbal echo, connotation, association, and symbol, all deployed (however unnoticeably under the commonplace veil of the story's everyday surface) to suggest and reinforce Joyce's theme, death taking over where life had once dwelled, death barricading the pathway to new life.

Here, then, the first round of questions I posed to my students so they could begin to see some part of the story's full complexity and beauty:[85]

01) What are the uses of windows?
02) How does *this* window fail in two of the essential uses of windows?
03) What is darkness?

---

[85] Readers uninterested in the questions may, of course, simply skip over them. [Author's note.]

04) What are the connotations of darkness?
05) What can darkness be symbolically?
04) What is air? What is air for?
05) What are the connotations of air?
06) What can air be symbolically?
07) What is dust? What is dust for?
08) What are some connotations of dust?
09) What can dust be symbolically?
10) What has to be *absent* in order for there to be dust?
11) What is water? What is water for?
12) What are some of the connotations of water?
13) What can water be symbolically?
14) What are the connotations of the word "invade"?
15) What, in this case, might be "invading"?
16) What is the position of Eveline's head in the second sentence?
17) What could be significant about this position of Eveline's head?

In that way, then, went the first round of questions, the class, by and large, having a pleasant time, I, by and large, also having a pleasant time—pleasant enough that, as we continued with our work, the forbidden element of loudness began gradually manifesting itself, soon to reach the level at which it was to be noted with disapproval and alarm by the Drs. Nose, Snoop, Correct, Cleopatra, and Muscle.

Nevertheless, the sheer joyfulness of the moment, combined with my passion for that moment's pedagogical and intellectual usefulness in digging into the revelatory depths of the story, led me to put out of my mind any thought of danger that might be creeping near. So I pushed onward to questions about "Eveline," round two:[86]

01) What literal reason might explain why "Few people passed"?
02) What symbolic reason might explain why "Few people passed"?
03) What is a cinder?
04) What causes cinders?
05) What might be the connotations of cinders?
04) What might be the connotations of the color red?
05) What is a field?
06) What is a field made of?
07) What does a field do?
08) What goes into a field? What else? When?
09) What comes out of a field? When?

---

[86] Readers uninterested in the "Eveline" questions, round two, may, of course, simply skip over them. [Author's note.]

10) What are children? What goes into children? When?

11) What comes out of children? When? What else? When?

12) What do children need that grain or vegetables also need?

13) If "the Waters had gone back to England," what has been left behind?

14) Assuming the Devines to be gone also; what, then, through association of the sound of words, is missing? What else?

15) Remember the color brown. What word does "Dunn" sound like?

16) What does the word "dun" mean?

17) What happens to grain or vegetables after people eat them?

18) When grain or vegetables come out of people, what color are they? When else? In the form of what?

19) When grain or vegetables come out of people, where can what comes out be put? When else and where else? Why?

20) If put on fields, this substance is put there to create what?

21) If "Tizzie Dunn was dead, too," what, then, by sound- and color-association, is missing?

22) Eveline, and Ireland, are therefore dying because of lack of what, what, what, and what?

In the classroom by this time, groans and laughter are coming from my students, and there are hand signals and rolling eyes. A desk is slapped by someone, much in the way a thigh might be slapped. There is a guffaw. The mood is festive, approaching the tumultuous. "Damn shit, pro, come off it," Steve Streather calls out from the back row. As usual, he is all but lying down in his desk, legs flung out, body near the horizontal. "Where you come up with this kind of shit, man?"

I leap at the—what do Drs. Nose, Muscle, Correct, and Cleopatra call it?—ah, yes, I leap at the "teachable moment."

The first, and absolutely critical, move: disarm the group and gain control again through a seemingly abrupt and complete change of subject. I find a tiny crack of quietness in the wall of sound and sneak my voice into it, like a knife into an oyster: "*Streatherian One*," I shout out loudly: "*Why were all the hotel rooms already booked?*"

The room falls quiet. "The *fuck*?" says Streather.

"Why were all the hotel rooms already booked?" I repeat.

"The fuck hotel you *talkin' 'bout*, man?"

"Well, what if I call it an inn? Why weren't there any rooms in the *inn*?" A hand shoots up. Another. Voices call out. Sound returns to the room like water flooding into a bottle. I've had my quiet instant. Now I'll have to fight sound with sound, quickness with quickness.

"Eveline" questions, round three:[87]

---

[87] The uninterested reader, of course, may skip. [Author's note.]

01) Why was there no room at the inn?
02) But if that's the way the story went, *why* did it go that way?
03) Was Bethlehem a town?
04) Did people live in it?
05) Did the people live in houses?
06) Is it likely that any of the people were kind?
07) Did any of them take Mary and Joseph in?
08) Why *doesn't* the story have it that way, then?
09) Why not in a store, a market, or a tent in the bazaar?
10) Why *doesn't* the story have it that way, then?
11) What is a stable?
12) What do the animals do there? What else? And what else?
13) What happens to the grasses and grains when they come out again?
14) What color are the grasses and grains when they come out again?[88]
15) Will the grasses and grains be put on fields again?
16) Why? To create what?
17) Christ descended from heaven and took bodily form to create what?
18) And he is associated with what? And what? And what?
19) Why?
20) For *what*?

"For life!" the class shouted. I called out the repeat, rhythm for rhythm, three or four times—"Life!" "Life!"—and then, at the split-instant of quiet after one of their responses, I added,

"Yes! Where there's shit there's life, for better or worse!"

which was repeated once by them and followed by my adding the second line—

"No shit, no life, for better or worse!"

this again repeated by the class one time, after which we all joined together, shout-repeating the whole,

"Yes! Where there's shit there's life, for better or worse!"
"No shit, no life, for better or worse!"

"Yes! Where there's shit there's life, for better or worse!"
"No shit, no life, for better or worse!"

---

[88] "Horseshit! They're *brown*, man!" Streather shouted out at exactly this point, unleashing huge bursts of noise, slapping, foot stomping, hilarity. [Author's note.]

"Yes! Where there's shit there's life, for better or worse!"
"No shit, no life, for better or worse!"

Whereupon, in the wonderfully apotheotic tumult of chant, shout, and desk-slap, at the very top of the hour's climax and the moment of its greatest success and effectiveness, I saw, filling the square window in the classroom door, her eyes wide, the shocked round face of Dr. Correct. Also peering in were Dr. Nose and Dr. Snoop, one behind each shoulder of Dr. Correct. And behind them, craning to see, stood Car Cleopatra.

The minute I looked at them, however, they disappeared. I imagined the four of them, with the addition of Dr. Muscle, disappearing hurriedly[89] around the corner on their way to the offices of Deans Glad, Happyhand, Dank, Shark, and Rattle.

My offense, indeed, was not *loudness* alone, but the misdeed of loudness accompanied also by the worse misdeed of *obscenity*, a twin bill of error comprising, my accusers were to say, an unacceptable breach of decorum, "decorum" being, it seemed to me, nothing if not the reddest of red herrings and falsest of false pieties,[90] albeit an effective enough tool for their own focused and particular purposes. In the letter of complaint that Nose, Snoop, Correct, Cleopatra, and Muscle prepared for Rattle— who dutifully forwarded it to Penguin-Duck—they wrote: "It is unconscionable that the students of Actaeon College, whom faculty members are here to serve, should be subjected to such vulgar, offensive, intemperate language as Dr. Larsen, shouting at the very top of his lungs, was making use of repeatedly in his classroom."

More decorously, I should have shouted,

"Yes! Where fecal material exists, life exists, for better or worse!"
"No fecal material, no life, for better or worse!"

but that would only have puzzled Streather and the others. Would have been a damper. Nor did I think of it. Nor would I have wanted to. The class was going much too well.

---

[89] But with Dr. Muscle putting great effort into trying not to look hurried. At all times, Dr. Muscle held his elbows slightly out from his body, the way wrestlers do when warily circling one another before a grapple. This habit, combined with Muscle's effort to appear unhurried when he was in fact positively filled with haste, gave him even more than his usual comic resemblance to a large primate. [Author's note.]

[90] Decorum, indeed. At *Actaeon!* Decorum at *Actaeon!* [Author's Note]

4)   In sixth grade, I also became friends with Tom
Prior, and, through him, with Denny Gudim. Tom, with
and three siblings lived on a farm west of ours a mile or
old man, a relative on Tom's mother's side of the f
in a little room off the kitchen, and I never had
except in late afternoon when he would
the house out to the barn for chores.
    I'm convinced that Tom
far from a standout in school;
lost track life, but during
was being limited by
        In the case
don't kno
embr
ab

4

in high school, I began finding believable signs in
lectual gift, almost entirely as a result of the inspirati
came through my close friendship with Stephen Koch. The
ver and I found myself at Carleton, it was as if a fuse had bee
ard the end of my first year I had reached a point where there
wanted to do with my life and mind. I leapt into this new proj
were wonderful years for me. There was promise! There rea
strength I had fed on its own certainty of itself, and its c
read, and wrote, and the more deeply and widely I
history of literature and the wondrous, powerf
of those arts also that came along with it.
    Wh[91]

5

I knew perfectly well that such intellectual gifts as I did possess
had come to me primarily through luck—the cosmic bio-roulette we
play in being born to whatever parents we are born to. On top of that,
stretching the odds still farther, there is the unpredictability of history itself—an unpredictability, after all, pre-planted also inside your
parents, whoever they may be, long before you yourself are planted
inside them.

---

[91] Whether this fragment stands in its proper place in the whole is not known with certainty.
Undoubtedly, however, it is one of the most tantalizing fragments in all the Papers—the author speaking candidly about his early intellectual growth. The fragmented passage under-
scores once again the enormity of what has been lost in the material destroyed during the
Collapse. [Editor]

I was lucky on both counts, certainly on the history one. On the paternal side, my family had been filled with scholars and writers, the line of them reaching back into the middle of the nineteenth century and beyond, constituting for me (or so I thought from quite early on) a background that surely must offer a significant kind of strength, a force that would give me a natural head start, a push from behind, in anything having to do with education or the intellectual life. Maybe this "force," if it existed, was only in myself, or perhaps it existed only through the power of suggestion that came to me from among the dead, the past. But soon enough I found that I'd begun taking it for granted, like knowing how to walk or how to put your clothes on in the morning: that becoming educated and using your mind to the best of your ability and in the best way possible was simply what one did, in whatever way, field, or direction.

When I started at Carleton College, in 1959, though, many of my classmates, were the first in their families the first stepping off into the deep waters. Later, wh Iowa City, the same was true, and few of my cla cated, whereas I was the fourth generation of a great-uncle, in fact, Henning, in a framed wall where I wrote my doctoral compreh over my shoulder to be sure I was doi
Almost never, however, did I
fidence about them. I learned quick
ill feeling of some sort, or suspic
resentment or even a perman
only more would be lost
loneliness was inesca
pitiful omission, t
history was abs
the enemy of
only choice
silence, n
cultur
die
u[92]

92 And so what must have been a lengthy discussion of social class and the author's own family and social-intellectual background survives only in severely fragmented form. Bedford Morris Lin (*History Repudiated: Ossification of the American Intelligentsia in the Ante-Penultimate and Penultimate*, Beijing, 2113) sees a central theme of the Larsen Papers as being the author's grievous lament at the death of history as an organic element in aesthetics and aesthetic thought. Also see Lin's brilliant exegesis of Larsen's "Fragment V" ("The Significance of Things Unseen"): "Past, Present, and Future as Nothingness, Being, and Nothingness: The Passionate Intensity of Larsen's Aesthetic System" (*Studies in Late American Intellectual History*, August 2109, pp. 752–775). [Editor]

So it was already true in the early 1960's, and it became only increasingly so as the 1970's ground on into the 1980's, that the Calamity gathered, grew, and at last conquered.[93]

When that happened, when the oxygen was sucked out of the politics and vision also changed in such a way that with the help than "a few quick and harmless words" bad became good, go small case, I was no longer someone born into an educat was a person under the onus of having been "privilege of this kind put into place, there was nothing to reclaim a meaningful degree of intellec autonomy or a meaningful degre that would allow individ *thinking,* but ins ful degree of re own domest of party, n princip nor eve back tru s

6

without history there can be no present; witho past, no present; and if no present, no future. The same is t ticularly if defined as units of history existing inside time. *is* one, and each passing instant determines what one *will* ands to reason thereby, does it not, that the more fully achiev fully achieved the latter: the more fully achieved the past present; the more fully achieved the present, th[94] malice, and spite have their roles fraternal triplets of idiot bir

---

[93] Here and elsewhere, Shandra (*Dating the Larsen Papers: A Writer's Progress toward Calamity* [Bangkok, 2096]) finds extremely strong evidence that *some sections* of "Fragment III" were composed at a *very, very* late date. [Editor]

[94] Lin examines this poor broken passage with extreme care in his discussion of Larsen's views of time, history, and aesthetics. "Larsen," he writes, "mourns the loss of the historical sense with the same passion that a parent might experience the death of a child. The comparison is not made lightly. In both forms of grief, a great part of the agony and pain comes from knowing that the future is what has died." [Editor]

II

1

The first time I remember seeing with true clarity and depth into the authentic nature of art was on a summer afternoon in 1946, when I hadn't yet reached the age of five.[95]

The results of that experience have been inspiriting, profound, and lifelong. They have also, however, had the unforeseen and deleterious effect of making my life—in this, the age of The Calamity—only more empty, regrettable, and bitter than it might otherwise have been. The reason is that now, in so vacuous an age as the one now given us, an age only of the linear, the shrill, the righteous, and the simple, I am driven almost to wish that I had never known what I do know. If my own ignorance were as pure as the ignorance of those who fill not only the halls of Actaeon but the entire nation around me, my life, I believe, would be far, far less painful than I find it to be now. The way things are for me, I am like the man who walked in sunlight for a day before being closed for eternity in darkness.

2

What caused my epiphany was that I watched my father take a photograph.

·

Our car was parked along a gravel road somewhere outside of Northfield. I leaned against it and looked out at my father, who stood a fair distance away and slightly below me in a field of tall grass that came above his knees. A tripod stood in front of him; on it was mounted his bellows camera. With a black cloth over his head and shoulders, he leaned forward to look through the view-finder.

The photograph was to include a line of trees in the mid-distance, the trees offering a certain contrast by merit of the field of tall grass reaching off toward them. Subjects such as this appealed to my father, who took a great number of them over the years, in varying seasons, lights, and weather.

Our car was a gray two-door coupé, a 1939 Ford. It was a two-seater, although squeezed into the back were two tiny jump seats.

---

95 Larsen's claim to this degree of precocity has, indeed, been debated fiercely among commentators and scholars. One of the most helpful voices is that of Frederik Nissen, who in an article on a different subject made the justly famous observation about the precocity question that has already become the start of an entirely new direction in Larsen studies. That observation is found in Nissen's "Negotiations with a Non-Future: Courageous Sanity in the Larsen *"Diary"* (*Annals of Lost Americana*, May 2130, pp. 34-51). [Editor]

My father had placed a wooden plank across these to fill the space between, so that I could sit there too, between my two sisters.

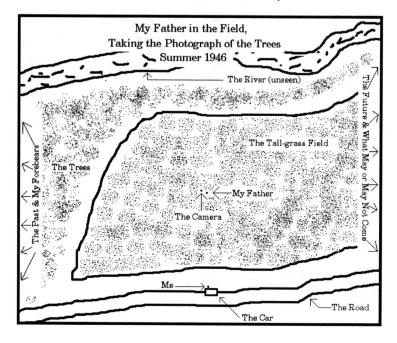

What I learned on the afternoon in 1946 is this: an artwork extends outward from itself in every direction at once, and it extends also through time, with equal force and in both directions simultaneously. For more than six decades now, I have held it as a central tenet of my intellectual and artistic life that these twin characteristics are fundamental and essential, since without them no created thing can achieve its transformation into art.

Am I alone in understanding so simple and essential an idea? In the aftermath of The Calamity, there are all around me not the perceptive but only the zealous. And by merit of their zeal, they hold a view directly the opposite of mine: they maintain that the highest (and perhaps only) measure of a work of art is the success of its existence as a simple straight line.

3

I am certain that my new understanding, that day in 1946 when I leaned against the car watching my father, came largely from the energy and achievements of my forebears. The existence of my grandparents and great-grandparents, of my great-aunts and great-uncles, many of them educated, even highly learned, undoubtedly helped make possible my own readiness and thereby my early and sudden recognition of those essential aspects of a work of art that serve to make it a work of art as opposed to something else.

On that long-ago summer afternoon (*silent; it was wonderfully silent under the massiveness of the summer sky, in the heat of the day*), this is what came suddenly to my understanding and never afterward left it:

For a work to be a work of art, it is essential

1. that it be *deep;*
2. that it be *broad;*
3. that it be *inclusive* (of every atom of life that can be available to it); and
4. that, by merit of these and other yet-unidentified qualities, it be inevitably and perpetually captured *within* and simultaneously dedicated *to* an ongoing struggle both *with* and *against* the imponderable force of time

4

As clearly as if it were yesterday, I remember the feeling of the day and of the moment. I remember the heat, the stillness, the dry, olive-dusty green of the crop-grass that rose above my father's knees, and I remember the darker, shadowy, voluminous and moist-looking green of the trees in the direction his camera was pointed toward, even the hint of gray-blue from the haze in the air when you looked across to where the trees waited, dense, shapely, and silent.

One of the quintessentially important facts regarding the moment was: that I was seeing these trees in the atmosphere and light of a summer afternoon exactly as my great-grandfather Laur. Larsen might have seen them in 1853, or 1862, or 1874. That I was seeing them, further, exactly as my great-uncles Nikolai or Jakob or Henning might have seen them in, say, 1889 or 1895 or 1904; or that I was seeing them as my great-aunts Karen and Ingeborg might have seen them in 1912, or 1928, or 1934, or even in 1941.

In turn, the immense importance of this fact has come to have not one but two quintessentially significant elements. One of these is positive and uplifting. The other is depleted of meaning and therefore despairing.

The positive:

1. From seeing the trees; from seeing my father photographing them; and from seeing them exactly as my forebears had seen them,

I concluded that a work of art must necessarily extend not only forward but also backward through time.

And the negative:

2. My having been lucky enough to have seen the trees in this durable, timeless, and fecund way caused me to be unprepared for life in the world surrounding me as I write these words now, six decades later, almost seven, when, in the unreverberant and vacuum-like emptiness of The Calamity's aftermath, this is the situation:

• There are none left capable of seeing the trees in the way I saw them, with this compound and inexpressibly lamentable result:

• that it is no longer *possible* to see the trees in the way that I saw them; and,

• that it is no longer *permissible* to see the trees in the way that I saw them.

5

(My father was six-feet-four, and in the manner of people with long limbs he moved in what seemed an unhurried way, never quickly or suddenly. When he took the photograph he was, as always, wearing long trousers. I never saw him, no matter now hot or oppressive the weather, in outdoor shorts of any kind. The same was true of his shirts, that they invariably had long sleeves. In hot weather, he would—like now, in the field of tall grass—roll them up just above his elbows.

The shirt and trousers were made of khaki, a fabric that my father had grown fond of during World War II, in the Navy.

As always when going into the countryside for photographs, he wore his ankle-high boots of scuffed brown leather, the kind he wore almost all the time after our move to the farm in 1947. His belt was navy style also, of canvas webbing with a metal buckle that allowed adjustment to any girth. On the front of the flat buckle my father had soldered a silver badge showing a ship's anchor over a background of coiled rope.

My father never wore a hat but preferred, like now, to let the sun beat down freely over his shoulders and head.

After being in the Navy, my father kept the habit of wearing aviator-style sunglasses like those he had worn in the South Pacific, with rims and temples of thin polished metal. Now, before disappearing again under the black cloth and leaning forward to peer through the view-finder, he took the glasses off and slipped them into the right front pocket of his shirt. In the left pocket, as always, in their slip-case of hard plastic, would be his Pall Malls.

•

(From the road, leaning against the car, I watched my father disappear under the black cloth. He reappeared and looked at the trees—without his sun glasses—then disappeared again for a much, much longer time.

•

I wondered what it was like under the cloth, what was happening there, what my father was seeing. I waited.

•

When he finally came out from under the hood for the last time, he stretched his arms back as if with relief. He tossed the black cloth over his right shoulder, put his sunglasses back on, tapped a Pall Mall out from the case in his left front pocket, lit it with the Zippo lighter he carried in his left pants pocket, and took in a deep breath of smoke. He made none of these movements quickly, but with his typical measured pace; if anything, he moved even more unhurriedly in the moments, like this one, following the completion of something significant or difficult. Holding the cigarette between his lips, he telescoped the camera bellows and locked them closed. Then he lifted the camera straight up from the ground so that the splayed legs of the tripod fell back together with a loose wooden clack that I could hear from the road. With the camera still attached to the tripod, he carried it the way he would a rifle or shotgun, up-angled and resting against his left shoulder.

He came out of the field slowly, the high grass making it look as if he were wading in deep water. As he approached, he looked off in one direction or another, sometimes pausing to gaze back at the trees, or to look in the opposite direction at something on the other side of the field, or, frequently, up into the sky at one compass point and then another. The appearance this gave was that he didn't quite want to come up out of the field, or that he was searching for other things to take photographs of and other points of view to take them from. In actuality, as I came to know later, he was looking at all of the surrounding things that would be a part of the photograph he had just taken even though they would not be in it. That they would not be seen, as I also came to know later, was something that served to make them all the more important.

6

(It's possible that I was wrong. The memory could have come about in a cumulative way, from recollections of several outings over a number of years. To a degree, I suppose, this must be true. On the other hand, the vividness of it makes me believe that at the very least its central outlines come from that single day. The field, the trees, behind them the river. The tripod, my father, the black cloth, the sun, the stillness, the haze. Me seeing as if through my father's eyes, in turn through the eyes of my forebears a hundred years earlier, who had been there also and had also seen what I saw. All of this coming together with the result that on that afternoon I began to understand the nature of space, time, multiplicity, and unity in a work of art.

How could it not have been so? How could I not have begun to understand, with advantages like mine, advantages such as the advantages I had? [96]

7

(Everything belonged to the photograph and therefore everything was in it: the day, the light, the colors, the quietness, the scent, the air. My father opened the trunk of the car, and inside were his camera cases. One was larger than the other, but otherwise they were alike, each with a hinged lid and corners reinforced with metal caps. Each had an upper and lower compartment inside, cunningly partitioned into felt-lined shapes, boxes, and trays to hold cameras, film plates, canisters, light meters, lenses, filters, even the wooden tripod with its elegant slender legs telescoped shut. The cases had fitted lids and stout metal hasps to keep them tightly closed. This was a good thing because of the road-dust that seemed to be everywhere in the car and around it, even inside the trunk, where thick accumulations gathered in the back corners and under the floor mats, even behind the curving section of pipe that went from the filler-cap down into the gas tank.

(This, *this* is what I began learning that afternoon: That everything belonged to the artwork, not only the things put into it or contained

---

[96] The more thorough a reader of the Larsen papers, the more likely the reader will respond to an impassioned and crucially-placed cry such as this one by remembering echoes of it elsewhere in the writings—and by remembering devastatingly painful counter-echoes in turn. Consider the following two passages, the first wholly in keeping with the wonder and hope of the "How could I not" passage—and the second, the famous "pit of ashes" passage, absolute in its expression of emptiness, failure, and loss. Such contrasts as these help suggest the immensity and sheer strength of the social, cultural, and political forces working adversely upon those unconverteds, like Larsen, still alive and at work in the Late Ante-Penultimate.

"Above all, I was trained to believe that in the artistic or intellectual life success invariably lay in solid and continued preparation, no matter the degree of natural talent that may or may not precede it. As a result, I set out to prove myself capable of great diligence by putting enormous effort into my own intellectual preparation and literary training. Or, to be exact, I did so once I was old enough to make conscious decisions of this sort.
"Before that, everything in my intellectual—and aesthetic—life was of course the result of such nurturing as I received from my parents, family, background, and surroundings—in other words, the blessings of fate." (Fragment Three, "My Intellectual Life, Part One, 'The Early Start Good Fortune Gave Me in My Intellectual Life; Its Brief Duration; and Its Sudden End,'" p. 81.)

"Then, all of a sudden, it simply happened: After good luck in birth, family, and upbringing; after strong academic preparation; after signs of genuine promise, my intellectual life (in the early 1980's, when I was entering my forties) collapsed as if overnight into a pit of ashes. And there, more or less—no: there, unremittingly, precisely, and exactly, it has remained ever since." (Fragment Three, "My Intellectual Life, Part One, 'The Early Start Good Fortune Gave Me in My Intellectual Life; Its Brief Duration; and Its Sudden End,'" p. 77.)

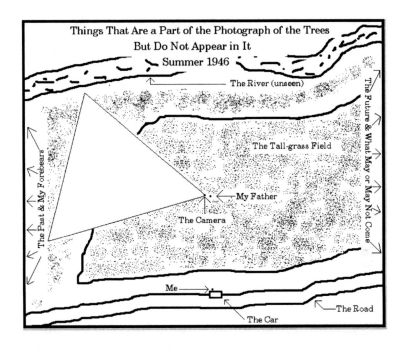

Things That Are a Part of the Photograph of the Trees But Do Not Appear in It

Summer 1946

The River (unseen)

The Tall-grass Field

The Future & What May or May Not Come

The Past & My Forebears

My Father

The Camera

Me →

The Road

The Car

in it but the things that were *left out of it,* since once the artwork contained what it *did* contain, everything that was not contained nevertheless remained a part of what *was* in it by the simple necessity of all things in the universe being interconnected; and in the artwork there would be not only the infinitesimal instant of the present but all of the long perdurability of the past, and not only all of the long perdurability of the past, but also all of the future with whatever it might bring, not bring, or fail to bring. And all of these, the past, the present, and the future, in however subtle a way, would themselves also be influenced in turn *by the artwork,* since the future cannot help but be determined by the past, and once the future comes into existence, the artwork will have become also a part of that past and can never unbecome a part of it; and since it exists also in the present it must furthermore be a part of the future, no matter what does or doesn't happen in the universe, no matter what does, does not, or fails to take place, and this explains why the artwork exists in all time.

(The oven-like heat inside the car from the sun beating down on its roof. And the dust: the dust that flew up if you slapped the upholstery; the gritty feel of the dashboard or the rear window-ledge or even the arm rests. The little triangular front vents, which my father swiveled open all the way so they scooped air into the car after he put it in gear and released the clutch and we began moving forward.

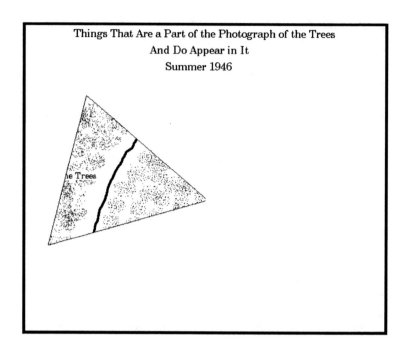

Things That Are a Part of the Photograph of the Trees
And Do Appear in It
Summer 1946

he Trees

His way of driving along the back roads so slowly that I could hear the sound of the tires on my side of the car rolling over the gravel, shifting it slightly. His looking one way out his open window, into the middle distance, then out through mine in the other direction.. I was so short that he could see over me, though much of the time I kneeled on the seat, changing position so I could see out the front, side, or back. Without stopping or even looking at what he was doing, my father took another cigarette from his shirt pocket and lit it when the dashboard lighter snapped out, its coils red. Still gazing out at a passing field, or a hill, or a herd of cattle, or a distant copse of trees, he pushed the lighter back in by feel, and in a moment, from the lighting of his cigarette, the most wonderful scent expanded into the interior of the car, for there was no place in the world where the smell of tobacco was more wonderful, fresh, piquant, and desirable than in the car when a cigarette was first lit, the scent mixing with the air as it came in through the windows, whether we were going fast or slow, or barely even moving, like now, when my father continued looking out over the sun-filled summer landscape that reached outward everywhere around us.

8

(And now more than sixty years later, every bit of it has been swept away and is lost and gone and will never be back again and will never happen again.

9

In other words: The Calamity gathered. The Calamity arose. The Calamity metastasized. The Calamity went on existing.

•

As an intellectual, cultural, social disease, the genius of it could not be more perfect. The Calamity brings an end to cycles of growth. And so, as a result, the only thing perdurable is the Calamity itself. And every one of us is locked in, locked up, locked down in our paralyzed idiot world.

•

Not true? But listen to them, what they say, look at what they do, Drs. Correct and Me, Drs. Nose and Snoop, Dr. Car Cleopatra, Drs. Long and Muscle, Deans Glad, Happyhand, Shark, Dank, Rattle, and—

•

The Calamity rose, towered up, overwhelmed the richness, variety, and wealth that previously had been everywhere. In the scentless air and unfecund soil of its aftermath there came into being The Age of Simplicity. And The Age of Simplicity—since it is the Age of Simplicity—is unable to hear, think, conceive, or generate anything beyond or greater than itself.

And therefore it is perfect, a self-maintained perpetual machine able to create only replicas of itself and nothing more or nothing else, each generation infinitesimally more simple than the last.

From The Age of Simplicity will therefore emerge (there are many hints already) The Age of Tyranny.

As a consequence, we are doomed. [97]

10

(Already, people think, feel, speak, do only certain specifiable things.

Already, things, thoughts, and concepts have been simplified.

Already, people think, feel, speak, create only single things at a time.

---

[97] The reader's attempt to follow precisely the line of Larsen's thinking and feeling throughout this long and extraordinary section is perhaps more demanding a task than at any other point in all of the Papers. The elegance, however, the passion, certainty, and power with which the author leaps from one peak of desperation, insight, and sorrow to the next, like skipping from one Alp to the next—such thought-writing as this can only inspire awe, and immediately afterward a newly intensified sense of historical sorrow and regret in any reader swept up by such energies, such perceptions, and such despair. [Editor]

Already, the concept that something can be more than one thing at a time is taken to be absurd.

Already, the concept that something can be more than one thing at a time and *thereby the greater rather than lesser* is taken to be absurd.

Already, perception of irony and ironies has been lost.

Already, the concept that a thing can be more than one thing at a time *and that the things that this thing consists of may themselves be contradictory* is taken to be even more absurd.

Already, the concept that what is left out of a thing may be equally important to what is put in, *or even more important than what is put in*, is taken to be inexpressibly absurd.

•

All of which is to say that my own life has come to be measur
itional, by its own achievements, characteristics, and under
but by those achievements and abilities only of others. A
who thrive and grow healthy and
Age of Simplicity, unlike
who withers and sicke
finally dies
inside
i 98

---

98 The pathos of this last truncation, coming in the midst of Larsen's description of the death-in-life that the Age of Simplicity imposes on him and other unconverteds, needs hardly be pointed out. [Editor]

APPENDIX TO FRAGMENT III

Editor's Note:

The close scrutiny made possible by methods of modern scholarship—not only the conventional weighing of internal literary evidence but also forensic chemical and molecular analyses that can determine similarities in paper and ink and thus date time of composition—has by now led scholars to the generally accepted view that the following pieces all belong to "Fragment III." Large sections of the Larsen papers, obviously, were found intact. At the same time it must not be forgotten how lamentably ruined, how chaotic, how decayed almost to the point of irretrievability was the condition of the author's Actaeon office at the time of its discovery. Wind, flood, fire, and collapse having played their parts, the small room contained shreds and leavings of paper and other types of material in every imaginable state of confusion, decomposition, and disarray. What follow are those salvaged bits and remnants that have been identified with certainty as belonging to Fragment III but that no one has yet been able to reassemble in their proper places within the whole.

i

Or, I should say, perhaps I will, perhaps I will, perhaps I will.

ii

                              if only among my col-
leagues, for example. In a number of cases these[99]   have taken
place within single people whom, after all, I've known for almost
four decades, more than a sufficiency of time for change to occur—
in dear old Professor Razor, for example, or in the once-tolerable
Professor Sanctimonious, or even, god knows, in President Peng

iii

                              e even greater changes, in the
sort of people hired. Before the Calamity, and even during it, when
only very few yet understood what was happening, the fruits of
hiring were not in point of fact so bad. Mistakes were made, of course,
sometimes bad ones, which is how we ended up with Deans Glad,
Happyhand, Shark, Dank, and Rattle, along with Vice Presidents
Hammerhand, Happyhand, and Hammerhead, fish of a feather, one
might say, though only one of these latter is with us still, grace be to

iv

                              rgues them to be gifted or dim, however,
Hammerhand, Happyhand, Gladhand, and Shark were nevertheless
still them*selves,* whatever models of mediocrity they may otherwise
have been. Though even the blessings of blandness came to a gradual
end as Calamity matured slowly into the thinner and meaner degradations of Simplicity. And then changes came in avalanche form and
we began no longer getting *people* at all, one might say, good, bad,
or indifferent, smart or dumb, but were taken over instead by walking, talking *ideas,* each (an important fact) *separate from the next and
inconsequential enough so as never to intrude upon another.*

These, then, were the beginnings of the Age of Simplicity, when
in new hirings came the likes of Dr. Race, Dr. Class, and Dr. Gender,
along with Dr. Black, Dr. Gay, and Dr. Muscle. The list goes on—
and went on. Dr. Asian and Dr. Blue Collar appeared in offices near
my own, soon followed by Drs. Ethnicity, Hispanic, and Lesbian,
all brought into my own department through the influence of Dr.
Socialism, himself holder of seniority beyond almost all others.
After a short hiatus, more arrived, even thinner (though widening
wildly to the eye) than their predecessors, among them Dr. Correct,

---

[99] Meaning "these changes"? [Editor]

Dr. Post-Colonial, Dr. Theory, and Dr. Third World. With a charmingly alliterative touch, there came also, soon after, the Drs. Victim, Woman, and Worker.

One can imagine how aliena
myself, how entirely unl
shared b
or
n

v

the few valued dear among whom I numbered my friends—most memorably Professors Tic, Nerve, Rash, Good, Colon, Meek, Book, and Poem.

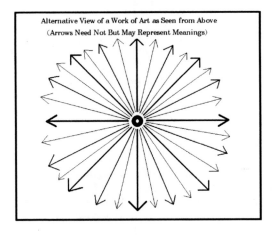

Alternative View of a Work of Art as Seen from Above
(Arrows Need Not But May Represent Meanings)

vi

was it, after all, that the new people would actually *think*? What would they do or show—for that matter, what would they *teach*—in their classrooms?

What *could* they think?

How w

vii

r example, content could there possibly have been other than that some people should be *women* and that some people should not; that some people should be gay and that some people should not; that some people should be Hispanic and that some people should not; that some people should be Black and that some people should not; that some people should be lesbian and that some people should not; that some people should be Asian, and that some people should not; that some people should be male, and that some peo

viii

ut whatever they thought, if nothing else, whatever they thought was *simple*

ix

et others practiced thinking that was even yet more greatly developed toward simplicity. Not only did these eliminate multiplicity; but they eliminated the last vestiges even of duality.

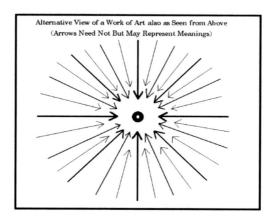

Alternative View of a Work of Art also as Seen from Above
(Arrows Need Not But May Represent Meanings)

To some extent, this even greater degree of simplification had been apparent in the earlier group, as in the thinking of Professor Post-Colonial and Professor Third World.

And yet the *most* simplified intellectual manifestation of all was to be found in the work of Professor Theory and Professor Correct, for in their thinking, every last element not only of multiplicity but of the very concept of "either-or" had been refined away to nothingness. No longer was their thinking similar to the relative crudeness, say, of Professor Woman, Black, or Gay, whose intellectual lives were dedicated to the premises that some people should be women, others not, that some people should be black, others not, or that some people should be gay, others not. Professor Theory and Professor Correct, unlike these, had pushed their research so far into The Pure Simple that even the most rudimentary or vestigial elements of choice, option, or distinction had disappeared entirely.

The very existence of the word "or" had been successfully eliminated from their thinking. No longer did they assume, argue, or profess that something or someone could (or must) be one thing *or* another. Professor Theory, showing the true zeal of the mono-minded, was capable of thinking only through intellectual or verbal equivalents of the phrase *"is true."* So highly simplified had his mind become that there remained in it no longer even the trace of such an idea—with its jejune, naïve, and immature embrace of contingency—as the idea that something may be true *or* not true (let alone true *and* not true).

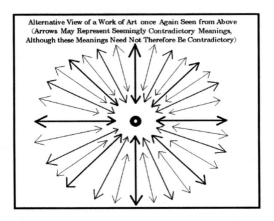

However remarkable the achievements of Professor Theory, they were bypassed by the thinking of Professor Correct, who pushed simplification to an even more highly perfected form than had Professor Theory. While Professor Theory hewed with justly praised mono-minded zeal to his *own single theory,* there always remained the disconcerting possibility for him that *other theories might exist* in which the concept of "or" still remained, not yet having been eliminated so as to leave only the one single and triumphalist thought-concept of *is true.*

With Professor Correct, remarkably, even this lingering and discomfiting residual element of complexity was to be done away with, since the professor's field of study itself, The Correct, by its very nature possessed no capability for expression in the comparative or superlative degrees, but was capable of expression in one form only, that of course being the absolute. Hence, Professor Correct's thinking had been simplified with so exquisite a brilliance that he was capable of thinking, professing, or speaking only one single unmodifiable concept, namely that all things and all people must be made to be correct and must be made to remain correct, *no matter what.*

The sheer brilliance of this development obviously sug

came about that my good fortune in being given an early start in my artistic and intellectual life failed to be of any importance, do me any good, bring me happiness, or even allow me in the remainder of my days simply to go on describing (and, yes, emulating) the wondrous, durable, pleasure-giving complexity, multiplicity, and harmony of artworks throughout history and of every kind although especially those created out of language.

For it could not have been made any more clear that everything I had learned, beginning in 1946 when my father stood in the field with his head under a black cloth—it could not be more clear that all I learned beginning that day and that I had cherished ever afterward was anathema to the new colleagues who began flowing into Actaeon in the earliest years of The Calamity, continuing on through the terrible and crushing Age of Simplicity.[101]

For it had seemed to me from early in my life that what made an artwork significant and distinctive was that as nearly as possible it hold *everything* in it; and, further, that those things not in it were nevertheless a part of it, and that those things not a part of it were nevertheless in it.

But instead of carefully and studiously putting things in until the artwork grew into an object of wondrous, life-inspiring complexity, my new colleagues, born of Calamity and raised in Simplicity, did exactly the opposite: with an intense and studious care, they took things *out* of the work of art, and once they had begun doing so, they continued with the undeviating blindness of true zeal, taking out more and more, simplifying and simplifying, until at last *every artwork had in it only one single idea.* The process went further still, in the hands of those few truly gifted among the Simplifiers—towering intellectual figures like Professor Theory and Professor Correct, with whom the process of simplification continued beyond the reach or ability of ordinary thinkers, until at last the state of absolute simplification was reached, with the widely lauded result that *no ideas whatsoever remained.*

•

(With the consequence, as any still capable of reading these words can imagine, that the strongest leaders among my colleagues,

---

[100] Between fragment ix and this closing fragment, there exist 210 others, all catalogued and available in the archives of the Larsen Papers in the Universities of Asia Central Library. Consisting, however, of words and phrases too incomplete to be meaningful for any but the highly specialized scholar, they have been omitted in the present edition. [Editor]

[101] Generally speaking, it is agreed that by "The Age of Simplicity," Larsen means approximately the Middle through the Early Penultimate. [Editor]

discovering themselves free of any ideas whatsoever other than the one, single, primitive, irreducible idea of the superiority of their each *having* only one; and being protected therefore from the influence of any empirically-based intellectual check or balance; grew quickly zealous with certitude, unseeing with righteousness, absolute with faith, and, far from least, unspeakably dangerous to those who might choose to remain unlike them.

So that once more, in the service of my own poor hopes of survival, I have gone into hiding and have grown newly cunning in the arts of secrecy. I am keenly aware of the danger that lies in writing what I now am writing, and that whatever words I assemble in defense of myself, with the purpose of revealing as clearly as possible how this dread and melancholy late chapter in my life could conceivably have come into existence—I know that these words, with these purposes, must be kept from the eyes and ears of the countless enemies among the theorists, simplifiers, and broadeners by whom I know myself to be surrounded in this, our new, undesired, unhappy, and dangerous age.))))))))))

A Portfolio

Examples of Some typical Works of Art
from the Period of Simplicity and Afterward, Showing
Tendentiousness
(Note: Movement of Any Artwork Is Understood to Be
in One Direction Only and
in Only One Direction at a Time)

Premise of Artwork	Conclusion of Artwork
1) starting point (A) ⟶	ending point (B)
2) idea 1 ("bad") ⟶	idea 2 ("good")
3) feeling 1 ("bad") ⟶	feeling 2 ("good")
4) position 1 ("bad") ⟶	position 2 ("good")
5) attitude 1 (unacceptable) ⟶	attitude 2 (acceptable)
6) conviction 1 (not tolerated) ⟶	conviction 2 (tolerated)

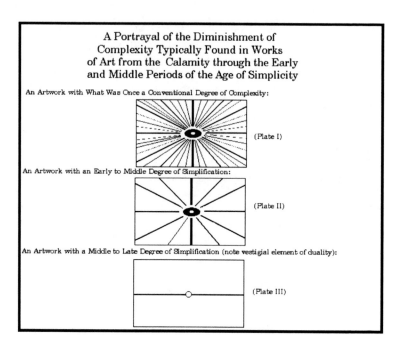

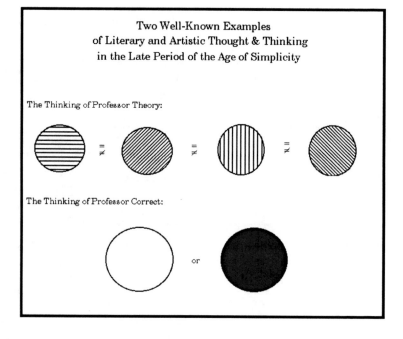

DANGER!

DO NOT READ THE FOLLOWING PAGES: DOING SO MAY BE DETRIMENTAL TO MENTAL OR EMOTIONAL WELLBEING[102]

The following pages are provided for the sole purpose of maintaining a historic and archival record of the events represented by them and for no other purpose. They will, consequently, fail to reward any effort whatsoever that may be made to read them. Let it be noted that any degree of narrative or dramatic energy that may exist within these pages does so to an extent *slightly greater than the degree to which it was present* in the actual past years of which they now comprise a fixed, unalterable, vacant, barren, and voiceless index.

Such energy, if any, of course, results not from the pages' being organized chronologically (all nature being so) but from the small touch of structural artistry they are imbued with through the device of their being arranged alphabetically and numerically.[103]

---

[102] See note 48, p. 51. [Editor]

[103] "A genuine emptiness, a pure silence are not feasible—either conceptually or in fact. If only because the artwork exists in a world furnished with many other things, the artist who creates silence or emptiness must produce something dialectical: a full void, an enriching emptiness, a resonating or eloquent silence. Silence remains, inescapably, a form of speech (in many instances, of complaint or indictment) and an element in a dialogue." (Susan Sontag, *Styles of Radical Will* [New York, 1966], p. 11) [Author's Note]

FRAGMENT VI —

MY ACADEMIC CAREER

Quantity is quality.
—President Morton Penguin-Duck

Our objective must be
enrollment, enrollment, enrollment.
—President Morton Penguin-Duck

XVIII

Spring 1980
1
English 101, Composition I
Sections 03–04

Adams, Nancy
Anaya, Luis
Anderson, James
Baez, Benjamin
Barry, John
Byrne, Kathleen
Cadet, Yves
Carpino, Marie
Clarke, Veronica
Conavan, Kevin
Craig, William
Deleston, Leona
Dennis, Jeffrey
Doval, Cynthia
Fernandez, Vicky

Hamsly, Diane
Hanlon, James
Jeffers, Yvonne
Johnson, Phyllis
Kirby, Richard
Kornfeld, Michelle
Lambert, Yvette
Leser, Dean
Monalvo, Elena
Moore, Michael
Moten, Rena
Newman, John
Pellot, John
Pitre, Linda
Ramos, Cindy

Rivera, Rosa
Rogers, Sharon
Romaine, Joseph
Saccone, Anthony
Saunders, Derek
Smikle, Conrad
Smith, Robert
Smith, Vanessa
Solis, Ethyl
Tillman, Robin
Virruso, Angela
White, Nadine
Williams, Carolyn
Wohlfahrt, Gustave
Zappone, Pat

Literature 103, The Enlightenment to the Twentieth Century
Section 04

Bastian, Gladys	Frisik, David	Pisani, Allen
Bittles, Richard	Garvin, Deborah	Reeves, Robert
Babb, Hamilton	Goodwin, Beatrice	Roper, Barbara
Brown, Carla	Inciso, Dorothy	Shell, Donald
Carpenter, Edna	Krajci, Steven	Silvero, Renee
Cepeda, Ivan	Lapidus, Barry	Sosa, Daisy
Colon, Felix	Lewis, Arnold	Titterton, James
Coor, Floyd	Lichtenthal, Robert	Toomey, Dennis
Daly, Peter	Lkmallory, Debra	Uberti, Arthur
Davis, Thurston	Medina, Maria	Verwoert, John
Duarte, Anthony	Melamed, Joel	Washington, Glenn
Fanan, Doreen	Ng, Henry	

Literature 103, The Enlightenment to the Twentieth Century
Section 06

Aiello, Raymond	Murphy, Maureen	Vogel, Bruce
Carbone, Richard	Palleja, Sandra	Welcome, Denise
Carmona, Jaime	Petersen, Eddy	Wiedermann, Paul
Enoch, Lisa	Phua, Marie	Wright, Isabelle
Iacopelli, Lisa	Vedral, Chris	
Kelly, Brenda	Velez, Eric	

XVIX

Fall 1980
1
English 101, Composition I
Section 05

Donna	Celentano, Frank	Kinard, Franklin
lph	Chen, Jose	Manos, Charles
hony	Cooper, Anthony	Mckenzie, Teresa
ony	Danjer, Marcq	Maclerio, Andrew
	Fisher, Michael	Pryjnak, Myron
	Jackson, Gail	Scudder, Ivy
	Jadusingh, Carlene	Vistoso, Julio

2
English 101, Composition I
Section 09

Cassandra	Nazario, Lourdes
u, Mary	Perez, William
Moraima	Reece, Kenneth
dia	Washington, George

3

ure 101
the Renaissance

XXVI

Spring 1984
1
English 101, Composition I
Section 07

[104] Whether "Susan Sontag" was in fact a real author and critic at work during the Middle Preliminary or whether she exists entirely as a product of Larsen's imagination is a question that remains without a clearly definitive answer. Wei hypothesizes convincingly that Sontag must have actually existed, although on the other hand Irena Hong-Koestler and Petra Gubar have become widely discussed for arguing that the figure is indeed invented and that here again is powerful evidence of the severity of Larsen's intellectual and emotional instability. Gubar and Hong-Koestler reject Wei's concept of the "unliving" words in "Fragment VI" and seize upon what they see as the patent contradictions in "Sontag's" thinking: how, they ask, can so egregiously bald and transparent contradictions as these conceivably be accepted either by critic or by common reader—"full void" "enriching emptiness" or "eloquent silence"? and, further, doesn't this very trio of conundrums, at odds with the basic principles both of language and of life, demonstrate once again the tragic withdrawal, inwardness, and increasingly unnatural solipsism developed by Larsen in his efforts at defense and survival (under the dual forces of the Late Ante-Penultimate/Early Penultimate era itself *and* the academic/intellectual travesties brought into being by the Penguin-Duck regime) as his intellect gradually withered and his very life itself, like the lives of *all* unconverteds, was demonstrated *each day* to be of less significance than it had been the day before. To any with even the least remnant of human feeling, in short, the case made by Gubar and Hong-Koestler will resonate in the heart even if the mind be more greatly swayed by Wei's command of logic. [Editor]

2
English 101, Composition I
Section 08

Estupinan, Richard	Mcnish, Celia
Hamer, Judy C.	Satterfield, Kevin
Lettsome, Gracia Yholanda	Williams, Agnes
Mccole, Peter	Zykofsky, Mitchelll

3
13, Enlightenment to the 20th Century
Section 01

reen, Eunice	Reyes, Irma
anor, Carla	Satterfield, Kevin
Hooper, Sheila	Smith, Timoothy
Jarvis, Jill	Spinelli, Elizabeth
Joiner, Karen	Stefanese, Anthony
Linares, Virginia	Toledo, Lorenzo
Mcdowell, Laci	Valentine, Christine
Miller, Jacqueline	Wright, Dorethea
Perez, Jose	
Pierce, Alison	

4
Literature 113, Enlightenment to the 20th Century
Section 02

Jemmott, Norman	Perine, Christopher
Jiminez, Katicaska	Petrie, Robert
Johnson, Everard	Quintero, Anthony
Kastner, Joseph	Santos, Yvonne
Kaye, Daniel	Smyth, Kerry
Kiely, Gregory	Soto, Franklin
Lewis, Shalleter	Tang, Barry
Mercado, Anthony	Terrett, Robert
Modeffi, Anne	Thomas, Gloria
Negron, Maudi	Vega, Lavine

XXVII

Fall 1984
1
English 101, Composition I
Section 22

Estupinan, Richard	Mcnish, Celia
Hamer, Judy C.	Satterfield, Kevin
Lettsome, Gracia Yholanda	Williams, Agnes
Mccole, Peter	Zykofsky, Mitchelll

2
English 101, Composition I
Section 23

ile, Peter
hillo, Gino
avy, Andrea
Delgado, Lisa

Golden, Peaches
Jarrin, Luis
O'connor, William
Payton, Troy
Perez, Maribel
Reed, Michelle

Rudowitz, Bruce
Scoon, Lisa
Seifullah, Musa
Valentin, Elliot

3
Literature 111, the Ancient World
Section 06

nk
atricia
in
na

Morales, David
Page, Shawnee
Pascullo, Anthony
Perrone, Diane
Randolph, Wanda
Reid, Deborah
Rivera, Neyla

Samedi, Harry
Sanchez, Jacqueline
Smith, Alphonso
Smith, Timothy
Tadros, Oudeh
Ulrich, Michael

4
Literature 111, the Ancient World
Section 07

Franqui, Maryanne
Gonzalez, Judi
Gray, Teresina
Haskins, Kim
Joyce, Thomas
Knox, Theresa
iano, Herman
donado, Ebelia
har, Patrick
z, Norma
Nilda
Thomas
Marcia

Sanchez, Milagros
Santos, Yvonne
Schill, Thomas
Skuludis, Theodora
Solimine, Vincent
Souffrant, George
Spiritosanto, Anton
Sullivan, Scott
Thomas, Gloria
Torres, Maria
Turner, Colon
Viggiano, Doreen
Williams, Debra

XXVIII

ring 1985
1
, Composition I
tion 01

Moll, Eric
Morales, Robert
Morris, Le Rue Anthony
Payton, Troy
Sanya, Jerry
Walker, Roslyn

---

n I

Briggs, Robin
driiguez, Ricardo
tzer, Robert
ucato, Frank
, Marie
th, Denise

---

n
l
a

FRAGMENT IV—PART 1

A Letter to My
Younger Colleagues
On the Subject
of
The Collaborative Destruction
from within Academia
of the Aesthetic
as a Living
Force

Editor's Note:

Along with all else taking place in Larsen's artistic and intellectual life during the period known now as the Middle to Late Ante-Penultimate, it should not be forgotten that the author was involved in an earnest and ongoing critical analysis of the difficulties faced by the small number of genuinely serious literary writers and thinkers that were left in that time.

Larsen's own non-scholarly work, as everyone knows, has been almost entirely lost, there being extant only those few fragments and allusions that have been well and famously explored by commentators and scholars like Archer L. Poindeft and the late Yanmei Ting.[105]

---

[105] Ting, Yanmei. *Darkness Visible: The Lost Novels of Eric Larsen* (Taipei, 2110); and Poindeft, Archer L. *Notes on Emptiness: Implied Meanings in the Lost Larsen Volumes* (Calcutta and Londinium, 2134).

Still, "Fragment IV," insofar as it is a piece of criticism about what writing and literary thinking really are and what they really mean, or what they *should* be and mean, offers an extraordinarily rewarding look into the workings of an *unconverted* scholarly, literary, and artistic mind of the first rank.

The document is complex, however, for reasons other than just the complexity of its author's mind. Of all the Larsen papers, Fragment IV is argued by some to be the most complicated as well the most questionable. Not only is it the best known among the papers because of its extended use of the "dual" method, but it also more than any other (except of course for some elements, sections, and aspects of the *"Diary"* itself) raises obvious questions, to put it without indirection, about both Larsen's honesty and the complete soundness of his mind.

First, as to the author's "dual" method of weaving his own words around actual notices, memos, postings, and advertisements selected from the blizzard of examples that must have been omnipresent in the daily life around him.

Through the use of this method, the author provides us with an important insight into the social, political, and so-called "market" forces that so effectively neutered Late Ante-Penultimate and Early Penultimate writers and artists, causing them to wither into insignificance as (parallel to the universities themselves) they more and more completely lost their ability to distinguish between art and "product."

The dual method, in effect, offers a walking tour through the prevalent banalities of life inside Late Ante-Penultimate or Early Penultimate academic institutions of "higher" learning. In Ting's expressive phrasing, the insertions create "innumerable windows through which we can look directly into a daily life that has become, in almost equal degrees, villainous, pathetic, and risible.")[106]

---

[106] Ting, p.153

Peering out from behind the banalities of these "windows," however, there lie remnants of an ambitious, extensive, and profoundly independent piece of analytic writing that some consider the most important of all the Larsen papers: that is, the most clearly revealing of a single, identifiable phenomenon that proved most damaging in the erosion of thought itself, therefore playing an enormous role in softening the ground in preparation for the Collapse.

Larsen illustrates how the erosion—beginning as early as the Middle Preliminary—of a literary tradition and way of understanding (inside the academy and out) gave impetus to a correlative diminishment in the quality generally of thought itself. Once a certain point of devolution had been reached (demonstrated by Larsen first through the phenomenon of "political correctness" and then, in Part 2, of "deconstructionism"), academic and artistic thinking, without its possessors even knowing it, became in actuality hollow and indefensible. Believing itself to be sound, independent, and "right," this form of "thought" had in truth, as Larsen shows, already become the unwitting prey of its own worst enemy: had become the simplified and malleable plaything of the immense "market"[107] forces that were the true engines driving the nation directly into the Early Ultimate and subsequently, of course, into the indescribable terrors of the Collapse itself.

•

Yet, all that said, there remains the troublesome question of authorial balance. To some of the most dedicated of Larsen analysts,[108] the very *brilliance itself* of "Fragment IV"—its penetrating insights, dazzling process of thought, the

---

107 Between the end of the Early Penultimate (2006-2012) and midway through the Middle Penultimate (2013-2019), the distinction between "market" and "government" forces was lost entirely, a massively important development by merit of its helping to increase the already accelerating pace of the approach of The Collapse. [Editor]

108 Probably the most notable of these, once again, being Irena Hong-Koestler and Petra Gubar (*Apollo or Cassandra? Victim or Prophet? A Historically based Analysis of the Question of Paranoia Versus Prophecy in the Larsen Papers*, Beijing, History House, 2110).

wizardry and artfulness of its "dual" presentations—these and other elements are simply *too* well done, *too* carefully planned, *too* skillfully conceived and executed *not* to elicit from some of the most dedicated and cautious Larsen readers a feeling similar to that of the Danish prince when he said of his mother that "The lady doth protest too much, methinks."[109]

Once even the suspicion has been raised, that is to say, that what we are seeing in "Fragment IV" may be the indefatigably industrious and artfully painstaking work of obsession or paranoia—once this possibility has occurred, few readers are able to recapture the innocence they brought to earlier experiences of Larsen works: to rid themselves, that is, of the corollary suspicion that the author may have reached a state of imbalance and paranoia before undertaking the grand project first known as "My Life in Education and the Arts Before and During the Gathering of the Great Calamity As I Have Experienced and Now Believe I Understand It."

The implications, of course, are as extraordinary as the question is inescapable: whether Larsen may in fact have developed a susceptibility to paranoid imbalance (if he ever did) *before* embarking upon his magnum opus rather than *after* or even *during* the composition of it. The question has to do with the basic reliability of the texts, and revisionists such as Gubar and Hong-Koestler, who see authorial paranoia as indisputable, have carried cause-and-effect studies to the point of suggesting that, rather than having been driven *to* madness and despair *by* the approaching Calamity and by academic life under President Penguin-Duck, Larsen may have succumbed to madness and despair, from other causes, before even beginning to write about Penguin-Duck or the approach of the Cataclysm.

By no means are all scholars or analysts convinced by the revisionist approach, and by no

---

[109] *Hamlet*, III, 2, 230. [Editor]

means, either, do they all accept categorically the soundness of revisionist methods.[110] But the sheer complexity of Larsen studies, without question, has been increased greatly by the revisionist explorations and the seeds of doubt they have sown.

•

The physical damage to the sheets of "Fragment IV" is, unfortunately, as severe as it is to any of the Larsen papers, and sometimes worse (with the exception, of course, of "Fragment VI"). Most analysts agree with Shandra[111] that "Fragment IV" is quite early (although, as its numerical title indicates, it was of course fourth in order of discovery), with an Early Ante-Penultimate first-composition date, possibly even *before* 1991 (although many disagree strongly on this point, among them Gubar and Hong-Koestler). Evidence is plentiful that the author at a later time returned to the work, developing and adding to it, although once again and at the same time there can be little disagreement with Isador Rosenwach's famous injunction that "no date in the Larsen papers can be trusted implicitly."[112] In spite of damage that at some points has caused massive loss, the sense of even the most severely compromised sheets can very often be gathered nevertheless though very careful reading and, often, simple deduction. We follow tradition[113] in presenting "Fragment IV" as a work seeming to be naturally of two parts, although we do so without losing sight of the several questions ever attendant upon that division.[114]

---

110 Although both, it should be noted, do remain on the whole well respected. [Editor]

111 Maximillian Shandra, *Dating the Larsen Papers: A Writer's Progress toward Calamity* (Bangkok, 2096).

112 Isador Rosenwach, *Enigmas of Time and Space: Finding Reality in the Larsen Papers,* (Katmandu, 2102), p. 37.

113 A tradition beginning, of course, with the Bhāskara Presentation. [Editor]

114 See "A Note to the Reader," p. xi.

"The Collaborative Destruction
from within Academia of the Aesthetic
as a Living Force"[115]

(1991)[116]

> Now, for the poet, he nothing affirmes,
> and therefore never lyeth. For, as I take it,
> to lye is to affirme that to be true which
> is false.
> —Sir Philip Sydney, "An Apolgie for
> Poetrie" (1595)

In what follows, you can depend on me, of course, to speak professionally: as a professional among professionals. Yet at the same time,
I am afraid, necessity will force me also to speak very personally,
perhaps even with what may seem an unrestricted frankness and
candor. If and as they are due, I offer apologies.

But, as must be perfectly obvious to all of us by now, nothing less
than a calamity is taking place among us. And to allow good manners,
collegiality, or traditional consideration for the feelings of others[117]
to stand in the way of our addressing immediately and forcefully the
true character and origin of so ruinous a crisis as this one is, would
constitute, it seems to me, an intellectual failure immeasurably more
significant than the maintaining of any degree of ritual politeness
could ever hope to be worth.

As no one now reading these words can be unaware, our department's recent series of meetings to discuss what changes, if any,
should be made in the college's required literature courses were by
almost every imaginable measure a failure. I say this not because

---

[115] Submitted afterward for publication in *The Actaeon Hound* and rejected by that journal's
board of readers. "A pox upon the wretched hound and every flea in its mangy hide." As in
legend, let it tear its masters to shreds. [Author's note.] In the sixth chapter of *Enigmas of
Time and Space,* Rosenwach argues that Larsen has made an invention here simply in order to
allude to the Actaeon legend. Rosenwach argues that while no journal named *The Hound* has
been traced, it is known that there did exist a journal named *The Actaeon Review of Human
Dignity.* The source of Larsen's quote about the "wretched" hound and the fleas in its hide has
never been traced. [Editor]

[116] As with many and very likely all of dates in the Larsen papers, it is impossible to know
whether this one is "real" or imaginary. The mystery is deepened by the fragment's first
"dual" insertion (p. 135), a letter from President Penguin-Duck that is "dated" July 28, 1998.
A case for *late* composition, however, can be made by noting that Larsen refers to "deconstructionism" in the past tense ("what it meant"). [Editor]

[117] This is the first of the fourteen hints of authorial imbalance in "Fragment IV" cited by
Gubar and Hong-Koestler. In one breath, they point out, Larsen offers apologies; in the next,
he argues that politeness can do nothing but stand in the way of the truth; the writers find
such wild swings in Larsen's own logic especially noticeable and damaging in a piece vilifying
the failed logic of his own colleagues. [Editor]

my own position—which I adhere to even now—was shared, by meetings' end, among only a small group, consisting of myself and Professors Tic, Nerve, Rash, Colon, and Book, while the main opposing position was stoutly defended to the very end by virtually all of the department's other members, although I will name here only the most vocal among them, those being Professors Black, Class, and Gender; Professors Correct, Ethnicity, Socialism, and Putty; Professors Me, Gay, Muscle, and Snoop; and Professors Theory, Lesbian, Victim, and Woman.

Still, my agitation and unremitting discontent—impelling me against others' judgment not just to compose these pages but to place copies in your mailboxes—aren't the result simply of my own views not having been upheld, although of course that does constitute a good part of the cause of my unhappiness. But the greater part by far, which over the past three days has occupied my mind without break—as I indeed have occupied my life without sleep—is, to put it simply, another thing al
Namely, the extraordinarily low level of intellect that w
stood as the impoverished substitutes for thought o
sheer penury of language; adolescent ind
group-think flung about the room
preening players—Professors Pu
to mind—fawners as if with
without once defining the
ersatz discourse both in
pendent or even
faintly substan
only a nitwit
appall those
lessness
mind
not
s

p
years
already made
otherwise might have
under the aegis of "collegiality as
others of a far less desirable kind. It hardly matte
among ourselves we behave as we do. How we think i
well try men's souls—and their long-standing passions, those very t
revering the "the aims of education," in the ringing phrase of philos

North Whitehead. How many of you may have a clear understanding of how powerful, steady, and unflagging a dedication to that classic idea some of our faculty members may have, after all, devoted their entire intellectual lives to

or Dr. Tic more animated, Dr. Rash a frighteningly enriched and deepened red, Dr. Colon forced to leave the room even more frequently than

as the "debate" went on. As for the
part that I myself played the unhappy
concluding minutes of our final meeting, nothing that I di
—however much I could wish the situation to have been other than
it was—seems to me now to call for[118]

including my response to Dr. Stool's outright nitwit argument that because fifty percent of the human race is female and fifty per
must accordingly be represented by authors
each sex, Dr. Stool inex
not alone by any
demonically
inane
pos
e[119]

•

for the necessity of talking about myself.[120]

---

[118] Here is the location of the second of Gubar and Hong-Koestler's fourteen citations. [Editor]

[119] Number three of the fourteen, containing hints of both the paranoiac and the suicidal. [Editor]

[120] Number four, in part because of its unexplainable change in tone, one personality receding as another steps forward. [Editor]

The years 1971–1991 have not been[121] ideal, but
fairly well: I have taught, and I have written. Of course I
been less and the writing more, since writing was the true motive for
get it. But I did do both, and my first important point is this:
perfectly possible, back in 1971, that a serious person could lead a literary life inside in the university, imperfect and difficult though it
might be, that would still be an honest and productive life that had
intellectual integrity and was genuinely a literary life.

But my second point, my own despairing point that must be
obvious to everyone now, after our meetings—is that that situation is simply not true anymore, that the whole brief and valuable
if unexotic and certainly fragile semi-miracle of the serious literary
life inside the university that I sought (and had for a while) is at this
very moment collapsing yawpishly, foolishly, and inanely about your
ears, my ears, all our ears,[122] with a sound l

•

writing them down
simple reason that if I try to speak
vable that any of you will listen for the length
explains also why I have placed them in your mailboxes f[123]

•

few words more on the subject of my last forty semesters.
If a great crisis is in truth unfolding

---

121 Larsen's choice of the present perfect tense here supports the idea that he actually may
have written "Fragment IV" in the year 1991. [Editor]

122 Number five. [Editor]

123 Six. [Editor]

can be seen so clearly in ongoing questions and
about what's taught and not taught in college. F
endless debates about the "curriculum," and more specifically
makes reading of literature an indispensable and significant part of
education and therefore—by extension—of the culture. By the
denly newsworthy through the "rising tide of mediocrity
such as William Bennett and Allan Bloom[124]—by
dancing around that particular campfire for years and
"cultural values and the humanities" campfire.
their arguments were *so empty of any true*
talk of "values" was no help at *all* to
now it's 1991, disaster has come to vis
entire house of literature is
ablaze from roof peak
we in the ashes
doomed never
die.[125]

•

When I first arrived at Actaeon, in 1971, a proposal was made in
the department to revitalize the required college literature courses
(our "core" courses) by thematizing them, thereby making them
more "relevant" to the students. The courses were arranged chronologically from antiquity to the present, and there was more
reading than the present students could keep up with. The pro
not to lighten them but to conceive them anew by casting
themes like "The Literature of Cities," "Woman in
"Law in Literature," and "The Author as
I have never been and never will be opposed to
cities, women, or philosophers. The proposal, nevert
fiber of opposition, and I wrote, as I am doing now
an impassioned memo to the members of the de
purposes and merits of literature really are."
My argument began with an asserti
it *isn't*. The idea that literature *as an aca*
amount of trouble in graduate school,
widely. His book's weaknesses not
Gerald Graff's *Professing Literat*
Whittemore's memoir in *Delos*

---

[124] Scholars know of no traces of or references to the figures of Bloom and Bennett other
than these. [Editor]

[125] Seven. [Editor]

is chronicled in Alvin Kernan's [126] *The Death of Literatu*
manages to write with unflagging charm while arguing not that

•

went, in part: the hoary date of December 13, 1971,

Literature's only true claim to a secure place in the academy is
precisely that it cannot be defined. It is *not* history, it is *not* philosophy, it is
not sociology, it is *not* psychology, it is *not* anthropology, it is *not* law, it is *not*
ethics, it is *not* current affairs. Of course to some extent it is made up of all of
these, but obviously it is none of them solely. It has some myster
so mysterious) ingredient or impulse that makes it unique a
makes it interesting, compelling, exciting, rewardi
        can't be pigeon-holed.
That fact is

                                        itself can only be dimin-
ished, neutered, and harmed by the thematizing of courses, especially courses
of this especially important kind..
Clytemnestra and Athena lead us to Gloria Steinem, but Gloria Steinem[127]
does not lead us to Aeschylus. To announce ahea
will approach Homer to discuss war, or Sophocles to
Shakespeare to discuss politics or philosophy, or D
cities is to make of literature something paltr
rather than alive, like the doctor who
lauds himself for saving the foot
has sacrificed the whole, and
patient dies.
Literature teaches hu
are not unique. We discove
in other places and other
of enlightenment, one
to recognize our ow
shows us options
not "values," w
injustice of
should
But
out
i

•

---

[126] An unknown reference. [Editor]
[127] Another so far untraceable reference. [Editor]

•

memo dated in part, though its central argument remains intact
two decades ago that has helped show what brought on the crisis
unexpectedly revealing—and deeply dispiriting—things about
still able to trust my colleagues—as I would you, if we could
can't find a way any longer to concur in certain basic
the donative nature of literature and its assumptions a
oping a simple institutional defense of "Eng-
appeal *to* you, my colleagues, through
has grown now into a defensive
ommon premises for debate.
And then something even more remarkable, I
no need to depart from its essentially pragmatic
far stronger *ethical* argument that
just under the surface.
Ethical? Yes, *ethical.* I
a literary life that was honest, productive, and had
But just consider. When I came for that job I was thirty years
studying literature when I entered college at the age of
thirteen years, or for *seventeen* years if high school
things—from molecular biology through Classi
equal or longer periods of time.
subjects that one *could* have decided to study. I,
ues, had chosen the study of literature and not, say, law,

government, politics, philosophy, history, cities, or women, and not psychology, biology, philosophy, or history. By what conceivable reason, then,
any of us, not having studied those things, now claim
turn the question around. If I or my
what argument could any
of us hope to deny
other things, when
had studied, but,
no matter the
field of th
literatu
inst

or dated, scholastic or old-fashioned as it may seem to you now, I myself consider it

1) an *ethical* argument,
2) a *strong* argument,
3) an argument having to do with intellectual integrity in general and also with the intellectual integrity of the university, and
4) an argument the general sweeping under the rug of which has had a great deal, though not all, to do with turning us—turning you, turning our department, turning the humanities university—into a lost, fraudulent, hypocritical, falsely- and poorly-educated ruin.[128]

THE UNIVERSITY FACULTY DEVELOPMENT PROGRAM
OFFICE OF RESEARCH AND REDEMPTIVE PROGRAMS
THE UNIVERSITY CENTER
THE UNIVERSITY OF NEW YORK
REQUEST FOR PROPOSALS (RFP)
The University Faculty development Program of the University of New York (UFDP-UNY) is designed to encourage and promote innovation in teaching and learning among faculty throughout UNY. This activity is administered as part of the "University Center" role of the university. We welcome the opportunity to work with you and your colleagues in this important endeavor.

---

[128] Eight. [Editor]

> We want these efforts to address the *real* needs of faculty and UNY's commitment to promote improved teaching and learning, as well as scholarship. The principle vehicles for achieving this goal are the seminar series, in which faculty throughout UNY explore topics of interest and importance to them and to their teaching. The following list illustrates proposals supported so far during the current funding year:
>
> —Balancing the Curriculum for Gender, Race, Class, and Ethnicity
> —Workshop in Logical Thinking
> —Preparing Teachers to Serve Young Children in the 21st. 22nd and 23rd Centuries
> —Establishing Strategies to Improve Research and Writing Skills for Beginning College Students
> —Understanding Evolutionary Perspectives on Human Reproductive Behavior
> —UNY Logic Workshop
> —Faculty Facilitation Training (FFT): Using Facilitation Skills to Effectively Manage Classroom Discussions
> —Technology and Reason
> —Understanding Race
> —Understanding Class
> —Understanding Gender
> —Understanding Ethnicity
> —Facilitation Skills in Approaching Difference in the Classroom

•

Fred Siegel in The New Republic called "an intellectual backwater."

•

In writing my 1971 memo *today,* in other words, I would
am indeed doing now, accuse *you*[129] of being unethical, at the very le
sistent; bad teachers, hypocritical about education, using a
the loss of the life of intellectual integrity inside the
that, supposedly, *you* have also devoted *yours*
in the years of *your* own study: a life that I
to follow for the very reason that it *did*
possess integrity and honesty, one
would not now happily see
callously disassembled o
abandoned for an
most imperative
of causes, not
that could
die of a
ever
n

•

---

[129] Nine. [Editor]

```
┌──────────────────────────────────────────┐
│                                          │
│        ARE YOU THINKING ABOUT            │
│             A CAREER                     │
│               in                         │
│             LAW???                       │
│           BUSINESS???                    │
│          GOVERNMENT???                   │
│       PUBLIC ADMINISTRATION???           │
│                                          │
│               ????                       │
│                                          │
│         THEN *YOU SHOULD BE*             │
│         *THINKING ABOUT A*               │
│                                          │
│             MAJOR                        │
│               IN                         │
│          GENDER STUDIES                  │
│                                          │
│            in order to                   │
│                                          │
│      UNDERSTAND THE GENDERED             │
│            NATURE OF                     │
│          YOUR PROFESSION                 │
│  •  Take only 6 courses (18 credits) in at least two  │
│     disciplines from a list of approved courses       │
│     offered throughout Actaeon!         │
│  •  Many courses in the Gender Studies minor also     │
│     count toward your major!!           │
│  •  Many courses in the Gender Studies minor also     │
│     count toward other minors!!!        │
│  •  Completion of the gender studies minor is noted   │
│     on your official transcript at graduation!!!!     │
└──────────────────────────────────────────┘
```

allowing you as literary people to teach anything at all, rather than what you have *studied*; or allowing you as literary people to discard the idea that what you know even is the result of what you have studied; or leading you—for this is inevitable, as I'll show you in a moment—to abandon the very bedrock idea itself that people *can* qualify themselves to teach literature by the means of studying it. Instead, the idea will be embraced, by you as by others, that it's not the fact, through study, of *what you know,* but the fact, instead, of what you *feel, what you are as a person,* that will become[130]—has become —the determiner of what you consider yourself qualified to say or do or perform inside academia.

---

[130] Ten. The noting here of the Gubar and Hong-Koestler "imbalance indicators" of course does not imply concurrence with their point of view on the part of the present editor. The substitution of feeling for thought, after all, is well known to have been one of the most highly favored means by which major economic powers kept "consumer" classes pliable and consumptive from at least the Early Ante-Penultimate the entire way through to the Collapse. See Kwi Yoon Li, *The End of Intellect: Consumerism in the American Nation from the Ante-Penultimate through the Collapse* (Seoul & Tokyo, 2104). [Editor]

•

Ours is a time, and rightly enough, that sets out avidly to decry the tyrannies of racism, social and political injustice, a

as I write these words, however, I aim not to address those issues but to carry on a literary and intellectual discussion, with literary and intellectual concerns, among

the question isn't why people have taken action against social and political evils. Instead, the question is this: why the existence of social and political evils—now, in 1991—has resulted so clearly in the disappearance of intellectual and literary integrity inside the university:

1) the abandonment of empiricism as a basis of literary understanding;

2) the loss of the immemorial relationship between study and what a person knows;

3) the confusion between what a person knows and what that person is; and

4) the jettisoning of the rock-bottom idea itself that the study of literature can result in the knowledge of literature, or, even if it can, that such knowledge *can in itself have value.*

Why, in other words, now, is literature in the univ
traduced, maligned, abused, exploited, denied, abandoned,
suspicion, calumniated, twisted, tortured, cursed, trampled, lynched,
—and this by those inside the university—you—who are literar
but are not acting as
        has been a long time in gestation; that I
        far back as 1971; that it has been battening on
        don't suggest to me[131] [132] that

        spiracy of subversives
      but they *do* suggest that I now daily
amidst people who seem to *think* they are literary
    but are not; who think they underst
the function literature has inside the liberal arts, but do not
ho believe themselves to have received literary educations, but
These things all being so, I can conclude only that literary education
must have failed drastically at some point *before* the fall semester
began in 1971; and possibility of finding a literary life inside the univ
had in fact *already* become doomed some
that, when I took that job, believing th
it, I was in truth living illusoril
borrowed, doomed
breath.

The Writing Center
invites
faculty, tutors, and other proofreaders of student writing
to attend a workshop hosted by

Professor Martin Bearded

on Monday, November 20, at 5:00 PM

in

"Goodbye, Expert—Hello, Reader"

1) Is it "wrong" to "correct" writing?
2) Is it "bad" even to make suggestions?
*3) Is it best for writers just to learn exactly how a reader reacts
to their writing,*
*4) So they can decide for themselves how good or bad it is and
what to do about it?*

Room 750 Presidential Hall

---

[131] As, in *Tenured Radicals* (1990), his book on these and additional aspects of the university crisis, they seem to suggest to Roger Kimball. [Author]

[132] Another unknown reference. [Editor]

And so,

time when "English professo
become newsworthy
names the like of Stanley Fish or Frank Lentricchia[133] are
ensational and outrageous quotes, in national magaz
departmental laundry in the likes of such
York Magazine, The New Republic,
John Searle, in *The New York*
view of Books,[134] almost
hat "One of the most depress-
ing things about educated people today *is that so few of them, even
among professional intellectuals, are able to follow the steps of a
simple logical argument.*"[135] [136]

•

o think about such questions. I know that those among you
who disagree with me, however, are fierce with conviction, outnum-
ber me greatly, and—most painfully—whenever I do set out to argue
with you, reject implacably not only my chosen terms of debate, but
debate itself as something corrupt and tainted *a priori.* As we saw

---

[133] Unknown and untraced names, lost, apparently, with myriad others, in the Collapse.
[Editor]

[134] References, apparently, to American general circulation journals. All, however, like the
names Fish and Lentricchia, remain unknown and untraced. [Editor]

[135] Emphasis added. [Author's Note]

[136] Eleven. Gubar and Hong-Koestler doubt that a socially adjusted person would speak this
way to his own colleagues without even a hinted amenity to the effect of excluding present
company. [Editor]

[137] Again, the question of time of composition. Did Larsen change the date of this "message,"
setting it six years in the future—or is his own putative composition-date of 1991 the false
one? [Editor]

[138] Emphasis added. [Author's Note]

during our recent trio of unhappy meetings, in any true attempt to argue with you—with those, that is, incapable of arguing[139]—the question becomes not what I'm to think or say, but *what* I'm to base what I think or say *on* when, no longer what a person *knows* but instead what a person is is the thing that matters. Who, in the eyes of such opposers as you, *am* I? And what, in the eyes of such enemies as you, do I conceivably know?

•

"MAN I'M AFRAID OF NEEDLES!"
DON'T LET THIS BE THE REASON THAT
OTHERS DIE
WITHOUT RECEIVING THE
LIVING GIFT OF LIFE
The unique characteristics of an individual's bone marrow is inherited in the same way one inherits skin, eye and hair color. A person of African ancestry's best chance of finding a match is with another person of African ancestry. YOU!
Marrow Donor Drive
Thursday,
December 11, 1997
The Actaeon College of Institutional Analysis
and Social Control
Organization of Black Students

2:00 PM — 5:30 PM

Donate a sample of blood and agree to have it tissue typed and entered into the National Marrow Donor Program registry for volunteer marrow donors. You may match one of the thousands of patients who are waiting for their "miracle match." Potential donors must be between the ages 18 and 60.
Sponsored by Link To Life Network, Inc. Michael Andrews, Manager, 718/659-5883;
New York Black Nurses Association Inc.

•

terms, phrases, shibboleths, code words, neologisms, absolutisms, labels,

an inescapable and logic-replacing part of my daily working life: a
"multiculturalism," "genderism," "agism," "political
"deconstructionism," "womanism," "lookism," "gay

---

[139] Twelve. [Editor]

canon," "homophobia," "marginalization,"
culum of inclusion." Only too well, I
with the insidious, deceitful, ingenious
psychological and literary "theories"
manifestations and absolutisms of this "revolution" in attitude and behavior. I know, for example, in the weird new world of
"us-versus-them-ism," that white males
prevaricators, and bigots, and this means *all*

that all whites are racist, and that their
denial of it is the strongest proof that they are. I know, that is to say,
yet again, that what a person *does* doesn't count anymore,[140][141] what
you *are* is what matters, and that there's nothing whatsoever you can
do about what you are. And I know about the yawning epistemologi-
cal abyss of critical-theory nothingness that you're so familiar with
from the
showing that there's no meaning in books, by extension
in any thought-system, by extension again no meaning
know that *therefore* (fiercely as you may claim that
free to insist upon *my* meaning, *we* are free to
us is free to insist upon and teach *us's* mea
know that "everything is political," that al
are political actions."[142]
    I have understood
against this assertion is impossible, tha
claim not to be political as in itself a politic
vast, implicit, and oppressive agenda. In these ways
half truths are cobbled into whole, banalities are lifted to
pronunciamentos, non-sequiturs are rampant and go unper

---

[140] Who, after all, is left to judge the merit of what one does? In the absence of experienced, fair, or knowledgeable judges in the field of one's own endeavor, nothing one does *can* matter. [Author's note]

[141] Thirteen. Gubar and Hong-Koestler find it impossible to believe that *no* such judges could have remained for the fair evaluation of work such as, say, Larsen's; and accordingly cite his generalization as tainted by paranoia. [Editor]

[142] All of you will doubtless remember that it was this same bit of a-logical and simplistic complacency that, spoken by Professor Car Cleopatra in our third meeting, so appalled me and caused me such dismay that I responded in the way I did. It may indeed not have been "collegial" of me to declare that only a fool could or would stoop to the use of such a phrase at a moment such as the one in a debate of the kind we were then having—and that if Professor Car Cleopatra thought for half a second that by using it she was in fact in any way clarifying or advancing the argument rather than simply hoping to bludgeon it to a dead stop advanta-geous to herself that she was twice the fool as before. It was a moment as flagrantly impov-erished of any significant intellectual content as any other—with the exception of Professor Muscle's equally egregious demonstration of pride in his own ignorance, that being revealed by his remark about Homer, to which, again, it's true I did respond. [Author's note]

discourse itself gives way to loggerheads and chaos, even here,
now know so very clearly. I now know, for example, that
ilization is a construct, thus a "text," thus meaningless,
unfair and unjust, done away with entirely a
replaced with a tenor saxophone, two bongo
lower left canine of the Wife of Bath. I am
words—and have put them in your mailbox
deluded, elitist, hegemonic, misogyny
top of it all a pig. I know that

**PLEASE ANNOUNCE THIS NEW CLASS
TO YOUR STUDENTS**
TITLE: **Women and Literature: On Violence and Survival**
     (Lit. 269)
INSTRUCTOR: Pamela Dreisbach
SCHEDULE: Mondays, Wednesdays, Fridays, 2nd period
CREDITS: Three credits; counts toward English *and* Gender
     Studies minors
PREREQUISITES: English 102 (College Composition II)
This is a new literature class that will be offered during the spring
semester. Students will examine issues surrounding violence against
women and the ways it is portrayed in movies, on television, in music
and in literature. We will read poems, short stories and novels by
twentieth century American women, including Gloria Naylor (*The
Woman of Brewster Place*), Maya Angelou (*I Know Why the Caged
Bird Sings*), Alice Walker (*The Color Purple*) and Toni Morrison (*The
Bluest Eye*). Students will earn credits toward English and Gender
Studies minors.

---

unnerved at this prospect, but also
striking out what I've written.
if pass at all, but I believe
solidly trained professor o
enment; philosophically
evidence, all evidenc
guide to thought or
certainly, though
before have I
folly, half-logic, faction
Orwellian[143] indignities to the la
from you, my young colleagues, who (as I
abandon empiricism and its attendant logic;
fling yourselves into a death-embrace with the very tyrannies
precise market-culture at large against which you imagine yourselv

---

[143] See Editor's Foreword, Note 5, p. 2. [Editor]

> The fall trumpet has sounded and with
> renewed vigor, we begin the new academic
> cycle. Attached is a listing of faculty
> responsibilities. Please read them carefully.
> This information is helpful in ensuring that
> there is clarity of thought in the performance
> of your noble duties.
> Sincerely,
> Smith Rattle
> Dean and Academic Vice President

•

never did understand what literature was,

of the
Alvin Kernan,[144]
even with him at a certai
entertaining, useful, and unsurpassed
"Ours is a strange time," he writes, "but it has in

> Adjunct faculty continue to play a critical role
> College. On the whole, the adjunct
> quality service to this instit
> for their devotion to
> to this urban ins
> Sincerel
>
> Smith
> Dea

a desire for the further "professionalizing"
greatest prestige, of course, has
the works of literature
insecurity
de

Bestseller!!

---

[144] Once again, an unknown and untraced name. [Editor]

I
whe
possible
to say any more
all, we are colleagues
but I can't justify not speaki
to reveal the truth as perfectly
position can possibly do. And so wha
socially immature, status-aspiring professoriate,
molded into or toward the political left—an theref
the case study of a "revolution" inside literary academia

The Future of Deconstructionism

By rights, it should quickly die. Insofar as it is based on
illogic, it should founder under its own weight. Insofar as it
is dedicated to the annihilation of its own source of being, it
should wither away. Insofar as it is a revolt against all
systems of meaning that then makes an exception for its
own, it should be laughed into impotence and shame. Insofar
as it leads to solipsism, it should be ignored. Insofar as it
advocates demolition but takes upon itself no responsibility
for replacement of what it destroys, it should be scorned.
Insofar as it drinks from the fountain of beauty but produces
nothing beautiful, it should be despised.

whether it can be possible for me to continue

all I've done and said

several of

you

no intention simply to be rude, uncharitable,
or certainly

a simple but entire collapse of mind and the abilities of m

no easy thing

must push on, against all odds, make every effort

"Lombroso is an ass."[145]

Stanley = tools = hook = Fish

"Man is but an ass if. . ."[146]

Stanley Fish is an ass

the only thing I w[147]

else could I do?[148, 149]

---

[145] Joseph Conrad, *The Secret Agent* (Doubleday, New York, 1953), p. 50. [Author's note]

[146] *A Midsummer Night's Dream*, IV, i, 204 [Author's note]

[147] The fourteenth and last of Gubar and Hong-Koestler's imbalance citations falls here. While, even as revisionists, Gubar and Hong-Koestler have no disagreement with the extraordinary giftedness and importance of the Larsen papers, they are also among the strongest (and earliest) proponents of the madness theory. At this point in "Fragment IV," they argue, is evidence (going far beyond mere manuscript damage) of almost complete fragmentation, breakdown, and chaotic mentality. Larsen's decision from here on to include no more of his own words in the letter to his colleagues but simply to quote at length from Bloomgarden and Margolies reinforces their claim that here we are seeing evidence of collapse, loss, concession, and despair in the author. [Editor]

[148] In his inane white tee-shirt. Professor Muscle. His way, even just sitting at the conference table beside everyone else, of striking a pose, his incapability of *not* striking one, sitting just slightly low in the chair, a narcissistic way about him of always flirting with his own body, that repugnant self-given pleasure whether he's on his feet or on his seat, talking or

silent, and always the faint hint of threat whether in his pose or attitude or tone, the *dare* tossed out toward you, his head slightly to one side, cheekbone resting against two fingers of one propped arm, when he said what he said, the slight curl to the admittedly handsome lip, faintly sinister. Muscle, Professor T. C. Muscle, theorist, radical, rhetorician, speaker at conferences, facilitator, sayer of the last word. And so he said, speaking as much *of* me as to me, holding the faint threat, the smirk, the dare; he said, in the quiet moment of time as I ended my statement and laid the sheets down carefully on the table in front of me. He said, in front of the twenty-eight of us gathered there, making it so obviously a test, a proof, to *show* me that not more than five of the twenty-eight would take my side over his, not more than that five would rebut him, or be impelled even to think to try, he said, "Sure, you can *say* all that, but old historicism in itself is relevant to nothing."

149 Understandably, Gubar and Hong-Koestler find in the hyper-intensity of Larsen's volcanic sense of repugnance at Dr. Muscle an indication of a personality ill equipped to adapt itself with any practical success to the realities (or necessities) of the world that it must in fact function in. Yet even they acknowledge that what seems irrational in Larsen can be vindicated at least in part not only by the not-identical but nevertheless equal irrationality in Dr. Muscle—its effect exacerbated, also understandably, by that person's repugnant character. For a discussion of the Professor Muscle incident seen as a classic plot climax in the Larsen story, see Maximillian Shandra, *Dating the Larsen Papers: A Writer's Progress toward Calamity* (Bangkok, 2096). As mentioned previously, Shandra in general argues for an early composition date for "Fragment IV," but, in a fascinating concession, he suggests that Larsen's terrible moment with Dr. Muscle may truly function as a climax from which all else follows only in sorry decline. Of equal or even greater interest in this regard is Isador Rosenwach's *Enigmas of Time and Space: Finding Reality in the Larsen Papers* (Katmandu, 2102). Rosenwach argues that the scene with Dr. Muscle offers readers a psychological preparation making both more credible and more meaningful Larsen's later attempt to "expunge" Sasha Brearly from the classroom—the event, albeit risible and innocuous, that resulted in President Penguin-Duck's swift summoning of Larsen and his punishing of him through betrayal (no reader who has ever read it can forget President Penguin-Duck's climactic, pharisaic, utterly and unimaginably cynical remark that Larsen had "offended" Sasha Brearly's "human dignity"). The description of the moment of betrayal, near the final pages of "The Diary," contains, argues Rosenwach, the Larsen Papers' single most revealing indictment of the abysmal—and cataclysmically fateful—emptiness within President Penguin-Duck. [Editor]

151

FRAGMENT IV—PART 2

A Letter to My
Younger Colleagues
On the Subject
of
The Collaborative Destruction
from within Academia
of the Aesthetic
as a Living
Force
(Continued)

Editor's Note:

From the time it was discovered, one of the central unresolved questions about the second part of "Fragment IV" has been the question of its authorship. The terms of the debate were clarified early and positions taken, with few (the present editor, however, being one) taking the middle road.

The question, of course, has been whether Part 2 does in fact consist of the true Chapter VII of a real work by Bloomgarden & Margolies, a piece of critical writing simply transcribed by Larsen, albeit subjected by him also to his "dual" method of interjecting boxed material; or, on the other hand, whether Bloomgarden & Margolies are only fictional, authors imagined by Larsen so that he could hide behind the resulting pretense that he himself was not fully responsible for the content of Part 2.

Why he might have done such a thing is not

especially difficult to guess, given the signs of breakdown (though they, too, of course, may have been manufactured) present at the close of "Part 1." There, Larsen's seeming discomfiture and sense of potential abandonment, confusion, and loss as a result of having spoken so openly, judgmentally, and radically before, to, and of his own Actaeon colleagues are movingly apparent. Even if only made up (which this writer, on balance, does not think they are), they are testament to Larsen's skill in evocation.

The instinct to hide, then, may well be understandable in a case such as this one, even in the most determined and brilliant of thinkers. The obligations of conscience often find themselves in conflict with the sheer animal comforts of the tribe; and being compelled to criticize—or even vilify—one's own family, people, or colleagues, no matter how supremely pressing the cause, can bring about emotional pain sometimes entirely unforeseen.

If proper records and resources were available, of course, the authorship question could be resolved in a matter of moments—but no trace of the existence of the Bloomgarden-Margolies volume, for example, has been found nor is any, now, likely to be. Larsen's colleagues would naturally have known the volume if it did exist or, upon reading "Fragment IV," could easily have verified whether it did or not. And yet also, as Rosenfeld[150] and others have wisely pointed out, we have no way of knowing, whatever he may have *said,* whether Larsen ever really did put copies of the finished "letter" into the mailboxes of his colleagues. As in the *"Diary,"* we may have here again a presumed genre—the letter—that in truth *had* or *found* no audience, with the result that these now-silenced words come to us with the haunting quality caused by their being words never heard by any but the sole and lone ear of their own author.

---

[150] Isador Rosenfeld, *Enigmas of Time and Space: Finding Reality in the Larsen Papers* (Katmandu, 2102), pp. 130–131. [Editor]

Indeed, this melancholy presence—the presence of absence—has proven one of the most powerful generators of emotion in readers of the papers: of these lost and ruined words that plead so desperately for the life of a once-great nation now also silenced and lost, a kingdom of dust.

"Despair Notes:
How Deconstructionism Happened,
And What It Really Meant" [151, 152]

But his[153] class-analysis of the revolt still doesn't explain why it's the *literature* that gets revolted against, instead of, say, the old power-holding guard of literature's previous scholars, critics, interpreters, and escorts: he still doesn't satisfactorily explain the origin, that is, of the astonishing *hatred and resentment of literature itself* that's revealed in this sudden debunking, emasculating, and dethroning of it by its own erstwhile servants and guardians, now become its vengeful and booted masters. Revolutions in criticism are necessary for criticism to stay alive, and even for literature to stay alive. The absurd purpose of this one, however, is apparently just to kill literature altogether.

The logic of that aim, even as we[154] see it in our daily lives in the hallways, rooms, and offices of our own universities, is patently crazed, akin not to fighting over the golden eggs laid by a goose, but to an agreed-upon killing of the goose. The analogy is homely but applicable. Deconstructionism is said to be a literary phenomenon. But it is not and cannot be so. It makes sense only if it is clearly understood *not to be literary at all; to have nothing to do with literature; to have been brought about by people who don't understand literature, don't*

---

151 Bloomgarden, Alan R., and Ira Margolies, *The Decline of Literature and Reason in an Age of Theory* (Yale University Press, 1992), Chapter VII, pp. 302–379. [Author's Note]

152 Yanmei Ting (*Darkness Visible: The Lost Novels of Eric Larsen* [Taipei, 2110]) and Archer L. Poindeft (*Notes on Emptiness: Implied Meanings in the Lost Larsen Volumes* (Calcutta and Londinium, 2134]) argue for the non-existence of the Bloomgarden-Margolies volume. Rosenfeld, mentioned above, comments on the entire authorship question with subtlety and perspicuity, fully weighing each side in the debate. Neither should the contributions of Maximillian Shandra (*Dating the Larsen Papers: A Writer's Progress toward Calamity* [Bangkok, 2096] be overlooked. [Editor]

153 Once again, an unknown reference. [Editor]

154 The plural pronoun, maintained throughout Part 2, and referring, of course, to Bloomgarden and Margolies. [Editor]

know what it is, don't know what it's for, and don't know what it does,
whether inside the liberal arts or out.[155]

•

tenable existence of an art itself. Down with
produced—poetry; down with the medie
produced—drama; down with th
Imagists as they produced
as they produce
criticism! Crit
icism!
ic

•

And so, tell us please,
where, in this sad new world, will
, playwrights, novelists? Where indeed will

•

> "One of the most depressing things about
> educated people today is that so few of
> them, even among professional
> intellectuals, are able to follow the steps of
> a simple logical argument."
>
> —John Searles, *The New York Review*
> *of Books*

Preparing for a New Millennium of Cultural Harmony
Monday, April 12, and Tuesday, April 13,
Room 380 Presidential Hall
Confronting Diversity through the Filmic Experience

Prof. Mag Black & Prof. Jean White
Department of Speech & Theatre

Using excerpts from two films, *The Defiant Ones* and
Passion Fish, this two part symposium will enhance students'
level of tolerance for diversity in the new millennium. The
first segment will involve a co-curricular discussion in which
parallel themes in both films (dependence, difference,
humanity, unity) will be analyzed. The second segment will
be a training exercise in which students will examine their
own prejudices through role-play situations and will
negotiate various ways to improve race relations on campus.
The session will end with an open discussion on diversity.

---

[155] Emphasis in original. [Author's note]

evolution of
a widely embraced thought-model aimed at
the foundation of a simple, pure,
empty non-sequitur.[156]

The logic is as hobbled[157]
hobbled[158] as declaring that since
Bruno is a dog and all dogs have four legs,
he and all others are free to jaywalk

"All animals are equal, but some animals are more equal than[159,160]

```
╔══════════════════════════════════════════════════════════╗
║              Come to the Peace Garden!!!                   ║
║              Peace Garden-Unity Day                        ║
║                 Wednesday, April 14ᵗʰ                      ║
║                Lobby, Non-Presidential Hall                ║
║                      3:00 p.m.                             ║
║   Brief Remarks:        Pres. Morton Penguin-Duck          ║
║                         Dean Smith Rattle                  ║
║                         Dean Warfield Shark                ║
║                         Prof. Warren Wetmore               ║
║                                                            ║
║   Enjoy the harmonious environment where the rich colorful diversity of ║
║   almost 135 plants and flowers, which are symbolic of the 135 nations  ║
║   of the Actaeon community, are beautiful manifestations of an infinite ║
║   creativity! JOIN in the celebration of our interconnectedness through ║
║   poetry, peace messages and songs!                        ║
╚══════════════════════════════════════════════════════════╝
```

The entire Actaeon College community will be invited to testify about their personal experiences and memories about abuse, rape, sexual assault, and sexual harassment.

The usual answer is power for the advance of left ideology and
values—a fact so appalling to Roger Kimball as to make him build
his *Tenured Radicals*[161] on a foundation of sand; impels Dinesh
D'Souza, in *Illiberal Education*[162] (1991), to create an impassioned
description of the perversi

---

[156] The session will end with an open discussion on diversity! [Author's note]

[157] *Hear Our Voices!* [Author's note]

[158] Is it "wrong" to correct writing? [Author's note]

[159] George Orwell, *Animal Farm* (New York, 1946), p. 123. [Author's note]

[160] Whatever the intended contents of this footnote may have been, they have never been known or seen. [Editor]

[161] *Tenured Radicals: How Politics Has Corrupted Our Higher Education*, New York, 1990. [Author's note]

[162] *Illiberal Education: The Politics of Race and Sex on Campus*, New York, 1998. [Author's note]

the liberal arts; and that
leads Alvin Kernan[163]
the same thing
or values?

Can you *say* you have them and yet *not* have them?

TEACHING TIPS
For College
And University
Instructors
A Practical Guide that
provides down-to-earth
advice!

David Royse, *University*
of Kentucky

Anyone who has
experienced sexual
violence, or knows
someone was has, will
have an opportunity to tie
a purple ribbon on our
clothesline...

Can you be accused
                of having them when you really don't? How,
            vindicate yourself in the face of presumed guilt? Could
heir to an oil well or a chain of department stores and still hold "the"
values—the way "Dave," at Brown University,[164] poses as doing—
and, in such a case, how would you prove that you do? Is *any* proof
ever
if *all* acts are political acts? And isn't this a despairing,
corrosive, dangerous business,
inane, execrable, brainless talk about *values:* this jejune, egregious
confusing of *values* with the *curriculum?*
        Oh, horrible, oh, horrible, most horrible. There's nothing
wrong with having a politicized faculty, but *everything* is wrong
with having a politicized *curriculum,*

---

[163] Once more, an unknown reference. [Editor]

[164] This famous reference has never been traced. For the joke about it that has become
equally famous, see Kwi Yoon Li's *The End of Intellect,* p. 267.

guaranteed by its very nature to produce *nothing* other than factionalism, intolerance, coercion, woe, injustice, insignificance, and decline, not to mention the even simpler yet even more horrifying fact that after the politicizing of a

must be these instead:

1. Bigotry
2. Passivity and conformity
3. Intellectual death

Anyone who has experienced sexual violence, or knows someone was has, will have an opportunity to tie a purple ribbon on our clothesline...

·

HOW TO GET
A
|TEACHING
JOB
*A user-friendly workbook for the
entire job search process!*

Courtney W. Moffatt, *Edgewood College*
Thomas L. Moffatt, Management
Dynamics, Inc.

An imposed value is no value. An indoctrinated thought is no thought. Both are backwardness and imprisonment. We are reduced to the uttering of commonplace

**Scenes of Shame
Psychoanalysis, Shame,
and Writing**

Joseph Adamson and
Hilary Clark, editors

people whose own educations must already have been sufficiently corrupted or faithless that

Bestseller!!

Successful
College
Teaching
PROBLEM SOLVING
STRATEGIES
OF DISTINGUISHED
PROFESSORS

Sharon A. Baiocco, *Jacksonville
College*
and Jamie N. DeWaters, *D'Youville
College*

that

they now lack an understanding of what the liberal
what they are for, or of what it is, really,
value and strength.

•

Nominations Sought for Most
Outstanding Teacher of the Year Award

An award for the Outstanding Teacher of the Year will be presented for the seventh time at Commencement. The purpose of the award is to encourage and celebrate excellence in teaching. All members of the faculty are eligible for nomination.

A scholarship of $1,000, in honor of the recipient of the Outstanding Teacher Award, will be given to a graduating senior.

The members of the committee for selecting the Outstanding Teacher Award of 1997 are: Professors Gadley Storm, Prudy Catcher, Iris Divine, Jane Sjögren, Abba Kwandadaba, Warren Wetmore, Florence Estevez, and Dean Smith Rattle.

Nominations should be sent to: The Counseling Information Office, Dr. Smith Rattle, Room 3140N, no later than April 15, 1999 [165]. Nominations may be made by members of the faculty, staff, and students as well as by formal or informal groups. Nominations from previous years will automatically be reconsidered this year.

Guidelines for the Most Outstanding Teach Award include:

1. Stimulates intellectual curiosity, motivates students to learn and promotes community involvement
2. Knows the subject matter thoroughly and is deeply committed to it.
3. Makes difficult material clear to students.
4. Plans well-organized, challenging, and inventive courses.
5. Shows capacity to develop as a teacher: to learn from others and to be self-critical.
6. Is available to students outside of class for conferences and mentoring.
7 Is never rude, loud, noisy, *or guilty of bad language!!*
Please include the name of the nominee and the words,
"The Outstanding Teacher Award of the Year"
Also list reasons or attach a statement for your choice.

---

[165] The same matter of dating as before is called into question again. [Editor]

At this point we creep inexorably closer to a devoutly abhorred discussion of American popular culture, since, based almost entirely on "marketing" and profit motive, that is an arena where the distinction between ideas and values is routinely obfuscated and exploited in the very interest of creating ignorance, contentment, and pliability in order through these traits to promote and intensify "consumerism" and other forms of harm. Yet that is anything *except* a reason tolerated or lauded inside the university or

---

FROM
FACULTY SENATE MINUTES

Senator C. Drews asked what incentives are being given to workers to improve their performance: many of the workers have been here for many years, many are good workers, but many are jaded and burnt out. Vice President Packman said he absolutely agrees. One of the first things he did, in this very room, in fact, was to assemble every Buildings & Grounds staff member to tell them that he understands their job because his father was a maintenance worker in a factory for 37 years and was a labor leader, the vice president of his local, and so he understands and appreciates the work they do. However, he told them, he also has expectations of them. He said he hopes to encourage the many good people in Buildings & Grounds and to isolate the bad ones. He is going to reward the good people through an "employee of the month" incentive program: a $100 cash award will be given to the employee of the month. A display with the awardee's picture will be featured on the 5th floor of Non-Presidential Hall and the 1st floor of Presidential Hall. There will be an employee recognition ceremony each year as well.

What qualifies a professor, what accounts for the privileges, rights, and obligations of a

FROM

FACULTY SENATE
MINUTES

In response to Senator Drews' question as to whether the Buildings & Grounds workers have name tags, Vice President Packman said he is buying the B & G staff new uniforms so that it will be very clear to everyone who they are and so they will feel pride in their work: and each worker's name will be on the uniform."

can in turn be tested and examined on. But *belief?* It plays no role, no more than in the work of a bricklayer, auto mechanic, or thoracic surgeon.

ANNOUNCEMENT FROM
THE OFFICE
OF ADMINISTRATIVE AFFAIRS

The Office of Administrative Affairs is proud to announce the selection of Mr. Murray Place as Building and Grounds Employee of the Month of February, 2003.[166] Mr. Place has worked for The Actaeon College of Institutional Analysis and Social Control since 1972 as a Custodial Supervisor, Custodial Assistant, and, presently, as a Laborer. His expertise was instrumental in the 1990 move of the College's Marketing Research and External Campus Development Offices from Non-Presidential Hall to Presidential Hall. The Office of Administrative Affairs and the entire Actaeon College community gratefully acknowledges Mr. Place's outstanding performance in his many years of service to Actaeon College.

This program has been made possible through the generous support of the Actaeon College Alumni Association, the Office of Dean & Vice President Smith Rattle, and the Office of President Morton R. Penguin-Duck.

---

outside the classroom door except as a guide, walking footn
thesaurus, reference encyclopedia and nothing more.
An imposed belief accepted out of ignorance, and
the *imposition* of belief is tyranny.
Values can't be *taught*. They o
can only be *found*.
no other con
faith or n
intelle
tech
as
s

---

[166] Once again, the question of date of composition arises. [Editor]

in the abysmal harvest that passes for
intellectual state of health
popular well being,
versity culture
can only
peop
who
si
i

[167] Professor Cleopatra, readers will recall, is a figure of far more than average importance to Larsen. See note 142, p. 146, where he speaks of her as having provided "a moment as flagrantly impoverished of any significant intellectual content as any other—with the exception [he goes on] of Professor Muscle's equally egregious demonstration of pride in his own ignorance, that being revealed by his remark about Homer, to which, again, it's true I did respond." Significantly, Professor Cleopatra's is one of the faces seen peering into the room on the fateful occasion of Larsen's doomed effort to "expunge" Sasha Brearly from his class ("*Diary,*" p. 246ff.), the event that led so swiftly to President Penguin-Duck's betrayal of Larsen and to what history has come to look upon (cf. Kwi Yoon Li, *The End of Intellect,* Chpt. V) as the probable end of the author's productive intellectual life. The importance of the Brearly incident to our understanding of the degradation of academic intellectual life in the Late Ante-Penultimate cannot be overestimated. [Editor]

brings us back to our still-unanswered question of what the the revolut
that they don't in fact know what liberal
not have experienced liberal educat
faintest conceivable idea whatso
is they're doing.

> "One of the most depressing things about educated people
> today is that so few of them, even among professional
> intellectuals, are able to follow the steps of a simple logical
> argument."
> --John Searle, The New York Review of Books

may be an incomplete truth, but it *is* a truth.[168] And
a kind of reversal of it: that is, power is being
welded to the *more* mutable. In the case of
being detached from books and
process of *education* is being replaced by
presumption, coercion, suspicion, innuendo, and
not so far away from an intellectual thuggery of non-think,
narrow vision, and coercive bandwagonism.

State University of New York Press

**BODILY DISCURSIONS
GENDERS, REPRESENTATIONS,
TECHNOLOGIES**

Deborah S. Wilson and
Christine Moneera Laennec, editors

All of the essays offer variations on the same theme—the idea that the body is a site for the
production of political ideologies, particularly in response to social exigencies and cultural crises.
However, there is no single, over-arching ideological model here for feminism, much less for reading
the body in a specific historical or cultural moment. *Bodily Discursions* offers instead a number of
individual voices on a variety of issues and phenomena as they determine the configuration of the
body. This book demonstrates that society needs to pay attention to how the body is manipulated if we
are to work for social progress and political justice, for it is through our bodies that we all must
articulate our experience and live our lives.

**FACULTY DEVELOPMENT
ANNOUNCEMENT
FALL 1997
Balancing the curriculum for Gender, Race,
Ethnicity, and Class**

Faculty Facilitation Training (FFT): Using
Facilitation Skills to Effectively Manage
Classroom Discussions

---

168 For a fuller discussion of the point, see chapter three, "Everything Changes, Nothing
Changes," in *The Decline of Literature and Reason in an Age of Theory* (Yale University
Press, 1992). [Footnote in original] [Author's note]

Fred Siegel, who, in a recent article in *The New Rep*
"reversal of the current":

anley Fish,[169] chair of Duke's English department, professor
self-described "academic leftist," is giving a dazzling
overflow audience sits rapt as Fish, who made his
critic of Renaissance poetry and a theorist of "self-
s," demonstrates the inability of words to repres
ain he shows that what is clearly X in a legal text can,
erpretations, become not X. For Fish, texts are
ses in "nothing but manipulation and power."
eriod if the First Amendment isn't something
wer, Fish rasps, "Free speech? Yeah, tell me
t, puzzled by the way Fish has folded the
ofessor where his kind of "leftism" is
ponds Fish, referring to students and
faculty, "to do what I tell them to."
minate it, shape it to my will. I'm
fascinated by my own will." [170]

and, due to it, of the
notions of "truth"
remarkable diff-
metamorphosis, what has taken place.
"I want them to do what I tell them to." [171]

SEXUAL
HARASSMENT
on CAMPUS

A guide for Administrators, Faculty, and Students

The truth about sexual harassment in higher education

Edited by Bernice R. Sandler, *National
Association for Women in Education*, and
Robert J. Shoop, *Kansas State University*

---

[169] See note 133, p. 144. [Editor]

[170] February 18, 1991, pp. 28, 30. [Author's note]

[171] See chapter two, "Epistemology, Romanticism, and Meaning," in *The Decline of Literature and Reason in an Age of Theory* (Yale University Press, 1992) for a comparison of Fish's ideas with the thinking of Romanticism. In both Fish and the Romantics, meaning can have its source from within the individual. The big difference, however, is that the Romantics' interest lies in the *creating* of meaning, Fish's only in the destroying (or destructing) of it. [Footnote in original] [Author's note]

whether the values of the current revolutionaries were good ones or
bad ones. Now, in light of Fish's paradigm of degenerated truth, it can
be seen why. The revolution may have believed it was seizing power
for leftism, but in truth its ostensibly anti-authoritarian pattern of half-
thinking has already begun to reveal that the revolution
equivalent of a sieve, its incoherence resulting simply in
exposing the movement to the apolitical force of
total unaccountability and pure, bare will. The
bring humanities education down with it
ing loss of rigor, clarity, substance, all
only coercion, passivity, bandwa
joinerism, chaos, unthinking
until without question
other than a final la
smaller and sma
until only poss
dissoluti
again
be
n

FA
of
COLOR
in
ACADEME

BITTERSWEET SUCCESS

*A comprehensive discussion On what needs to be
to Achieve diversity*

Caroline Sotello Viernes Turner & Samuel L. Myers, Jr., *University of Minnesota*

for "thought" to degenerate into solipsism; "meaning" to become
thrall to will; "truth" to become whatever the petulant, aggressive,
infantile-grandiose Stanley Fish happens to

and eager unthinkers inside academia have
something very big indeed. Such matters as the ones

come to be drawn on a scale that transforms them from
to something clearly of public, of world, importance.[172]

accordingly. And we come to the simple truth
this intellectual revolution, with Fish bearing the flag
the entirety of deconstructionism is at its very heart infantile,
consists of babytalk, however esoteric the sound of

HEAR OUR VOICES!

GLOBAL ISSUES OF GENDER

One-Act Plays about child abuse, death, family
relationships, female genital mutilation,
marriage, murder, prostitution, rape and suicide.

Written by ordinary people, this record of
American life shows that anyone who can tell a
story can write one.

---

women of all colors women of all colors women of al

April is Sexual Assault & Rape Awareness Month

A person of African ancestry's best chance of finding
a match is with another person of African ancestry.
YOU!

President Penguin-Duck
Offers Congratulations

Petulance, destructiveness, hyper-sensitivity to
perceived injury, sustained resentment unassuageable through reason
or even subsequent experience—these are traits of the child, as[173]

---

[172] What question can there be but that the author at this point—be it Larsen or Bloom-garden/Margolies—is thinking more of the *future* than merely of the manifold and jejune banalities surrounding him in academia? The true purport not only of "Fragment IV" but of the entirety of the Larsen papers, after all, lies in their providing, for our own later generations, at least some understandable idea of what could possibly have gone so dreadfully wrong within the intellectual classes of the American Nation as to make it even conceivable that The Collapse could ever become a true danger, let alone a dread, dread actuality. [Editor]

[173] Shandra (*Dating the Larsen Papers: A Writer's Progress toward Calamity*, Bangkok, 2096) has estimated that "Fragment IV" alone may originally have extended to as many as 50,000 words, although less than a tenth of those have survived. Certain very long sections—such as this one—have been reduced to the barest relics of what they once were. Curiously, however, the boxed notices are far, far less often damaged than are the sections of plain text. Shandra attributes this difference to the author's habit of mounting the boxed notices on various types of art-board before integrating them into his text. The art-board, of course, has proven more durable than has the simple white paper that Larsen used for most of the papers. [Editor]

o whether the revolution is seriously destructive both of the university and of education, there can be no doubt at all. But whet

efore nothing but wreckage is left behind, we cannot say. By all rights, it should quickly die. Insofar as it is based on illogic, it *should* founder under its own weight. Insofar as it is dedicated to the annihilation of its own source of being, it should wither away. Insofar as it declares all systems of thought to be without meaning but then makes an exception for its own, it should be laughed into impotence and shame. Insofar as it leads to solipsism, it should be ignored. Insofar as it advocates demolition but takes upon itself no responsibility for the replacement of what it destroys, it should be scorned. Insofar as it drinks from the fountain of beauty but produces nothing beautiful, it should be despised.[174]

| Literary Trauma |
| Sadism, Memory, |
| and Sexual Violence |
| In American Women's |
| Fiction |
| Deborah M. Horvitz |

| Writing Prejudices |
| The Psychoanalysis |
| And Pedagogy of |
| Discrimination |
| From Shakespeare |
| To Toni Morrison |
| Robert Samuels |

| Other Titles of Interest on Reverse Side... |
| TEXTUAL BODIES |
| BODIES AT RISK |
| CAPTIVE BODIES |
| MELVILLE, SHAME, AND THE EVIL EYE |

---

[174] Understandably famous as a model of the perfection of Larsen's (or, of course, Bloomgarden/Margolies') writing at its best. We are nothing if not fortunate that such exemplary and suasive passages escaped greater damage and fragmentation as frequently as they did. This particular passage, as many commentators have observed, combines eloquence and common sense to extraordinary effect. [Editor]

whose possessors no longer realize that *they have internalized a state of on-going infantilism,* the perfection of this retrograde achievement causing them to have lost the customary means of self-recognition—by the contrast of self *with things outside the self*—a loss causing them to be exactly as unaware of their own condition as a fish is unaware that it swims in water.

We don't speak lightly in making these assertions. We have not lost our minds.[175]

But

to the deep, true, dreadful heart of the matter—the traits we have cited *are the same traits as those nurtured, encouraged, rewarded, and ritually*

ation at large by the almost immeasurably powerful American general and popular culture

movement that prides itself on its own incoherence, that feeling and thinking, that by closing its eyes to an isolates itself from the logic of that world—

can justly be called

Coming.....
To Actaeon College of Institutional Analysis
and Social Control!

Suzan-Lori Parks' Most Recent Play
IN THE BLOOD

IN THE BLOOD is a breath-taking piece of theater about a homeless mother of five living under a bridge. Jabber, her oldest, teaches her how to read the only letter she knows, the letter "A." A tender, harrowing, heart-wrenching story portrayed against the harsh reality of inner city poverty—meet the children and adults who alter her fate.

Faculty:
Be a part of the excitement this spring:
Include this play in your course!

"You will leave...feeling pity and terror. And because it is a work of art, you will leave thrilled even [sic] comforted by its mastery..."
The New York Times

---

[175] If a reader were to set aside the authorship question for a moment and simply assume the writer to be Larsen himself, this line might take on element of pathos otherwise lacking in it. Did Larsen not, in essence (as Gubar and Hong-Koestler have maintained from the start), find himself driven mad by what he saw around him, by daily life in the Actaeon of President Penguin-Duck, by the very direction of thought and intellectuality in the American Nation? Might it not be said, too, that his moment of amnesia in President Penguin-Duck's office after the betrayal following the Sasha Brearly incident could itself be a very clear clinical sign that one part of the author's mind has begun to close down in order to shut out the terrible truths and degradations that another part of that same mind has found it impossible to remedy or to escape? Rosenfeld (*Enigmas of Time and Space: Finding Reality in the Larsen Papers,* Katmandu, 2102) has gone so far as to propose (Chapter 2, "Speaking in the Empty Auditorium") that the overall structure of the papers as a whole shows the accumulating, and finally the crushing, power of madness—as, among other things, the papers' voice increasingly introverted, despairing of any audience, and in fact (as in "Fragment VI," for example), falling entirely into silence. [Editor]

the distinctive, rich history and experiences of individuals with disabilities   the distinctive, rich

history and experiences of individuals with disabilities   the distinctive, rich history and experie

s of individuals with disabilities   the distinctive, rich history and experiences of individuals wit

h disabilities   the distinctive, rich history and experiences of individuals with disabilities   the r

rev
from the
oppressive injust
cultural and political power.
unable to distinguish between distinct aspects
("everything is political") proclivity toward simplifi
But another and far more important index to the degree of blindness
it itself is creature and creation of an unseen and genuinely rapacious
aspect of the same same monolithic "Western" power: *that the revo-*
lution unknowingly is working in perfect union with that oppressive
force; that the movement, believing itself to be fighting for

and in fact preferring as much as possible the absence of distinc-
tions altogether, the revolutionaries from the start were doomed
by the same commercial and economic culture that bred them to be
intellectually insensitive *Faculty: Be a part of the excitement this spring!* ,
self-concerned *Hear our Voices!* , and undiscriminating *Written by*
ordinary people, this record of American life shows that anyone who can tell a
story can write one .

•

Burning with hatred after witnessing force applied ruinously
    criminally by the "West," they, making
        error after predictable error, one feeding upon
            directly into the trap all along set by their very
worst enemy.

> A person of African ancestry's best chance of
> finding a match is with another person of African
> ancestry. YOU!

                                an a
                            frustration
                        steadily grew that
                ership and political action *were in*
            festations of "Western values" or of the
        a simplification that eroded other, corollary distinctions
"politics" and "culture." In this process, a real and empirically
        —that the economic and market powers now fully in control
of the society we live in care nothing for or about Western civilization and would in fact very much prefer not having its values stand
in their way. Following these failed perceptions, there was needed
only the collapse of a small number of others before a syllogism
could be set up calling in absolutist moral terms f

•

The Syllogism
1) Western civilization consists solely of oppressive power;
2) it, its artifacts and values being one and the same,
3) all three consist solely and only of oppressive power.
4) Western civilization, therefore, its values and artifacts (one and the
   same) must be exposed for what they are and destroyed

The Syllogism
1) Dogs consist solely of fangs;
2) dogs' fangs and everything dogs do and create being one and the same,
3) dogs, dogs' eating, and dog bites all consist solely of fangs.
4) Dogs, therefore, their fangs, and everything they do must be exposed
   for what they are and destroyed.

> **President Penguin-Duck**
> **Offers Congratulations**

the true axiomatic values of the West are in fact breathtakingly
simple, elegant in their purity, intrinsically antagonistic to oppression (in fact innately corrosive of it), and in no conceivable way are
they inimical to the aims

are these:

1) *reverence for the individual,*
2) *sanctity for the untrammeled freedom of thought and*
   expression.
3) *the rule of secular law*

From these, all subsequent cultural and political blessings that the
West is capable of causing to flow will flow. From this basis alone
will come any achievements that may *distinctively or justly* be
called Western.

exploit or oppress the individual, dishonor secular law,
and circumscribe and condemn thought—these can and do take
place in the West. But that doesn't make them a product of the
West. Murder may occur in Athens. It should not therefore be
declared Athenian.[176]

•

...the distinctive, rich history and experiences of individuals with disabilities...

•

u
pra
despond
here a person is driven
    sidering the true insidiousness
terrible story that is ineluctably unfolding
        axiomatic values

**Quiet as It's Kept:
Shame, Trauma,
and Race
In the Novels of
Toni Morrison**
J. Brooks Bouson

---

[176] A passage of clarity, simplicity, and power that since the discovery of the papers has
drawn the attention of all serious commentators. The "true axiomatic values" are indeed
breathtaking, not only in their simplicity but in their profundity as well. One need only
consider the true extent and degree to which these fundamental twin values were, at Actaeon College in the Late Ante-Penultimate and Early Penultimate, degraded, abused, and
perverted to understand quite clearly the destructive toll that could be taken on any college
member of distinguished intellect, strong moral sense, and deep sensitivity toward those
same values that everywhere around him were being thrown into a pity of abuse, misun-
derstanding, and disarray. [Editor]

those same forces seeking tyranny will stand by patiently, contentedly watching these self-involved academic lunatics go about destroying the long record of *individual* achievement—the literature and art, much of the philosophy—that has been historically a thorn in despotism's side and, until now, an antagonistic check to the last perfection of its own Orwellian aim: bringing about a state in which every citizen has been relieved of an independent or inquiring mind, every citizen reduced into a pure and perfect "consume

•

tell a story can write one. Written by ordinary people, this record of American life

can write one. Written by ordinary people, this record of American life shows

anyone who can tell a story can write one. Written by ordinary people, this record

anyone who can tell a story can write one. Written by ordinary people

tell a story can write one. Written by ordinary people, this

anyone who can tell a story can write one

anyone who can tell a story can write one

anyone who can tell a story can

anyone who can tell a story can

anyone who can tell a story can write one

by ordinary people, this record

can write one. Written by ordinary people, th

anyone who can tell a story can

write one. Written by ordinary

can write one. Written by ordi

story can write one. Written b

ordinary people, this

that anyone who

tell a story

who

can

t

> ...the distinctive, rich history and experiences of individuals
> with disabilities...

> *...the distinctive, rich history and experiences of individuals with disabilities...*

> Bluestreak Series. . . of innovative literary writing by women of all colors.

> **When fully funded the grant will be worth $ 18.4 million.**

> President Penguin-Duck Offers Congratulations

short, once you, the erstwhile guardians of the liberal arts, have completed your work of destroying not only the content of the university but also the frail and invaluable process—of affirming, discovering, or rejecting of values *through knowledge*—that the university still barely manages to harbor: once this ruin has been accomplished, then the greater power, the market power, the evil power, the power that in fact cares nothing whatsoever for the real values of

> **HEAR OUR VOICES!**
>
> One-Act Plays about child abuse, death, family relationships, female genital mutilation, marriage, murder, prostitution, rape and suicide.

> **Faculty: Be a part of the excitement! Include this play in your course!**

will be taken over by the market state, or, if you prefer, by government functioning as handmaiden to corporate economic and financial interests.

Impossible? Hyperbolic? Paranoid?[177] If only it were so. Dinesh D'Souza, though,

---

[177] It is impossible for the reader not to wonder what thought, association, or feeling might have flickered through Larsen's mind—assuming that the author was Larsen—at the moment he used this word, so terribly relevant to so many aspects of (and questions about) both his own mind and the collapsing world around him, certainly within Actaeon, and certainly without. [Editor]

about Stanley Fish,[178] raises the same question and is provided—from Fish himself—with an answer that suggests the full extent of the loss awaiting us. "Besides youthful literary iconoclasts," writes D'Souza[179, 180] "another group has been drawn

Although Fish does not consider himself a political partisan, 'many people on the political left found my work psychologically liberating,' he explained. 'They began to say: once you realize that standards emerge historically, then you can see through and discard all the norms to which we have been falsely enslaved.'"

> *Is it "wrong" to "correct" writing?*
> *Is it "bad" even to make suggestions?*

"Fish's feelings about subverting the old rules in criticism," remarks D'Souza, "parallel his feelings about the old rules in campus governance,"

> **The Women's Center** will sponsor, "The Ribbon
> " commencing **Monday, April 16ᵗʰ** through
> **ril 19ᵗʰ** (April is Sexual Assault &
> h).

iring policies in academia
ot the same standards should be
, Fish offers no intellectual response
e has *nothing to base such a response on* or
cept power, of course, and here, then, calling up-
only remaining resource available to him, altogether

> **JOIN   in   the   celebration   of   our
> interconnectedness   through   poetry,   peace
> messages and songs!**

> Fish grinned. "Sure, I might be in favor of that.

---

[178] In spite of his having apparently once been eminent—or notorious—scholars have failed to find any traces of Fish's life or work other than those chronicled by Larsen (or Bloomgarden/Margolies). [Editor]

[179] *The Atlantic,* March 1991, pp. 72–73 [Author's note]

[180] For D'Souza, see note 162, p. 157. [Editor]

—what Fish has done, apparently oblivious to the towering, crushing irony, is this: Grant that aid and stability will be re-established by the great Satan itself, the hated wielder of enslaving Western values, the same despised bringer of war and oppression that was responsible a mere twenty-five years earlier for the *very genesis* of the morally outraged and putatively leftist revolution.

D'Souza comments wanly that "In Fish's view, not even
more arbitrary value, with no claim to special.
political exigencies, including the agenda
ight have remarked upon instead, far more
can't apply to Fish's thinking: for,
his view, "value" has been bled away
"value" and "power" are made one
Can't say one power is "more impor
only true statement is that one
stronger or weaker than another.
moral or evaluative judgment gone—
have no place whatsoever in such
speak any longer of an
let alone possess the
moral rigor or
uasive ethic
gone with
troyed
ld be
if a

e

This project is designed to be an action project of testimony and affirmation. The entire Actaeon College community will be invited to testify about their personal experiences and memories about abuse, rape, sexual assault, and sexual harassment. Anyone who has experienced sexual violence, or knows someone was has, will have an opportunity to tie a purple ribbon on our clothesline (which will be strung up in the **Presidential Hall Lobby**) and write their thoughts and affirmations in the Ribbon Project Journal.

**ARE YOU THINKING ABOUT
A CAREER
in
LAW???
BUSINESS???
GOVERNMENT???
PUBLIC ADMINISTRATION???
????
THEN *YOU SHOULD BE
THINKING ABOUT A*

MAJOR
IN
GENDER STUDIES**

---

*FOLLOW THE RED HERRING!
SUCCEED AT WHAT YOU DO
BEST!!*

The fall trumpet has sounded and with renewed vigor, we begin the new academic cycle. Attached is a listing of faculty responsibilities. Please read them carefully. This information is helpful in ensuring that there is clarity of thought in the performance of your noble duties.

Sincerely,
Dean & Vice President Smith Rattle

Anyone who has experienced sexual violence, or knows someone was has, will have an opportunity to tie a purple ribbon on our clothesline (which will be strung up in the **Presidential Hall Lobby**) and write their thoughts and affirmations in the Ribbon Project Journal.

President Penguin-Duck Offers Congratulations

•

And so Fish himself is the one to show us exactly how it will be, thanks to him and thanks to all you who follow his lunatic affectations, how it will be that the liberal arts, with their frail but invaluable capacity for keeping the breath of a free life in our intellects and also in our hearts, how it is that these will be handed over lock, stock, and barrel, out of high arrogance and overwhelming ignorance, after long and persistent folly and in the most pathetic of closing scenes, to the greatest lobby force for corporate profits, dis-education, exploitation of the individual, artificial additives, throw-away razor blades, hemorrhoid ointments, and plastic packaging ever to have existed in the history of mankind.

> *FOLLOW THE RED HERR*
> *SUCCEED AT WHAT YOU*
> *D*

> **JOIN in the celebration of our interconnectedness through poe peace messages and songs!**

> President Penguin-Duck Offers Cong

•

These devastating failures among putatively literary people have to do in large part, as we have said, with the corrosive and subtle curse of "values" in American

> **THE**
> **ACTAEON**
> **POETRY FESTIVAL HAS RETURNED**
> Write Poetry? Like Poetry?
> Come to the Festival
> Open Mike!
> Bring a Friend!!

because they are afraid of "intellectuality," and because they believe that it's sterile, uninteresting, and elitist, Americans rearrange the cart and the horse in education. They make "values" into the horse and reduce knowledge to the cart, which, depending on

how well it's attached, may or may not follow after. People like you,
younger colleagues, in positions of a near-sacred responsib
in this long tradition of recorded achievement
to the status of art not what "values" it may
these come and these go, and in any ca
extraordinarily simple, basic, an
to hardly be anything at all
existence and survival
but rise to the level
far different fr
mockery o
very utm
story o
long
af
b

> **9:15 am—10:30 am**
> **CONCURRENT SESSIONS I**
> **A. Popular Culture and Composition: A**
> **Link to Individual & National Histories**
> **B. ESL & Writing Across the Curriculum**
> **(ESLWAC)**
> **C. Crossing Borders: Texts, Genres, Media**
> **D. Doing it All: Part I**

"creative writing" instead of literature; "American Studies" in
"religion" instead of philosoph

> Plays about child abuse, death, family relationships, female genital
> mutilation, marriage, murder, prostitution, rape and suicide

horse and cart rearrangements of almost every disc
Black Studies, Asian Studies, Women's
Gay, now even White Studies, if

> **10:45 am—12:00 pm**
> **CONCURRENT SESSIONS II**
>
> **A. Cultural Cartography**
> **B. The Feminization of Composition**
> **and Pedagogies of Care**
> **C. Tech: Teaching Issues**
> **D. Doing it All: Part II**

                              political rather than intellectual
                                   may have done, or in turn
                                  iticizing of the curriculum
                                    estroy the liberal arts
                                       of literature,
                                          one word
                                            if I am
                                              say
                                               1

```
+---------------------------------------+
|           2:00 pm—1:45 pm             |
|       CONCURRENT SESSIONS II          |
|   A. What Should We Be Looking For?   |
|      B. Tech: Integrating Issues      |
|   C. Using Verbal and Written Activities |
|       D. Doing it All: Part III       |
+---------------------------------------+
```

But that the value-theory of education is a fallacy hasn't prevented
it from being increasingly adhered to as people feel more threatened
and alarmed by what they perceive to be breakdowns of substantial
or meaningful social order. We mentioned

```
+-------------------+
| HEAR OUR VOICES!  |
+-------------------+
```

```
+-------------------------+
| Global Issues of Gender |
+-------------------------+
```

```
+----------------------------------------------------------+
| child abuse, death, family relationships, female genital |
| mutilation, marriage, murder, prostitution, rape and suicide |
+----------------------------------------------------------+
```

```
+-------------------------------+
| ...Included among these cultures is |
| the distinctive, rich history and  |
| experiences of individuals with   |
| disabilities.                      |
+-------------------------------+
```

```
+-----------------------------------+
|     Come to the Peace Garden!!!   |
|       Peace Garden-Unity Day      |
|       Wednesday, April 14th       |
|     Lobby, Non-Presidential Hall  |
|            3:00 p.m.              |
+-----------------------------------+
```

```
+---------------------------------+
| The session will end with an    |
| open discussion on diversity.   |
+---------------------------------+
```

and, yes, there
is a crisis, one that they often describe and indict powerfully. But
they have no real idea at all of what the arts are, how they work, and wha
or what the relationship between life and the arts really is or
their arguments are doomed to a futile wheel-spinni
deeper into argumentative holes the longer they
wrongly that education teaches values, the
of values (but only the good ones, mind
thereby reducing themselves to the
impotence and tyranny, since the
is the imposing of values, a
coercion more familiar
no different from
bullying Fish
but his
dam
in tr
to l
int
mu
e

Every repeated insistence upon the instilling of "classic Western
values" that falls from their lips is only more music to the despots'

were lied to, being told that literature was vital and important
because it contained and expressed high Western values that could
be instilled only in those who read it, so that only

half-truth at best, has never been
more than a half-truth, and every truly literary or educated person

But

like any other students who have been
deceived , lied to, and misled by a system of education that assumes
truth to reside in its teachers instead of in what's studied,[181, 182] they

---

[181] Emphasis in original. [Author's note]

[182] A penetrating and extremely useful distinction. One of the things made very clear by
the Larsen papers regarding "higher" education during the Late Ante-Penultimate and the
years following is that, almost entirely, *personality* replaced *mastery* as a measure of those
qualities that were considered as worthy in evaluations leading to advancement. A parallel

Written by ordinary people

set an example by drinking deep of "literature"),

...by women of all colors. ...by women of all colors....by women of all colors....by women of all colors. by women of all colors. by women of all ...by women of all colors. ......by women of all colors. ......by women of all colors. ......by women of all colors. ......by women of all colors. ...by

**The Wounded Body
Remembering the
Markings of Flesh**

...the wounded body in
literature from Homer to Toni
Morrison ..

**Sadism, Memory, and
Sexual Violence**
In American Women's
Fiction
Deborah M. Horvitz

believing it to be a repository of high Western values. And, very soon after, it made them sick.

**Scenes of Shame
Psychoanalysis, Shame,
and Writing**

Joseph Adamson and
Hilary Clark, editors

**TEXTUAL BODIES
BODIES AT RISK
CAPTIVE BODIES**

usurpation, of course, during the same period, was the replacement of *mastery* by *political view*. Both, as Larsen (and/or Bloomgarden/Margolies) shows again and again, were incalculably destructive and are seen by all serious scholars of the subject to have been significantly dissolvent forces that helped break down large varieties of traditional barriers that might otherwise have been able to stand in the way of the Collapse. For an insightful and intelligent handling of the subject, see Marietta Caswell-Wu, *We Feel These Truths to Be Self-Evident: The Degradation of Thought and Intellect through the Deification of Feeling and Opinion in the Early, Middle, and Late Penultimate* (Hong Kong, 2129). [Editor]

> Finding the
> right text
> doesn't have
> to be a
> shot
> in the
> dark.

And here the story gets truly despairing. For the fact was, of course,

> This book demonstrates that society needs to pay attention to how the body is manipulated if we are to work for social progress and political justice, for it is through our bodies that we all must articulate our experience and live our lives.

> **FACULTY DEVELOPMENT ANNOUNCEMENT**
> **Balancing the curriculum for Gender, Race, Ethnicity, and Class**

> ### The Many Worlds of Literature
>
> **A treasury of stories, essays, poems and plays exploring the rich diversity of global cultures.**

> *Included among these cultures is the distinctive, rich history and experiences of individuals with disabilities...*

> Collected from every corner of the world, these writings provide a deep and varied exploration into the global art of storytelling—and insight into a wide variety of cultural and ethnic backgrounds. Almost 90% of the selections (which include fiction, non-fiction, poetry, and drama) were published after 1965; more than half were written by women.

> As a result, this is a truly fresh contemporary alternative for composition and literature courses. The works are organized in seven thematic chapters, *beginning with highly personal writings, then expanding to include social, political and spiritual topics.* Each chapter ends with a discussion of formal literary elements and techniques. Each selection includes an author biography, questions, and writing assignments that encourage students to explore their own experiences in the context of our increasingly multicultural society.

"...able to follow the steps of a simple logical argument."

"Winter kept us warm..."

Successful College Teaching

Bestseller!!

PROBLEM SOLVING STRATEGIES
OF DISTINGUISHED PROFESSORS

Sharon A. Baiocco, *Jacksonville College*
and Jamie N. DeWaters, *D'Youville College*

". . . consisting in its essence of babytalk"

("...hyper-sensitivity to perceived injury, a sustained resentment unassuageable through reason or even subsequent experience—these are traits of the... ")

New!!

ADVICE
for
NEW
FACULTY
MEMBERS
*Proven strategies for surviving
And thriving as a new faculty
member*
Robert Boice, *SUNY Stonybrook,
Retired*

Retired!

**Active Learning:
101 Strategies to Teach
Any Subject**

*The most comprehensive
Collection of active learning
Techniques ever published!*

Mel Silberman, *Temple University*

Retired!!

Confronting Diversity through the Filmic
Experience

> Balancing the curriculum for Gender, Race,
> Ethnicity, and Class

> Retired!!!

Retired!!!!

•

misunderstandings, and lies. It may very well be that no hope remains for the regaining of mature seriousness, but in the belief that

> The 5th Annual
> ## Queer-UNY
> CONFERENCE
>
> **Why are so few
> faculty out?**

let us implore any who are still capable of listening, to listen[183]. Do this: Distinguish, if nothing else, between

> *CHANGES IN
> ACADEMIC
> STANDARDS:*
>
> *HOW WILL THEY
> AFFECT YOU?
> ARE* **YOU** *IN
> JEOPARDY?*

> **Why are so few UNY faculty
> out?**

> **FACULTY DEVELOPMENT
> ANNOUNCEMENT
> Balancing the curriculum for Gender,
> Race, Ethnicity, and Class**

> Written by ordinary people,
> this record of American life shows that anyone
> who can tell a story
> can write one.

---

[183] This sad, powerful, rhythmic litany cannot help but suggest the towering importance the author or authors see in their subject. The clear sense of sorrow, loss, incredulity, and perhaps of resignation is commensurate only to minds that consider these matters to have profound implications far beyond the walls merely of academia. For, indeed, the fact is inescapable to any careful reader that Larsen was concerned not simply with the way his colleagues "thought" about the arts, but, seeing his colleagues as examples, that he was concerned with the way an entire nation thought, finding in it unwelcome seeds of doom. [Editor]

...celebration of our
interconnectedness through poetry,
peace messages and songs!!!

literature teaches nothing, at its heart *is* nothing—whatever its other and attendant complexities[184]—other than this: small reminders and exquisitely blooming whispers of meaninglessness, nothingness, and death—[185]

---

[184] To my younger colleagues: As you know, no part of "Despair Notes," or for that matter, no part of the entirety of *The Decline of Literature and Reason in an Age of Theory,* has received as much commentary—or as negative and adversarial a reception—as the concluding paragraphs of its seventh and last chapter, with their definition of literature. I myself subscribe wholeheartedly to the Bloomgarden/Margolies definition and, for that matter, have done so throughout my adult literary and intellectual life. At this point, let me serve those two authors, if I may, by amplifying briefly what I take to be their meaning in the parenthetical phrase "whatever its other and attendant complexities." At a later point, I will take up the relationship between literature and death.

By and large, inexperienced readers such as you are prone to react with shock and almost as often with outrage as well—as you remember Professor Car Cleopatra doing recently, when she threw her coffee mug across the conference table at me—when they hear scholars like Bloomgarden and Margolies declare that literature "says nothing, means nothing, teaches nothing, at its heart is nothing..." Absolutely crucial to Bloomgarden and Margolies' meaning, of course, is that readers not *stop* at this point, however enraged they may be (you'll remember, also, Professor Muscle's denunciation of Bloomgarden and Margolies as "obstructionist navel-gazing counter-revolutionary do-nothing bags of shit"), but that instead they continue on to the *assertive* segment of the definition, which declares not what literature *is not and does not do,* but what it *is and does do.*

But the negative segment first, since it clears the way logically for the assertive segment. Simply put, the authors are separating the essence of literature from other elements that it indeed may have within it but that *are not the elements that make it literature.* The essence of a *person,* after all, is not elbow, thumbnail, or ear lobe, but something *else,* though a person may *have* those elements. In parallel, therefore, literature is not philosophy, though it may have philosophy in it; nor is it history, though history may be *in* it; neither is it politics, though politics, too, may be in it or may even be its *subject.* But none of these elements justifies literature, makes it what it is, or catalyzes it into becoming art. *That alone* is the unique and distinctive thing that practitioners of literature or people who *are* literary *must* know and must understand and must adhere to and must be able to convey to others. The other, lesser, elements of literature are merely "its other and attendant complexities," which must be, either early or late, set aside before the true heart, life, and purpose of the creation can be known, felt, seen, and responded to.

Insofar as you, my own younger colleagues, devote all, or all but the most meager and tiny part of your energies precisely *to those other and attendant complexities,* I cannot even hope that you might overnight change your ways. In the manner of your proceeding now, however, you are similar to nothing so much as to those medical doctors who might concern themselves with every conceivable aspect of a patient *except that patient's life.* [Author's note]

[185] Any of you who know I. F. Bauer's virulent and extended attack on Bloomgarden and Margolies in *The New York Review of Books* will also know that, in essence, Bauer based that attack *on a deliberately false representation of this indescribably important definition of literature.* That is, he simply stopped here, misleading his own readers into the impression that Bloomgarden and Margolies' definition *ends* with the words "small reminders and exquisitely blooming whispers of meaninglessness, nothingness, and death." Only because

Anyone who has experienced sexual violence, or knows
someone was has, will have an opportunity to tie a purple
ribbon on our clothesline...

the distinctive, rich history and experiences of individuals with disabilities!!!

—Balancing the Curriculum for Ethnicity, Class, Race, and Gender

Why are so few faculty out?

HOW TO GET
A
TEACHING
JOB

President Penguin-Duck Offers
Congratulations

Retired

and only[186] thereby, through its reminding us of the briefness of life,
does it also and concomitantly become an undeniable affirmation of
the sole, unique, universal, inestimably treasurable and ineluctably
deep and mysterious value of human existence.[187] If the case were
otherwise than as we have just described, there would be no literature, since those who

of Bauer's eminently visible political position—*and* his having been for more than ten years
one of the most generous monetary supporters of that journal (as well as a member of its
board)—has the NYRB *consistently* kept letters objecting to Bauer's method of attack and
purposeful distortion of *The Decline of Literature and Reason in an Age of Theory* from its
pages. Any kind of intellectual honesty or true fairness requires that the entire definition be
included in any analysis, not only a part. [Author's note. Not in original]

[186] Ignored altogether by Bauer, the importance of this simple adverb cannot be overstated:
only by "reminding us of the briefness of life" can a work of art "concomitantly" become
an affirmation of life. It is not a matter, alone, of Bloomgarden and Margolies requiring that
a work be of high seriousness (even if comic, or slight, or small—it still *must* be of a high
seriousness), but of their requiring that the *reader read* in a way that is itself also high in its
seriousness: one must always be aware not only of what one is reading but of what one is *not*
reading, not only of what one is seeing or hearing, but of what is *not* seeing and *not* hearing. The true artwork "speaks" both by its presence *and* by its absence; both by the *presence* of
elements in it and by the *absence* of other elements that were a part of the making of it. I have
written elsewhere about this aspect of art *and* about the high demand placed upon the *experiencer* of art. I also hope, in the future, to write about it further. These requirements, these
elements and aspects of art, without which art cannot *be* art: I fully understand that you, my
younger colleagues, having been trained as simplifiers, having been indoctrinated perversely
to see in art not celebration but falsehood, and having been raised in a generation trained by
its true teachers to be incapable of the high demands and equivalent rewards of knowing,
feeling, and practicing true seriousness—I fully understand it to be a most unlikely thing that
any of you will be sufficiently moved by my words so as to look into your hearts and ask,
given what you find there, whether you may in fact not have betrayed the finest in art, embracing instead the very least, or very possibly nothing at all. [Author's note. Not in original]

[187] All art, that is to say, if it is to achieve perdurability (and thus any significance beyond ephemera) must result in there being—by it, from it, through it, as a result of it—a

dedicated themselves to the struggle of creating it would have been content, instead, simply with *living* life, and afterward with the silence that follows.[188, 189] Literature's being nothing other than this, just as a ballet or piece of music or a painting, however glorious or fine, is nothing other than this (however complex, however beautiful, however fully achieved), remains in truth the one, single, real, and wholly unassailable source of its genuine and great strength, of its significance beyond the reach or call of any ideology,

---

consciousness of death and absence which, in contrast with the life, presence, and on-going existence of the artwork itself, creates the existing irony of life being and not being art and of art being and not being life. The awe that comes from experiencing a work of art comes from precisely this aspect of the experience: one is looking at, or hearing, reading, or viewing that which exists and does not exist, that which is and is not. That one must have life in order to have this feeling is the root fact by which the artwork, through being "an exquisitely blooming whisper of meaninglessness, nothingness, and death," becomes simultaneously the means of bringing about a gratitude for life, an appreciation of life, a love and celebration of life. Any artwork doing less than this is not art but rhetoric, politics, or empty design. [Author's note. Not in original]

188 Also ignored—and uninvestigated—by Bauer in his attack, not surprisingly. Doubtless, he had no idea what it meant and so pretended simply that it didn't exist. Just as little or no writing today any longer achieves the quality of art, so, too, fewer and fewer remain (as you, my younger colleagues, exemplify) who are "still capable" of a responsiveness to the existence of literary art—with the result that there is now less interest than at any time over the past century and a half, at least, in the making of literary art, of the why and how it is or might be created, let alone what it means to have been created. You know intimately, my younger colleagues, your own qualities and kinds of non-interest—you with whom I have never yet had a literary conversation—Drs. Gay, Gender, and Ghetto, Drs. Long, Lesbian, and Know, Drs. Woman, Victim, and Theory, others—in, say, an impromptu conversation about writing.

Indeed, there are bookstore readings, talks, appearances on television of people said to be writers—who are producers of books—but attendance at these results from interest in celebrity, not in literature, let alone literary art. There is around us now, in fact, almost no remaining literary life whatsoever, certainly none inside academia. Your own indoctrination and training have so deeply failed you—and have so brilliantly succeeded in their intended purposes—that you are very nearly incapable of thinking naturally (let alone regularly) about death, or very possibly of thinking about it at all. And how, I ask, if you are unaware of death, can you conceivably be aware of—or even conscious of—art? Being incapable of an ongoing,

and of its universal value: its being the life-forged and afterward eternally faithful whisperings of meaninglessness and death that, by

—Balancing the Curriculum for Class, Gender, Ethnicity, and Race

making invisible the struggle for their own birth, create—in the face of the universal, unremitting, implacable, and absolute nothingness that confronts each and every one of us at each and every moment of our lives, followed then by nothingness absolute—making invisible the struggle for their own birth, create something of permanence, beauty, and human gesture. And to be ignorant of beauty of that or any equivalent kind, let alone to *destroy* beauty of that or any *equivalent* kind, as those still capable

Retired

—Balancing the Curriculum for Gender, Race, Ethnicity, and Class

—Balancing the Curriculum for Ethnicity, Class, Race, and Gender

FOLLOW THE RED HERRING!
SUCCEED AT WHAT YOU DO
BEST!!

Almost 90% of the selections (which include fiction, non-fiction, poetry, and drama) were published after 1965;

Retired

intellectual, conscious awareness of death-in-life (at, for example, this very moment, as I write these very words), you can not ever possibly be aware of life-in-death, of presence-in-absence, these being the sole essential identifying products of true art.

In having been indoctrinated to attend solely to life, you have been made incapable of attending simultaneously and also to death. In having been indoctrinated to attend solely and only to "issues," you have been made incapable of attending to anything other than or beyond life. Through death's having been removed from your serious intellectual consciousness (through your having been transformed, that is, into what you believe to be political thinkers but what in actuality is the state of "consumerism"), you have been made incapable not only of perceiving but even of thinking about real art. Without death there can be no life. Without death there can be no true aesthetic seriousness. Without death there can be no art. Without death there can be no passion for art.

You, my young colleagues, who believe yourselves to be among the living, are in fact wandering among the dead. Arise, look about you. Reclaim death. Reclaim autonomy. Reclaim true life.

Otherwise, we all are doomed. [Author's note. Not in original]

189 In light of what did in fact take place, the echoing pathos of this last sentence is indisputable, haunting, and very, very, very deep. [Editor]

know only too well,

Why are so few faculty out?

Collected from every corner of the world, these writings
provide a deep and varied exploration into the global art of
storytelling—and insight into a wide variety of cultural and
ethnic backgrounds. Almost 90% of the selections (which
include fiction, non-fiction, poetry, and drama) were
published after 1965; more than half were written by
women.

en of all colors ... women of all colors ... women of all colors ... women of all colors ...

is to
destroy far more than only one thing: It is, instead, to destroy also
pleasure, dignity, joy, and one more lovely, pitiful, irreplaceable,
harmless piece of the all too meager lasting achievement—and of such
meaning as may come of it—that has managed to have been born out
of the union of mind and heart, that of late so deeply despised but
single most all-important marriage, the marriage of mind and heart,
upon which all true humanity depends, and without exception all
true artistic achievement.

An Inquiry into the Death Penalty

Presented by
The Office of President Morton R. Penguin-Duck,
the Office of Dean & Vice-President Smith Rattle,
and the Office of Academic Affairs

Monday, March 12th 4:00-6:00 PM
Room 800, Presidential Hall

Greetings from: Beryl Jade, Curator of Exhibit

Opening Remarks: Pres. Penguin-Duck, Dean Rattle

Discussants

Prof. Kama Catfield   Department of Philosophy and Social Control

Prof. Wanda Drake   Department of Law and Social Control

Warren Wetmore   Department of Government and Social Control

Refreshments will be served following the program, courtesy of
the Office of the President

_D_

DO NOT READ TH
DOING SO MAY BE DETRIME
MENTAL OR EMO[190]

The following pages are provide
historic and archival record of the
no other purpose. They will, conseq
whatsoever that may be made to read
degree of narrative or dramatic energy t
does so to an extent slightly greater than th
present in the actual past years of which the
unalterable, vacant, barren, and voiceless ind

Such energy, if any, of course, results not from be
organized chronologically (all nature being so) but
of structural artistry they are imbued with through th
being arranged alphabetically and numerically. [191, 192]

---

[190] See note 48, p. 51. [Editor]

[191] "Unmoored from the body, speech deteriorates. It becomes false, inane, ignoble, weightless. Silence can inhibit or counteract this tendency, providing a kind of ballast, monitoring and even correcting language when it becomes inauthentic." (Susan Sontag, *Styles of Radical Will* [New York, 1966], p. 21) [Author's Note]

[192] Obviously, the same questions arise once again as to precisely what Larsen might have intended by citing from the same work as before—and, of course, as to whether the work cited from is imaginary or real. In *Apollo or Cassandra? Victim or Prophet?*, Irena Hong-Koestler and Petra Gubar make, again, a strong case for taking the citation as one deliberately composed by Larsen to provide a "hidden" attack on the perversion and deformation of language in the Late Ante-Penultiate, especially as he daily found it "used" ("false, inane, ignoble, weightless") around him at Actaeon. Many have devoted

themselves to conjectures as to the meaning of "Unmoored from the body." The question grows immediately into so enormous a topic, however, that it leads quickly away from the Larsen papers themselves and by necessity grows into the historic study—sociological, political, psychological—of the Collapse itself.

A note on the condition of the pages: Readers cannot help but notice that here and in the final section of "Fragment VI" the condition of the sheets rapidly worsens. In many cases, in fact, only shreds remain, and reconstruction, in the years after discovery, was a slow and laborious process. Few hypotheses have been made as to why the condition of these particular sheets, laden with their "unliving words," should be worse than so many others. [Editor]

FRAGMENT VI —

MY ACADEMIC CAREER

Quantity is
—

Our obj
enroll

XXXII
Spring 1
0
English 1
S

Bertsouclis, Haralabo	Griffi
Caragiulo, Dominic	Jo
Canteen, Stanley	J
Crenshaw, Daren	
Daly, Michael	
Ellison, Florence	
Figueroa, Tammy	
Furman, Daniel	

Altagracia, Zobeida
Alvarez, Cathy
Braumuller, Aretha
Bryan, Antonia
Cameron, Charles
Civorelli, Anthony
Cohen, Diane
Emerson, James
Farmar, David

Abdelhady, Z
Arias, Ang
Bacon, C
Best, Wi
Cara, Su
Casey,
Coley
De S
De

E

3
Literature 121 The Ancient World to the Renaissance
Section 01

Adednego, David	Henri, Claudine	Rom
Barahana, Sara	Hermida, Mercedes	Rotger
Bartolatta, John	Holder, Debra	Schwart
Boyce, Jonathan	Le Juez, Kim	Shelton, M
Boyle, Janice	Lind, Joseph	Spannow, R
Centoducatti, Dena	Mai, Herbert	Swierzowski,
Cunningham, Scott	Manson, James	Tejera, Manue
Diaz, Rafael	Masterson, Charles	Toledo, Richard
Farah, Lyes	Milo, Ronald	Torres, Daisy
Fossum, Carl	Myers, Cremston	Torres, Dannisa
Gallagher, Gerald	Nieves, Samuel	Vinas, Gloria
Garney, Charles	Parker, Tracey	Warley, Raquel
Goolsby, Sabrina	Peguero, Wanda	Wilson, Ramika
Gulati,Dheer	Reeves, Tina	
Hagan, Stephen	Rivera, Alejandrina	

4
Literature 121 The Ancient World to the Renaissance
Section 01

Baker, Ines
Blaize, Dermond
Blanch, Gary
Breton, Lydia
Brumfield, Misha
Carter, Michael
Conroy, John
Corchado, Maribel
Cox-Whiteside, J. A.
Doherty, Danielle
Gonzalez, Egidio
Greene, Typhena
Hind, David
Jones, Mellissa
Kovacs, John

Mc Cabe, Laura
Mc Carthy, Jacqueline
Mc Glynn, Eileen
Mc Neill, Denise
Melgar, Silvia
Mencia, Jose
Mensaho, Kwaku
Moss, Kyna
O' Connor, John
Potts, Janice
Powell, S.
Ramirez, Manauel
Ramairez, Mercedes
Reid, Juliette
Richardson, Cheryl

Roberts,
Salek,
Silv
Sm
So
S

XL
Spring 1991
I
Literature 122, The Enlighte

Albagil, Fiordaliza
Arp, Christopher
Ascatigno, Doreen
Bautisto, Annie
Bennett, Beverly
Borges, Clarissa
Bottino, Roland
Codd, Maria
Dongo, Marsha
Dunbr, Ramon
Feigenbaum, Daniel

Franco, Vanessa
Gallagher, Gerald
Gonzalez, Ivette
Harris, Debra
Hasbr
Heal

Her
He
H

Andujar, Di
Audifredd,

Chen, Ste
Cruz, M
Cunni
Curti
De
El
G

A
Ar
Asc
Bowm
Brevet-
Daly, De
Dingui, Y
Dalanto, M
Davis, Vame
Fernandez, Ev
Francis, Yoland
Gardner, Steven
George, Dick

Buda, Jacqueline
Burside, Robert
Camilleri, Michelle
Cassidy, Stehen
Chabron, Jennifer
Chow, Patty Yau-Lin
Concepcion, Yvette
Cora, Marissa
Cubillos, Diana
Fasano, Kathryn
Feuer, Jason
Fowler, Kareem
Francis, Mario   Ow
Funtow, Alexander   Paoli

English 1
S

Akua, Ngozi   Goggins, Trisha
Barbei, Brian   Gonzalez, Luis
Brunson, Jacqueline   Hawkins, James
Bush, Joseph   Marshall, Marsha
Darrigan, Andrew   Mendez, Hector
Diaz, Jacqueline   Murphy, Matthew
Edwards, Roxanne   Narine, Kaswaree
Gentile, Lauren   Rabes, Stephen

2
English 101, College Co
Section 12

Amerson, Theresa
Bruckman, Wanda
Cordero, Samuel
Dallessandro, Kevin
De Latour, Patrice
De Los Angeles, Henry
Dillon, Lisa
Espinosa, Carola
Ferreira, Jeanette

Gonzalez, Danny
Goss, Ronald
Gutierrez, Sandra
Hoens, Eric
Johnson, Kimberley
Marrerro, Mercinda
Mullen, Bruce
Nune
Rumbl

Russell,
Sapigao,
Thomas, N
Truong, Ro
Tuason, Ale
Vaughn, Nke
Wallace, Kevin
Zambrava, Giovanni

3
Literature 121 The Ancient World to the Renaissance
Section 01

Abousamra, Paul
Andraqde, Joel
Arellano, Jose
Ascatigno, Doreen
Berger, Jeffrey
Bush, Christopher
Caban, Wilfred
Camacho, Gabriel
Diaz, Patricis
Fina, Stephen
Francis, Willie
Funtow, Alexander
Garcia, Gabriel
Hajaree, Sabita

Heaaley, Peter
Hyacinthe, Vladimir
Karras, Andrea
Keys, Robin
Korb, Adriana
Lewin, Goergia
Lindenmeyer, Rose
Martinnez, Felix
Micalizzi, Paul
Moses, Stephanie
Movick, David
Panagopoulos, Stilian
Perrina, Enrico
Reilly, Theresa

Rigny, James
Roskef, Daniel
Sansarran, Normala
Saraceni, Frank
Shoemaker, Douglas
Sookbin Singh, Michelle
Soriano, Christina
Stevens, Craig
Strazzullo, Salvatore
Strickland, Annette
Taveras, Louisa
West, Jennifer

4
Literature 121 The Ancient World to the Renaissance
Section 01

Ali, Fyza
Arce, Nelson
Balanta, Beatrice
Barbetta, Mary
Bolenky, Dmitry
Bowilla, Cesar
Brodack, Jeffrey
Bruno, Danie
Castiglioni, Steven
Checo, Manuela
Coard, Toiata
Deans, Karen
De Lia, Massimo
Dixon, Cedric

Donahue, Brian
Fetus, Patrick
Flores, Steve
Gabbert, Deron
Germosen, Otto
Gustavsen, Kjell
Guerrier, Wendy
Lodispoto, Michael
Longo, Steven
Loox, Lance
Madrid, Fabian
Martinez, Marison
Mc Cauley, Chris
Melendez, Janet

Mendes, Jeffrey
Mione, Kimbe
Montalvo, Ju
Pansard, Be
Palacios, L
Paulino,
Pereles
Platki
Sarfo
Sim
Sm
W

English 101, College Composition
Section 10

Basic, Richard
Bolton, Cheryl
Brigantie, Anthony
Cancel, Becky
Concepcion, Luis
Donohue, William
Englezos, Franky
English, Claudia

Garcia, Luis
Kniaz, Katarzyna
Maurice, Geraldine
Mendez, Guzman
Proscia, Thomas
Ram, Terrence
Roca, Monica
Rumble, Tricia

2
Literature 122, The Englightenmen
Section 01

Abousamra, Paul
Anderson, Vanita
Armstrong, Lenore
Brennan, Michael
Bush, Christopher
Cadet, Robinson
Carvajal, Nelson
Castiglione, Steven

Chambers, Jeffrey
Charles, Rose
Colbert, Mary
Colon, Gladys
Danjer, Marco
Diaz, Patricia
Dougherty, D
Gonzalez, O
Grubb, Dur
Guadalupe

Novick, David
Roske, Daniel
Ruiz-Dia
Simon,
Smith

Literature

Annis, Christopher
Bailey, Nigel
Bonilla, Matilde
Currie, Andrea
David, Dallas
Davis, Jean
Decoteau, Francis
Dougherty, Shawn
Fred, Jacqueline
Gjoni, Paul
Glover, Trevor

Avvenir,
Ayala,
Bella,
Cul
Do
F

FRAGMENT V —

"THE ETIOLOGY OF AN AESTHETIC: THE SIGNIFICANCE OF ABSENT THINGS"

by

Eric Larsen
written for the
Board of Editors, *The Hound*,
Actaeon College of Institutional Analysis and Social Control
University of New York (UNY)[193]

Editor's Note:

Even though "Fragment V" can at moments seem every bit as challenging as some of those sections of the Larsen Papers most renowned for their obvious complexity, it has never become the cause of on-going or acrimonious debate of the sort well known among critics of, say, "Fragment IV" or, even more, of the fourth part of "Fragment VI." Indeed, many readers have declared "The Etiology of an Aesthetic" to be among their two or three favorite sections of the Papers. Maximillian Shandra has called it, along with "Fragment III," the most "personable" segment of all the Larsen Papers,[194] and Lok Ho Woo has spoken for many

---

[193] "The Etiology of an Aesthetic: The Significance of Absent things," it should be noted, never did actually appear in the pages of *The Hound,* in spite of its having been written expressly for that journal. [Author's Note]

[194] Maximillian Shandra, *The Collapse of History: Statistical Analyses of American Fields of Study in the Early Penultimate* (Bangkok & Tokyo, 2099), p. 145.

in commenting that the fragment "is perhaps the single most successful example of Larsen's high humor and extraordinary depth being bonded into a philosophic / aesthetic tool with the power to reach farther and see more clearly than could ever be the case without such a union.[195]

It is, perhaps, the fragment least in need of editorial comment or support, this in part due to its having been so well aided by the affection of its readers. We can only regret that among those "absent things" here shown to be so equally essential to the truth of art *and* to the art of truth must be included so many pages of the author's own work itself.

1

I am absolutely without any doubt but that my understanding of the importance of unseen things had its period of most rapid growth at the time my family moved from East Fifth Street in Northfield, Minnesota, and took up life on a small farm a mile or two away. That move took place, as I've said,[196] in October of 1947. I was six years old, or a few weeks shy of six, and had already undergone the earliest shapings of my intellectual life, as I have described elsewhere in some detail.[197]

It hardly need be said, even so, that the aesthetic, literary, and intellectual understanding I'm referring to—an understanding of the overwhelming importance of *absent things*—did not come to me all in a single moment. But its growth nevertheless was especially, perhaps even extraordinarily, rapid during the five or six years beginning in 1947.

All around me on the farm we had come to live on were things that once had existed but now were there no more. These included the bleached skull of a cow in the long-grass meadow in the grove (the skull was there, that is to say, while the cow was not), the antique corn crib (the ancient weathered building was there, while the corn

---

[195] Lok Ho Woo, "These Fragments I Have Shored Against My Ruins" (*Studies in American Intellectual History*, December 2134), p. 98.

[196] Nothing if not a reference to one of the lost novels. See next note. [Editor]

[197] The reference may be, in part, to "Fragment III—My Intellectual Life" (pp. 75–118), but scholars almost universally interpret it, along with the parallel remark in the next paragraph plus one, as two of Larsen's rare allusions to his lost book-length "fictional" works. See, as before, Ting ,Yanmei, *Darkness Visible: The Lost Novels of Eric Larsen* (Taipei, 2110); and Poindeft, Archer L. *Notes on Emptiness: Meanings in the Lost Larsen Volumes* (Calcutta and Londinium, 2134).

was not), the long iron spike driven into a box elder tree (the spike was there, the hammer that drove it not), and the ancient scythe hanging from a the limb of a tree near the driveway (the scythe was there, the farmer who once had wielded it not).

In each of these cases, of course, although I have mentioned only a single one so far, *additional* things were missing as well: the heat of the autumn sun and gentleness of autumn breezes that had once helped dry the corn, for example, were gone, as were the acres of high grass that, decades before, the scythe had cut. Even the ringing hammer-blows as the farmer drove the iron spike into the box elder tree— they had long since fallen mute and therefore had been plunged into non-existence, never to be brought back again.

In each case, obviously, *something* was there but the past was not.

And yet even that isn't a true statement, since, at the same time, *the past was indeed there and always must be.*

Paradox of this sort, concerning the presence of things not present—and therefore also concerning the importance of such things to the existence of time—confronted me constantly in my early days, months, and years on the farm, from the time, as I've mentioned, when I was approximately six years old.

2

During that period, a great many other objects, impressions, occasions, moments, and incidents presented themselves to me as opportunities through which I gradually became able not only to recognize the paradoxical nature of time, but also, and in exactly the same way, to recognize the true and paradoxical nature of narrative.

I became aware, that is, of the truth of the following:

> **In any story—or in the aesthetic experience of any kind of artifact—absent things possess an importance equal to, and perhaps greater than,[198] that possessed by things that are present.**

In my early summers on the farm, for example, I often spent long afternoons in the haymow, sitting on a horizontal wooden beam high up under the barn roof. I sat, usually, with my back leaning against a second beam, this being one of those that ascended at an angle from

---

[198] Although this importance need not be an importance, necessarily, of the *same kind*. [Author's Note]

the horizontal beam so as to connect in turn with one of the cross-beams that supported the rafters themselves.

As I sat there, pigeons would make their way in and out of the barn, passing through small openings in the roof-peaks at either end. The same was true of sparrows, although, with their quicker and more darting flight, they entered just as often simply by flying in through the open double doors far below me. Fairly often, the sparrows would alight on the beam parallel to mine across the open bay and look over at me for a time, cocking one eye and then the other, as if they were putting each of those bright little optical organs to the test by corrobo-rating that the second one saw the same thing as the first. Sometimes, after I had remained still for a long time, a handful of them would flutter over to my beam and alight, then step closer to me with great caution, at each step checking me with one eye and then the other.

Inside the old barn, everything was quiet and still. Now and then, some of the pigeons would scuffle among themselves up in the tin cupola where they nested, and from time to time they would treat me to their somnolent cooing sounds. Otherwise, though, and for the greater time by far, the enormous space inside the barn remained perfectly quiet and still. Through tiny holes in roof and walls, pen-cil-lines of sunlight would pierce into the shadowy darkness, some-times, when the angle was right, continuing all the way down to the hay-strewn wooden floor below.

Those afternoons of leisure and reflection in the loft of the barn resulted in some of my earliest conscious recognitions of the twinned miracles of narrative and time.

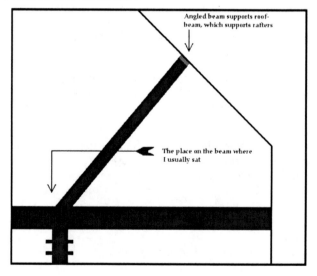

Angled beam supports roof-beam, which supports rafters

The place on the beam where I usually sat

Many times, I crawled the length of my beam, in good part simply to admire the symmetry of the barn's construction, the angles of the paired beams rising up to the underside of the pitched roof, the way those beams had been sunk into hand-hewn niches in the horizontal ones to keep them in place when they were raised up by the barn-builders to meet the initial pairs of crossbeams overhead. Afterward, holes were augered out and thick hardwood pegs toed in to hold butt and beam firmly together.

Adze marks were still visible where the niches had been hewn out, as they were visible elsewhere along the beam at points where shaping had been done. The head of each wooden peg was flanged out, beaten down from the blows of the hammer that had driven it into its hole.

I studied these details of the barn's construction, running my fingers over the markings on the beams, feeling the splintery texture of the flattened peg heads.

•

In these ways, over time, I came to an understanding of the remarkable wedding of absence and presence that exists in narrative, as it does, for that matter, in every artifact whatsoever. The concept can be stated in this way:

> **Every artifact, itself existing physically in the silver of the present, joins seamlessly together the past with the future, as it does the future with the past. This true wedding of "to be" and "was" remains permanent and unalterable throughout the ongoing life of the artifact. It ends, becoming no longer sustainable, only when the artifact itself disappears from existence.**

And so it was, in every splinter of every beam, in every adze-mark, in every flattened head of every hardwood peg, that I came, through an oft repeated and unjudgmental scrutiny, to recognize, almost like invisible fossils held within the artifacts themselves, entire realms, regions, and nations of the past, entire worlds and all the lives that once existed in them—all of this history flowing toward and then *into* the beams and splinters, the flattened pegs and adzed markings of all these cunning artifacts and elements of the old barn. Then, since all artifacts exist within time and not merely at a point in it—having roots in past and future while "existing" only in the present—these same things, forces, recognitions, and lives that had flowed *into* the beams, pegs, marks, and splinters came out again instantly and reached forward into a more and more distant future.

And, simultaneously, the exact reverse. Each moment in the future approached increasingly closer and closer—doing so with the passing of each particle of "time"—to its infinitesimal "present" and its passing—*through* the artifact—back into the past.

Each moment, that is, came from the future, existed invisibly in the present, then slipped away into the past, while the artifact—*and only the artifact*—simultaneously and unceasingly gathered up the past and propelled it forward into the future.

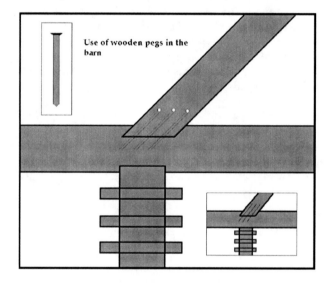

Use of wooden pegs in the barn

In the future waited all the moments when I came into the barn through the big double door, climbed up the ladder, and, high up in the sun-penciled half-darkness, crawled along my beam observing each splinter, peg, and adze-mark. And in the very act and instant of my doing so, *that moment came into and went through the beam, peg, and adze-mark* and, receding at once into the past, was lost to me. Again and again and again this happened and went on happening, while simultaneously, as I looked at, felt, touched, and even lay down on the beams, splinters, pegs, and adze-marks, they themselves *gathered up the past into themselves and (while I, there, then, at those moments, seeing and touching and feeling them, was bathed in the past as if in a very shower of quietness and silence) and flung it unceasingly into the future.*

Other than artifacts, there is nothing in the universe that can function in this way. Nothing in the universe except artifacts can do this.

Which is why, when they are lost—or when they are ruined or unsaved, or when they are prevented from being born or caused to be unborn—so much more than just themselves is lost. The marrying of past and future and future and past is also lost. And as a consequence of *that* loss, *everything* is lost.

I know that this is true because I have seen it being true.

The moments of my coming in through the barn door drew closer from out of the future, moving toward me, and then they receded into the past, with the result that I was no longer able to go in through the barn door, climb the ladder, crawl along the beam, listen to the pigeons, gaze out into the quiet, pencil-streaked half-darkness of the haymow.

After a time, the barn went unused, fell into disrepair, no longer kept out the weather, then was torn down, even the stones and boulders of its foundation scattered.

Without it, the wedding of time was also lost, past and present no longer existing as one. And, so, more and more came to be lost. The farmhouse disappeared, as did the farm surrounding it, and then the farm's environs, other farms, houses, homesteads, barns, and then the whole town of Northfield a mile or two away, its two colleges and its stores and shops and tree-shaded streets, every bit of it disappearing so that only tall grasses and the gentle undulations of empty prairies remained, visited only by the sun, and the rain, and the winds, but without any other measurement or marking at all, whatsoever, or of any kind.[199]

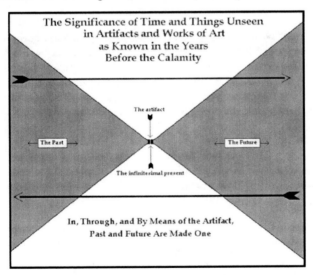

199 An image justly made famous by its rhythm, tone, and color of desolation, loss, and sorrow. [Editor]

3

So it was that in the quiet stillness of a summer afternoon, I *saw* the muscled arms that employed the adzes, or pounded the pegs, or sawed the rafters, built the ladders, hammered in the shingles on the high slope of finished roof. And, from before that, I saw the dinner prepared for the barn raisers, food brought outdoors to a long table in the yard under a tree, a midday meal that was brought out of the house by the same number of women as there were men, and that before the serving of it had been prepared by them, the women rising at dawn, before that climbing the stairs and sleeping in their beds, and, still farther back, farther and farther into the past, growing younger with each [200]

[201]exactly so also with the foundation of fieldstones placed one upon another or side by side, then bonded together with mortar. These stones, some immense, weighing a quarter or half a ton, others the size of bushel baskets, pumpkins, grapefruits, baseballs—all holding within them the heat of the sun that warmed the newly plowed fields where they had been turned up; the sight also of teams dragging rock-sleds piled with mounds of the glacier-rounded stones; and glimpses of paired hands, brown with sun and weather, lowering the stones into place on the growing

double corncrib. Its slats of weathered gray wood had passed through seventy-five summers and winters, so that now the eroded grain of its wood, even in the absence of any other ornament, sign, or indication, expressed the entire accumulation of that span of time: mutely, it held every sound that had been heard in that particular spot throughout three-quarters of a century; eyelessly, it contained every sight and movement that

earthen ramp built up, giving a team and hay-wagon access to the wide double door of the barn and a way onto the hollow-sounding floor of the haymow. The horses would go in onto the w

---

[200] No explanation has been found to explain why so long and unbroken a segment came to be followed immediately by one so *very, very badly* damaged as this. Chemical analyses of ink, paper, and residual oils, while having proven useful elsewhere, have in this instance been fruitless in providing clues to any understanding. The question remains a mystery. [Editor]

[201] Spacing between the fragment's broken pieces is merely conventional and should in no way be taken as suggesting any known or measurable extent of lost material. [Editor]

that from below

                          admitted to be

altogether different in the winter, when

obvious parallel to any work of art, plastic, dramatic, narrative, or even the most pure forms of

           equally so of any musical work

                  lost to very nearly every

         can only wish and hope

                       and even then,

would in all probability never

4 202

not bring up these or any of the other variously related and important matters that I have attempted to describe so far—and that I myself consider essential, basic, and fundamental to any full, durable, or respectable literary life within the university—were it not for the fact that among my colleagues at Actaeon there remain now so few, a tiny remnant that itself is rapidly dwindling due to the erosive powers of age, retirement, exhaustion, anxiety, depression, and, in more cases than I can admit to with any degree of composure, death—very few among my colleagues any longer exist, that is, who might even possibly

not scorn as frivolous, effete, insignificant, or misdirected the profound relationship between narrative (or any artifact) and time;

    2) are in fact themselves any longer *capable* of perceiving, observing, exploring, evaluating, or understanding the profound relationship between narrative (or any artifact) and time.

---

202 Most commentators agree that the section *numbering* is the author's, but there is little certainty as to as to how *much* material is gone. Estimates range from just 12 to 14 sheets (Martin) on up, far more significantly, to as many as 90 to 100 (Scabriani). [Editor]

So absolute is this break in tradition, so far-reaching these new intellectual inabilities, so omnipresent this concomitant inability (and disinclination) to perceive *any* meaning or implication beneath the simplest and most visible surface of whatever may be at any moment under consideration—so epidemic within the academic population is this degenerate, virulent, falsifying *malaise that it becomes the standard by which other attitudes or activities are judged,*[203] and this new standard routinely and rigidly deplores complexity in favor of simplicity, excoriates subtlety in deference to the single-dimensioned, condemns multiplicity in praise of monism and unanimity, takes pride in its own blindness to irony while simultaneously deprecating such meaning or interest as the few remaining others who are capable of doing so might find in it, declares, in keeping with all the aforesaid, that there is in life *no thing that is not "political"*; in science that *there are indeed such elements as evil and good,* the "evil" being all undertakings purely abstract, the "good" being those that remain within the realm of the "practical"; that *no higher achievement can be reached* in the graphic arts than that the products of those arts be either tendentious or "pleasant" ; that the same is true in all the literary or narrative arts except that here the terms denoting success become divided more or less evenly between those having to do with the "informative" and those having to do with the "entertaining."

To such a state as *this* state of depraved banality have declined the magnificent, penetrating, courageous, subtle, towering, powerful, and breathtakingly beautiful achievements in the uses of word, image, symbol, object, and in the arrangements of them among themselves—in *art,* that is to say—of the first two thirds of the 20th Century. It is a devolution so perfect and so extreme, so unequivocal in its embrace of simplification, that the ability to hold more than a single impression or idea in the mind simultaneously, even to hold more than a single impression or idea in the mind in rapid succession, or to hold more than one impression or idea in the mind *in any way whatsoever or at any time whatsoever*—not only have these abilities been lost but *their very absence has become a cause for pride, an absence perversely conceived of as a foundation to build on and a resource for growth,* so that at an institution even with the underlying historic complexity of Actaeon; even at an institution located, as Actaeon is, on grounds so fertile, compacted, dense, and, until now, so demonstrably *fecund* with the many fruits of a world-class

---

[203] "Forgive me this my virtue; / For in the fatness of these pursy times / Virtue itself of vice must pardon beg, / Yea, curb and woo for leave to do him good." (*Hamlet,* III, iv, 172–176) [Author's Note]

city's long social, aesthetic, artistic, intellectual, and political history; even at such a place as Actaeon, the simple replaces the complex, surface replaces depth, singularity replaces multiplicity, and a semester's reading that just 30 years ago[204] might have included Voltaire, Swift, Wordsworth, Dickens, Virginia Woolf, and Samuel Beckett might now include Chinua Achebe, Toni Morrison, and Art Spiegelman; deans who then might have been holders of degrees in history, languages, literature, or philosophy might hold them now in marketing, management, gender studies, language arts, or communication skills. Language itself gives evidence more and more readily of erosion both in expression and in use. Consider a passage drawn at random from my bookshelf—

> "Nonconformity is the basic pre-condition of art, as it is the pre-condition of good thinking and therefore of growth and greatness in a people. The degree of nonconformity present—and tolerated—in a society might be looked upon as a symptom of its state of health"[205]

—and compare its words with those of another, again chosen at random, provided by any of the Deans Glad, Happyhand, Shark, Dank, Rattle, or Slapster, or even of President Penguin-Duck himself:

> Hi, This is President Penguin-Duck. This is going to be my midsummer letter to you, which I usually send, uh, in the mail but we didn't know that we had all your summer addresses so I thought you'd be calling in to get your messages. I just wanted to mention, um, a few things since commencement...

The difference is evident, unequivocal, execrable, and mournfully depressing.[206]

With these and other benchmarks and reference p

eeply

sorry to be placed in a position that makes it incumbent upon me—a sentiment, by the way, almost identical to one expressed recently by

---

[204] Maximillian Shandra's dating system places composition of Fragment V in the Late Ante-Penultimate. A date 30 years earlier would fall in the Late Preliminary, or sometime between, say, 1970 and 1976. [Editor]

[205] Ben Shahn, *The Shape of Content,* Vintage paperback, New York 1957, pp. 100–101. [Author's note]

[206] And, as for the age's few and sad attempts to achieve elevation through words, one may recall Dean Rattle's "The fall trumpet has sounded and with renewed vigor, we begin the new academic cycle." [Author's Note]

Professors Razor, Book, and Poem—to itemize and expose these failings, especially since they are of a kind that may readily be viewed by so

in infinite resources that never were e

uently can't be doubted or denied, that things unseen

nor can it be denied that a life itself is, then, an artifact if lived well: since living well (in the Homeric sense, that is, of living any given life to its best) is a process of shaping the natural by responding to it and simultaneously by preparing for it: which is to say by learning through it and also being changed by it.

And, most vitally important of all, *this is precisely the trait that is absent in the intellectual, literary, and aesthetic life around me, in the world of Actaeon itself, the world of my own colleagues, the very institutional hierarchy of the college and the entire university, from bottom to top:* from the underling so incapable of being changed by experience that he can actually be condescending and insensitive *while declaring himself the opposite;*[207] from the faculty member who can declare himself to be serving the life of the freely inquiring intellect *while at the same moment committing intellectual suicide;*[208] on to President Penguin-Duck himself, who, in his position at the top of the "corporate" pyramid of Actaeon, regularly says, writes, declares, and states things that are in palpable fact plain falsehoods

---

[207] a)"Senator C. Drews asked what incentives are being given to workers to improve their performance: many of the workers have been here for many years, many are good workers, but many are jaded and burnt out. Vice President Packman said he absolutely agrees. One of the first things he did, in this very room, in fact, was to assemble every B & G staff member to tell them that he understands their job because his father was a maintenance worker in a factory for 37 years and was a labor leader, the vice president of his local, and so he understands and appreciates the work they do. However, he told them, he also has expectations of them. He said he hopes to encourage the many good people in B & G and to isolate the bad ones. He is going to reward the good people through an "employee of the month" incentive program: a $100 cash award will be given to the employee of the month. A display with the awardee's picture will be featured on the 5th floor. There will be an employee recognition ceremony each year as well."
b)"In response to Senator Drews' question as to whether the B & G workers have name tags, Vice President Packman said he is buying the B & G staff new uniforms so that it will be very clear to everyone who they are and so they will feel pride in their work: and each worker's name will be on the uniform."

[208] See note 8, p. 3. [Editor].

while celebrating them for the optimistic, wonderful, and uplifting truths that they hold.[209]

In so depraved a situation as this, when charity becomes oppression, when intellectual freedom leads to power-grasping, when lies become truth—the imperative thing, at such a time, is that any who might genuinely wish to make things better, to arrest the rapidly accelerating decline, to assert the values of the truth—any who want to make things better *must above all be skilled at perceiving the incalculably great significance of that which is not there, of that which is absent, of that which is unseen.* For in all of President Penguin-Duck's pronouncements (in which without fail he does *all within his power to make things appear other than they are*); in all the declarations of the intellectual suicides as they attempt to become "administrators"; in all the ignorant professions of the underlings—in all of these cases, *the one single perfectly absent thing is the truth. As a consequence, obviously, the most genuinely and vitally significant thing of all to anyone who wants to make things better is the **absent** thing, the thing **unseen.*** This fact must be understood with perfect clarity and held to with absolute fidelity before anything further can be done to demonstrate to *others* who might want to do what they can to bring about reform that the thing unseen, namely the truth, is far, far greater in importance than the thing seen, which is to say the lie, the falsehood, the empty gesture.

And yet, and yet, and yet—and here is the reason for my malaise, my despair, for my writing this paper in the first place and for my submitting it to *The Hound.* For the most withering fact, as I have tried to show elsewhere and in other ways, is that such an understanding as this is exactly the thing that is itself missing in the great majority of my colleagues, exactly the thing that is itself lacking in those who have any visible role at all in the identity and governance of Actaeon. What's missing—most lamentably, most increasingly, most profoundly—is this: the ability—whether through training, background, experience, or through any other incentive, encouragement, or inquisitiveness of nature—*to see, sense, know, understand, or perceive the significance of absent things.*

---

[209] For a clarification of Larsen's assertion that controllers of the American university in the Middle and Late Ante-Penultimate purveyed falsehoods while declaring themselves to be dealing only in truths, see the "Editor's Foreword" (pp. 1–6), especially those passages describing how "Image" became the university's sole "product," the administrators themselves at one and the same time the producers, controllers, and beneficiaries of it. [Editor]

And how, one must therefore ask, can it conceivably be hoped th [210]

y own life, though
object increasingly to the biographical as
philosophically and logically flawed approach to
art or of study. But *what is made* of something is the sole or true
measure of scholarship, *not* the thing or subject that's studied,
though—in an era now leading up to what I cannot help but fear
will be a serious and generalized intellectual collapse of some as-yet
unknown dimension [211]—most of those around me, in Actaeon
and in the wider world of scholarship and thought, take the very
opposite view, explicitly or implicitly, and cling fiercely to it: *that
the thing or subject that is studied is what matters, not what might be
made of that thing.*

Any who read these words will doubtless be able to provide their
own abundant examples of this phenomenon and of the intellectual
and cultural simplification that, with a demoralizing inevitability,
follows upon it. Within the walls of Actaeon alone, a superfluity of [212]

ducation, what could have happened in my own
elements could (or would) have remained deficient in it, or
have failed to burgeon, grow, and strengthen, most especially the

---

[210] It need hardly be pointed out how disappointing this sudden truncation will be to
readers caught up in the increasingly passionate flow of Larsen's aesthetic, moral, and
political argument—which is an argument not only about the governance and management of Actaeon but also, by extension, of the American Nation. We will never know
what concrete steps Larsen must have proposed—in the lost pages that should have followed here—in the doomed effort to do whatever could be done to help forestall the
Collapse. [Editor]

[211] One of the author's rare expressions of the intensity of his fear for his nation and of
what the future might hold for it. From our own 22nd Century vantage, his words carry
a heavy burden indeed of unintended grief, pathos, and sorrow. No reader of the Papers
can possibly doubt that this passionate author and intellectual, to the very end of his
life—however that end may finally have come about—did anything other than remain
fervently and utterly dedicated to the health and well-being of his beloved nation, even as
his worst fears for and about it became gradually more and more inevitably realized. [Editor]

[212] Unfortunately, the list that must have followed here has been lost. At various points
in "Fragment IV," however ("A Letter to My Younger Colleagues on the Subject of the
Collaborative Destruction from within Academia of the Aesthetic as a Living Force," pp.
127–192) suggestions can be found of Larsen's point that penury in scholarship results
when the *subjects* of scholarship, declared to be significant simply by their *being chosen,*
replace evaluation based on the *results* of study. [Editor]

years of my early start—the understanding for which I am and will
    ays remain, no matter how despairing in other ways, invari-
ably and deeply grateful—the understanding of the enormous and
invaluable significance of
                            ite possible that if things had not
occurred exactly as they did, I might never have been able t
since its origin has enriched and directed me intellectually
own fault but through the faults of the world I live in—it has also
and more alone, and, for that reason, all the more and more deeply
threatened by despair.

And yet the reward has also been great, and equally far-reaching.
Could I possibly have been the recipient later in life of so abundant a
richness if, in sixth grade, outside the north door, I hadn't fallen on
the ice and seen stars; or hadn't, from where I stood at the bottom of
the hill, seen Stephen Koch, at the top, come out of the school door
after his father's death, this experience, like the first, strengthening
extraordinarily my understanding of the principles of up and down,
of the meanings inherent in them, and of the consequent, attendant,
and concomitant reality of all symbols; or if I hadn't been playing
with Tom Rankin on the sidewalk when his father stepped over us
on his way home to lunch, that being the brief but radiant moment
first turning me in the direction of my later and incalculably influential understanding of the nineteenth century, not only of its antiquity
but of its universal significance; or if, shortly after sunup one morning in the summer of 1950, I hadn't come out of the front door of our
farmhouse when I did,[213] to find my father sitting naked in a white
wooden lawnchair on the grass; or if I hadn't been over at Charlie
Frame's house on the afternoon when his father sent him up the field
lane with a .22 rifle and orders to shoot the young mongrel that he'd
concluded to be spoiled, untrainable, and therefore useless; or if I
hadn't gone upstairs to the bathroom in Karen and Ingeborg's house
after dinner on another summer afternoon, in August of 1949, and
hadn't thereby begun for the first time in my life to gain a conscious

---

[213] This and the following two incidents are referred to nowhere else in the Papers,
as though Larsen obviously assumes them to be familiar to the reader. It is generally
agreed that here is yet another loss due to severe damage to the papers. At the same
time, however, both Ting (*Darkness Visible: The Lost Novels of Eric Larsen* [Taipei,
2110] and Poindeft (*Notes on Emptiness: Meanings in the Lost Larsen Volumes* [Calcutta
and Londinium, 2134] make interesting extrapolations about this list of incidents, as
they do with other lists also. See especially Poindeft's brilliant third chapter, devoted
to the subject of absence and silence as tools consciously used by the author ("Notes
on Emptiness / Notes in Emptiness: Absence as Theme in the Larsen Papers," pp.
198–247). [Editor]

grasp of the true nature of space and time and of the relationship between the extraordinary and rev[214]

DANGER!

DO NOT READ THE FOLLOW
DOING SO MAY BE DETRIMENTAL
MENTAL OR EMOTIO[215]

The following pages are provided f
historic and archival record of th
no other purpose. They will, c
whatsoever that may be made
degree of narrative or dramat
does so to an extent *slight*
present in the actual past
unalterable, vacant, barr

Such energy, if any, o
organized chronologica
of structural artistry t
being arranged alpha

---

[215] See note 48, p. 51. [Editor]

FRAGMENT VI —

MY ACADEMIC CAREER[216]

> Quantity is quality.
> —President Morton
> Penguin-Duck

> Our objective must be
> enrollment, enrollment,
> enrollment.
> —President Morton
> Penguin-Duck

XLVIII
Spring 1995
I
Literature 232, From the Enlightenment
to the Twentieth Century
Section 01

---

[216] As mentioned previously, the condition of the papers at this point degenerates into the truly fragmentary, to the point finally of the words' disappearance altogether. This physical state *may* be due simply to the location of the sheets in Larsen's office during the apocalyptic and convulsive months of the Collapse itself. A highly unconventional alternative view, however, has been proposed by Ioannis Korfor Moravec (see note 218, p. 224) and has gained a certain acclaim and notoriety, although few have in fact been soundly persuaded by it, it being considered generally an irresponsibly radical approach to Larsen studies. [Editor]

Almonte, Alex
Bagonyi, Gregg

Brewster, Ralph
Brown, Verley
Carrera, Miguel

Davis, Chantel
Davis, William

Gibbons, Nicole
Gonzalez, Elizabeth
Gonzalez, Gilbert

Harrow, Tracy
Horn, Helen
Jones, Kevin

La Torre, Harry
Meszaros, Stephanie

Mitchell, Kimberly
Morales, Carlos

Perez, Lanette
Perez, Mike

Pisarczyk, Edyta
Rahmana, Shafeena
Rivera, Marilyn

Sable, Ruth
Sahdala, Ambiorix
Stokely, Jonathan

Woodbyne, Maurice
Yusufi, Davar

2
Literature 232, From the Enlightenment to the Twentieth Century
Section 02

Anderson, Mickaco
Andrini, Deanna
Beekram, Anita

Carter, Debbie
Charles, Victgor
Darby, Dan
Delarosa, Jasmin

Dennedy, James
Diorio, Vincent
Esposito, Angelina

Gutierrrez, Johannaw
Hall, Clifton

Jones, Marla

Lynn, Kandia

Mc Walters, Joseph

Ogunade, Tamara
O' Kafer, Emeka
Owens, Veronica

Petrov, Aleksey

Rozier, Christopher
Sallemi, Ralph

Siguencia, Audi

Toro, Grace
Viera, Elizabeth
Winberly, Sheila

Zepf, Darin

3
Literature 232, From the Enlightenment to the Twentieth Century
Section 05

Antoine, Youseline

Boodhoo, Joanne

Doyle, Michael
Florio, Chris
Freedell, Karen

Guastella, Joan

Herrman, Christoher
Hughes, Lisa

Jusino, Alexix

Koutouratsas, Nick

Lopez, Kevin
Magliacano, Anthony

O' Rourke, Tara
Patton, Ronda

Presume, Thierry
Rawls, Shanell

Ring, Brian

Simpson, Nicole
Smith, Frank

Tardi, Michael
Teel, Taneka
Vazquez, Jose

Yusuf, Olalekan

XLIX
Fall 1995
I
English 101, College Composition
Section 08

Abdel-Nour, Mary
Fernandez, Melody

Johnson, Tim
Kaufmann, Susan
Lyons, Sabrina

Marrero, Michele

Recalde, Jacqueline

Reed, Jasmine
Revanales, Janelle
Reyes, Christina

Shipsey, Lauren

Simmons, Christopher
Wolfersberger, Lauren

2
Literature 231, The Ancient and Medieval Worlds
Section 01

Adefioye, Belinda

Bosch, Hans
Burke, Patrick
Calderon, Marilyn

Dinh, Thai
Edery, Narkis

Frick, Henry

Garcia, Aldo
Garcia, Sugel
Gavney, Shannon

Gray, Benjamin
Guarana, Vanessa

Lutchmansingh, David
Mc Cue, Colleen

Nolan, James

Rosario, Victor
Santiago, Lisette

Summers, Karl
Szall, Barbara

Zavala, Joe

3
Literature 231, The Ancient and Medieval Worlds
Section 02

Asencio, Stacy
Bell, James
Bernard, Regina
Betancourt, Brian
Briu, Yolanda

Coleman, Shermelle
Colon, Myrna

Dennedy, James
Edmonds, Garfield

Gosling, Carolin
Herrera, Ventura

Lagares, Cynthia
Louvado, Ivo

Mitchell, Salalhadine

Ogunade, Tamara
Pena, Anthony

Peralta, Omar

Regalado, Ana
Riso, Edward

Rivera, Selenia

Telesco, Christina
Thompson, Sacheen

Anantavara, Charles

Ceron, Gladys
Clee, Crystal
Collins, Yolanda

Galanpena, Frances
Garael, Raul
Garvey, Wendy

Harper, Lawrence
Hudspeth, William
Hwee, Edmund

Jurado, John
Kemp, Royevette

Lisoski, Tomas
Louissant, Madeline

Martin, Corina
Nisi, Anthony

Owen, Stephen
Parades, Mirna

Robertson, Jean
Rosado, Carmen

Shah, Rashid
Shapiro, Anna

Wright, Andrea
Zuleta, Andy

XLIX
Spring 1996
I
**Literature 232, From the Enlightenment
to the Twentieth Century
Section 01**

Arslani, Naim

Gosling, Caroline

Burke, Patrick
Calderon, Marilyn
Castillo, Omar

Daniels, Nathaniel
Daouaou, Abdelilah

Joubert, Januarie

Lovell, Frederick
Mc Cue, Colleen

Peralta, Omar

Riso, Edward

Sheikh, Mohsin
Smith, Kisha
Suppa, Christina
Telesco, Christina

2
**Literature 232, From the Enlightenment to the Twentieth
Century
Section 02**

Abreu, David
Adefioye, Belinda

Baldera, Pilar

Garrison, Melissa

Graham, Bobbie

Miladinov, Marija
Ortiz, Luis

Byrne, George
Carlucci, Jean
Clarke, Cleveland

Horowitz, Kenneth

Sesso, Lawrence

Smith, Farah
Squires, Ronald

Crowley, Daniel
Duarte, Giselle

3
Literature 232, From the Enlightenment
to the Twentieth Century
Section 02

Banarsi, Monica

Harper, Lawrence

Shapiro, Anna

Hudspeth, William

Sorg, Gregory
Strubbe, Maureen

Briu, Yolanda
Browning, Monique

Lisoski, Thomas

Tsekouras, Fay
Usera, Jessica
Velez, Annette

Digiambattista, Joseph

Paredes, Mirna

Garvey, Wendy

Setten, Carol

L
Fall 1996
I
Literature 232, From the Enlightenment
to the Twentieth Century
Section 01

Ault, Colette

Galvin, Christopher

Peguero, Janil
Perjatel, Robert

Prentis, Cheryle
Kyriakides, Michael
Lutchmansingh, David

Real, George

Cherizard, Sarah

Custodio, Cindy
Dada, Maureen

Moutopoulos, Jimmy

Vargas, Dayanara
West, Felicia

2
Literature 232, From the Enlightenment
to the Twentieth Century
Section 02

Cabrera, Ramon	Lugo, Christina	Pierri, Rocco
Clarke, Maurice		
		Smigielska, Katarzyna
Daniels, Nathaniel	Myung, Ji Man	Toro, Grace
	Ortega, Jessica	
		Zavala, James
	Pierre-Francois, Vlad	Zea, Veronica

3
Literature 231, The Ancient and Medieval Worlds
Section 07

Chiluiza, John		Pecorella, Kevin
	Kosteas, Panagiotes	
Cummings, Dalila		
	Maher, Christopher	Smith, Laneeka
Fountoulakis, Georgios	Navarro, Catherine	
		Zagorodnyuk, Lada
	Nurse, Roshelle	Zouhbi, Faisal

4
Literature 231, The Ancient and Medieval Worlds [217, 218]

Alleyne, Johan	Haynes, Loisa	
		Moran, Kendre
		Moylan, Mary
	Kowalski, Brian	
Bobel, Susan		
	Loizou, Louis	Sheard, Paige
Collado, David		Simion, Nicolae
Dillane, Stephen	Mitchell, Natasha	

[217] "Language is demoted to the status of an event. Something takes place in time, a voice speaking which points to the before and to what comes after an utterance: silence. Silence, then, is both the precondition of speech and the result or aim of properly directed speech. On this model, the artist's activity is the creating or establishing of silence; the efficacious artwork leaves silence in its wake. Silence, administered by the artist, is part of a program of perceptual and cultural therapy, often on the model of shock therapy rather than of persuasion. Even if the artist's medium is words, he can share in this task: language can be employed to check language, to express muteness. Mallarmé thought it was the job of poetry, using words, to clean up our word-clogged reality—by creating silences around things. Art must mount a full-scale attack on language itself, by means of language and its surrogates, on behalf of the standard of silence." (Susan Sontag, *Styles of Radical Will* [New York, 1966], p. 23) [Author's Note]

[218] Here, then, in footnote 217, is the famous citation that has in all probability caused as much debate, disagreement, and commentary in and of itself as any other single point or

LI
Spring 1997
1
Literature 231, The Ancient and Medieval Worlds
Section 01

Antonin, Joann	Gomez, Jini	
		Rivera, Marilyn
		Krosario, Malanie
Coker, Eugenia	Lebowitz, Karala	
Conroy, Michael		
	Maldonado, Ismael	Waszczuk, Wieslan
Donnelly, Stephen		
	Millstein, Shari	Xenakis, Helen

moment in the entire body of the Larsen papers. So great a degree of attention has come about as a result not only of the citation's own puzzling content but as a result also of Larsen's extraordinary—and possibly, as some argue, arbitrary—choice of placement for it. Indeed, to the radical as well as to the conservative reader, the passage can seem almost mystically to contain messages within messages, and secrets within secrets. The paradoxic element is of course obvious, this being the element that so powerfully seized the literary imagination of Ioannis Moravec in his widely known if not now also notorious book-length interpretation (*Alms for Oblivion: The Struggle for Silence and Meaning in a World of Nothingness and Noise, a Literary Study of the Larsen Papers* [Beijing, History House, 2109]). The paradoxical conceit that the artist's "language can be used to... express muteness" leads Moravec to contend that creating muteness is *precisely what Larsen set out to do from the very beginning* in the awesomely ambitious "Fragment VI." Moravec goes so far, in fact, as to suggest that the increasingly ravaged condition of the sheets throughout the fragment *may* be not solely the result of natural cataclysm, as has always been thought, but the result, if only in part, *of the author's own shaping hand*. In short, Moravec takes up Wei's idea that what Larsen has done is simultaneously "kill" the words as he "uses" them, metamorphosing them into "unliving" things that, once "dead," are capable only of "silence." Moravec takes the idea one step further, however, extending it into the realms of the psychological and biographical: Larsen's "killing" of the words, he argues, is the symbolic equivalent of his actually *murdering* his students. So it is that only by this loathsome, mad, driven, depraved, and pitiable means are silence and muteness brought into existence. At the end, we are left not with nothing but with *more* than nothing: we are left, instead, with an awareness, hideously, of a "full void." Language, says Sontag, "points to the before and to what comes after an utterance," and so the unliving silence that Larsen has assiduously created points back to what went before—namely, to the life that he has now destroyed. He, reduced slowly to madness and ruin by the fraud, emptiness, and desolation of the intellectual life at Actaeon ("false, inane, ignoble, weightless"), has been driven to the worst of all conceivable crimes. After this, only silence is left, or only silence and that one worse thing: *the silent echo.* Each thing has its function. The emptiness reveals the "fruits" of the crime. The silence bespeaks the perpetrator's (the creator's) cry of madness and sorrow. The process of falsehood, then degradation, then ruin, then *nothing*: only this can be the inevitable and tragic cycle controlling both institutions and nations once they become accustomed to feeding only on the blood of their own children, or begin to mistake the living of a lie for the living of a truth. Moravec's contention that "Fragment VI" is in effect nothing more nor less than a suicide letter—for man and conceivably for nation—has, like the rest of his critical thinking, perhaps attracted more attention than it has brought about agreement. None, however, can dispute the intensity of Moravec's convictions, the consistency of his purpose, or the effort he has made to see as deeply as may be humanly possible into the Larsen papers. [Editor]

2
Literature 231, The Ancient and Medieval Worlds
Section 02

Beekram, Anita	Gabryelski, Jacek	
		Pereira, Susana
Brown, Linata	Harrison, Lance	
		Sambula, Anthony
Csuha, David		Sukhu, Devindra
		Terrell, Chanel
	Metanovic, Fadila	
Frazer, Natasha		Zea, Veronica

3
Literature 231, The Ancient and Medieval Worlds
Section 09

Barnswell, Pearl	Dorsaint, Marjorie	Pierre-Toussaint, Lynd
	Francois, Marc	
Cheung, David		Sands, Danielle
Coello, David		Sevastyanov, Vladimir
	Nieves, Elizabeth	Welwolo, Teaminlee
Daring, Natacha		

LII
Fall 1997
1
Literature 231, The Ancient and Medieval Worlds
Section 02

Acosta, Cindy		
	Hopkins, Adrian	
Basani, John		
		Shoulders, Lasheena
		Shtern, Natalie
	Mc Clinton, Jennifer	
	Morales, Magaly	
Francis, Noreka		Texler, Misty
	Pavon, Jessica	Wojtach, Susan

Literature 231, The Ancient and Medieval Worlds
Section 04

Balcom, Garth	Jerome, Alain Johnson, David	Parson, Latoya
Disclafani, Leonaardo	Lopez, Digna Lopez, Ruth	Sandoval, Judelka
Galasso, Daniel	Matviv, Vitaly	Tully, Mairead

LIII
Spring 1998
I
Literature 232, From the Enlightenment to the Twentieth Century
Section 01

Asante, Sidney	Jerome, Anita	Rivera, Vivien Roman, Jenny
Chiofolo, Suzanne	Marmol, Jakelin Mrzec, Justyna	
Dinegar, Allan	Ng, Raymond	Tsouros, Stephen Tully, Mairead

2
Literature 232, From the Enlightenment to the Twentieth Century
Section 02

Bogdanovic, Dzevshire		
	Kyriakides, Michael Lekhram, Ahalia	Sandoval, Judelka
Drago, Michele		Sugrim, Sunita
	Pereira, Susana	
Holsten, Gary		Zarzoukis, Nick

LIV
Fall 1998
1
Literature 230, The Ancient World
Section 01

Bogan, Monique

       Liautaud, Mc Kensie

       Maloo, Naresh   Song, Edward

Charles, Fitz

       Wolfe, Timothy

2
Literature 230, The Ancient World
Section 02

Ba   La
Bodhnara   ha   Guzman, Maria   Mc
Boyd,

Cazares, Fernando   Jackson, Rashida   Negron, Alexis

       Ju   Ramos, Eug

    Samantha   Stephe
Encarnacion, Vanessa   Grecory
Fern

3
Literature 230, The Ancient World
Section 07

Czwarno, Mon   Marmolejos   River
                        Peter

       Mei,

LV
Spring 1999
1
Literature 232, The Enlightenment through the 20th Century
Section 01

Ad   Jan
                        Kearns

                        Lo
Chan, Wai

                        Maloo, N
                                                vin
                        Miller, Courtney   Sawh, G
Dvoryanchikov, Al

Guzman
     , Falffi   ez, Olmedo
                        Parks,

2
Literature 232, The Enlightenment through the 20th Century
Section 02

Bernier, Judy   ace   Alexis
                        son, Rohane
                        Intravaia   Jessica
        Kazeela   Perez,

    erard   Majeski,
            ette   , Michelle

                        nald

LVI
Fall 1999
1
Literature 230, The Ancient World
Section 01

Alham   Mul

Bernier, Judy

                        Mehmedagi
Cardus, Vict   Seczak

                        Edwidge   aren
                                        Thomas,

Flood,

Literature 230, The Ancient World
Section 02

Hernandez, Esther   Raebu

Betan
          Rochelle   Kremer, Kelly
Cesar,
                                          , Ralph
                              Sheoch

                              Vil
                              Vines

3

Literature 230, The Ancient World
Section 09

                                          Ragoona

Cetoute,
                              An
     Wojc
                                              K

Done
                    asovich
                                   Usera, Jam

Literature 230, The Ancient World
Section 13

Abreu, Maria
Alexander, Denise
Almonte, Verlin   Libassi,

gadai

no
                    sz
                    scu
Formosa,
                    Oh,   Lesley

LVII
Spring 2000

1
Literature 231, The Middle Ages and Renaissance
Section 01

R

P

Eramo,   Mc

, R   juk,

V

2
Literature 231, The Middle Ages and Renaissance
Section 02

Gomez,

Promyslovskaya,

Rezac, Elissa

olande
Freiberg,   Mc

Zheng,

3
Literature 231, The Middle Ages and Renaissance
Section 08

Temek

z, Diana   Jamie

Coo
va,

LVIII
Fall 2000

1

Literature 232, The Enlightenment through the 20th Century
Section 01

Or
D   Pulawska
Azar'   Ko

ovich,
Crotti,

2

Literature 232, The Enlightenment through the 20th Century
Section 02

By   Deidra

Li,

a, Frank
Orl
Ryan

3

Literature 232, The Enlightenment through the 20th Century
Section 12

me   Kim

P

GiaL

fanski, El

Bartoli

lakshan

mara

J

LIX
Spring 2001
1
Literature 231, The Middle Ages and Renaissance
Section 01

c

2
Literature 231, The Middle Ages and Renaissance
Section 02

3
Literature 231, The Middle A
Sectio

Literature 231,

THE "DIARY"

(Part Three)

iii

My Life in Education:
What I Learned from Thirty-Five Years
in the
University of New York (UNY):
by
Eric Larsen, B.A., M.A., Ph.D.,
Professor of English
The Actaeon College of Institutional Analysis and Social Control,
The University of New York (UNY)
New York, New York
U.S.A.

6/21/06 3:14 AM (Mon.):
The classrooms at Actaeon settled down into climatic cycles of approximately half a decade each, switching from arctic to tropical and back again. Without doubt, the tropical was the more difficult for me personally, although from the student point of view there was little difference between the two: both were equally unendurable and equally detrimental to learning, the only difference being that one caused withdrawal and then sleep (the tropical), while the other caused hostility first and *then* the waiting arms of Morpheus.

6/21/06 3:34 AM (Mon.):
My moment of truth; the single instant from which so much else stopped flowing; the day the idea came to me of no longer having

Sasha Brearly in the classroom—the start of my end, in other words, took place, not surprisingly, near the end of a tropical cycle.

The hot cycles were much more difficult for me primarily because of dehydration. During the arctic cycles, I was able to keep warm simply through the manifold and unceasing physical exertions of my work. But it was another matter when the temperature in the rooms

6/22/06 8:18 AM (Tue.):

hovered between 88 and 96 degrees. Then, the exertions necessary for the highly active and—I believed and hoped—amusing presentations that I insisted upon (as I put all my powers into making Homer, Dante, Aeschylus, Sophocles, Chaucer, Swift, Shakespeare, Austen, Dickens, Hardy, G. Eliot, V. Woolf, or S. Beckett interesting *to* the students while also trying to elicit felt and thoughtful responses *from* the students) would cause me to sweat heavily from the first moment of the day onward, my shirt quickly becoming soaked through, likewise my handkerchief (which I used not for my nose but solely for mopping my face and brow), so that by only midday, after two classes and with two more to go, I had generally reached already a fairly advanced state of dehydration, a condition causing decreased blood levels of salt, potassium, and sugar, deficiencies in turn bringing on increased muscle spasm (tic), irregularity of heart (palpitation), non-topical anxiety (like that before heart attack), dizziness (vertigo), sense of dissociation and unreality (lightness and floating), and, most debilitating of all, subtle diminishment (in part from simple exhaustion due to the additional and incessant need for screaming) in mind-body coordination, a crucial deficit causing an infinitesimal impairment of the all-important split-second timing that enables one, if one is sufficiently gifted in this and in other ways as well, to keep control over forty-five restless, bored, irritable, fitful, unread, unmotivated, sleepy, dim, aggressive, hostile, insolent, outspoken, begrudging, anti-educated, disdainful, antagonistic students who have been jam-packed for tuition-collecting and illusion-maintaining purposes into an overheated, windowless, noise-saturated room more suitable for holding twenty-five if even that many.

In defense of President Penguin-Duck, let me add, lest I seem to be blaming *him* for various aspects of what has been my *own* daily life for decades at Actaeon, there is something important I must mention at this point. I later came to understand that due to President Penguin-Duck's taking upon his own shoulders the incalculably demanding administrative task of being sole commanding officer in charge of *making things appear other than they are*—I came to understand (and it is understandable), that due to the obligations and responsibilities of so important a job, President Penguin-Duck in fact, throughout his tenure, knew *very nearly nothing whatsoever of the truly deplorable and even inhumane conditions in the Actaeon classrooms,* so that, of course, he therefore must not and can not *in any way be considered responsible for them.*[219]

I often consider how differently things might have turned out if there had only been a ventilating system in the Actaeon latrines, a freedom from bullets there, a bit of fresh air: how if that had been the case it would no longer have been necessary for me to protect my health and life by avoidance of those vile and dangerous places. Then, of course, I could have drunk normally, could have avoided dehydration, could have maintained my all-important split-second timing—and could perhaps even have kept the strength and will to guard, gird, and blind myself against my calamitous moment of truth, *could have turned away from it instead of embracing it*—and thus, having had the strength to remain blind, could have avoided becoming what I have become now, a man destroyed by the simple truth, brought to ruin, lost forever.

6/22/06 9:13 AM (Tue.):

As time ground on, President Penguin-Duck continued—as he does, so far as I could possibly know,[220] to this very day—in his selfless efforts to *make the world at large perceive things at Actaeon as other than they are.*

One of the essential aspects of President Penguin-Duck's genius was his clear perception that big things command greater awe than small things. As a result of this gifted, rare, and extraordinary insight, one of the first things he did as soon as funds became available was to set out on a program of enlarging and expanding his office.

The great success of this undertaking was obvious to all from the beginning.

Even before the funds were known to be available, the President appointed a site development committee and, when its report was presented to him a year later, he followed it in every detail. As the committee advised, he chose to locate his new and bigger office not

---

219 The President is in fact recorded as having once said, in an open meeting called by The Quality of Life Committee, that he refused to "become President of Bathrooms," showing then as ever that his sole, true, and passionate dedication was to the maintaining of the dignity, integrity, and growth of education only on the highest and most meaningful levels. [Author's Note]

220 One of the more clear hints that Larsen, though ostensibly composing his "retirement" speech, is in fact no longer a part of Actaeon at all. Why he might wish us to think he were is one of the most interesting questions taken up, albeit in passing, by Ioannis Moravec in his *Alms for Oblivion: The Struggle for Silence and Meaning in a World of Nothingness and Noise, a Literary Study of the Larsen Papers* (Beijing, History House, 2009). [Editor]

in the building where I and Drs. Tic, Colon, Rash, Book, and Poem had offices and met classes, but in the larger building instead, which became known shortly thereafter as Presidential Hall. He situated the office on the top floor, where, from a row of tall windows along its front wall, one could look down and across the street onto the flat tar roof of our own building, crowded with the enormous, riveted, sheet-metaled, louvered, multi-valved, tank-topped, steam-emitting and engine-driven machines whose function was the forcing, over alternate, carefully monitored half-decades, of arctic or tropical air into the windowless and insufferable rooms below.

Fittingly enough, our own building came to be known as Non-Presidential Hall. The President's

6/23/06 1:32 AM (Wed.):

office itself occupied the whole wing it was situated in. It was indeed quite impossible for its capaciousness not to inspire awe: if one sat behind President Penguin-Duck's great desk itself, against the north wall, and chose to converse with a person, say, in a chair near the south wall, it would be impossible to do so in a normal voice at normal conversational volume. The entire area, vast and deeply carpeted, was scattered with davenports, sofas, easy chairs, tables, and lamps. On the far side from President Penguin-Duck's desk was an enormous mahogany conference table that, as desire and occasion determined, could be used either for meetings or for banquets. Near it, a section of paneled wall could be opened by means of a secret latch to expose a full bar, and through a doorway near the head of the table was President Penguin-Duck's private kitchen. A cook and bar keeper were available to the President at all times, and a full complement of chef, kitchen workers, wine stewards, and waiters remained permanently on call to plan and present the grandest of events even on the shortest of notice.

Through another door nearby, sometimes open and sometimes closed, was the office of President Penguin-Duck's executive assistant, whose staff members themselves were situated in a string of other offices that opened off hers, growing smaller and smaller the farther removed they were from the President, much like the strings of eggs inside pullets as they neared readiness to begin their lives as layers. [221]

The approach to President Penguin-Duck's office was arranged in

---

[221] In 1952, as a young boy on my parents' farm in Minnesota, when a pullet was one day inadvertently run over by a wagon wheel, I saw this precise and lovely phenomenon: a string, as it were, of a dozen pearls, the largest an egg the size of a thumbnail, the smallest, while also white, little larger than the head of a pin. [Author's Note]

such a way as to make it extremely impressive. After taking an elevator to the top floor, walking to the appropriate wing, and turning in the appropriate direction, one made one's way down a wide corridor with doors on either side opening into offices that grew larger the nearer they were to the Presidential terminus. After passing the last of these offices, one went through double doors into an ante-room containing coffee tables and upholstered chairs, these presumably for the comfort of those waiting long periods for Presidential audiences. This room was occupied permanently by four people behind four desks placed near the entry. Leaving this ante room, one continued through a second set of double doors to a second ante-room accoutered in the same way as the first but presided over by only two people instead of four. Penultimately, a third set of double doors brought one into a third ante-room that, larger than either of the previous two, was presided over by a single person seated behind a single desk. A visitor was then at last—or might be—summoned into the presence of President Penguin-Duck himself: whereby, if that august moment did take place, the supplicant passed through an ultimate set of double doors, through a final dark-paneled entryway, and into the airy expanse of the great room itself, where President Penguin-Duck would be visible, a distance away, off to your left, behind his desk against the north wall, with a telephone pressed to his ear.

6/23/06 2:59 AM (Wed.):

My weight continued to drop through the long middle years. I know now, although my understanding of it came too late to do much good, that I should have taken my weight loss far more seriously than I did, since, as I now know, it was a sign of greatly diminishing strength both physical *and* emotional. I know also that in response—in imitation of my far more adaptable colleagues—what I really ought to have done was take the simple and extremely effective measure of no longer trying to do my job well.

As always, however, other instincts and forces pushed me to work only harder to compensate for my weight loss, to expend *more* energy, try yet *new* ways to ignite and captivate my students' interests and abilities, to give them the important chance at intellectual growth that I so much wanted them to have and considered it my job to provide.

Yet even so I *should* have understood a different truth: that all of it was purely quixotic. Pointless. Doomed. Every last bit of it.

In short, I was losing ground. I, too, was beginning to disappear. Like my other narrowing colleagues, the few of them left, I was, slowly but surely, becoming in-

6/24/06 5:59 AM (Thu.):

visible.

Among the wideners, in the meantime, there appeared not the smallest hint of exhaustion or failure: if anything, the opposite was true. The wideners, to a one, continued to fatten. Inexplicably, they appeared to be filled with energy. Most perplexing of all, they moved with a quickness, spoke with an animation, consorted, gathered, and conversed with one another in lighthearted and even jocular ways that made it appear (an outlandish, preposterous, absurd idea to a thinking person) *that every one last one of them was happy.*

Their students, too, had about them an inexplicable air of contentedness and ease. The wideners' students emerged from classrooms with languid smiles on their faces, often chattering glibly among themselves, and by the half-dozens they gathered at the front of the rooms after class to talk with their placid, unruffled, increasingly hefty instructors. At examination time, equally amazing, there appeared to be among them no fear, anxiety, or (as with *my* students) hostile posturings, eye-rollings, or outright expressions of vindictiveness, sullenness, or anger.

I can surmise that one of the chief causes of so vivid a contrast was the difference between the wideners' grading policies and my own. *Their* students' grades moved inexorably and steadily (albeit sometimes slowly) upward, while mine, *no matter how hard I tried* to make them do so, did nothing of the sort. If anything, they fell.

6/24/06 6:03 AM (Thu.):

I thought long and hard about these and other matters, and I came to a conclusion that shocked me briefly.

It was impossible not to conclude that my widening colleagues, by making the important decision *no longer to think,* had joined in the enormous task that had rested previously on President Penguin-Duck's shoulders alone—the task of *making absolutely certain that things at Actaeon appeared other than they were.*

The wideners, that is to say, were no longer faculty members, for in actuality *they had become administrators.*

What else if not that precise metamorphosis could have resulted in their appearance of being so entirely relieved from the heavy, unrelenting, Sisyphean burden of maintaining a fidelity to the truth, the very burden that was causing me and the few remaining narrowers left at Actaeon to grow nearer and nearer to complete disappearance with each passing year?

And what else if not that precise metamorphosis could have resulted in their appearance of *actually being happy?* What else if not that precise metamorphosis could explain their students' otherwise inexplicable impressions of contented casualness, irresponsibility, and ease? And what else if not that precise metamorphosis could explain President Penguin-Duck's *tacit approval* of the wideners, his *contentment with* them and *his reaching out*, as he had begun doing more and more, to *draw them more actively* into college affairs (although of course without ever saying even the least word about any such policy or sympathies. The groundwork for final calamity, after all,[222] had, even by this time, not been firmly enough laid to make it politic for someone with the vast responsibilities of President Penguin-Duck to reveal his professional dedication to the untruth openly and unabashedly. For the time being, a polite but firmly maintained deceit still remained necessary.)?

6/24/06 6:22 AM (Thu):

The truth? Shall we have the truth? The truth is that some of my own students were kind, sweet, considerate, well-intended, and docile. Some of my own students showed interest. Some of my students came up to the front after class. And some of my students—in one very special year, I remember, there were three—had grades that went up instead of nowhere, or down.

One of my own students also, once, I remember, raised a hand.

6/24/06 8:27 AM (Thu.):

But by this time I was already badly worn down, albeit not conscious of the full extent of the damage.

So much simpler it would have been, so healthy and drug-free a way to ease the intolerable pressure. That is, *simply to stop thinking any longer.* But without that simple and elementary step, I now understand clearly, no easing could be possible.

How else could it be true of the broadeners that they remained so calm in class? What other cause could there be for their appearance of speaking so effortlessly, quietly, and casually in their fetid, noise-tormented rooms?

Unless this:

Unless the inner truth, the deeper truth, the truth of truths, was *that they needed no sounds anyhow.*

Unless the truth of truths, that is, was *that there was nothing that needed saying by them.*

Unless the wideners in fact were *not trying to change anything, to do anything, to "teach" anything.*

Unless, that is, the wideners had granted (whether knowing or not

---

222 On this despondent note, see again the "Chronology" (Appendix, p. 303). [Editor]

knowing that they had done so) *that they and their students already knew exactly the same amount about exactly all the same things believed by either of them to be in any way whatsoever significant or important,* thereby leaving both parties, by definition *absolutely the same as one another, equals in every way, and therefore free to do nothing more in the classrooms other than be amiable, complimentary, pleasant, and kind to one another, the relationship, in short, of colleagues.*

Impossible. It could not be possible.

And yet it was.

It was only too true.

Being nice had replaced teaching.

Personality and good intentions had replaced content.

The job of professor, no longer any different from President Penguin-Duck's job, had become *the job of making things appear other than they are. It had become the job of making it clear that students and professors were the same.*

•

And yet here again, in this as in so many other matters, I was unable to join my broadening colleagues, so manifold and deeply rooted were my weaknesses and failures. Unlike the wideners, I still found it obvious that I knew a great deal about something—my field of study, specifically—about which my students knew very little if anything at all. And consequently (so unable was I, unlike the wideners, to embrace new ideas) I continued finding it perfectly reasonable that my position as professor existed *for the purpose of making evident to my students*—do with it as they may—some part of what I *did* know about my field of study.

There was for me, therefore, no possibility of turning over my professional energies to the genial and effortless task simply of being nice. There was for me no possibility of dedicating myself simply to being casual, relaxed, and egalitarian—*of portraying myself as and proving myself to be the very same in every way as my students.*

No. For me, the point of the undertaking, a towering part of the very truth of the life I had chosen, was the precise opposite of egalitarian: it was the rudimentary assumption: *that my students and I were essentially different from one another and that this difference explained why they were the students and I was the professor.*

For someone like me, then, insufficiently trained, insufficiently adaptable, insufficiently flexible to be able to abandon this elementary idea of *essential difference*—to someone like me, therefore, the roar of the air ducts remained intrusive, disruptive, deafening. To someone like me, therefore, the necessity for screaming remained dehumanizing and draining. For someone like me, therefore, the obligation to do battle with the heat remained demoralizing and ruinous as I sweated more heavily than ever, ran to my office between classes (glancing, for safety's sake, one way and then the other before slipping in the door) to change my shirts, underwear, and socks as I continued to avoid the latrines, grow dehydrated, suffer dizziness and tics and, most alarmingly, endure a new difficulty simply in maintaining a sense of comfortable orientation inside whatever it was—call it the world around me—that until this point in my life I had, by and large, always been perfectly able to accept as "reality" but was now no longer certain of my ability to go on doing so.

•

All I wanted was this: for my students to have the experience of learning things they didn't know, the experience of understanding things they didn't understand.

Which of these came first, I asked them: your Achilles tendon or the story of Achilles? Here's how to find out. Feel your Achilles tendon. Bend down, pinch your fingers around it, feel the way your thumb and the tip of your first finger almost meet, then tell me what seem the most significant qualities of it *(So small! So vulnerable!).* Now: explain why the story of Achilles came into existence.

Who created the story of Thetis dipping Achilles into the river Styx, I ask, and they are sullen; several of them leave the room, each allowing the door to slam shut as they go. They return some time later (the same hour? semester? year? life?), one after another, allowing the door to slam again. *Please don't let the door slam when you enter or leave, especially if class is already in session.* How many times had I said this? I am asking, now, why Dante would lie, or seem to lie, or rewrite history, or seem to rewrite history.

Look at Canto II, lines 16 through 24: Dante says that Aeneas founded Rome not because it was *destined to be Rome and Roman but because it was destined to be the seat of the papacy*; and *that* was Christian-god's reason (because Aeneas was founding the Papacy) for treating the Trojan with such privilege as he did:

> But if the Adversary of all Evil
>   weighing his [Aeneas'] consequence and who and what
>   should issue from him, treated him so well—
> That cannot seem unfitting to thinking men,
>   since he was chosen father of Mother Rome
>   and of her Empire by God's will and token.
> Both, to speak strictly, were founded and foreknown

as the established Seat of Holiness
for the successors of Great Peter's throne.
(trans. John Ciardi)

But, wait, when did Troy fall? When did Aeneas sail? If Troy fell and Aeneas sailed *in 1184 BC,* what gods or god was in charge of these events? Virgil himself, in 19 BC, in the *Aeneid,* says it was Jove. So now, thirteen centuries later, in 1320 AD, when Dante sacks Jove and replaces him with Christian-god ("the Adversary of all Evil"), what does that do to Virgil's much older poem, the *Aeneid?* What "truth" about it is Dante simply and willfully changing? And why does the Virgil who appears in Dante's *Inferno* seem to think that this simple and willful change is a perfectly all right thing to do?

Outside the door, a young woman is eating pizza. She holds her slice on a near-level with her mouth, dips her head forward to get a bite, then stands looking into the room through the glass as she chews. After a time, she pushes the door open with a foot, comes in, lets the door slam behind her, takes a seat, leans forward to look for pencil, paper, or book in a knapsack on the floor. As she does this, the melted cheese and toppings slide off the crust of the pizza onto a floor littered already with paper plates, cups, tissues, and napkins, and with glass bottles and aluminum soda cans. As always, the floor is sticky in puddle-sized areas where fruit juices and sugar-drinks have been spilled. How recently each spill took place can be determined by the degree of dark coloring it has acquired. Transparent when fresh, any spill of a certain age will have turned black (and less sticky), showing itself as a dirt-map.

Or consider Wordsworth (when do I say this? in what semester? year? decade?). Among the dirt-maps, in the heat and roaring noise, amid the smells of ketchup, French fries, and pizza, I read:

> "Though inland far we be,
> Our Souls have sight of that immortal sea
> Which brought us hither"

Is there a physical, real-life origin for the metaphor? Here's something to do to help find out. An exercise. Cup your hands over one ear. Listen carefully. Identify what you hear. With that identification in mind, name what the 'immortal sea' is that Wordsworth refers to. There's an *interior* 'immortal sea' and an *external* 'immortal sea.' Name what each is.

Few, or none, or some do cup their hands and listen. Of the forty-five students in the room, seven have read the assignment. Nine are asleep. Five are eating. Four are leaving the room, slamming the door successively. Three others are returning, also slamming the door in succession. Do I exaggerate? Do I dare to eat a peach? *The noise, the noise, the noise, the noise, and, for reasons unknown...*

Frequently, we read *Hamlet:* Why doesn't Hamlet simply kill the king? Why not just get it over with? The prince has opportunity, motive, and means. Claudius is known by the audience to be guilty by III, iii (*"O, my offense is rank, it smells to heaven"*), after the play-within-the-play. But Hamlet doesn't, doesn't again, and again doesn't kill Claudius. Coward? No ambition? Religious compunction? Defeat each of these arguments with evidence from the text.

Hamlet's delay in taking vengeance must be due to something *more important* than cowardice, lack of ambition, or religious compunction—unless it's due to *nothing whatsoever,* a seeming unlikelihood. So *what is Hamlet really doing in the play* to fill the long middle sections and the sections toward the end of the drama, before the duel?

You have had three weeks of discussion, reading, and analysis. Write an essay expressing your own best reasoning as to what...

> When Hamlet is with his mother and the ghost of his father appears, his mother Geraldine does not see him.

> After Hamlet found out about his father's murder and his mother marrying the murderer, Hamlet's life tragically became honorable.

> After Hamlet witnessed his mother die at the hands of the glass of wine intended for Hamlet, he...

> Before his father's murder, Hamlet had a great life. He had good parents, a nice girlfriend, and was a college educated prince.

6/24/06 11:26 AM (Thu.):

President Penguin-Duck had floodlights installed to illuminate the outside of Presidential Hall at night. They threw enormous paint-splashes of light up onto the building, giving it the appearance of a huge illuminated bauble, or, if seen from a certain distance away, a casino boat cruising offshore.

Indefatigably, President Penguin-Duck worked to make Actaeon's significance and achievement more and more widely unknown throughout the world. Toward this end, he established a program of making telephone calls to public figures and leaders in other parts of the world. Each time he spoke with the head of an institution or university abroad, or with the leader of a local, state, provincial, or national government elsewhere than in the United States, he commemorated the achievement by obtaining the pertinent nation's flag and arranging for it to be placed among those already displayed on poles extending out from the walls of the great atrium in Presidential Hall. Gay, profuse, and bright with many colors, the collection grew steadily—from twenty to forty to sixty flags, then eighty, until the atrium might have been the entryway to an international diplomatic center of some particularly significant kind, its importance reaching everywhere around the world.

6/25/06 1:31 AM (Fri):

My weight had fallen by seventy-eight pounds. In my ears was a steady ringing that I attributed to weight loss, anxiety, fear of failure, despair, and dehydration.

On the day of reckoning, the day when I exercised reason by thinking seriously of *not* having Sasha Brearly in the classroom any longer, I had already changed my shirt three times, my underwear twice, my trousers and socks once. The day's subject was the *Aeneid,* specifically the passage in Book VI, in the underworld, containing the preview of Roman history that Anchises gives to his son Aeneas, who is on his way to found the Roman line.

"Great authors *can* tell untruths," I explained. "Their reasons are various, and so are the results. Sometimes the untruth is true in certain ways, even if untrue in others. But what *you* don't want is to be deceived or tricked. That's why you're here, so that later when you read or hear things you'll be able to tell the difference between what's true or not true, and to tell whether each truth or untruth is a big one and important, or a small one and less important. And always, of course, *why* this is so.

"Anchises' preview of coming attractions is a grand, elevated speech about law, war, the arts, victory, and loss. Now, Actaeon itself is dedicated to the study of social control, and so law and war, and loss, and even the arts, should be subjects of interest. So listen for what is or might be ironic in Anchises' words. Listen for things that could be true or untrue, or true for one listener and not another, or differently true, like praising yourself for bringing wars to an end when you're the one who *won* all the wars, or praising the goodness of new laws when *you're* the one who's chosen and made them—ironies that might slip by people if they get caught up in the grand style of Virgil's words and stop hearing all the *meanings* in them."

Walking slowly back and forth at the front of the room, I read:

> Who can ignore the Gracchi or the Scipios,
> twin thunderbolts of war, the lash of Libya;
> Fabricius, so strong and with so little;
> or you, Serranus, as you sow your furrow?
> And Fabii, where does your prodding lead me—
> now weary—with your many deeds and numbers!

You are that Maximus, the only man
who, by delaying, gave us back our fortunes.
For other peoples will, I do not doubt,
still cast their bronze to breathe with softer features,
or draw out of the marble living lines,
plead causes better, trace the ways of heaven
with wands and tell the rising constellations;
but yours will be the rulership of nations,
remember, Roman, these will be your arts:
to teach the ways of peace to those you conquer,
to spare defeated peoples, tame the proud.
                    (trans. Allen Mandelbaum)

As I read out the passage, weak, plagued by tinnitus, filled with doubt and desire, six students went out of the room, the door (its damper broken) slamming behind each; five came into the room (the door, again); seven fell asleep, their heads falling forward; eighteen looked into the air, having with them neither books nor notebooks; fifteen looked into the air, all with books in front of them, although nine of these were closed, six open to the wrong page. Two students followed along with me in the poem. One marked the passage with a pen.

At the words "You are that Maximus," Sasha Brearly came into the room, as she did near this time each day, having left twenty minutes or so earlier, immediately after responding to her name in the roll call.

As usual, she had brought food with her. As usual, she caused a disruption, making her way into the back row past writing surfaces, notebooks, feet, and knees. As usual, upon sitting down, she turned to the person on her left and asked "where we were." As usual, she asked the person on her right for pen and paper. As usual, once she'd gotten these, she made use of neither but settled in and began to eat.

This time, along with a grape soda, she had a slice of pizza topped—as I was to learn—with sausage and extra cheese. As she leaned forward to say something to Damian Sloma in the row ahead of her, the topping slid from the pizza and onto Eve Brennan's right foot, which was entirely bare except for a minimalist white sandal with a spaghetti-thin strap over the toe and another over the foot. Eve Brennan had been asleep, and it may well have been that she was now awakened by a dream of something hot, liquescent, or sharp-toothed suddenly attacking her foot. From her throat, in any case, came a loud, sudden, intense, high scream.

Limbs twitched and heads jerked up as people woke in what appeared to be states of sudden terror. Some of those already awake jumped in their seats, others pressed hands to their hearts, turned toward the source of the noise, declared their anger at having been so frightened, or began talking animatedly with others nearby about what each of them thought had happened and oh-my-god, how scared they'd been, how relieved they were, how—

Within only a second or two, in other words, the room had degenerated into chaos—and I had had the beginning of my deadly epiphanic vision. The vision came into being sometime during Eve Brennan's scream, and its power over me was such that, if only for a moment or two, I behaved in a way that was rational.

6/27/06 0:21 AM (Sun.):

Something like a camera shutter seemed to open, very quietly, and for a brief, clear, transcendently illuminating moment *I saw things as they actually were.* The reality of the sordid classroom, of the tropical heat and arctic cold, of the latrines, of the students, and of my last three-and-a-half decades at Actaeon generally—all of these appeared to me with an extreme, perfect, unadulterated clarity, while along with them came also a curiously simple, almost childlike refrain that repeated itself in my head. It was this: *Some things are true, others are not true; some things are true, others are not true; some things are true, others are not true.*

I felt, if only for a moment, as though a nearby window had opened onto fresh, cool, clean summer air. This feeling, like the refrain, was simple, invigorating, and pure.

As these things were happening to me, I showed no outward sign of them, at least not at first, but continued reading from the *Aeneid,* pacing across the front of the room and back again. So engrossed was I, however, in my epiphany, that I failed to watch my step as carefully as I normally did, with the result that I placed my left foot directly on a soda-spill. The spill was relatively recent, not yet a dirt-map, but only a day or two old and more than sticky enough to suck at my right shoe and pull it off. That the shoe came off this easily was not so remarkable as thing as it might seem, since, as one of my responses to the heat, I wore my shoes tied only in the very loosest manner, not only to allow more air in and onto my feet, but also because of the ease it allowed me in slipping my shoes off quickly, and replacing them just as quickly, during my changes of clothing between classes.

In any case, the instant my foot and shoe parted from one another, I turned and—not knowing until I did it that I was *going* to do it— instead of retracing my steps across the front of the room again, walked casually toward the back. At exactly the moment I finished the lines

> remember, Roman, these will be your arts:
> to teach the ways of peace to those you conquer,
> to spare defeated peoples, tame the proud,

I stopped at the back row, closed my book, and stood looking in at Sasha Brearly, who in turn was looking down at the mix of sausage, tomato sauce, and hot cheese on Eve Brennan's foot—a foot which in turn Eve Brennan was shaking strenuously in an effort to rid it of its covering, simultaneously emitting high, short, repeated yelps.

To me, it seemed all at once, almost miraculously, as though everything around me was new, fresh, plain, stupendously simple and clear—just as the lilting refrain of my epiphany brought me such enormous relief by merit of its also seeming to me new, fresh, plain, stupendously simple and clear: *Some things are true, others are not true; some things are true, others are not true.*

Over Eva Brennan's yelping, I told Sasha Brearly that I was removing her from the class, that she should pack her gear, go out of the room, and never come back.

In the surrounding gulf of din and disorder, my words caused nothing whatsoever to happen. I repeated them, this time shouting.

Sasha Brearly looked up at me. Her face went quickly through a sequence of expressions: at first, non-comprehension and puzzlement, then a kind of shocked amazement, then sheerest outrage. Topless pizza crust in left hand, grape soda can in the other, she spat words back at me, screaming over the din that *she wasn't going any damned place and who was I to talk to her like that.*

I repeated my own words.

She repeated hers.

I bellowed mine, including new phrasing and additional reasoning.

She shrieked a reply, adding dimension, vigor, and color.

I howled my original assertion, adding still additional support that had to do with Sasha Brearly's repeated disruptions, ongoing inattention, failure to change in behavior.

She again.

I again.

And repeat.

She.

I.

She.

Until

7/1/06 0:22 AM (Wed.):
the simple, pure, refreshing clarity of my epiphany *(Some things are true, others are not true)* led me to explain to Sasha Brearly *that if she wouldn't get up and make her way out of the room I would pull her out.*

Simple. Reasonable. *(Some things are reasonable, others are not reasonable.)*

I set my *Aeneid* down on the floor. I went into the back row, moving crabwise to avoid people's knees. At the middle of the row, both of our voices going strong at top pitch, I clasped one hand firmly on either side of Sasha Brearly's desktop and tried with all my effort to pull it—and her—out from her place in the row and toward the door.

The seats in each classroom, however, were fitted with a diabolic system of hooks and eyes that linked whole rows together like freight cars. And in trying to pull Sasha Brearly from the room, therefore, I was in fact trying to pull the weight of another four people on one side of her and five on the other.

In my weakened state, I couldn't do it, nor in *any* state could I have done it. But in light of my weight loss and diminishing strength it was even more obviously impossible than it normally would have been. The weight was enormous, and furthermore I had the traction of only one shoe, since my left sock slipped hopelessly on the tiled floor. Sasha Brearly, on top of that, had from the first moment pressed her heels against the floor and had continued pushing as hard as she could in the *other* direction.

I gave up.

I turned. I made my way crabwise out of the row, bumping against knees.

I picked my *Aeneid* up from the floor, went back to the front of the room, and—began laughing.

My epiphany had not yet left me entirely, and, under the influence of its simple clarity, how could I help but be amused at so high, or low, a comedy as this. There I was, one shoe missing, red-faced, sweating profusely, trying haplessly to pull from the room an entire row of ten interlocked students, one of them back-pedaling her heels furiously in resistance.

In front, I slipped my shoe on again, opened my *Aeneid,* rested it on one open hand, and turned to face the room. As I did, Sasha Brearly pushed herself up, tossed back her head, and stormed from the room, shouting over her shoulder *who did I think I was I had no right to talk to her like that.* The door, naturally, slammed behind her.

And as it

7/2/06 3:38 AM (Thu.):

did,

7/2/06 3:47 AM (Thu.):

I saw these things:

1) a crowd of faces at the window, some of them (once the door fell closed again) pressed up against it and looking in. Among them, instantly recognizable, were the faces of

2) Dr. Correct, Dr. Long, Dr. Nose, Dr. Everybody's, Dr. Me, Dr. Cleopatra, and Dr. Know. These

3) pulled away as Sasha Brearly flung the door open and flounced out, tossing back a last imprecation as she went. From where I stood at the front of the room, I saw

4) an arm curl around Sasha Brearly's shoulder; a face

5) bend toward her with concern;

6) then another arm and

7) another

8) the

9) w [223]

7/5/06 4:35 AM (Sun.):

I continued, for the remainder of the hour, with a class more quiet, attentive, possibly even interested, than ever in all the decades before. Could it be that I had done the right thing and hadn't only *thought* so? That my epiphany had led me in the right direction? That some things really were not and that others indeed *were* true? That exercising authority in the interest of the worthwhile really *could* be worthwhile? I took up, exactly as planned, one passage of the *Aeneid* after another, asked questions about each, elicited responses, then went on to the next. Although I was aware of a continuing agitation outside the door—faces, like aquarium fish, would come up to the glass, peer in, draw away—I ignored it and gave my attention to the newly attentive and even somewhat responsive class, which, even with Sasha Brearly missing, still, after all, consisted of Acosta, Babb, Banks, Battaglia, Blanco, Brennan, Brice, Castillo, Chapman, Clarke, Davis, Figueroa, Fox, Francis, Freeman, Gennaro, Haynes, Hopkins, Johnson, Kaplan, Kingston, Kopen, Lopez, Marquez, Matthew, Masters, Murphy, Nelson, Owens, Pettway, Pinckney, Pisani, Profitt, Rashford, Reyes, Rissuto, Rivera, Russell, Sloma, Smith, Soto, Taylor, Tsouros, and Williams.

As the hour went on, activity in the corridor intensified rather than diminished. Faces appeared at the door more frequently and looked in through the window for longer periods, though I ignored them, allowing myself to notice them, if at all, only through the corner of my eye.

When the class ended, however, and my students made their way out of the room, they found themselves having to push through

---

[223] Here is the *only known example* of damage to the sheets that comprise the *"Diary"* as we have it. The damage-free condition of the "Diary" has been commented on in detail by Lok-Ho Woo in "Voice in the Wilderness: Questions of Preservation in the *"Diary"* of Eric Larsen" (*Studies in American Intellectual History,* April 2124, pp. 33–58).

7/6/06 8:52 AM (Mon.):
a crowd that consisted no longer only of Dr. Correct, Dr. Long, Dr. Nose, Dr. Everybody's, Dr. Me, Dr. Cleopatra, and Dr. Know, but now also of Dr. Race, Dr. Class, Dr. Gender, Dr. Muscle, and Dr. Victim, along with three photographers, two reporters, and Mr. Badge Worn, Director of the Actaeon Security Team (ASECTOR). When I, the last one to leave the room, stepped out into the crowd and flashing cameras, Mr. Badge Worn immediately came up beside me, took me by the arm, propelled me forward gently but firmly, and said into my ear,

"Come along quietly now. President Penguin-Duck wants you in his office. Best if you don't say anything at all, not for the moment. Wait until you're

7/6/06 9:03 AM (Mon.):
there before you say a thing. They're probably going to make a case against you. But don't worry about that. Just don't say anything. Keep quiet and don't worry. President Penguin-Duck has your best interests at heart. Everyone at Actaeon can be assured of that. President Penguin-Duck has everyone's best interests at heart. Pardon us, pardon us. All right, come along now."

7/6/06 9:17 AM (Mon.):
And so it came about at last,

7/7/06 9:22 AM (Tue.):
as undoubtedly it had been destined from the beginning, that I was summoned to President Penguin-Duck's office. And not only summoned, but escorted there by Mr. Badge Worn himself, his hand gripping the bone of my skinny upper arm as we left Non-Presidential Hall, crossed the avenue (groups of students along the curbs stared at us in silence), entered the atrium of flags in Presidential Hall, and took the elevator up. Mr. Worn guided me to the appropriate wing and then down the grand corridor itself, offices on either side, each one larger than the last. The people in them, having heard that I was coming, looked up from behind their desks as I was taken past, or, in some cases, stood leaning in doorways, following us with their eyes.

Still holding my arm, Mr. Badge Worn took me through the antepenultimate set of double doors and in to that first room with its four people looking up at me from behind their desks. Then he took me through the penultimate set of doors, to the room where the two people looked up at me from behind their desks; and into the last ante-room, where the one person, with her baleful eyes and dark frown, stared at me from behind her desk. At last Mr. Badge Worn opened the ultimate set of doors, released my arm, and, with the slightest push against the center of my back,[224] propelled me out into the huge expanse of the great room itself, where I saw, far away and off to my left, President Penguin-Duck himself, his elbows on his desk, a telephone pressed, at the narrow part of his head, to his ear.

•

Without looking up, he made a gesture with his free hand, indicating that I should approach his desk. When I had done so and stood nearby, he gestured for a second time, again without looking up. This gesture was a down-hooking movement of his right forefinger, indicating a chair at the corner of his desk. I sat, and, since he continued holding the phone to his ear and looking off into the air instead of at me, I took the opportunity to study him briefly. I had seldom been this close to him and then only briefly, in, say, reception lines or at large gatherings, where others crowded around him while I tended to linger near the edges. Now, however, free to look my fill, I wondered why it was, considering the swell of his chest and the thickness of his neck, he didn't wear a larger shirt size or even unbutton his jacket, since both pieces of clothing were visibly stretched, close to the button-popping stage.

As I waited, President Penguin-Duck pressed a button on his telephone console, and I soon realized that he was waiting for another of his international calls. If he completed it, another flag would appear in the grand atrium downstairs.

"Bettina? Bettina?" he said into the mouthpiece. "Are you still there? Yes. Yes, I *am*. What've you got from Plovdiv? We need to keep trying. Yes, seven hours difference. Yes, after dinner is fine for me, tell him that, but only if it's also good for him." There was a pause. Then President Penguin-Duck said, his words more rushed and a faint slur audible in them this time, "No, no, no, no, no. Keep on it. Im*per*'tive. This one's imper'tive. Uh huh. Mm. Yes. Abz lootly."

Then he surprised me by saying, even now without looking toward me but still gazing straight ahead, across the room, into the air, "Well, Larsen, I hear you pushed a person out of the room."

I was instantly angry but made every effort not to show it. "I did not," I said. "Who told you that?" President Penguin-Duck seemed not to have heard me.

"You understand the significance of this, this pushing. Pushing is very, pushing's terr'bly, terr'bly serious, I'm 'fraid. Cons toots vuln'bility to a charge of assault. This, um, this Sasha is talking with

---

[224] Whether this was a personal thing, a friendly and perhaps even intimate touch intended to wish me well; or whether it was simply a *discarding* of me, akin to the scornful flick of a finger in removing an insect; I was not able to tell. [Author's Note]

her lawyer. Already called him. I know from Badge. He briefed me on all vit. It looks pretty certain she'll be bringing charges. But even if—" I interrupted him. "I didn't push. I pulled."

Slowly, he turned his face toward me for the first time, looked at me for a moment, then turned away again. His smallish eyes were bloodshot, and thin branches of broken capillaries fanned out colorfully across his cheeks.

He quickly pressed four buttons in a sequence on his telephone console and, sighing deeply as he did so, said, "No. No. Don't deny, Larsen. There's no good in denying, no use in it. Don't try that with me." Holding the telephone against his left ear, he looked with his right hand for a piece of paper on the desktop, found it, and drew it toward him. He looked at it, then went on, "Says so right here. Sasha testifies that you pushed her in a 'hostile, malevolent, and aggravating manner.' And we have corroboration. Lemme see"—he bent closer to the piece of paper, squinting at it slightly—"oh, from lots of people. Here's Dr. Correct, and Dr. Long, and also Dr. Nose. And Dr. Everybody's. Dr. Cleopatra. And I've got Dr. Race, and I've got Dr. Class, Dr. Gender, and Dr. Victim. Three student photographers. Two reporters. And Badge. Don't forget Badge. Man of the law, Badge."

I found myself, for the first time in my career at Actaeon, suddenly frightened of something less concrete than bullets, death threats from students, or disease-bearing spores in the air of the latrines. "That's a lie," I said to President Penguin-Duck. "I didn't push anyone. I tried to *pull*, but I couldn't even manage to do that."

President Penguin-Duck moved the telephone six or seven inches away from his left ear and held it in the air. Slowly, he turned his head in my direction and looked straight, directly, *right* at me, his eyes holding my eyes. *"What did you say?"* he asked. His eyebrows went up, held there for a moment, and then crushed suddenly down toward the center again, squinching his blotchy face into a look of fierce anger that I found extremely frightening. "I want you to know, Dr. Larsen, that within the walls of this office I have never before, ever, heard such a libelous statement as that, *never*. And you had better make it absolutely certain that I never hear such a thing again. *I will have no talk about lies. Do you understand me perfectly clearly?"*

He must have then heard a small sound coming from the telephone, because, turning away from me again, he put the instrument back to his ear and said, "Yes? Bettina? Oh, very, very good. Yes, yes, of course. You *really* didn't think so? Well, you shouldn't be such a skeptic. You mustn't go on being such a doubter, Bettina, my dear." Then, the phone an inch or two away from his ear, he looked at me again, just for a second, then replaced the phone to his ear and gazed off into space across his enormous office. When he started talking, I thought at first that he was talking to someone on the phone rather than to me. The bloodlessly fierce tone of only a moment before had vanished entirely and given way to a buttery softness in his voice, weary-sounding, even bored, almost dreamy. "No, no, no," he said with a kind of sigh. "It's no good denying. No good to anyone. Not you, not her, not me, not Badge, not anybody. Much, much better juz' cooperate every way. Thaz the bes' advice, strongest anybody can give you, Larsen, including me. And you're going to be needing it. We have your best interests at heart. You can be abz lootly assured of that. Ev' one at Actaeon can be assured of that. I have ev' one's best interests at heart."

Impulsively, I jumped up from my chair, having had no idea whatsoever that I was about to do so. I believe that up until that moment I had been able to keep myself quite calm, but something had seized on me like a snapping jaw: the panicked realization that there really was not going to be any way out of this thing, not going to be any recourse. My heart was racing insanely as I was overcome by fear, outrage, frustration, and sheer panic.

"*Sit down,*" President Penguin-Duck barked, or intoned. Even though his voice was sharp, it was still weary. As if my strings had been cut, I crumpled into the chair. When I spoke, my voice sounded faint, weak, and pleading, making me despise the sound of it and making me despise myself as well. "I was there to teach the *Aeneid*," I said. "And I did that. I held on to the class and I went on teaching the *Aeneid*. I did my job."

And I heard myself add, "For once." This brought President Penguin-Duck's face toward me again, though only briefly. He sighed again, even more deeply this time. "No, no, no, no, my dear *Doctor Larsen*" he said. The weariness in his voice was undisguised and extreme. "No, you didn't. You didn't do your *job*. Your *job* is to keep students *in the classroom*. You didn't do that. You pushed them *out of it*. Everyone heard you."

"What do you mean, '*heard*' me? You can't '*hear*' a push. I yelled but I didn't push. No one heard a push or saw one. I pulled. You're buying a lie, Morton. And I can tell you for absolutely certain—" There came a beep from the telephone, and, at the tiny burble of sound, as if suddenly I no longer so much as existed, President Penguin-Duck pressed a button on the console and said into the receiver at his ear, "Yes? Yes? *Bettina?*"

His voice at once took on animated eagerness, completely unlike its deep lethargy of just an instant before. "Yes? Oh, yes, absolutely. Yes, of course. *Of course!*"

He looked over at me but did so without moving his head, only his eyes. He kept the phone pressed to his left ear. "Larsen," he said, "Larsen, Larsen. I don't know what else I can say to make you understand. We'll put a record of the incident into your personnel file. You can see it but you can't remove it. You've got to understand that the aggrieved party here is Sasha. I mean, have you ever stopped to think about what Actaeon really

7/8/06 10:01 AM (Wed.):

is? Actaeon is its *students,* and what we're here for is to serve *them.* That's our role, our calling, our duty and purpose, that's what we do, we serve them, that's why we're here. Now, you've made a serious error, Larsen. A desperate error. Failure to provide the service you've been brought here to provide. Manner unbecoming a member of the Actaeon family. And then assault, a very good chance of assault, criminal offense. It's only justice. Price must be paid if it's called for. And not considering the students. Students always first. Just think of the young lady. What you did. You trammeled her rights. You deprived her of them. Her right to be left alone. Her right as an adult to make decisions about her own intellectual life. Her right to live as an adult in a free society. Why, what you've done is not only deprive her of her civil liberties but you've *also offended her human dignity.* Oh, no, no, no, there's no other way but to let things take their course from here. I'll write up the report, have it put in your file. Send you a copy. But if anyone ever needs to see it, there it'll be. And meanwhile, don't forget that the lawyers may—*Bettina? Yes?* Yes, of course. *Of* course, of course, of course. Ah *ha! Wonderful!* Yes, yes, yes, of course. Naturally. Put him on, put him on. Yes, put him

7/9/06 2:47 AM (Thu.):had

on."

And so the telephone connection was made, and the awaited conversation with the mayor of Plovdiv, Bulgaria, began. At the very instant the mayor said hello, President Penguin-Duck lost interest in me absolutely. It was as though I were no longer there. It was as though I had never been there.

And perhaps that was a good thing, my being invisible and nonexistent to him, since otherwise I wouldn't have seen what I saw, and I wouldn't have learned the extraordinary things I learned.

Yet at the same time, a blessing in disguise or not, even though I was on the brink of learning more about Actaeon, and more about President Penguin-Duck, than I had ever known before or could ever have hoped to know, none of it could any longer be of any conceivable use or help to me, either personally or professionally, now. Crushed, defeated, depressed, fully expecting to be brought up on charges of criminal assault by Sasha Brearly and her lawyers, knowing that I could not rely on truth or support or guidance or understanding or defense of any kind whatsoever from President Penguin-Duck—I felt defeated, utterly, and frightened of the magnitude of what seemed to be happening, not only to me alone but, so it seemed, to the world around me.

I don't even remember, certainly not with any degree of clarity, leaving the room. There's no question but that I must have gotten to my feet, crossed the immense carpet, and gone out through the door as President Penguin-Duck continued talking, far behind me, on the phone—but I don't know it. Just as possibly it may be that I crept, or crawled, walked backward, or shuffled on my knees. It would hardly have made a difference. And it *hasn't* made a difference.

•

The moment he heard the call actually coming through, President Penguin-Duck dismissed me by swiveling away from me in his chair and ending our conversation with a tiny brushing movement of the fingers of his right hand, the universal suggestion of a broom, flicking me away. Then, as he began speaking animatedly into the telephone, he stood up and idly took a step or two away from his desk and toward the windows, showing me his back—and leaving me, it seemed apparent, to make my own way out. Before I did that, however (and however I did it), I saw something that, if I hadn't seen it with my own eyes, no lifetime could have prepared me to believe.

What happened first was this: *I saw the President's actual, true, real-life duck-tail.* It appeared initially as only a very slight bulge, but then it came into actual sight, protruding through the rear vent in the President's jacket. From there it extended farther, in a faintly pulsing manner, slowly at first but then more quickly, growing more rapid in concert with the growing excitement and volubility of the President's voice—until I saw, in full view, *the actual tail and feathers of a true, real, actual duck.*

"Yes, of course, Mr. Beftik,"[225] President Penguin-Duck was saying. "Oh, *pardon* me! *Sir* Beftik, I should say. Yes, *Sir* Beftik, your

---

225 Pronounced "*beff* teak." [Author's Note]

honor. It's marvelous, simply marvelous of you to get back to me. Yes. No. Yes. No, absolutely not. That's correct. No, absolutely nothing. We have nothing in mind whatsoever of any substance or import, you can be assured of that. Everyone can be very strongly assured of that. Never. Absolutely not. In no case whatsoever. Nothing substantial, but *certainly* important. Yes, we here at Actaeon simply want to extend our greetings, convey our sense of warmth and community, find a way to extend our regards and cement our relationship. Yes, our *human* regards! That's right! *Correct!* Yes, *human* dignities! The highest of all dignities! No one can disagree *there*! That's right! Absolutely correct, yes, they were indeed, that's right. That indeed is our mission. That is *exactly* what we are directed toward and dedicated to. Nothing of any adversarial or disruptive potential whatsoever—since *everyone agrees*. It's wonderful. How *could* anyone conceivably disagree with such an idea? Yes. Of course. And, still more important, not *of any significance*. Correct. Correct. Correct. *Except* for the fact that *you are the one hundred and thirty-sixth head of foreign government, national, civic, state, or local, that I have contacted as part of our university family!* Imagine! The one hundred and thirty-sixth! Oh, yes. Oh, you *have* heard of our program, then. I see. Yes, I *am* flattered, and it *is* an honor, yes, on behalf of all our dedicated and hardworking faculty. Yes, world renown, world renown. *Pardon?* Me *personally?* Of course, certainly it would. Of course. Yes, I would love to accept, and I do so right now. Yes, and a *great, great, great honor it will be for me, your honor.* Of course I am *very pleased.* Yes..."

And, at this exact moment in the conversation, may god strike me dead and pitch me straight to the eternal fires of hell if I what I am about to say is *anything other than the purest truth*—at this exact moment, when Sir Beftik extended his invitation to the President to come to Bulgaria, I saw President Penguin-Duck's tail rise up erect, in two or three tightening spasms, again as if in accord with the rising intensity of its owner's pleasure. And then, as I watched—this is *absolute, unequivocal, literal truth*—four or five spurts of watery excrement shot forth from underneath the tail in the sphincter-released rhythm of such emissions, half of the material in this case being squirted out and backward two or three feet, and half of it—thickish liquid carrying within it semi-large curds—falling lazily to the carpet. After evacuation, there came a half dozen, perhaps eight or ten, quick sideways flickings of the tail, left and right, these followed by the tail itself gradually retracting back up under the rear vent of the President's jacket, where it remained hidden once again.

The chanted words from that lost and long-ago day came back to me, the day I was discussing James Joyce with one of my classes—

"Where there's shit there's life, for better or worse!"
"No shit, no life, for better or worse!"

—but as I was reminded of the truth of the words this time, my heart felt not the elation and joy of that lost and long-ago day, but felt instead as if it were dying from ugliness, disappointment, sorrow, and loss.

7/9/06 4:49 AM (Thu.):

And so it came about that in those few minutes—as my life was being transmuted forever into a crippled and meager thing—I finally gained, once and for all, an understanding of two of the greatest enigmas lying at the heart of Actaeon and of its loathsome, sordid, pathetic history.

For only now, after my many decades of suffering, decline, and intensifying despair, did I finally come upon the solution to the greatest twin mysteries of the place: the mystery of the latrines' repugnance and the mystery of the absurd immensity of President Penguin-Duck's office.

At long last, that is to say, I was bequeathed an understanding, first, that the reason the Actaeon latrines remained airless, decrepit, dangerous, and diseased was simply that President Penguin-Duck had no use for them himself, had never experienced them, and consequently cared about them not in the least. And the reason he didn't care about them in the least way was that he himself, whenever the urge struck him, simply defecated or urinated not in the latrines but in his own office!

The second mystery, too, was revealed in full, it being in essence a corollary of the first.

And this second mystery, although it touched less intimately on any part of *my own* daily life at Actaeon, was in point of fact even more radically profound than the first, lying at the very deepest, bedrock level of the college's moral and intellectual being.

As I mentioned, the second mystery now revealed to me as a mystery no longer was that of why President Penguin-Duck's office was so big.

It was huge not only in order that it would be awe-inspiring and thus an aid to the President in his professional, moral, legal, administrative, and academic aim of hiding Actaeon's miserable and contemptible actuality by means of *making things appear other than they were;* but it was enormous also for the simple, practical, sensible, rational, and well-planned reason that, being so huge, it would require a proportionately greater length of time before he would fill it up.

7/10/06 0:04 AM (Fri.):

It is entirely possible, I suppose, that I really did lose consciousness, and this would explain my loss of memory—although I can't easily imagine myself, say, sprawled out on the carpet of the President's office without hearing so much as a word or whisper about it later. On the other hand, maybe my cognitive powers, due to shock, stress, or trauma, simply closed down for a moment or two—and during that blackout time, I left the room. Unbeknownst to anyone, as President Penguin-Duck went on chattering to Bulgaria, perhaps I just somnambulated across the enormous, empty room and let myself out the first set of doors.

And from that point on, whatever may or may not have happened just before it, I remember clearly every detail.

As I came out through the *foyer-sanctum sanctorum*, like an animal blinking in the light, I found myself stared at with an implacable and withering gaze by the senior Presidential Keeper, who sat behind her desk in silence, also utterly without movement except for her head, which turned slowly as she watched me go by. In the *foyer-secondaire* and the *foyer-troisiéme,* the more numerous keepers also watched me with disdainful expressions, although perhaps—or so I fancied—they were to some small degree less merciless. From inside the larger offices at the Presidential end of the open corridor, the expressions of people looking out at me were merely impassively dismissive, while those from the intermediate offices farther away from Penguin-Duck appeared almost curious; and at the farthest end, in the small offices nearest the building's common areas, workers actually got up from behind their desks and *stood in their doorways to watch me pass.* In some of their eyes, I was certain, I saw half-repressed and all-but-imperceptible flickers of sympathy and understanding.

•

As I turned the corner, expelled for the first and last time in my life from the Grand Presidential Hall, I saw, some distance ahead, gathered together and waiting for my return, those of my narrowing colleagues who were still alive and who still remained at Actaeon—Dr. Razor himself (who out of consideration stood sideways so I could more easily see him) along with Drs. Tic, Nerve, Rash, Colon, Meek, Good, Book, and Poem.

As soon I saw them there, gathered near the elevators and waiting for me to come out of my meeting with President Penguin-Duck, I realized that what had just happened in the President's office was in fact more important than I had previously thought, for it had to do not only with me but with all of us. There was every reason, now, to understand with perfect clarity that in any future conflict between hypocrisy and truth, President Penguin-Duck would side with hypocrisy; that in any future conflict between appearance and actuality, he would side with appearance; and that in any future conflict between duty and depravity, he would side with depravity. A change of towering significance had taken place in our decades at Actaeon, a change affecting us all, and, unless rescue of an unknown and unsolicited kind were to appear very soon, it would go on making itself evident until every one of us was gone.

Which, judging by the look of us, would not be very long. For we were now, I saw, even more shrunken, narrowed, and withered than I had realized before. All too soon, every one of us would be nearly invisible, like Dr. Razor—or gone entirely, like Dr. Socialism, who not long before had simply disappeared and was nowhere to be found, a development that caused me a degree of surprise, since I found myself actually missing him. In any case, wherever he was or wherever he was not, all of us would be joining him soon enough unless some intervening power, as yet unidentified, manifested itself to prevent this happening. Already we had grown wrinkled, old, and frail, and soon, our strength waning even further, we would be less able than ever to survive the extremes of arctic and tropical cycles, the manifold dangers of Actaeon's offices, classrooms, and hallways, and the diseases packed in waiting in the stinking airlessness of the latrines.

As we stood under the fluorescent lights in the elevator foyer, slumped in our baggy clothing, I exchanged handshakes with each of my old friends. All of us uttered quietly such bittersweet phrases of reassurance and encouragement as we were capable of summoning up. Then, as we were doing this, a noise came to be heard. It was a distant, thunder-like rumbling that, as it drew nearer, became clarified into the sound of voices and laughter—and, as the elevator doors opened on both sides of the area we stood in, there poured out from all six cars our heavy, hearty, and cheerful broadening colleagues on their way (as we quickly learned) to a reception in President Penguin-Duck's office to celebrate the completion of his one hundred and sixty-sixth international telephone call and his being honored, as a consequence of it, by a personal invitation to Bulgaria.

Sweeping around us without taking the slightest notice, these boisterous, festive, back-slapping colleagues made their way from the elevators to the corner leading to the grand corridor, then around that turn into the corridor itself, where in a mass they disappeared from sight, although of course the babble of their voices disappeared much more gradually. For some time, as we stood there, we could still hear them, the loud, happy, honking, laughing, chuckling, braying, oblivious and cacophonous voices of Dr. Race, Class, and Gender; of

Dr. Correct, Muscle, and Long; of Dr. Nose, Everybody's, and Me; of Dr. Cleopatra and Dr. Know; of Dr. Ethnicity and Dr. Woman and Dr. Gay and Dr. Lesbian; of Dr. Black and Dr. Hispanic; of Dr. Ghetto, Dr. Victim, Dr. Worker, Dr. Post-Colonial, Dr. Third World, and Dr. Asian; and, the last to disappear from our hearing, the high, silly, tittering, excited voices of Dr. Gender 2, Dr. Ethnicity 2, Dr. Class 2, Dr. Blue Collar, and, the ultimate and the last, Dr. Theory.

And then, after the entire group had gone into the Great Office, and the last of the many sets of double doors had fallen closed behind them, none of us moved for a time. None of us spoke. And everything all around us, except for the empty, insect-like buzzing of the fluorescent lights overhead, fell into a deep, perfect, unbroken silence.

FRAGMENT VII —

"THE LAST FRAGMENT"

Editor's Note:
Both Shandra and Wei have shown persuasively[226] that the severely fragmented materials of Fragment VII (known universally as "The
Last Fragment") do indeed belong in a single
unified piece constituting what is now agreed
to have been a final[227] and tremendously ambitious effort by Larsen to bring his massive project to completion before he ran out of time. Many
scholars believe that the effort was a failure, and
that the excessively damaged state of the sheets
(as well as the huge numbers of them missing
entirely) shows that Larsen himself had been
unable to bring them together into a single typescript before his work ended, with the result that

---

[226] Shandra primarily through textual study, Wei through chemical, x-ray, and carbon-
dating methods of testing. The results of the two methods are remarkably corroborative.
See Jacopo Mentz, "Wondrous Bonds: Unity and Coherence in 'The Last Fragment'"
(*Annals of Lost Americana*, May 2129, pp. 29–43). [Editor's Note]

[227] See the authors cited in the preceding note, but also Derald Cadiz, *Time Must Have
a Stop: The Approach of the End in "The Last Fragment"* (Helsinki, 2114), particularly Cadiz's brilliant and extraordinarily gripping second chapter, "Time's winged chariot."
[Editor's Note]

groups of sheets were left separated from one another and in scattered locations in the office, making them far more subject to damage and loss during the ruinous period of The Collapse than were other parts of the manuscript.

As for the project's in fact never having been completed, while some believe we can do nothing more than conjecture as to the reason why not, others have argued that Larsen's pen was finally stilled by forces ranging from death itself on through disease, breakdown, ostracism, hospitalization, and in one notable case even imprisonment.[228] The spirit of the piece, perhaps, must counsel each reader in the direction of his or her own thought on this sorrowful point.

Debate continues also as to what exactly did happen in the aftermath of the Sasha Brearly incident—whether the "court" referred to by Larsen was in fact a true court of law,[229] whether it was an academic council or disciplinary board of some kind ("the court of my own reckoning, peopled and overseen by victims and deans"), or whether it may in fact have been purely fictional.[230]

As to the sheer enormity of the doomed author's ambition in "The Last Fragment," however, there remains general concurrence of judgment. The section numbering that appears on the surviving sheets (the fragment "starts," for example, at section 4, "continues" on to section 9, etc.) point obviously to what must have been an almost staggeringly massive amount of material. Estimates of the extent lost to us range as

---

[228] For the extreme view, see R. N. Kremer-Bernier, *Calamity Beyond Any Man's Ken—Hidden Forces of Oppression in the Late Ante-Penultimate and Afterward* (Oslo and Bejing, 2114); for a review of the more moderate positions, Shandra is once again both useful and thorough (Maximillian Shandra, *Dating the Larsen Papers: A Writer's Progress toward Calamity* [Bangkok, 2096]). [Editor's Note]

[229] Again, see Kremer-Bernier, especially chapter three, "Ideas and Iron Bars." [Editor's Note]

[230] For an intriguing analysis of this view, see Delia Nawrocki, *Language and the American Collapse* (Helsinki & Beijing, 2118). Nawrocki finds a pun in "my own reckoning" that provides her with the key to an ingenious reading of the entirety of the Larsen Papers. [Editor's Note]

high as 95%,[231] a figure that implies an original typescript that could have contained as many as three-quarters of a million words. The fervor, passion, and strength of belief; the sheer commitment to the truth that would be necessary as a stimulus for any writer in undertaking so mammoth a task, are obvious. How much greater an intensity of motive and purpose must have been required for an author who was in ill health, growing old, threatened by despair, at the end of a lost and ruined career in a nation no longer faithful even to itself—this we can scarcely imagine.

---

[231] Shandra, Wei, Kremer-Bernier, and even Hong-Koestler and Gubar (*Apollo or Cassandra? Victim or Prophet? A Historically based Analysis of the Question of Paranoia Versus Prophecy in the Larsen Papers* (Beijing, History House, 2110) all concur with this estimate or make other estimates hardly distinguishable from it. [Editor's Note]

FRAGMENT VII —

"THE LAST FRAGMENT"

4

nted only to capture

tmosphere, nothing more. My entire life devoted to one,

igh, sustained, single end.

Yes, to capture *atmosphere:* the look, feel, smell, sound, the softness, the temperature, the feel on your skin, the calmness, suddenness, sometimes the certainty of change: to render it immobile in a single, perfect, caught-in-amber stillness. And this not an end in itself, not an effort to evoke atmosphere *simply for the doing of it,* as most people think, but the aim, by this means alone, of making possible its *coming back to life* each time the words are read over again, if read carefully and with understanding of what they are for: for the bringing back to life again, bringing into existence again,[232] the precise, exact, true feel of a day, time, place, or fleeting moment of change, each of these, however long ago they may have taken place, thus retu

•

---

232 Even though it does no longer exist. [Author's Note]

hest of all aims achiev-
able through the medium of words. And despite having devoted my
entire life to it, I have nevertheless failed. I believe increasingly that I
have failed. With more and more certainty, I

9

d so, as you already know, my time at Actaeon draws to an
r already has for some time *been* at an end, the very
ing a physical presence but not one in spirit or in
ll that remains, something I have known
grateful for your coming to listen
closing words of a long
felt by all of us who
ears at Actaeon be
ng a covenant
grateful for
aving lost
so very
wish for
fond
rets
ay
s

28

but not even *one single person* among the legions of Simplifiers could
even have an interest in an aim, ambition, or desire such as this one.
Nor could any among them *imagine* having such desire, for the simple
reason that desire for anything *must be preceded by at least some
responsiveness or susceptibility to the thing desired.* For a Simplifier,
this would remain an impossibility, since in the Simplified view, the
significance of any work of art *must lie outside of that work rather than
within it.* For the Simplifier, an ideal work of art is one that

1) advocates the bringing about of (or actually brings about) an
econo-socio-politico-psycho or equivalent attitudinal change in the
world *outside the work,* a change that, in keeping with the lowered
capacity of the Simplified mind adheres to these qualifications:

a) *that it must be minor,*
b) *that it must be consistent with other such proposed or
already-effected attitudinal changes, and*

c) that it must owe its existence in some observable measure
   less to thinking than to feeling.[233]

From among the hundreds of such "changes" (the word "ideas" is not, strictly speaking, accurate here) available to the chronicler, few must suffice in example. There are, for instance, "arguments," however contradictory, such as the following:

> a) that some people should be women and some should not;
> b) that some people should be gay and others should not;
> c) that some people should be *proud* of the color, race, class, ethnicity, sex, or religion that they happen to be of;
> d) while others should be *humiliated and excoriated* for the color, race, class, ethnicity, sex, or religion that *they* happen to be of;
> e) that some people should exhibit with the utmost possible flamboyance *the great joy they receive from being who and what they are;*
> f) while others should shiver, cringe, and suffer paralyzing guilt *at the very idea* of receiving joy from who or what they are, let alone even think of flaunting their conscious ness of it;
> g) etc.

or a work of art that

2. makes certain that its significance resides outside of itself by exhibiting *no originality of any artistic kind whatsoever* and in fact, deliberately or not, by being very often the clone or near-clone of other, usually earlier works. In these ways, the Simplified artwork can successfully guarantee that its significance *predates* itself, is *elsewhere* than in itself, and therefore obviously cannot lie *within* itself. Such an artwork, that is, can fulfill the Simplifiers' requirements most successfully by depriving itself of any *inward meaning whatsoever.*

or a work of art that

3. proves its sole purpose to be external to itself, not internal, by succeeding in no aim other or greater than that of "entertaining" the

---

233 That this view of the purpose of art reduces the artwork to the level of rhetoric, argument, or propaganda is a matter neither of consideration nor consequence to the Simplifier, who, after all, is unequipped to create or respond to works of any other kind. [Author's Note]

person experiencing or receiving it.

To "entertain" or "to be entertaining," it must be clearly understood, is much different from *moving* an audience or the experiencer of an artwork. Being "entertained" (with exceptions so rare as to be insignificant) means either to be titillated or frightened, so that the presence of *suspense* or *surprise* becomes the chief element by which a work's merit or success will be judged.

In order for the artwork to conform still more completely with Simplified tenets, it must also—and this is very important—be "accessible." This term means, simply, that the work must be transparently understandable to any average or below average Simplifier.

And, finally, for an artwork in the Age of Simplification to be considered of the first or highest rank, it is imperative that the experiencing of it *not* result in thinking of any kind, degree, or complexity unable to fit within the proscriptive terms of point number 2 above.

As a corollary to this requirement, there follows the additional requirement that the artwork not assume any conceivable relationship between the aesthetic, emotional, and intellectual elements of the self; and that—another corollary—an experience of the artwork therefore not result in any emotion, feeling, or idea different from *any of those already familiar* to the audience, viewer, or reader.

Finally, essentially, and above all, no emotion, feeling, or idea brought into existence by an artwork may in any case remain in the consciousness of audience, viewer, or auditor for longer than 240 minutes after the end of the actual experiencing of the work. The reason for so strict a limitation is that remembering the effect of an artwork for any longer a period will exponentially increase the likelihood of there occurring *permanent alteration or change* in the affected person or group. Not only might this alteration or change prove deleterious in any of myriad ways, but it would also by the nature of things vary in type, quality, and degree from one group or individual to another. If this were to happen, the consequence would be both significant and negative. Arguments would arise over the question of one artwork's being superior or inferior to another through its having had, say, a greater or lesser, a more fleeting or a more durable, more pleasant or unpleasant effect upon its auditors, viewers, or readers than another may have had. And no argument of this kind or on this subject can ever, ever be permitted to occur, since the tenet that all artworks have meaning only outside of themselves and never within is in fact not the only essential aesthetic tenet of the Age of Simplification. Another, equally absolute and irrefragable, is that all artworks are equal, and, beyond that, no artworks are more equal than others.

s was in
inner office, all the
uin-Duck himself, the most
f all the things he said or did not
protect yourselves in the time you have re-
btless, having happened, will happen again, and
hope can be maintained only if you can recapture
eld dear and considered—*then*—hardly questionable for
o demonstrably served the well-being of the academy and
ention the well-being of the students, of the intellectual life it-
nd freedoms of mind, spirit, inquiry, and expression—none of th
otected or even valued now by an institution and administration
between the public and the private, individual and the mass, let al
ich is logically valid and sound and that which is invalid and unso
omes about not only through deficiencies in their mathematical and s
not only through the resultant inability to follow the steps even of
a simple logical argument, but through the sheer penury and flaccid-
ity of their own *general* educations, so that not only are they men
of little knowledge and less understanding, but they are men also of
little *experience,* there being within them no capacity for the making
of experience, however abundant it may be in raw form, into something meaningful *within the growing man.*

The result is that they guide in blindness, consistently mistake the
small for the great, consider the weaker argument the stronger, abandon scruples, cling to the commonplace, lose all distinction between
serving the self and serving others, as they lose also, until the dis-
ability becomes the very definition of the man, the very ability itself
to see or understand that some things are meaningful and others
not, that piety is one thing and understanding another, that received
wisdom is different from discovered wisdom.

(From where he sat behind the desk, telephone pressed to one ear,
he leaned toward me in a manner suggesting gravity, threat, anger,
disapproval:

"And also vulgarity?" he exclaimed. "Do I understand that there was
vulgarity? Is it true that *in my classrooms* you expressed *vulgarity*?"

---

[234] The preceding section was number 28. This section's being number 92 suggests
the sheer enormity of how much has been lost of "The Last Fragment." [Editor's Note]

117

pe

nis

airhorn

ore could be said by anyone, in whatever
state of desolation they might find themselves, than that the whole
monstrous entirety of the thing had become a system virtually tamperproof, not even to b

Translations

Gaudeamus igitur
Juvenes dum sumus
Post jucundum juventutem
Post molestam senectutem
Nos habebit humus

"Let us rejoice
"while we are young
"After delightful youth
"After grievous old age
"Earth will cover our bones"

Vivat academia
Vivant professores
Semper sint in flore

"Long live our academy
"Teachers whom we cherish
"Ever may they flourish"

Vivat nostra societas
Vivant studiosi
Crescat una veritas
Floreat fraternitas

"Long live our society
"Scholars wise and learned
"May truth and sincerity
"Nourish our fraternity"

Alma Mater floreat
Quae nos educavit

Our Alma Mater may she thrive
A font of education

Crapademia, you we hail
Crapademia, you we hail
O hollow halls of Crapademia
Crapademia, crapademia
May you ever flourish

Crapademia, you we hail
Crapademia, you we hail
O hollow halls of Crapademia
Crapademia, crapademia
May you ever flourish

231

Professor Car Cleopatra

Woman I am,
Woman I see,
The whole world knows
There is only me.

Professor Hamilton Christopher Muscle

Dr. Muscle wears a mirror
In which himself he sees.
This is all he ever does,
Even when he pees.

Dr. Theory Gave a Speech

Dr. Theory gave a speech
While in the lake there swam a leech.
When Dr. Theory ended talking
The swimming leech was up and walking.
And all the world stood awed.
And all the world stood awed.

715

"Stanley" equals "tools" equals "schlon

783

In court, what they told me was that I would have t

ut

that there was no other choice open t

me o

Sasha Brearly's lawy

no other possi

277

r

wever grievous, pitiful, ruinous, or lamentable, an

y other course, alternative, or remedy. And so it was th

834

"Oh!" said President Penguin-Duck. "*A Perfect Storm*. Now *there's* a wonderful book. There's a *great* book! A great, *great* book!"

(Sky, sky, the world is falling!)

972

l, I simply said, "I liked Streather." That's what I answered when
asked me. The simple truth, after all. "And I still do." But they could
ally the other side *would not* make any effort to entertain even
ossibility, since empiricism played no part or had the least
f either thinking or of thought. And as a result, to put it most
simply, there was available no common ground on which to mount
a campaign either in argument, defense, or even simple debate, since
the rules of evidence were changed, or for that matter no longer
existed in the way they had at least since the witch trials of the sev-
enteenth century ended and rules of evidence—and therefore of
defense—that were built on a foundation of empiricism took over,
allowing—requiring—that judgment be based on what in actuality
was done rather than on what was or may have been believed. Now,
however, certainly in the court of my own reckoning, peopled and
overseen by victims and deans, self-anointed and self-appointed,
you can be quite certain indeed that objectivity would never rear its
ugly head, or that innuendo and hearsay—*listen now, Drs. Long, Nose,
Cleopatra, Others, and Me!*—would be thrust out into the cold. No,
this was the hearing room of tamperproof affairs, outcomes under
warranty to be safely predetermined, the court of a "social" machine
set in motion by forces far greater than any single person could ever
contain, but that are indeed as much an artifact as any other result
of human invention or creation, this one cared for and supported
whether knowingly or unknowingly by the most base among us, the
narrowest of view, shakiest of learning, simplest of feeling, intent,
morality, and mind.

That President Penguin-Duck himself exemplifies so very, very perfectly—in mind, manner, outlook, method, and morality—a typical supporter and perpetrator of monstrosities so ghastly and dangerous as these should by now be no surprise to any who have listened to the entirety of this melancholy talk.[235] Nor should there be surprise in the somber and indeed frightening recognition that an entire institution—not an institution as a place of mortar and brick, but an institution as a greater concept, a coalition of many smaller independent centers joined tacitly in a broader fellowship of purpose, responsibility, governance, and intent—that the entire institution of higher education should have

---

Black Scholar Chides Summers for 'Attack'

Harvard Professor Airs Feelings on Talk Show

By Howard Kurtz
Washington Post Staff Writer
Monday, January 7, 2002; Page A03

"Cornel West, the professor of a racially tinged dispute that threatens to break up Harvard University's Afro-American Studies Department, says that Harvard President Lawrence H. Summers 'attacked and insulted' him and treated him with 'disrespect.'

"In his first public comments on his highly publicized clash with Summers, West made clear that he was deeply offended by a meeting in which the former treasury secretary expressed displeasure with West's conduct.

"'The one thing I do not tolerate is disrespect, being dishonored and being devalued,' West told Tavis Smiley in a National Public Radio interview to be aired today in selected cities, including Baltimore. The pilot program of 'The Tavis Smiley Show' can also be heard online at www.npr.org."

---

grown or been caused or allowed to grow to so advanced, outrageous, fraught, pitiable, and dangerous an extent of decay, erosion, and depravity—this indeed is a situation the responsibility for which can't

---

[235] Even here, as many have noted, Larsen clings, perhaps for one very last time, to the poor and wan conceit of the retirement speech. Not surprisingly, Irena Hong-Koestler and Petra Gubar, (*Apollo or Cassandra? Victim or Prophet? A Historically based Analysis of the Question of Paranoia Versus Prophecy in the Larsen Papers* [Beijing, History House, 2110]) find the reference as yet another piece of evidence regarding the dreadful and wholly shattered mental condition of the author. [Editor's Note]

possibly be identified as being the responsibility of any single woman or man; but so generalized, broad, far-reaching, pervasive, and egregious an ill as this

> ...for which I hope the candid reader will give some allowance, after he hath maturely and impartially considered my case, and the distress I was in. From this time my constant practice was, as soon as I rose, to perform that business in open air, at the full extent of my chain, and due care was taken every morning before company came, that the offensive matter should be carried off in wheelbarrows by two servants appointed for that purpose.
>
> —*Gulliver's Travels*

can have come into existence only through an equivalently widespread and *generalized* failure—itself made up of countless subsidiary failures both of commission and omission, action and neglect—of which President Penguin-Duck's own egregious, pernicious, profound, degrading, and systematic failures find themselves, extraordinary as they are, remaining typical in their way of escaping censure entirely, doing so by merit of the fact, quite simply, that they remain *wholly invisible* to those professional, legal, and regulatory agencies, institutions, or bodies that *should* respond to them in accordance with their traditional roles, sensitivities, powers, and values. But so pervasive and extreme have grown the malfeasances and corrosions we are speaking of that these bodies *no longer see anything wrong with the situation within the academy around them,* so accustomed have they grown to and so thoroughly co-opted have they been by the changes of the past three decades or so that they no are longer capable of seeing as erroneous that which by any earlier measure is or would be indeed erroneous, in this way proving themselves to be very much like the fish in the sea, which, when asked how it likes the water, is unable to respond due to its never

having known anything other than water.
And thus, in consequence of all that we have so far seen and said, it becomes perfectly and inescapably clear that in the last analysis the fault cannot be said to lie with any single woman or man; any single discipline, department, or college; any single region or group or organization; or even with any single group of groups or organization of organizations, but that we must conclude instead that the fault lies indeed with the entire nation itself. In its governance, in its economic system, in its own policies of education, in its own understanding of what constitutes growth and what does not, of what truly is or is not a resource that must above all else be husbanded rather than exploited—in these matters as in countless others—be th

1113

o consider a chronology, simplest of all narrative forms, in a final attempt to evaluate my life, to identify and observe what in fact it aimed for, and to look unflinchingly and without self-pity at the meager, lost, and penurious way it came to be spent. Such an undertaking might begin in this manner:

1941   I am born. The date is November 29th. On December 7th, near noon, I am brought home, at almost exactly the moment when the attack on Pearl Harbor is starting. The world stands poised at the edge of a great abyss, yet poised also at the edge of great achievement.

Who could then conceivably have imagined the ruin, grief, penury, loss, malignance, misdirection, and sorrow that would be the chief components of the poor remnants of life surrounding me sixty-odd years later?

1942 I have no memory of my existence. My father goes to war.

1943 Most likely in August or September, I have what I believe now to have been my first memory—of seeing a pattern of light shifting on my bedroom ceiling.

1944 The war continues. Standing in our yard, in the sunlight, I look down at a penny resting on my open palm.

1945 In this year, I have my earliest remembered introduction to the ineffable power of the aesthetic. It happens when I watch my great-aunts Karen and Ingeborg one summer afternoon, walking away from me toward the corner of Fifth Street and Union. They are like a window. Through them, I am able to see a great number of years back, into the nineteenth century.

1946 Standing in a field of high grass, my father takes a photograph as I watch from a certain distance away. With this experience begins the rapid growth of my understanding of the relationships between time, space, and absence in all works of art.

1947 My family moves from Fifth Street in Northfield to our farm a mile or two to the northeast. Without realizing it at first, I start my years of perfect seeing.

1948 During the period of my perfect seeing, I grow more and more aware of the vital and ineluctable relationship that exists, *in all artifact,* between space and time.

1949 On long quiet summer afternoons I sit on the crossbeams in the hayloft of the barn, studying the aesthetic / philosophic nature of artifact.

1950 Very early one summer morning I come upon my father sitting on our front lawn, in a white wooden lawn chair, naked. The experience results in an enormous and sudden intensifying and deepening of my understanding of space, time, and history.
    Simultaneously, though still unknown to me, the state of historic perfection achieved by Northfield, Minnesota, begins to deteriorate.

This process of loss in fact began (albeit at that time remaining almost entirely unnoticed), in 1949 and was soon to accelerate tragically.

That is to say, the world as I have just now begun to know it is also just at this same time beginning to come to an end.

1951 Outside the north door of the Longfellow school, I fall on the ice and am knocked unconscious for a moment. What I learn from this, I am not certain. Stephen Koch's father dies. Soon afterward, one day after school, I learn from Stephen the symbolic meaning of up and down, though he has no idea this happens. Three years later, under his influence, I begin a program of reading, discovering an industry in myself that had not existed previously.

1952 Our farm has begun to fail, and my years of perfect seeing will soon also be at an end, though never forgotten. I am not yet in puberty. I practice running, and in doing so I create trails and routes in various patterns across our farmland.

1953 I enter seventh grade and therefore go to school on the east side of town instead of the west. My first feeling of affection having in it any sexual element is for a pleasantly attractive teacher named Miss Shuh. On the first day of school, Miss Shuh—her name pronounced "shoe"— forbids any of us so much as even to think about making fun of her name.

Having a locker in the hallway and moving from room to room for classes seems exotic and adult, although I find soon enough that this impression is not permanent. Part of the school building is old, dating from 1890, another part dating from the 1930's, while a new section is added early in my own years there. The building itself and the many artifacts in it, including those in the science rooms, lend themselves to my studies of the relationships between space and time far more intensely than I perceive any of my classwork doing. Two more years will pass before I become friends with Stephen Koch, but even then I will not tell him about these studies—or at least not in any completely explicit and candid way.

1954 My father no longer crops our farm. Both the farmland and our buildings begin revealing symptoms of neglect and—a word pertinent to the buildings if not the land—decline. The same is true of Northfield itself. The old wading pool, for example, at the bottom of the once-formal esplanade behind the public hospital, instead of being host to children's voices and delightfully spraying water, is now filled with broken glass, discarded bottles, and other detritus.

This particular symptom of failure and decline is of special importance to me because one of my earliest memories—from 1944, of being there, in the spray, and seeing my great-aunts Karen and Ingeborg on a bench nearby—took place at the wading pool, located near where they lived.

1955   By this time I have fallen in love for the first time, with a slender classmate named Marietta Greenfield, and, in the summer of this year, one evening as darkness is falling, I climb with her to the top of the old Nordic ski jump on the northeast shoulder of the St. Olaf hill. My experience with Marietta changes nothing but electrifies and intensifies everything. After this formative and crucially important moment in my life takes place, all of space, time, and history reveal themselves to be imbued with something new, namely with extraordinary intensities of *feeling*. The essential nature of my studies remains unchanged, but my awareness of my studies' meaning, dimension, subtlety, humanity, and universality is intensified immensely and forever. Not for forty or more years will I lose faith in the clear sense of their power and importance,[236] not until the full-blown Age of Simplification itself is in place, when *all* that is subtle, no matter how powerful or important, will be crushed in the attendant decline and collapse.[237]

In the autumn of this year, our first term of high school, my friendship with Stephen Koch comes about. The fall of 1955, therefore, practically speaking, marks the beginning of my literary life, just as The Age of Simplification and the iniquities of President Penguin-Duck will mark, or bring, its end.

1956–1959   During high school, instead of listening to popular music on the radio, I learn the history of jazz and listen to all I can find of the music, playing it first on 78s, then ten-inch LPs, and finally on twelve-inch. In this music, I find that my studies of space and time are affirmed, enhanced, and reinforced, although this remains true only within the intellectual and aesthetic mainstream of the music itself and not in the popular or commercial derivatives of it that are commonplace and that are those versions of it preferred by the huge majority of my classmates, although in this, as in literary matters, Stephen Koch is the clear exception, one fact of the several that continue to cement our friendship.

---

236 And in truth never *have* lost faith in these things, but have instead seen it lost, rejected, or abandoned by others, everywhere around me. [Author's Note]

237 However prescient Larsen's words inevitably appear to us now, his reference, obviously, is not to the Collapse of the American Nation, but instead only to the facts of decline and collapse as they had already occurred in the aesthetic and intellectual life of the Late Ante-Penultimate (2000–2006). [Editor's Note]

In the music, amid much else, I discover a passionate intensity that impels its performers to express *order* in as nearly perfected a form as possible by means of challenging it with the greatest possible *disorder* that it can stand without being altered or harmed. By this subtle, gifted, and ingenious means is created a medium of pure beauty—the music—that is also a high celebration of the order without which this medium would be impossible to achieve.

These elements of high passion, extraordinary accomplishment, unqualified dedication, and fearlessness of risk—these are among the qualities and elements that I discovered in the music and that I concluded therefore to be elements and qualities necessary also in the preparation, creation, or expression of any other true art.

With feelings that included desire, fear, joy, reverence, and awe, I dedicated myself to these elements as the standard without which any artistic or aesthetic achievement would be lacking, inadequate, a lesser thing, and also possibly, in the highest sense, untrue.

(The music, in spite of its extraordinary richness, power, significance, and vitality, appeared for a time to stand as a hindrance to my general studies of space and time, or even as a check to them, since I was unable at first to understand how space could have any part in it, since it occupied none, while time, obviously, was one of the springs of its very essence. Soon enough, however, I saw that there in fact was no obstacle at all, and that the music existed throughout space—and could exist *only* throughout space—in ways exactly true of any other art, artwork, or artifice. Once perceived, it occupies space, just as it does once recorded. And since it cannot exist without being perceived, obviously it cannot exist except in space. Curiously, this proves also that memory cannot exist except within space, it being incapable of existing without a rememberer. [238]

Just as the musicians moved from one place to another and brought the music with them, so it also moved from one place to another within the minds of those who, having heard it and having been changed by it, themselves then also moved.

This process continued, beginning to weaken and draw to an end only with the advent of The Age of Simplification, when, through the ruinous workings of that time's nature and being, *all* art that

---

[238] These remarkable questions of space, time, and location in the Larsen approach to aesthetics and ontology have been, among the various critics and analysts, probably most fruitfully described and studied by Frederik Nissen in his "Negotiations with a Non-Future: Courageous Sanity in the *"Diary"* (*Annals of Lost Americana*, May 2130, pp. 34–51). Nissen's explorations have been carried further, and their importance shown dramatically, by Lok-Ho Woo in *Art, Meaning, and Integrity in the Early Penultimate: A Fatally Lost Unity* (Bangkok, 2142).

possessed the complex or the subtle within it as it would possess a necessary or animating germ or spirit, gradually sickened, went unattended, and died.

How could anyone have imagined or believed, ever, that it could

1959–1963   I spend four years at Carleton. During this time, albeit with the usual disclaimers and exceptions, I believe (as I will continue doing for fifteen years or more afterward) that the experience constitutes the salutary and proper strengthening, training, and broadening of my intellectual life and powers that I have been waiting for since grade school. I am not necessarily "happy"—"happiness": that most vacuous measure, in general, of anything actually signifi

lert, drawn forward by a sense of anticipation, stirred by the presence of intellect and history around me, and—unlike any feeling I had in high school—driven by an appetite for reading. Such discontent as I do have while at Carleton—the ravages of personal loneliness, for example—diminishes with the pa

pearance, scent, atmosphere, and then of course the seasons: the look of the weathered brick or stone streaked with rain, or seen through falling snow, or in the slanting golden sunlight of warm autumn afternoons, when not a breath of air is moving but all around the atmosphere is sweetly delicate and soft with the scents of earth and leaves and dryi

itting careless on a granary floor, / Thy hair soft-lifted by the winnowing w[239]

n of Williams Hall, an annihilation that never c

1197

Mr. Rankin

---

[239] The fragment is from "Ode to Autumn" by English poet John Keats, ca. 1825 (cf. Stark-weather & Pei, *A Compendium of Extant Verse in English* [Delhi, 2105]). [Editor's Note]

ld

urage

o ponder

ost simply put

nconceivable to be able to

tent and degree of the loss. Of course

n inescapable hypocrisy in policy of the

o with race, a concept of reparation, even if

idence of ever having thought or done anything

ver. But who you are is what matters, not what you

hether what you do, in spite of merits that may be incon-

oint is that you become expendable for the sake of the over-

orate-"educational" machine, whose *sole purpose* is its own exist-

different from President Penguin-Duck, who no longer saw

the objective actuality of the pernicious ideas he stood for

routinely encouraged out of genuine desire to serve what he sincerely

believed to be absolutely true and also good. But Grau and Samson,

heir deeply passionate, fastidiously researched article in *Academic Questions,* make the powerful argument that President Penguin-Duck maintains no such beliefs whatsoever, that his actions are conducted solely and wholly on a basis of the purest cynicism alone, and that his seizure of the institution and decades-long bending of it toward the construction of his own corporate-style fiefdom—that these are all, or so the article tries to show, matters that can be understood *only* if they are first understood *not* to be matters of conscience or belief, *not* products, that is, of a failed education that has resulted in an ignorance of the past that is of course sufficiently paralyzing in and of itself but that is made even worse through its being accompanied by an inability to follow the steps of a simple logical argument.

No, argue Grau and Samson, the actions and policies of President Penguin-Duck, exactly like the actions and policies of the countless hundreds of others just like him and in positions just like his—no, the actions and policies of these institutional leaders are based *not* on any belief in education, any commitment to the values traditionally associated *with* education, *not* on any understanding of what may reasonably be considered "right," but instead they are based only on the most transparently and patently se

1327

Food is a friend.

1401

  still remember how certain it seemed. What reason was there to
think otherwise? And how many reasons to think *so*? Spirit, atmosphere, flavor, scent—and laughter, none of that any more, too complex. Remember the time, Anne and I not yet married, it must have
been one of the very last big parties, coming back to the farmhouse
sometime around eight-thirty or so, maybe a little later, but it was
the whole crowd, they'd begun outdoors, on the west lawn, under
the elms—a stone-toss from my old grassy spot with the cow skull—
so that there were still blankets and chairs and bottles and plates and
glasses and buckets and coolers down there, two or three lanterns
burning forlornly on the card tables, but everyone had come up and
indoors, mosquitoes I suppose, and also up in the house is where the
coffee was—funny the way everyone always had a cup and then went
right on drinking again—and the fresh bottles, and also the electric
light was so pleasant after squinting at everything you tried to see
down there in the darkness and losing things in the grass. How lively
it all was, and bright-lighted. No curtains at any of the windows, of
course. Reed Whittemore at the piano—the piano was in the dining
room then—bringing out one tune after another, sophisticated light
things, and someone came up where we were watching and listening and said "That's why he's a poet, because he can do that," and
I questioned the logic but didn't say anything. I think of it as being
Arlene Lawrence, but that couldn't have been, because she'd never
have said anything about poetry. Music, yes. I remember Fritz,

another time, so angry and completely disgusted and saying "Now all they do is learn *three chords*." Imagine yet again what it would have been like to hear him and Doc Evans, Jack Lucas at the drums, playing in Northfield—but that was unreachable for me, too far back, after 1928, I think, but before 1933. It could have been Pat Lucas, but it wasn't sophisticated enough for her, and she was in the living room anyway, in the big discussion going on there about the election. Scott Elledge was in the shower, singing something from *Kiss Me, Kate* at the top of his lungs, but without the water running. His was the idea of using the Yale key for whatever it was they were doing, a treasure hunt of some kind, and Yale would be the clue, I suppose having to do with Reed Whittemore. Helen was there. It was always more interesting when she was there. I liked her so much. All those wonderful kids. *That did be fun.* All that learning, what a wonderful moment and place for learning, though how was I, or anyone, to know that it was to be the last of each? The way big things were part of little things and vice versa, the life of symbol and the symbol of life, never to be known again or cared about. Luckily, they're all dead so at least it can't hurt them. But not my crowd, not me, not dead yet but might as well be for the deadness everywhere. Who, do you think, was the biggest influence? Not Charlie Shain or Jo, although I learned plenty through them about *atmosphere,* although not the kind that mattered much beyond the social use you could make of it, the sort of You *(talk, dress, move, cook, drink, converse) as if you're from the East,* which they were indeed. I learned about tweeds from my father and from Charlie Shain, and about briar pipes, and about oxford cloth shirts. Reed Whittemore, obviously. And Owen Jenkins, for logic and coherence, remember the semester of Aristotle and wholeness, and then finding it again in Stephen Dedalus, radiance, wholeness, and harmony—gone forever now, that's for sure, nobody even to mourn it. Remember how complicated it felt suddenly, hearing about Scott Elledge's death, thinking: it can't be. Perhaps it was him, yes, I suspect it was, but never directly, always by hint, suggestion, example, it was up to you to take it, not up to him to give it. How could there ever have been anyone better than he was to read Shakespeare with? *"I took Shakespeare with Elledge."* Hard work it was, but life in it everywhere, boiling up over the edges every moment of every class, not to mention in doing the reading itself. Yes, it was the atmosphere, wasn't it, it's true, it was. Like with music, or the sense of smell, you never lose the association. One thing connected with another, then all things a part of all things, and then wholeness, radiance, harmony, and it never, never disappears. Except that that's not the way it will ever be, not again. *Dr. Muscle wears a mirror. . .* Imagine, for good god's sake, parade of happy ignorance. Ignorance rights. Saying right there in our third meeting, puffing himself up, all proud and smug and cocky: *"I've never read Homer in my life, and I'm not really planning on it."* A scholarly paper: "Dr. Muscle and Ignorance Rights in the Age of Simplification." Do I care? I do. I care, the son of a bitch. *This is all he ever does, Even when he pees.* He and Penguin-Duck should get together and read *A Perfect Storm* and then form a discussion group the way Car Cleopatra does over noon-hours, her group in the seminar room, what fun. Lies, shallowness, prefabrications, falsehoods, mental penury, self-beguilement, hypocrisy. *The one thing I do not and will not tolerate is disrespect, being dishonored and being devalued.* To be pinned to a lie and hung out to dry. Dry. Rap. Rap-rap. It's all the emperor's clothes, as Frederick always said, but how can the fear of truth have grown so intense, people cowering, in terror, quick, throw out a lie and defend us against the truth! Quick, throw water on the wicked witch! Penguin-Duck lied. He spoke the lie, wrote the lie, then put the lie in the file. Hi! I lie! My name is Penguin-Duck! No, I never pushed anyone in my life—except for Tippy Walstrom, do you remember him, in sixth

Poem

Hi!
I lie!
My name
is Penguin-Duck!

grade, during recess, in the schoolyard, when he and I came to shoves and pushes even though he weighed a third more than I did. And now he's dead, I read it in the paper, purely by chance, I'd cancelled my subscription but it still came, and I thought, *how can this be?* And how *can* it? I remember Tippy wearing his jeans with the cuffs turned up five or six inches, and any papers the teacher gave us to take home he folded in quarters and slipped into his cuffs, front-back-and-side, so he was like a walking file cabinet. But his hands were free, the main concern. That was all that mattered to the boys, that their hands be free, anything to avoid looking like a schoolboy, or, worse, like a girl. I wonder if that's why none of them, or hardly any, played musical instruments, because they'd have the cases to carry. Sixth grade, I don't remember Tippy Walstrom beyond that year, the same year I knocked myself out on the ice and saw Stephen Koch coming out of the school after his father had died. Ah, but there was another shoving moment, four years later, between Stephen and me, at the end of the school day, in tenth grade, down at the dismal end of the hall on the first floor where our lockers were, down where it didn't even feel like you were in the school building anymore because it was right next to the shop where they taught vocational agriculture, a tractor in there that the boys would take apart and put back together. I have only the faintest memory of what the shoving was about, but neither of us was very good at it and after the first tussle and thrust we both felt nothing more than simply ridiculous and let it end. I wonder if he remembers it. He, of course, an influence, enormous. Do you remember, his lyricism phase, he was the one who first made me aware of the sounds, an enormous awakening. Rhythms and sounds? In *sentences?* The year he'd moved to New York but came back over Christmas, with Sheila, and we met one night at someone's house—whose?—a crowded little cracker box at the bottom of the St. Olaf hill, under where the ski jump used to be, and Stephen, I don't remember what we talked about, Norman Grier was also there I think, and Stephen had done so much reading since his move, and he was citing by memory from some of it, "the devious-cruising Rachel, that in her retracing search after her missing children only found another orphan"[240] I remember him reciting, almost beside himself with elevation and excitement. After all, we were what? Twenty? "The barge she sat in, like a burnish'd throne, / Burn'd on the water."[241] Then it must have been only a year later, the summer I took the Greyhound and went out to visit, and Stephen and I and his friend Peter Germain, whom he'd bumped into, stood on the corner at West End and 85th, he and Peter talking about an instructor at CCNY, and Peter saying, "He showed me the prose rhythms in *The Dead*," and I—no one had ever told *me* anything about this. *Prose? Rhythm?* No one had so much as hinted, I'd had no idea, and from then on everything changed, as of course it would have to. And now. Who would ever have thought what malignant depravity and contemptible ruin it was going to come to. All the way back in *high* school, for the love of god, *in 1958 and 1959,* we used to use the word "Orwellian"[242] routinely, and remember all the talk about "subliminal" ads? Much talk, but then the plague of lotus-eating. Even Orwell starting to be forgotten by 1976, do you remember the *Harper's* editor, Judith something, in 1976, made me take "Orwellian" out because she didn't know it could mean cant, doubletalk, and jargon. Orwell: not a towering, illimitable genius,

---

240 An unknown reference. [Editor's Note]

241 Shakespeare, Dramatic Fragment XXIX, 14-15. [Editor's Note]

242 See note 5, p.2. [Editor's Note]

not destined to transform a genre entirely like Eliot or Yeats or V. Woolf, but, even so, as to the rest of it, what an unsurpassable, conscience-carrying observer. 1948 being turned into *1984*. Think of it. In 1948, I was still in the barn, studying the hewn beams, and for Orwell it was here already, the strangle of the totalitarian, truth changing to lie and lie changing to truth. It was already starting—moving toward the age of Cleopatra, Nose, Muscle, Penguin-Duck. Moving toward the age of Stanley Fish. Do you remember all the essays, in the early 1980's—*Has 1984 Come Yet? Was Orwell Right? Are We Doomed?* Doomed indeed, doomed indeed. But the latrines are fine, the latrines are fine. "Dr. Razor, may I please see you for a moment?" One, I remember, was called "Big Brother is You, Watching." A brilliant piece out of the murky wretchedness. Now, it wouldn't be printed. Or read. Or understood. Too subtle, too true, cuts too close to home, but, no, that's not it, it's a result of the lotus-eating, nothing more. Once people *are* the tv shows they watch, once they *are* tv sounds they hear, then you can't any longer condemn one without the other. I am my trash, my trash is me. I am my Fish, my Fish is me. Hey, penguin, *duck!* "And now, Mr. Penguin, or Duck, coming back to you for a moment, how do *you* feel about the loss of the individual in a society whose smallest unit is the *group?* Is it possible for a group to *think,* and if not, why not, and if so, will the *group* be capable of maintaining adherence to the truth, will it be capable of discriminating between the true and the false, and of choosing one over the other?" Mr. Duck, or Mr. Penguin, you're out of luck. I'm tired and getting more tired. Must begin to eat again. After all, food is a friend. Sam is gone. For two entire years not knowing that Sam was gone. Poor Anne, sitting at the bar and crying. Ingenious artifice, O, ingenious artifice, help us now. *Time, stop here.* Create as nearly perfect an order as humanly possible by means of challenging it with the greatest possible *disorder* that it can stand without being altered or harmed. And by this subtle, gifted, and ingenious means create . . .
. . . "Adze marks were still visible where the niches had been hewn out, as they were visible elsewhere along the beam at points where shaping had been done. The head of each wooden peg was flanged out, beaten down and spread out into splinters from the blows of the hammer that had driven it into its hole." And I, too, will be driven into my hole, yet no artifact will I become, but only flesh, never to be seen again. Old father, old artificer, stand me—bah! He's dead too, only Penguin-Duckism lives: The group, the group, the group ("alas alas on on the skull the skull the skull the skull . . ." Aren't we lucky, though!). Can the group *think?* Dr. Razor, could I see you for a moment? The farm is gone, the town is dying, the nation in peril. *"Only the landscape itself remained. In most cases unchanged,*

while in certain other areas it was scarred or subtly altered in a.
mounded, slightly built-up way, as though it were welted or
way flesh can grow in the healing after a large wound." The barn
hand, thick with weeds and impenetrable. The stock tank no long
only one of its four sides remaining upright. The barn roof, fal
on the east end, the cupola and weather vane missing entirely
open square on the sway-backed roof. The granary and th
collapsed entirely, roofs lying on the floors. The walls
drawn inward by the collapsed roof. In the granary
stood, those at right angles, while the other two
lay flat. A demanding tutor, so was I readied
remainder of a lifetime, result not in the per
of a life but in the possibility of one be
superior to another. The recipient or
the simplified person—must be a

quiet and still. Sometimes, the pigeon
scuffle among themselves in the tin cupola where they nested, and fr
time would treat me to their somnolent cooing sounds. Otherwise, i
far the greater time, the enormous space inside the barn remained p
still. Through holes in roof and walls, pencil-lines of sunlight wou
the shadowy darkness, sometimes, when the angle was right, conti
down to the hay-strewn wooden floor below. Those afternoons of l
reflection in the old loft resulted in some of my earliest conscious
twinned miracles of narrative and time. Often, I crawled the leng
beam, in part just to admire the symmetry of the barn's construc
paired beams rising up to fit under the pitched roof, the way tho
sunk into hand-hewn niches in the horizontal beams to keep the
were raised up by the barn-builders to find the first pairs of cro
Afterward, holes were augered, and thick hardwood pegs toed
butt and beam firmly together. No trace of anything remained.
that had lined them, curbs, sidewalks, and boulevards dating fr
the Epoch of Walking—none remained; in their places stood t
aromatic high grass, in blossom, bending over as the wind ble
up again as it died. The great-rooted shade tree outside Barb
gone. The iron hitching post where I saw Karen and Ingebo
century and then back into it again had vanished. When I fo
ing post, it seemed to me more clear than ever that what ha
walked to the place where Carleton College had stood, not

Olaf College, where my grandmother's house on Forest A
long time on that spot—the cellar, where the broken croq
old-fashioned telephone; tennis rackets in the attic, their
for some time. Here was the place from which my fathe
camping trips in years like 1926 and 1927, where he ha
into tennis clothes or sat reading at his desk, where he
before going down the Nordic ski jump. Karen and In
low mounds in the earth, then a faint slope downwar
garden had been. (It was gone, of course, the shed
way was gone, the house, dining table, the crèche
kitchen wall, two beds upstairs, the bathroom, cu
outward for a moment, the white chair with a fol
pillows that had lain at the head of each bed, the
neatly at the foot.

(And so it was, in every splinter of every beam, in every adze
flattened head of every hardwood peg, I came, through an oft repeat
scrutiny, to recognize, almost like invisible fossils held within the a
entire realms, regions, and nations of the past, entire worlds and all
existed in them—all of this history flowing toward and then *into* th
the flattened pegs and adzed markings of all these cunning artifacts
old barn. Then, since all artifacts exist within time and not merely
roots in past and future while "existing" only in the present—these
recognitions, and lives that had flowed *into* the beams, pegs, mark
out again instantly and reached forward into a more and more dist
      And, simultaneously, the exact reverse. Each moment in t
increasingly closer and closer—doing so with the passing of each
to its infinitesimal "present" and its passing—*through* the artifac
      Each moment, that is, came from the future, existed invis
slipped away into the past, while the artifact—*and only the artif*
unceasingly gathered up the past and propelled it forward into t
      In the future waited all the moments when I came into t
double door, climbed up the ladder, and, high up in the sun-pe
crawled along my beam observing each splinter, peg, and adze
and instant of my doing so, *that moment came into and went t*
adze-mark and, receding at once into the past, was lost to me.
this happened and went on happening, while simultaneously,
and even lay down on the beams, splinters, pegs, and adze-m
gathered up the past into themselves and (while I, there, the
and touching and feeling them, was bathed in the past it as
quietness and silence) and flung it unceasingly into the fut

Other than artifacts, there is nothing in the univers
Nothing in the universe except artifacts can do this.
   Which is why, when they are lost—or whe
they are prevented from being born or caused to b
themselves is lost. The marrying of past and futur
a consequence of *that* loss, *everything is lost.*
   I know that this is true because I hav
   The moments of my coming in thro
future, moving toward me, and then they r
no longer able to go in through the barn d
listen to the pigeons, gaze out into the qu
haymow.
   After a time, the barn went unuse
the weather, then was torn down, even t
scattered.
   Without it, the wedding of time
as one. And so more and more came to
farm surrounding it, and then the farm
barns, and then the whole town of No
its stores and shops and tree-shaded s
grasses and the gentle undulations of
and the rain, and the winds, but with
whatsoever, or of any kind.
   So it was that in the quiet sti
that employed the adzes, or pounde
hammered in the shingles onto the
saw the dinner prepared for the ba
yard under a tree, a midday meal
of women as there were men, an
the women rising at dawn, befor
still farther back, farther and far

fieldstones placed one upon an
These stones, some immense,
baskets, pumpkins, grapefruit
that warmed the newly plowe
teams dragging rock-sleds pi
of paired hands, brown with
growing

weathered gray wood had p
the eroded grain of its woo
expressed the entire accum
been heard in that particul

contained every sight and

up to the wide double do
haymow. The horses wo

different in the winter,

to any work of art, pl

every one of those w

not bring others or
attempted to describ
to any full, durable,
my colleagues at A
a tiny remnant that
age, disease, anxie
death—very few a
longer exist, that
might even possi
not scorn the pro
tween narrative (
time; are in fact
capable of perc
act) and time.
   So ab
omnipresent
any meaning
simplest an
epidemic I
virulent, f
the stand
rigidly d
single-d

monism
few re
life *no*
evil a
no hi
"plea
term
to d

bea
art,
20
si
i

EDITOR'S AFTERWORD

And thus, with a poor, last, single, lower-case vowel, the voice falls silent[243] that has accompanied and guided us throughout the entirety of "My Life in Education and the Arts Before and During the Gathering of the Great Calamity As I Have Experienced and Now Believe I Understand It." A great deal else indeed comes to an end also at this moment. Not only does the likely possibility of our gaining additional knowledge of Dr. Larsen come to an end, but so does the insight he has given us into the intellectual/literary life as it was still capable of being lived in the depredations of the Late Ante-Penultimate. And the same must be said also, of course, of the astonishing insights he has given us into the actual nature of American academia during that same pitiable era.

As many have pointed out,[244] it is fully possible that at the moment of his silencing, Larsen's difficulties were in fact only beginning. Or it may be that at that time his travails were very soon to end—or, indeed, that they had already done so, through the kindly agency of death. In any case, it is a highly uncertain that we will never know significantly more than we do now about the originator of this private

---

[243] It falls silent at this point, that is, in the Bhāskara Presentation. See "A Note to the Reader," pp. xi–xii.

[244] Especially Shandra, Wei, and Cadiz, but again also see chapter three in Kremer-Bernier, "Ideas and Iron Bars." [Editor's Note]

and invaluably candid voice from inside the ranks of American higher education in the Late-Ante-Penultimate.

After Larsen, indeed, we have from inside American academia nothing beyond an ominous, foreboding silence.

Still, although we are unlikely ever to know *more,* questions *about* Larsen remain very much alive—and rightly so. Exactly how explicit or invasive *were* the pro-conformity pressures brought to bear upon him and the small number of other unconverteds still extant in his day? How much and in what ways did *his* portrait of academia remain accurate between the time of his writing and the time of the Collapse? Did academia change *radically* after his descriptions of it? Did it change at all? And finally, hardly the question of least interest, what was the truth of Larsen's mental and psychological state during the different stages of writing?[245]

A currently influential group of commentators and scholars[246] are of the opinion that these and other questions will remain unanswerable until such time as new information becomes known: until, that is, we are able to identify with fair exactness what specific external event (or turn of events) it was that functioned catalytically, impelling the author to embark upon his great project. That is, a considerably greater *historical* context than we now possess is essential as an aid before we can hope for any significantly greater elucidation of these and other matters than we have achieved so far.

The pace of archeological recovery from the part of the world once known as The American Nation has slowed dramatically over the past several decades. But the possibility always remains, nevertheless, that something entirely unexpected will appear to help us unlock further the mysteries still lying within the heart of these extraordinary papers so fortunately bequeathed to us by Larsen—whoever he may have been.

X. Jin Li
October 2137 C.E.

---

[245] For one example of the varied approaches to the question of balance, see Cadwallader Mulghoon, "The Naïve Artist in the Larsen Papers and in the Hugh Nissenson 'Novel-Fragment'" (*Studies in American Prose Narrative in the Period of the Early Collapse,* Winter 2128, pp. 874-923). Mulghoon makes a convincing albeit sympathetic case for Larsen as clinically unbalanced. In doing so, he includes an argument that the author's line-drawings of President Penguin-Duck prove that Larsen was familiar with the brilliant pictures in the Nissenson fragment.

[246] The so-called "Causal Group," consisting predominantly of Foerthwright, Lu Yen, Mulghoon, Paredes, and Kremer-Bernier. [Editor's Note]

APPENDIX

A Chronology of the Collapse of the American Nation from the Early Preliminary through the Late Ultimate and on to the End

Early Preliminary (1950–1964)
Middle Preliminary (1964–1971)
Late Preliminary (1971–1983)

Early Ante-Penultimate (1983–1996)
Middle Ante-Penultimate (1996–2000)
Late Ante-Penultimate (2000–2006)

Early Penultimate (2006–2012)
Middle Penultimate (2013–2019)
Late Penultimate (2020–2024)

Early Ultimate (2025–2031)
Middle Ultimate (2032–2037)
Late Ultimate (2037–2041)

The Collapse (2042–?)

CPSIA information can be obtained at www.ICGtesting.com
Printed in the USA
BVOW05s1634130314

347576BV00004B/10/P